SPHERES OF INFLUENCE

The Stellar Heritage Series

by Bob Mauldin

Legacy

Spheres of Influence

Far Horizons

When One Door Closes

SPHERES OF INFLUENCE

Stellar Heritage

Book Two

BOB MAULDIN

Publishing Company

Published in the United States by
Blade of Truth Publishing Company, Forsyth, Montana

Cover art: Covers by Christian

Contact the publisher via email at:
chadd@bladeoftruthpublishing.com

ISBN-13: 978-1-64248-012-2

PROLOGUE

Rentec do' Verlas, Minister for Spatial Affairs to the Shiravan Polity, usually enjoyed his visits to Minister Foran's offices because he'd noticed of late that the minister's secretary was showing more than passing interest in him. As a high-ranking, unattached male in the expanding Shiravan space program, he was, he knew, a "good catch," and therefore tended to view any female advances with a great deal of skepticism. But this secretary of Minister Foran's was different. Hired just over a year earlier from the common labor pool, she'd come to the minister's office with the highest recommendations from her superiors in Personnel Placement. This had occurred at just about the same time he'd been elevated to his father's post by the bomb that had killed his father and severely injured his mother.

The shy young woman with the amazingly red eyes had never said anything to him that was not strictly within the bounds of Shiravan protocol, but every time he entered a room she was in, she began to drop things, or stutter, or trip. And though he usually discounted the rumors that inevitably abounded anywhere so many people co-existed, his interest had been piqued by the stories passed to him by co-workers, who said she oh-so-casually asked about him on occasion. Perhaps it was time he did something about it. His mother wasn't one to let a son go unattached forever, and if he didn't find a mate on his own, there was no telling who she'd saddle him with.

"Good morning, Ramannie," he said, staring at her frankly and taking a chance on getting lost in her ruby gaze. "Is the Minister ready to see me yet?"

"Yes, M-minister do' Verlas he is," the girl said as papers spilled off the stack in her hands. "He canceled his morning appointments r-right after you called. You may go right in." Twice missing the button that opened the door to the inner office, she had to look down to find and press it.

"Good morning, Minister Foran," the younger man said as he entered the office.

"In this office, you may call me Mondel, Rentec." He turned to a device on his desk and spoke into it. "Ramannie, please bring in a tray of refreshments." Looking back to his guest, the older minister asked, "And how is your revered mother this morning?"

"As well as can be expected, sir. She had to have a lung replaced and quite a bit of skin grafting after the explosion, as well as a few weeks in a regeneration chamber, but she's mending well. Of course, she still mourns the loss of my father. And she won't stop trying to find me a mate. I sometimes think she does it just to irritate me. Oh, and she sends her regards."

"Those things are ever a mother's province, Rentec, and not a thing you can do except find a mate on your own. Thank you, Ramannie," Mondel said as the woman entered with a tray.

Ceremoniously setting two wooden cups in front of the two men, she carefully poured a green liquid into each cup from a crystal decanter.

"Take my regards and condolences to her when

you next go home, and tell her I said you're filling your father's position quite well," the minister said. "So tell me, what made you go to the trouble of making a formal appointment this fine morning?"

"It's about Colony Ship 478. You may remember that five turnings ago a scout ship came back from Descaret Four, and all the data showed it to be nearly perfect for colonization. Its light is a little too much on the yellow side and gravity's a bit higher than we would have liked, but otherwise it's a great prospect. Since we had a colony ship nearly completed—number 478, the *Dalgor Kreth*—we sent it out as soon as it was crewed. All the senior officers and most of the crew were veterans. Only twenty were new personnel. It took just over a turning to get there, another turning to get the infrastructure mined from the asteroid belt, and another turning to return. By our best estimates, the ship should have arrived over half a turning ago. We've had no word of any kind, and according to standard operating procedures, I, as Spatial Minister, have to formally list the ship as 'missing.' To that end, it's my duty to request that you, as Minister of Colonization, order any and all ships to begin searching for the missing vessel and crew."

Mondel silently gathered his thoughts as he watched the young woman putter around, cutting small edibles, which she set on plates and placed in front of each man. She then looked expectantly at the older man.

"Thank you, Ramannie, you may go now," the Minister for Colonization said. "There's no reason to bore you with any of this." The minister looked at the younger as the office door closed. "While it *is* my responsibility to order such a search, it's yours to know if a vessel is available to perform the search."

"I'm sure you received my report about the colonist ship that had to return because the *Dalgor Kreth* wasn't in-system and had apparently not been there at all since no work had been done to receive the colonists."

As they spoke, both nibbled at the platter on the table before them.

"Survey Vessel 264 has just finished its latest refit. The captain and crew would be happy to engage in such a search, and the thought of a salvage bonus has been dangled in front of them."

"Salvage bonus is *always* a potent argument," the minister said. He looked down into the cup in his hand "How is it that kemwood can impart such an intoxicating flavor to anything poured into it and still leave one perfectly sober afterwards? Ah well, one of the little mysteries of life."

Mondel stood and led Rentec to the office door. As he opened the door, he said, "I'll authorize 264 to embark as soon as they can be provisioned. But understand, not one other vessel can be spared at this time. We'll have to await their report before I can authorize other craft away from their duties. I'll suggest that they proceed directly to Descaret Four first. The captain will have discretionary powers to alter the schedule as she sees fit after exploring the area."

As Rentec took his leave of his elder, he stopped at Ramannie's desk. Looking into her eyes, he said, "Good day to you Ramannie kep Gillas. Perhaps one day soon you'll do me the honor of having dinner with me."

"I-it would be my p-pleasure, Minister do' Verlas," she said without raising her eyes from her desk.

CHAPTER ONE

Chaos reigned supreme on the *Galileo*. Lucy stood on the bridge, swaying as if she'd been sucker-punched. *Simon dead?* All the away team's bio-monitors were red across the board. Lucy shook herself visibly and turned to the monitors showing Kitty's condition. There was far more red than green for her liking, that was for sure.

The aftermath of what was quickly coming to be known as "the debacle at Camp David" was that the United States was now short a vice-president, leaving Speaker of the House Dennis Hastings to move into the second most powerful position in the land. The event had also left the country deeply divided, sending the world on a witch hunt.

In addition to the vice-president, ambassadors from Russia, Great Britain, China, France, Spain, and Portugal had died in the explosion, along with representatives from half a dozen third-world countries. The list also included an unknown number of "covert operatives" from a little-known outfit called the Defense Intelligence Agency, whose members were beginning to scurry around like a bunch of cockroaches exposed to the light. This agency's chief operative, known by a variety of names—the latest of which was John Anderson—was nowhere to be found and was presumed to have died in the explosion, although most members of the intelligence community weren't taking bets.

Losses on the American side included five Apache helicopters and their crews, as well as some two dozen Marines assigned to Camp David's perimeter defense force. Losses on the Terran Alliance side were one shuttle, one Mamba, four dead, and one critically injured.

Dr. Penn wasn't sure how Kitty had managed to survive the explosion, much less the transport back to the *Galileo* and then the trip to sick bay. He'd had her placed on the table farthest from the door. It was part of the *Galileo's* original equipment—a solid rectangular pillar slightly too high for humans to work comfortably. Up until then, it hadn't been a problem since patients were rare due to the extremely reliable nature of the technology they'd acquired.

With the help of a portable x-ray machine he'd brought aboard, he began his examination. Thirty minutes later, he delivered a harrowing diagnosis to Lucy.

She looked at the body of her friend, now supreme commander, and quaked with each word the doctor uttered.

"Two broken legs, the right one in two places, cracked pelvis, spine broken in the lumbar region, three broken ribs on the left side, left arm broken in two places, and a massive concussion. In addition, her corneas are burnt, most likely from her proximity to the explosion. Her left lung is punctured, and considering the obvious pounding her body's taken, there's bound to be bruising to many of her internal organs. I won't know for sure until I can get a better look. What she needs is a state-of-the-art medical facility, but I won't even consider moving her until I can get her stabilized—*if* I can do that."

Several hours later, after turning the sickbay into a makeshift surgery, Dr. Penn had dealt with the punctured lung, set the various broken bones, taped her ribs, and administered what medication he could to make her comfortable and combat the shock. When he felt he'd done all he could, he sent his two assistants off to clean up and stepped into the corridor to call Lucy. Breaking a major rule, he left the door to sickbay open, pulled out his commlink, and lit a cigarette. He nodded to the two guards who'd been placed there to keep the corridor clear and took the first satisfying drag, exhaling in relief. As he did so, he heard a sound that reminded him of airbrakes bleeding down and turned just in time to witness a sight that left him speechless and raised the hairs on the back of his neck.

Dumbfounded, Dr. Penn watched as a transparent cover slid out of an as-yet-unnoticed hole in the wall, covering Kitty's body and meeting a semicircular piece rising up out of the base of the table. He now realized what the two recessed tracks along the long sides of the table were for but wished he didn't. Hermetic sealing was nothing new to him. He punched in Lucy's comm frequency, and as he waited for her to answer, he saw panels opening up in the table's surface along Kitty's body and watched, horrified, as *things* came out of the holes and attached themselves near her ankles and wrists, including a darkened patch that covered her eyes, nose, and mouth.

Lucy answered as a light mist began to fill the

interior of the... device. Shock making his voice rock steady, all he could say was, "There's a problem with the captain. You should get down here right away." Finally noticing the forgotten cigarette, he snuffed it out with shaking hands and dropped it in a disposal.

A flustered Dr. Penn was bent over the casing that enclosed Kitty, stethoscope pressed against it, when Lucy stormed into the room. Sliding to a halt, she asked, "What the hell have you done, Doctor?"

"I haven't *done* anything," the doctor replied indignantly. "At least, nothing I wasn't supposed to do, which was to make her as comfortable as possible and get as much done as I could before transporting her downside. She needs specialists now. I'm not experienced in spinal injuries, and she needs a real specialist to work on her pelvis."

"Well, what's happening?" Lucy demanded as she tried unsuccessfully to peer into the cover.

The doctor described what he'd seen and pointed out the places—visible once he knew where to look in the mist—where hoses and tubes had come out of the table and either connected to or entered Kitty's body. There was something covering the area around her pelvis. There were four black bands that circled her arms and legs just above her wrists and ankles, with tubes a quarter-inch thick running down into the table. And a black band covered her mouth, nose, and damaged eyes.

"We have to get her out of there!" Lucy exclaimed.

"That was my first response also, Captain, but I'm no longer sure of that. What I can see shows me that she's still breathing. If there was a limited amount of oxygen in there, she'd have already used it up. If you look closely, you can see her chest rising and falling regularly. Slowly, but regularly. And whatever is in charge of this process has attached cuffs to her arms and legs at optimal points to access arteries for flushing the blood of toxins or administering drugs."

The doctor fiddled with the Zippo he'd pulled back out of his pocket. "What's controlling this process and whether or not we should take her out of there is anybody's guess. At any rate, she doesn't seem to be any worse off than if she were out of there."

Lucy laid a hand on the container. "For the time being, since you feel that she's in no danger, we'll keep things as they are. I don't like it, but it doesn't look like we have any choice. I'll have the engineers look into this situation, and I expect you to keep me apprised of any changes in her status. That is your top priority. Understood, Doctor?"

Dr. Penn drew himself up to his full, not inconsiderable height and said gravely, "Captain Grimes, I consider Captain Hawke to be a *most* important patient. With the death of her husband, she's the single most important person in our organization."

"I'm glad we agree, Doctor." Lucy took one more look at the container. "All I can say is do the best you can with what you have available. Now, there are several things I need to see to." As she left sickbay, she looked at her watch and noted that it was only two p.m.

Forcibly pushing Kitty's situation to the back of her mind, Lucy headed back to *Galileo's* ready room. Hating the thought of sitting in Simon's chair, she did so reluctantly and picked up the personnel roster she'd ordered. Anxiety tingling her thoughts, she looked for someone—*anyone*—who could take over command of the *Galileo*.

Her commlink chimed, interrupting her thoughts. Picking it up, she snapped, "Grimes."

A nervous ensign, bucked up to second watch by the loss of crew transferred to Libra Base, stammered, "M-ma'am, communication from the *Heinlein*. Captain Kane's compliments, and she says they plan to dock with the *Galileo* within two hours."

Lucy sat up with a start. *What the hell*, she thought. *Marsha was in the belt the last I heard.*

Aloud, she asked the ensign, "How is she going to dock in two hours? Where *is* the *Heinlein*?"

"Ma'am, scan reports the *Heinlein's* beacon at two hours out. That's all I can tell you."

Lucy's first order of business had been to send messages to all bases and the *Heinlein,* informing them of the disaster. She hadn't expected anyone to show up in much less than a week, and she'd certainly have questions for Marsha about how she'd managed this feat.

As for what was going on down below, the United States was reeling. Kitty's two antimatter missiles, combined with the shuttle's power core blowing up, had taken out a sizable chunk of real estate. At the present time, government estimates as to the number of people killed were fifty-six, not counting dignitaries and Simon's team. And of course, that number being revised upward was a very real possibility because there were generally no remains with an antimatter explosion. So, for the time being, that total was going to remain a guesstimate, albeit a close one.

Lucy had tried several times to reach Galway but had received no answer on the special comm circuit set up just for him. She'd decided to beam down and call his private number when word of the *Heinlein's* arrival reached her.

Her commlink chimed again. She sighed and picked it up. "Grimes," she said in a resigned voice.

"Captain, this is Commander Nellis, Senior Computer Technician," a hesitant voice said.

"Yes, Commander?"

"Normally, ma'am, I'd be bringing this to either Captain Hawkes' attention, but..."

"Go on, Commander. I understand your problem. We'll all be dealing with it for a long time," Lucy prompted.

"I just want to report some strange occurrences in the computer core."

"Define 'strange' for me, will you?" Lucy asked. *With all the surprises I've had today, what's another one?* she thought and forced herself to take a calming breath. "And tell me why you feel the need to bring it to my attention right now."

"Well, Captain Hawke left standing instructions that any time we found something new about *Galileo*, we were to report to him immediately. And since he's... since you're... I didn't know who else to report to."

"We're all having a hard time right now, Commander," Lucy said, consoling the nervous crewman. "So, what did you discover?"

"Well, you know that when we first started to activate the *Heinlein*, we were downloading programs from the *Galileo* to the *Heinlein's* computer core.”

“Go on,” Lucy urged.

“We left out a lot of stuff, of course, because the new ships don’t need to have information about how to build bases and factories and things like.”

“I understand. Go on.” Frustration was becoming apparent in her voice.

“Well, Captain, there was a section of the core we couldn’t read. It seemed to be locked. We couldn’t download it to anything else, and we couldn’t read it or access it in any way. We assumed it was a locked file under some code we hadn’t figured out or possibly a voice lock that belonged to the previous captain. Anyway, that section is now active and doing... something”

Lucy felt a chill run up her spine. “When did you notice this section of the core become active, Commander?”

“About an hour and a half ago, I noticed some unusual activity around the file area, ma’am, but it wasn’t ‘til about half an hour ago that it actually started doing anything that caught my attention as far as the locked file itself.”

“A half hour, you say?”

“Yes, ma’am.”

“Well, thank you, Commander. Keep me informed of any changes, and if I have any questions, I’ll call you. Thank you for your attention to this matter.”

The conversation had reminded her that she needed to get in touch with the engineering department, so she called them immediately and asked the chief engineer if he would please be kind enough to go down to the sickbay and look into the matter of how they could possibly disengage Captain

Hawke from the equipment. "I need to know everything you can tell me about the device we're dealing with here. I don't like being sandbagged."

Lucy was beginning to feel very tenuous; like a cloud on a summer day, her attention and time were being nibbled at from one direction and then another. Handling the problems of her own ship was a headache in and of itself. Now, she had to solve the *Galileo's* problems, too.

Both ships were overcrowded. The one she was now on had no commanding officer or first officer, and she didn't see anybody farther down the chain of command ready to take over in anything less than six months. To make matters worse, radio and television from Earth was having a field day with the situation. Half of them were looking for some government official or other to hang, and the other half wanted to launch strikes at the "aliens in our skies."

Stephen had been standing back, in as much shock as everybody else. He'd understood before anyone else that the situation wasn't going to get better without people working to make it so. Simon, he realized, had always known. He'd been bull-headed, stubborn, and something akin to a force of nature when he got his mind set. Kitty was his lighter side, his motivator and his brake, when needed. She took what he created and somehow made those she came in contact with feel that it was the right thing to do. What he saw now was a rudderless ship with one chance to get back on track. *That* was why he had, even before Lucy, sent word out to all the bases with the suggestion that Kitty be put in charge "for the duration."

The *Heinlein* finally matched orbit with the two ships already circling the stunned planet, and Lucy, Marsha, and Gayle shared a tearful reunion. When the three women broke apart, Stephen took his turn commiserating Gayle.

"I didn't know him as long as you did, but you can't work with someone for three years without something developing. I was going to ask him to be my best man when he got back from this trip."

Gayle held him tight and said, "I saw the bond grow between you two, so I know you're hurting too. Wait… best man?" She pushed him away and held him at arm's length. "Is that a proposal?" At his nod, she said, "Lucy, Marsha, wanna be bride's maids? This skunk just proposed! His timing sucks, but I think I'm gonna take him up on it just to teach him a lesson."

People could only talk about a painful subject for so long before they had to get away from it for at least a little while.

After agreeing to be Gayle's bride's maid, Lucy turned to Marsha. "Okay, how did you get here so fast?"

"Actually it was something Kitty said on our shakedown cruise," Marsha answered. "She was the one who thought about the idea I call 'micro-jumps.' I wouldn't try it out in the belt, but coming into Earth orbit was no problem."

They sat in the *Galileo's* ready room, and Lucy brought the others up to date on the goings on aboard the two ships, and as far as she could with what was going on downside.

"I'm willing to bet this whole thing was set up by

that bastard Anderson," she said and glanced around guiltily, recalling a very unpleasant ass-chewing she'd received in this very room for losing her temper once before. "I'm guessing he died in the explosion, but I'm wondering about Galway. He's not answering the commlink we gave him, so I'm going to have to go down eventually and try his private number. It looks like Anderson is going to be their scapegoat. His name and face are already beginning to show up on television. The White House is trying to put the best spin on it they can. They're saying Anderson was a rogue agent and that he had Vice-President Reese fooled. Communications is picking up transmissions aimed directly at us asking for contact, but I haven't responded yet."

Marsha ran her hands through her hair, gave her head a shake to settle her pageboy cut back into place, and asked, "Okay, so what do you want me to do?"

"What do I want you to do? What do *I* want *you* to do?" she repeated, voice rising. Picking up three pieces of paper and waving them at Marsha, she read, "Libra Base, Captain McCord commanding: How can I help? Gemini Base, Commander Gardner commanding: What can we do to assist? Orion Base, Commander Baylor commanding: Our deepest sympathies. Just ask. Whatever we can do, we will.

"And now *you* hit me with 'What do you want me to do?' Just who decided that all this shit was supposed to land on *my* shoulders? Simon was the one who had the vision, and Kitty made people want to... well, she just had confidence oozing out of every pore. And every time you stood next to her or she looked at you, you caught it. She led by 'being' as much as 'doing,' and I'm here right now because

Stephen's and Gayle's 'smoke and mirrors' got our attention at that first meeting in Denver. But it wasn't the smoke and mirrors that kept us, or it wasn't what kept *me*. I'm here because Kitty made it feel right. Simon said, 'Let's go build a base in the asteroid belt,' and Kitty didn't blink an eye. Build a second base? The right thing to do. Command of the first ship to come off the line? The right thing to do. Take out the ship that tried to take out Orion, the right thing to do. (Okay, she went a little loopy there, but she's human.) Negotiate for bases on Earth? It was the right thing to do. But for *this* to happen… for her to see Simon dead, for her to be hurt this badly. And for her to be in that… that… thing. To be in *storage*. You haven't seen her. I *have.*" And with that Lucy finally got to break down and have her cry.

It's said that catharsis is good for the soul, and Lucy came away from her experience a new person but still unwilling to take any kind of command beyond the *McCaffrey*. "I'm only twenty-five for Christ's sake," she said.

Stephen, as the only male in the room, felt it incumbent on him to say something to try to help. "You know, Alexander the Great set out to conquer the world before he was twenty-four."

Lucy considered that for all of two seconds and then laughed. "First of all, Alexander was absolute ruler of his empire. If you happen to have an empire laying around here for me to be absolute ruler of, I might consider it. Second, his two biggest problems were elephants and the Alps. I'm going to have to deal with spaceships and aliens—at least,anyone who sits in this chair for any length of time will have to deal with it. And third, he *failed*."

"*Wonderful* analogy, Stephen," Gayle said.

"Well, my point is that Alexander tried. He didn't just roll over and curl up into a ball 'cause his daddy died. Uh, I mean..."

"Well, you still can't expect me to take command of this... this bunch," Lucy wailed.

"Yes, we can," Marsha said gently, "and here's why. One of the things Simon tried to teach us was the chain of command. And by us, I mean those of us young enough not to have any military experience and young enough to not know what following a chain of command meant. Which, if you think about it, is about ninety-eight percent of us out here. I talked to a couple of people on the way in, and they told me some interesting things about the chain of command. One is that you can't be in overall command unless you've been in a fighting unit or come up through the ranks of a fighting unit. In other words, the head of the Quartermaster Corps can't go out and command an army in the field. He's not trained for it, although he has the rank. So nobody on the space bases qualifies to be in command. Right now, there are three other captains, and one is critically injured. And you've been a captain longer than me, Lucy. That's why you're it—not because somebody ganged up on you and not because nobody else wants the job, but because if we're going to follow this thing the way Simon wanted, that's the way it'll have to be. I've heard of something called a council of captains, and we can think about that one. Call it an advisory board or delegating authority."

"Well, if I'm going to be senior captain," Lucy said. "I can't command two ships. That's my rule. My number one moves up and gets his own ship a little sooner than expected. We'll have to name his new number one. And by the time that's all done, there are going to be three ships ready and waiting for crews. I don't know if anyone else has seen the bottleneck, but I have. What I want to see done is that in the next open spot we build a freighter with room for four hundred passengers and simulators. Figure the crew yourself, Stephen, since your job is to design a new ship. And this new ship's job is going to be to go to Earth, fill up with passengers and go crew a ship. This ship will also have a transporter in it, and it will be armed. It will carry two flights of Mambas and have shields. We'll try to fly her with an escort whenever possible. Gayle, Miranda Lee, and Robert Greene will be captaining the three new ships."

Immediately after this revelation, Lucy's commlink went off. "I've been getting this all day," she said, "and I'm getting tired of it."

The *Galileo's* chief engineer, Titus Safer, reported to Lucy. "As you know, Captain, we've been mapping out the *Galileo's* inner systems for over two years now. This just goes to show that we can still be surprised. We had no idea that any of these systems or equipment existed. What we have is some very sophisticated medical equipment whose monitors are piggybacked off sensors that are connected to the bio-monitors in our wristbands. We managed to get inside the pedestal below the tabletop, but I'm not willing to monkey with the equipment we found there—not with the captain's life at stake. As for the rest, that was all in what amounts to a concealed room next to the sickbay. Apparently, what the system does is identify when someone is in critical condition, then takes over and begins repairs on its own."

CHAPTER TWO

Roland Daniels, FBI, on special assignment to the *TAS Galileo*, looked around and saw nothing but destruction. Actually, the destruction was a short way from where he sat in a copse of trees and brush while acrid smoke drifted through his hiding place.

His original intention had been to tweak the noses of the Hawkes when he left the *Galileo* unobserved because of the sensitive material he was carrying—material he was sure they wouldn't let him leave the ship with because a lot of it concerned the weapons and propulsion systems he wasn't supposed to get near.

He *had* managed to get near them, though, and he'd done that by the simple expedient of removing his wristband. He'd been sure that doing so would have raised a flag in the computer, but nothing had happened. Of course, it had taken McNalley's help, and the only reason he'd been able to convince McNalley to help him was because he'd taught him to read and then helped him pass his ratings test.

A grateful McNalley had fabricated a fake wristband for him that he could wear around, and just so the computer wouldn't get suspicious, he carried his real wristband around in his pocket to show that he was going about his daily activities, except, of course, when he wanted to be someplace off-limits, like weapons bays, engine rooms, shuttles, etcetera.

Thinking his bosses would be very pleased with him, he'd managed to acquire one of those neat little hand lasers, and not the model they used in their Z-tag games. Being a fan of the old-fashioned methods, as well, he'd managed to get McNalley to fashion a taser, which he stashed in a hiding place along with the laser and the phony wristband.

His new-found freedom came in very handy the day he found out that Simon was going down to talk with the vice-president at Camp David. In the days leading up to that mission, he'd kept a close eye on the comings and goings of the technicians and other personnel working on the projects deck. The night before the flight, he'd secreted himself, along with his cache of weapons and information, in a storage locker near where he expected the shuttle to be prepped. He'd drilled several small holes for air and surveillance, and settled down for a long, uncomfortable wait.

A loud clang woke him from an uneasy slumber, and he peered groggily out one of the holes he'd drilled the night before. As he'd guessed, the shuttle was being prepped not far from where he'd chosen to hide—only fifty yards, in fact—and he waited patiently while the technicians came and went. Finally, the last preflight check had been made, and the last technician had gone off to lunch.

He'd slipped out of the storage locker and made his way to the shuttle. This would be the hardest part of his plan—no place to hide and no excuse for being where he was. And if he'd miscounted and there *was* somebody aboard…

The shuttle, designed to hold a pilot, co-pilot, and eight passengers, was empty. During his last three months aboard, Daniels had found time enough to inspect these particular vehicles several times and knew there was a space in the engine room large enough to hold him if no concerted search or inspection was made. He'd passed through a thick door in the aft bulkhead and slid it shut. Calling on his training in the service, he'd then slipped into a light doze and waited.

Muffled sounds and nearly imperceptible vibrations had brought him back to awareness of his surroundings. He made out what he thought were the sounds of people entering and then the definite sound of the shuttle door closing. Engines powering up left no doubt that they were about to depart the *Galileo*. It was the thought of having no control over what was going to happen in the descent and landing that had almost made him reveal his presence, and it was training that kept had him quiet.

His original intention had been to exit the shuttle immediately after the Terran Alliance contact team left it, depending on the taser to overcome anyone left aboard and his credentials to get him past any guards posted by the Camp David commander. But that intention was blown to hell by the rocket that streaked past Simon, blowing three of the contact team to pieces.

Daniels had opened the aft hatch a crack to see Simon walking down the ramp and managed to slam it shut when he saw the trapdoor spring up and a camouflage-clad soldier lift a shoulder-fired rocket launcher into position. Opening it again proved to be a problem. Warped by the explosion just on the other side, it required all his strength to get it open enough to squeeze through, but hearing urgent voices getting louder, he decided to stay put and instead peeked around the edge of the door. He saw five men racing past the sprawled body of Simon for the shuttle ramp, weapons firing into the interior. Stepping back into the shadows provided by an extinguished light, he was able to see into the main section of the shuttle and recognized parts of bodies here and there around the interior. With his gorge rising and skin crawling at the smell of burning flesh, he pulled the laser pistol and taser out of his waistband and waited.

Crouching down behind a cluster of power conduits near the doorway, he heard the screams of injured men and shuddered. Almost immediately, he heard feet thundering up the access ramp, and knowing how he would divide his forces had they been his, he pointed his laser at the door. Seconds later, he saw fingers reach around the door and try to slide it farther open. A rifle barrel poked its nose in and sprayed a fan of slugs into the room, which provoked an outcry from the front of the craft.

"That's the engine room, asshole! Do you want to blow us all to hell?"

The soldier slid through into the room, and Roland Daniels joined the opposition when he raised the pistol and silently burned a hole through the man's temple.

As he crossed the hatchway, pistol in hand, he could see the backs of two men standing at the controls. Wondering where the other men were, he angled himself so he could see out the hatch and down the ramp. Seeing Simon's body lying there with a camo-clad body next to him, Daniels had a pretty good idea where the fifth body lay. Quickly stripping off the dead soldier's shirt, he put it on, casting uneasy glances out the hatch.

After repeated explosions from outside the craft, he noticed that the heavy weapons' fire was diminishing. *The Mambas are probably taking out the gun emplacements*, he thought. He also knew that it would be a matter of moments before the Mambas turned their attention to the shuttle to keep it from being hijacked. As the thickening smoke drifted across the helipad and compound, he picked up the soldier's rifle, shoved the pistol in his belt, and stepped out of the hatchway.

Three quick strides took him to the ramp, and he raced down it, stopping beside Simon's body. Kneeling, he checked the neck for a pulse as he scanned the compound, looking for any indication that he'd been discovered. The drifting clouds of smoke reassured him that he was still relatively safe from both parties. Finding a pulse, he shouldered the rifle, lifted the limp body in a fireman's carry, and staggered off into a pall of smoke. Glancing up, he saw the shapes of the Mambas, slicing through the smoke like vengeful sharks through a murky sea.

As he tottered away, he glanced back and saw a Mamba come to a stop just feet off the ground. Kitty's voice came from *inside* the shuttle, and he realized it must be some sort of relay.

"Attention Earth forces inside the shuttle. This is Wing Commander Hawke of the *TAS Galileo*. You have two choices: surrender or die. That shuttle only leaves the ground with *TAS* personnel at the helm."

Hearing her threats to destroy the shuttle made Roland redouble his efforts. Having spent the better part of a year aboard the *Galileo* while being exposed to all the talk about antimatter and exactly what it could do added impetus to his headlong flight. He stopped behind a gardener's shack only long enough to secure his hold on Simon.

When he almost ran headlong into a fence on the backside of the compound, he figured he'd only traveled some two hundred yards. With his free hand he pulled the laser from his belt, used it to burn a hole through the fence, and continued on at a shambling run. He began cursing every one of his sixty-one years with each step, and finally, when his legs and back were on fire and he could move no farther, he wormed his way into a tangled thicket among some trees and dropped his load.

Simon was in miraculously good condition... for a man who'd been hit by four bullets. One had entered the upper left thigh and Roland could find no exit wound. Another had gone in and out the left shoulder and seemed to have missed the artery there. One had creased the scalp for about four inches above the left ear and was probably the cause of his unconsciousness. And the last one seemed to have hit the wristband on his left wrist. "Seemed" was the only word for it. Simon's wrist was discolored, swollen, and flopping loosely, and his wristband was hanging by a thread.

Roland held the wrist down and pulled the remains of the wristband off, placing it in a pocket. Slipping the dead soldier's shirt off, he began to rip it into strips. He wrapped Simon's wrist, then did what he could to stop the blood flow from the other two major wounds.

Taking stock of assets and liabilities was part of Roland's training. First, he considered the clothes on his back. He pulled the patches and rank insignia off both himself and Simon and put them in the same pocket with the wristband. Next was his wallet, which contained sixty-five dollars he hadn't expected to need, a Visa card that was surely invalid since he hadn't made a payment in almost a year, his identification, and a driver's license. Then there was a taser of "alien" manufacture, a laser of equally unlikely origin, a military rifle with eighteen rounds, and an unconscious man in shock and oozing blood. Best of all, he'd managed to bring along seven medium-sized diamonds "scavenged" from a collection tray in the factory section of the *Galileo* during one of his interviews. No one had seen him scoop them from the collection tray, and he'd figured they'd go a long way towards proving to his bosses just how lucrative a venture space could be. Added to all that was his being in a strange state, knowing almost nobody, and the fact that the unconscious man was the leader of the "opposition."

When you get into deep shit, Daniels, you do it in a big way! he told himself.

During his brief rest, the sounds of traffic finally penetrated his mind, and Roland loaded a still-unconscious Simon up, moving toward those sounds. What he found was a paved two-lane road bordered on both sides by trees and scrub. Sitting along the road, he waited for just the right vehicle. Roland Daniels, FBI, had just become a terrorist on the run.

Here I am rescuing people whose way of life is detrimental to all I've believed in all my life, and now I'm planning to shoot out a tire so some poor schmuck will have to change it so I can sneak into the nation's capital and hide the very person I rescued. And to top it off, I can't go to any government source!

After shooting out a tire with the laser, Roland got Simon up into the backend of a disreputable stake-bed truck loaded with questionable-looking barrels of something-or-other. Roland had noticed the transport logo on the truck's door and figured it would be headed into the city's commercial district since it was headed in the direction of DC. Already, a plan was forming in his mind, one that dealt with a lot of ifs. But with luck, he could pull it off.

He'd looked at things as more of a game than anything else when he climbed into that storage locker on the *Galileo,* and luck had been riding with him from the first. Now, though, he was going to have to *depend* on luck, and that could be very disconcerting.

Simon had been drifting in and out of consciousness over the past several hours as they made their way into the commercial district. Roland had been able to stop the bleeding using parts of the dead soldier's shirt as a compress, but the stains on his shoulder and thigh were a dead giveaway. The only thing that helped at the moment was the black material of the uniform Simon wore.

The driver pulled his rig into a nondescript cartage company's holding yard and went to report to the freight master. Roland chivied Simon to the edge of the truck's bed, jumped out, and helped him down. Using one arm to hold Simon up without appearing to do anything except keep him on a straight path, and with the other hand holding a paper bag filled with rubbish from the truck's bed to simulate a bottle, Roland and Simon staggered out of the yard without being spotted and down the street to an alley Roland had noticed on the way in.

Taking the calculated risk of leaving Simon in the alley, Roland walked back to the cartage company and asked to borrow a phone book. Checking first for a local Goodwill store, he then called a taxi and squandered some of his precious cash. He had the cabby drop him off two blocks past the store, paid him off and watched him turn the next corner.

Buying two sets of clothes that would make them look more rural than anything else, he used the store's phone to call another cab. Using the same deception, he let this driver drop him several blocks from his destination and walked to a convenience store. There, he bought bottled water for the resealable containers and several sandwiches, and headed back for the alley.

He was relieved to find Simon's condition unchanged and managed with some success to get him to drink some of the water. With the remainder of the soldier's shirt, he tried to get most of the blood wiped off Simon's face and neck. He then proceeded to strip the blood-soaked shirt off and replace it with one of the shirts from the Goodwill store. The water seemed to restore some of Simon's energy, and he seemed to rest easier, although he didn't regain full consciousness.

Roland waited impatiently for dark and then walked back to the cartage company. Finding it dark, as he'd hoped, he used the laser to cut a link in the chain locking the gate and slipped inside. Through the darkened glass of the door, he could barely make out the alarm sensor and, setting the laser at a lower intensity, he managed to fuse it so it wouldn't go off. He'd seen the key box when he made his earlier visit, so he had no trouble finding the key he wanted—the one to the truck that had brought them there. Praying that it wasn't sitting on empty, he climbed in and checked the gauge. He found it to be half full, and sighing with relief, he started the engine.

Opening the gate, moving the truck through, and closing it again took all of three minutes, including welding the link back in place. Moving out of the area without arousing suspicion was of prime importance, so he kept everything as legal as possible.

Except for breaking and entering, grand theft auto, harboring a fugitive, breaking my oath to the United States, and who knows how many other charges that could be filed against me, he thought.

With some difficulty, he got Simon into the cab of the truck. He then went back to pick up the water bottles and food and changed clothes. That hurdle passed, Roland headed for his next one—getting clandestine medical help for a wounded man. He drove the truck back to the area of the Goodwill store. In this district, a person could find liquor stores, crack houses, whorehouses, and rescue missions, all within easy reach of the capitol building, Roland realized with a shake of his head.

He pulled the truck into an alley behind a rescue mission where he laid Simon down on the seat, locked the doors, and went inside. Realizing his appearance was a cut above what passed for normal for this place, even though he'd "dressed down," he walked up to a middle-aged man who was industriously pushing a broom across the floor.

Obviously down on his luck, and equally obviously bound and determined to pay his way with the only coin he had, he asked, "Who's in charge around here, bud?"

"That'd be Father Timothy," the man said. Pointing with his chin, he added, "You can find his office down that hall."

The man turned away without another word and went back to his sweeping, leaving Roland standing there. He watched the man sweep for a few more seconds, then went in the indicated direction. At the third door on the right he saw a cardboard nameplate held up with masking tape that said simply, "Father Jeffers."

Knocking on the door brought a muffled, "Come in," and he opened the door.

Father Timothy was not what he'd expected. In his forties, black, balding, and heavy-set, he didn't sit in his chair as much as inhabit it. Nor was he dressed as one would traditionally expect a priest to be. He had on a grey sweatshirt that showed a frayed cuff as he moved a piece of correspondence from one stack to another.

"Can I help you?" he asked, moving an appraising eye up and down Roland's body.

Roland hesitantly asked, "Father Timothy?"

The man behind the desk said, "I have either that honor or cross to bear, depending on whether you bring me good news or trouble, my son. How may I be of service?"

Roland looked back out the door, stepped inside, and pushed it shut. "Father, I'm afraid it may be a cross for you to bear as what I have is nothing but trouble."

"Sit down, my son, and tell me what the problem is. I'll be the judge of whether it's trouble or not."

"Well, now I'm beginning to wonder if it was such a good idea for me to come here at all, Father,"

Roland said. "I have an injured friend, and at this particular point in time I can't take him to a hospital."

Father Timothy said, "When you have trouble with the law, my hands are pretty well tied, my son."

"Well, there's different kinds of trouble. Sometimes it not so much with the law as it is with the people who make the laws."

"Could you be a little more specific?"

Roland reached into his hip pocket, pulled out his wallet, and let the priest see his badge and ID card. "Father, I'm under cover, and my partner has been shot. I can't afford losing a year's worth of investigation by going to a hospital. They'll ask questions I'm not prepared to answer at this time. I need a doctor to patch up some holes so I can move him to a safehouse. Father, I really hate to put you on the spot, but it amounts to this: we go to a hospital, my partner dies. There are... others out there who would kill us both before we could walk back out the doors. And if we don't get him some medical attention soon, he dies anyway. His, and my, only chance is to find, shall we say, alternative medical help. I was really hoping you might know someone I could deal with quietly."

"How badly off is your partner? I can't say what I can do until I know that much, at least," the father said.

"He has a bullet in his thigh, a hole through his shoulder, a broken wrist, and most likely a concussion from a bullet graze."

The Father thought for a moment or two, then sighed. "There's a man I can call. He's a doctor, but he won't be able to show you a license. Helps me out with some of the addicts and usually I can get him to work for free, but for this he's going to want to be paid."

"Father, I'll pay you, and *you* can pay him. That way, you'll be able to keep the largest portion of this." Roland reached into his pocket, felt among the stones there, and pulled out what felt like the largest, about the size of a pea. "This is an uncut diamond. There's no blood associated with it, and if you want to get right down to it, I'm the one who found it." He thought back to scooping them out of the retrieval tray along with the other six in his pocket. Never would he have guessed at the time what use he'd be putting them to.

"Now, you wouldn't be lying to a priest, my son?" Father Timothy asked.

"Father, I wasn't raised Catholic, but what religious upbringing I have won't let me lie to a priest. I'm with the FBI, we'll get killed if we go to a hospital, I found that diamond, and our situation is desperate and urgent."

Father Timothy said, "Without indications to the contrary, I'll have to take you at your word, and I can call the doctor right now. I need to know your partner's condition one more time so he'll know what to bring."

Roland repeated, "A bullet lodged in his upper left thigh, a broken left wrist, a through-and-through in the left shoulder and a bullet graze over his left ear. I don't know his blood type."

Having reached a decision, the priest came alive and took charge of the situation. "So where is your partner?" he asked in a brisk and business-like manner.

"In the alley behind this building," was the instant

response "And it would be best for all concerned if as few people as possible know we're here."

"Then I suggest we go get him ourselves," the father said. "We can leave him in the care of Sister Celestine until the doctor arrives." Picking up the phone, he called a number from memory and spoke persuasively for about two minutes. Then, to Roland, he said, "Let's be about it. As the Bard would say, 'Twere best were done quickly.'"

The two men stepped out into the alley and Roland unlocked the truck. Grabbing Simon's feet, they slid him out, caught a shoulder apiece and hurried him into the mission.

As he was being laid down on an examining table in the mission's infirmary, Simon's eyes shot open. Seeing the priest, he exclaimed, "Who the hell are you?"

Roland spoke quietly. "You're in good hands, Simon. You got shot, remember? You're safe now. Just rest. The doctor is on his way. This is Father Jeffers," he said, a placating tone in his voice.

Simon turned his head and focused on Roland with difficulty. "You're... Daniels."

"That's right. I'm Daniels, your partner. Go to sleep now. The doctor will be here shortly."

Simon slumped in the priest's arms, and Roland helped get him onto the table. Father Jeffers called a nun into the room.

"I need you to sit with him, Sister. Do what you can for him until the doctor arrives."

The sister, dressed as unconventionally as the priest, complied silently. She went first to the sink, got a wet towel, and began to wash Simon's face.

"We'll leave your partner in Sister Celestine's

capable hands for now. Let's go back to my office for the time being."

The priest sat down and dialed a number again. "I need you here an hour ago. The patient has a high fever and probably a massive infection, so antibiotics, an intravenous saline drip, and a plasma bag would be in order. We'll discuss your compensation later." He listened for a few seconds and then said, "Don't forget you're speaking to a man of the cloth. You'll not be cheated, and you know it."

Hanging up the phone, Father Timothy rummaged through a desk drawer and came up with a business card. He dialed the number and leaned back in the chair. As he waited for the connection, he told Roland, "We can expect the doctor within the half hour." Turning his attention back to the phone, the father said, "Michael, I know it's late, but I have a small item for you to look at. If you'd be kind enough to bring your experience and a jeweler's loupe around to the mission, I'll say a prayer for you at Sunday Mass." At Roland's raised eyebrows, Father Timothy hung up the phone and said, "Some of the people who come through here don't live their lives on the streets, but they do occasionally find themselves in untenable circumstances. The church is there to give a hand up where it can, Michael needed to be put back on the straight and narrow, as it were." He gave a small chuckle. "His marriage broke up and his wife took the kids. He thought the world had ended, but I showed him it hadn't. And now, he helps me out from time to time."

"I assume then that Michael is a jeweler," Roland said in a conversational tone.

The father smiled. "In a manner of speaking. A lot

of people who come through here have items of... questionable history. And Michael is adept at dealing with that type of material."

"In other words, he's a fence."

"Michael," the priest said, "is a pawnbroker with his own unique interpretation of the rules of ownership. He makes money on the deal, money comes into the mission, people stay fed and clothed. As you can tell, I, myself, have my own interpretation of right and wrong. And as long as nobody's getting hurt, I'm willing to overlook some of the niceties. Now, I *am* bound to tell you that you won't realize as much from this," he pushed the small gem around on the desktop, "as you would if you went to a reputable jeweler."

Roland hastily said, "I'm not looking to realize anything out of this. That's yours."

Father Timothy looked at Roland said, "You're going to have to learn not to argue with a stubborn man, my son."

Roland replied, "And you're going to have to learn not to look a gift horse in the mouth, Father. You can feed, clothe, and help a lot more people, and you can do it better with reliable heat, good plumbing, blankets for all, and things I haven't even considered in my whole life. Anyway, at this particular moment I have an errand to run. I need to return that truck before someone gets upset over my having borrowed it."

"I must admit," the father said, "the idea had crossed my mind that you'd be attending to that in some way or other."

Roland gave Father Timothy a crooked grin. "Well, at least I'm not going to try to sell it to Michael."

The father laughed heartily. "That is a mark in your favor, my son. Indeed it is."

Parking the truck about a block from the cartage company's yard, Roland walked back toward the mission. He disposed of the keys in a storm drain and walked down the stairs into the subway, checking a map on the wall for the exit nearest the mission.

When he finally stepped back into the mission, he felt the tension drain out of his shoulders. A place of relative safety, he could relax somewhat. He walked down the corridor to Father Timothy's office and tapped on the door. After hearing a scrape and footsteps moving toward the door, it opened a fraction.

"I realized after you left that I never did get your name. And the doctor arrived shortly before you did. We should be hearing from him shortly," the priest said as he stepped back and opened the door.

"Roland Daniels, Father." His eyes took in the guest sitting at Father Timothy's desk—a smallish man in his mid-thirties. He was using the desk lamp as he put a jeweler's loupe to his eye. "You must be Michael," Roland said.

"I've been accused of it at one time or another in my life. You must be the man who belongs to this stone."

"That, for a fact, I am," Roland replied.

"So where did you get this little beauty?" Michael asked as he gazed into the depths of the stone. "Not a flaw, not an inclusion, uncut and a beautiful blue-white."

"I'm not at liberty to tell you where I got it."

"Then I've got news for you. I can only get about ten percent for a hot stone."

"I can guarantee you," Roland said, "that you'll find the stone in your hands has never been reported stolen. You're only the third person to ever lay eyes on it—myself and Father Timothy being the first two."

Michael looked up from the diamond in his hand. "So, you're telling me I can go up to the City, go to any jewel buyer on the Street, and they'll give what this stone is worth?"

"I don't see why not. What *is* it worth?"

Michael looked up at the father. "You know I get ten percent, right?"

"Michael, we've been associates for a long time now. Besides, you'll be the one taking any risks. We'll take your word on the price, and you'll get your ten percent. I just want you to know that if you cheat me, you're cheating God, too."

"Father, I wouldn't do that to you," Michael said a bit hastily. "But what we're talking about is twenty thousand dollars or better. And that's just for the rough stone. Imagine what it'll be worth after it's been cut!"

"How long do you think it'll take you to make a deal that'll bring Father Timothy here some cash?" Roland asked.

"Forty-eight hours, maybe seventy-two."

"Tell ya what." Roland reached into his pocket and pulled out two more stones. "If you can turn that into 'twenty-four, maybe forty-eight,' you can add this one for me, keep twenty percent, and keep the third one all to yourself."

Father Timothy's mouth fell open. "My son! Are you sure about this?"

"Father, without your assistance, I'd be dead, along with my partner," Roland said, "so yes, I am."

"I can leave for New York first thing in the morning," Michael said, "and find out what I can get for these on the Street." He stood up and pocketed the stones. "I can probably be back late tomorrow evening with cashier's checks that will require jaw surgery for the both of you."

Shaking his hand, Roland wished him a safe trip and watched him pull the door closed with a soft click, leaving the two men with nothing to do but wait.

As they waited to hear from the doctor, the father's eyes were drawn to a small television set flickering in the corner, volume down. He glanced at his watch and said, "Would you be kind enough to turn the volume up a bit? It's almost time for the eleven o'clock news."

With a great deal of trepidation, Roland reached over and turned the volume up, listening to what amounted to the tail end of a recap of that morning's events, as there'd been nothing else on the news since then. What little he did hear was enough to chill him to the bone. Then, the top of the hour brought a dose of reality he didn't know how to swallow.

An appropriately sad-faced commentator sat inside the little flickering box and announced to the world the death of the American Vice-President, British ambassador, Chinese, Pakistani and Russian ambassadors, ambassadors from half a dozen third world countries, and various and sundry US military forces to the number of fifty-six, at present count. "The problem with this type of explosion, I've been told, is that while there is no release of radiation," the commentator told a disbelieving world, "according to scientists, an antimatter explosion is tantamount to a total energy conversion, so there are no bodies and remarkably little debris to sift through for clues. Cameras with telescopic lenses set up outside Camp David were able to record what happened.

"First, one of the deadly little ships known as 'Mambas' seemed to magically appear above the helipad at Camp David." The scene cut to one of the Mambas, and the reporter continued as a voice-over. "Shortly thereafter, at a slightly more sedate pace, the other four craft appeared and squared off against the Apache helicopters on patrol above the compound. In a bizarre game of aerial 'chicken,'" the camera zoomed in on Kitty's ship, "one of these 'Mambas' and one of the helicopters traded moves in a display that was obviously initiated by the helicopter. Just minutes later, the shuttle purportedly carrying the contact team from the 'Terran Alliance' landed."

The scene switched to the shuttle landing in the center of the helipad. "Supposedly headed by the Captain Hawke featured in the transmissions that blanketed the world just a few days ago, shown here in this footage is the one individual who managed to exit the craft before it was attacked by soldiers secreted in hidden spaces below the ground ringing the helipad. As you can tell, he bears a striking resemblance to the 'Captain Hawke' in the video transmission." The screen split in two and showed an enlarged three-quarter still image leaving the shuttle beside one of Simon from his video message to Earth. "Again, in what was obviously a move initiated by US military, a simultaneous assault was launched against the shuttle and the five Mamba craft."

Roland was treated to a montage of helicopters firing on Mambas, gun emplacements opening fire on Mambas, and soldiers jumping up out of concealment, one of them launching a shoulder-fired rocket past Simon into the shuttle itself. Simultaneously, other soldiers cut him down and still others made a determined rush to gain access to the shuttle.

"This obviously orchestrated attack has been laid at the feet of the White House. White House Press Secretary John Gower released a statement just hours ago."

The scene shifted to the White House press room. "The president and the late vice-president had no knowledge of anything pertaining to this morning's unprovoked attack on the members of the Terran Alliance delegation that landed at Camp David. The attack was orchestrated by rogue members of an intelligence department known as the Defense Intelligence Agency under the command of a John Anderson, who was responsible for issuing the orders that activated a select elite unit for guard duty at Camp David this morning. The apparent motive for the assault was to gain access to technology that the United States and several other countries were going to negotiate for. The President deplores the regrettable incident and wishes to express his condolences to the survivors of all those who lost their lives in this most heinous act."

The scene cut back to the reporter. "Democrats and Republicans alike have united for almost the first time in history. And in an apparent effort to assure the world at large that this was not an attempt by the United States to steal technology that was promised to the entire world, they've called for not only a congressional over-sight committee to look into the matter, but to establish a multinational tribunal to deal with the situation and to deal fairly with the Terran Alliance. In a unanimous vote, US Ambassador William Kent has been appointed as US representative to the proposed tribunal, but as of this hour there has been no response from the ambassador's office.

"It is this reporter's opinion that the instantaneous and overwhelming response to the assault on the shuttle has given not only the American military but the military forces of the world in general reason to hesitate before acting in such haste again. And it is also this reporter's opinion that two specific incidents in this morning's debacle are responsible for the instantaneous change of opinion." The scene cut back to an image of the shuttle's landing. Once more, the shuttle was shown landing, the ramp coming down, and the captain walking out. Once more, trapdoors popped open, bodies emerged, a shoulder-fired rocket was launched into the shuttle, and Captain Hawke's body was seen to fall. Once more, the blast wave was seen to explode out of the shuttle. "This scene, and the one just before the final explosion," the reporter said as the scene changed again to one of the shuttle beginning to lift, "shows the shuttle clearly beginning to take off. The fact that it can take that much damage internally and still function shows the durability of this craft, and it is just a *transport!*

"The other fact to consider is that the Mambas were hit on more than one occasion by rockets fired by the Apache helicopters." The scene shifted again to a montage of rockets fired from Apache weapons pods. "And aside from momentary confusion on the part of the Mamba pilots at these unprovoked attacks, there seems to have been no damage at all. In what was obviously intended to be a devastating and overwhelming assault to gain technological advantage for the United States, the military has received their blackest eye in its history. Within five minutes of the first rocket attack, these five small, deadly craft showed why they've been named 'Mambas.'" Scenes of laser beams lancing through the thickening smoke and flames, midair antimatter explosions, and wreckage flaming from the sky assaulted Roland's eyes. The images of gun emplacements exploding, sending sandbags, dirt, and unidentifiable pieces of men and machines flying in all directions brought back memories he wished had stayed securely under lock and key.

"All of this happened with a near-surgical precision that would have taken out only the combatants," the reporter continued, "but for one fatal error on the part of the assailants. We have been made aware that one of the restrictions on the release of technology to Earth at this time is on weapons and propulsion technology. The attempt to seize the shuttle was designed to circumvent that restriction at the cost of all other technology we might acquire." The scene changed to show Kitty's Mamba down on the deck, preparing to fire through the shuttle door. The screen went white and then back to the reporter.

"All that's left in an explosion of this type is a big hole in the ground. Again, the physics of what can only be an antimatter explosion is that it's a very local phenomenon and there is no radioactive fallout. Miraculously, while severely damaged in the explosion, the Mamba that fired the missiles seems to have survived." The scene cut to a shot of the four remaining Mambas surrounding Kitty's ship and lifting it out of camera range. "At last estimate, American losses number fifty-six, including the vice-president and the various ambassadors there to receive the Terran Alliance delegation.

"In other news tonight..."

Father Timothy indicated that Roland could turn the television off, which he did with a sense of relief, sitting back in his chair.

After a few moments of contemplative silence, Father Timothy said, "You appear curiously unmoved, my son." The priest reached into a drawer and pulled out two glasses and a bottle of scotch, pouring a double shot for each of them.

"Unmoved, Father? Let's say I'm... conflicted. I am sad, I am angry, and I'm shamed and humiliated by my government's actions. To think of what we could have had and now won't—technologies to help clean up our air and water; no more reliance on fossil fuel; cheaper, cleaner sources of energy; safer ways to remove toxic and radioactive waste; the ability to feed the hungry throughout the world. And that's not even taking into account gaining access to the stars. And now, because of the stupid actions of a few greedy people, we stand a very good chance of losing all of that."

Father Timothy had a speculative look on his face. "Well, what do you think of the concept of people not having things they haven't earned by the sweat of their own brows, so to speak?"

"Did I say you're in the wrong business, Father?" Roland retorted. At the raised eyebrows, he continued, "The people you help here, they deserve their places to sleep and the food they get because they're human beings, but they haven't earned these things by the sweat of their brows, as you put it. And just what would you do with a ten-dollar bill you found lying on the ground and no way to trace its owner?"

"To answer the first part of your question, my son, a compassionate man cannot watch others go hungry if it's within his power to help, and as for the second part, while I understand what you mean by the finding of a ten-dollar bill, I personally would put it in the poor box or use it to feed some of these people here… some of my flock."

"Well, the people out there found their spaceship. That's their ten-dollar bill. And they're compassionate enough to be willing to share it with the entire world. It's just that in this particular instance, it's a bill of such a large denomination that measures must be taken to safeguard it first."

"I see your point," Father Timothy said. "But what about the many industries destroyed by these new technologies coming along? Large industries with large numbers of people who'll be out of work?"

"Every time a new invention or innovation comes along, someone gets hurt. Look at the light bulb. Do you have any idea how many candle makers and lamp makers and oil transporters and natural gas companies went out of business? I certainly don't, but it must have been a lot. How about the automobile? How many industries went belly up? And how many were created? And the railroad and the telegraph, followed by the telephone. Sure, a lot of people lost jobs, but look at all the *new* jobs that opened up. We have so much to look forward to, Father. A little disruption is a small price to pay."

"I'm beginning to think *you* are in the wrong profession yourself, my son," the father chuckled. "You'd have made a great priest with that kind of conviction. Do you mind the observations of a tired old man?"

"I don't mind the observation of any man, Father. What is it?" Roland asked.

"Actually, I have two. The first is that you seem to know an awful lot for a simple FBI agent. And the second is that your partner bears an amazing resemblance to this 'Captain Hawke.' In all my years as a priest—and there have been quite a few of those—one of the things I've learned to do fairly well is read body language and facial expressions. Now, your body language says you're holding something back, and the expression on your face gave you away when I mentioned the name Hawke. So, do you have anything to tell me that I should know about?"

"Well, Father, I can't tell you *how* I know *what* I know, but I can say that I've noticed the resemblance myself, and I'll have to leave it at that for now."

It was at this moment that the doctor chose to make his appearance. He sank down into the only other chair in the room and said, "Timmy, I do hope you have more of that rotgut stashed in your bottom drawer."

"I'll thank you to show some respect for fine scotch," the father responded. "At no time in history has Chivas Regal ever been considered 'rotgut.' Would you care for another, Mr. Daniels?"

"This once, it might not be such a bad idea," Roland said dryly.

As the father puttered around with another glass and the bottle, the doctor turned to Roland. "Your partner, I presume?"

"Yes, he is," Roland answered. "And if you'll excuse me for being rude, will you not beat around the bush? I need to know how he is."

"Well, as for how he is, he's shot to hell. Beginnings of a good-sized infection, broken wrist, lost a good bit of blood, concussion, dehydration, and a crease in his scalp that it wouldn't hurt to have a plastic surgeon look at or he'll never have hair growing there again. The in-and-out in his left shoulder needs to drain, and it's been irrigated and dressed. You'll need to change bandages twice daily for about a week, then go to once a day for a while. I set the wrist and pulled a bullet out of his left thigh. That will also need to have the dressings changed regularly. He's now resting comfortably, although he seems to want his cat. Do you know anything about that?"

Roland said, "Excuse me? His cat?"

The doctor said, "He kept calling 'kitty, kitty.' That's a first for me."

Roland temporized by saying, "I don't know. Concussion can do strange things to a person's memory, I've heard. Maybe he's remembering a lost cat from his childhood?"

"Well, anyway, I appreciate it when people are a little more forthcoming with me than you seem to have been. And I'm beginning to believe you haven't been all that forthright with Father Timothy here, either."

Roland took a sizable swallow from the drink Father Timothy had set beside him. "I'm sure I don't know what you're talking about, Doctor."

"Really?" retorted the physician, reaching into his

pocket. "I get called into cases like this because sometimes I'm the only doctor people can find without going to the hospital... like you tonight. So I see all kinds of things and pull all kinds of things out of people. And this," he said, tossing a slug down on the table next to Roland's drink, "is a 7.62MM NATO slug. I pulled it out of your partner's thigh. There aren't very many criminals who use this type of round, although there *are* some out there. But it's a military round. And to be perfectly honest with you, the only military action recently has been at Camp David. This morning. This says you two are hotter than a two-dollar pistol."

"Okay, I'm going to talk to you man-to-man. There's no FBI agent here, no doctor, no priest. The more you know about this situation, the more trouble you're in. That *is* Captain Hawke in the other room. I was on the shuttle, too. I managed to get off just before the craft was destroyed, and I picked him up in the smoke and confusion. As soon as he's fit to travel, we need to move. How long will that be, by the way?"

"If he's got the constitution I think he does," the doctor mused, "and if he doesn't do *anything* strenuous, I'd say three days. And he can travel if all he has to do is sit and maybe walk from a car to a motel room. If it's going to be more strenuous than that, it will be weeks. And the more he moves, the more you'll need to change his bandages. In three days he should be able to *hobble*, and please note the stress on the word hobble, on that leg for very short distances. But because of the broken wrist, he can't use crutches. Just what is it you're planning to do, mister?"

Roland thought swiftly, took a sip of the scotch in

his glass, and said, "Head west." More silence while the other two men looked at each other. "Back to where it all started. Which is in Montana and Colorado. That's where a large portion of their recruits come from."

Father Timothy closed his mouth with an audible snap. "So they truly are Earthmen?"

"Yes, Father. Every one of them. There are almost three thousand of them up there on three bases and three ships. They're planning one more base, and they want to have dozens of ships, so they're going to need even more crew."

"And I'm sure they need guidance, too," the father said as his eyes focused on a point far beyond the walls that confined the three men.

"Well, everybody has their own interpretation of guidance. I've spent the last year living with them, studying them to make a report to my superiors... to the Office of the President. With their knowledge, mind you. My presence on the shuttle and saving Captain Hawke's life was a purely fortuitous situation. The simple fact of the matter is that the man you just patched up, Doctor, is the head of their organization, and with him 'dead,' his wife is in charge. And after this morning, there's no telling *what* she's going to do. I've known her for over a year now, and I think she's a pretty levelheaded woman, but with this shock, who can say what she'll do to the country that 'murdered' her husband."

"Let me get this straight," the doctor interjected. "You say this 'Terran Alliance' is composed of human beings, and they're taking *recruits*?"

"I do. That's how they've gone from the original three who were lucky enough to find the first ship and smart enough to recognize the opportunity, to the thousands who operate three ships and three bases, with plans for drastic expansion in the near future. And there are two more ships just waiting for crew to be assigned. But this little fiasco this morning puts a hell of a crimp in *those* plans.

"Look, they think they've got four dead, and one of them is alive in the next room. And he's their number one man. I don't know what they'll do now, but I know what they had planned. One, take enough people out to the third ship to get it back to Earth orbit and then do it again for the fourth. They also need to get their main ship, the *Galileo*, back out to the belt and build their fourth base, the big one to make some of the bigger ships. That will put the big ship away from Earth for almost a year. Now, though, it's anybody's guess. All I am sure of is that we need to get to Denver where their recruiters are. If we can find them, we can get him back to his people and save something out of this mess."

The doctor zeroed in on two points. "What do you mean by 'belt,' and when does it leave?"

Roland thought for a moment. "They could leave any time. Whether they will or not, well..." He looked at the two men and shrugged. "I know that *he* knows the recruiters in Denver. Maybe when he's able to talk, we can make a call and set something in motion. But they—the folks in Denver—have the radio and what they call locator disks that will let them locate and beam Simon back aboard the big ship. And by 'belt,' I mean asteroid belt."

"Beam?" the father asked. "Like in 'Star Trek'?"

"I'm afraid so, Father," Roland said ruefully.

The doctor leaned forward as excitement and

animation took years off slumped shoulders and a fatigued expression. "You know, I could do some good out there."

"What? You have work to do here, Brian Jeffers! You can't go gallivanting around the solar system or whatever! Besides, you know you don't have..."

"And you haven't had the same thoughts, Timmy? What did you just get through saying? 'I'm sure they need guidance, too,' wasn't it?" Doctor Jeffers pointed out. "You and I both grew up on Buck Rogers and Flash Gordon, and we both couldn't wait for the next Amazing Stories. I'll tell ya now, big brother, I'm for helping these two out and joining up when we get there. You know I only lost my license for writing prescriptions I shouldn't have because I cared too much."

The doctor looked at Roland. "So how many doctors do they have? What kind of facilities? General practitioners? Surgeons? Dentists, for God's sake? Somebody has to look after the sanitation and general health of that many people. Who is it? And how about mental health? Not to mention the fact that you're spread out all over the solar system, for crying out loud."

Roland held his hands up. "Whoa there, Doc. I don't know the answers. I was there studying them as potential adversaries and found out they'd make better allies. But I didn't look into their health. Everybody *seemed* healthy. Just the normal sniffles and broken bones. I only saw one real doctor aboard though. Quite a few medics and paramedics. Still not enough to do the job, if I had to make a guess."

"Well, it's a profession you need, and there's another profession you need across the desk there," the doctor said. "How many priests or rabbis or whatever do you have up there?"

"Again, I have no idea. Are you talking about going to Denver with us?" Roland asked incredulously.

"Can you think of better camouflage than a priest and a doctor?"

"Wait a minute, Brian!" Father Timothy said, panic in his voice.

"You know you can get a replacement here in a couple of days. The Cardinal owes you," Doctor Jeffers said. "You haven't had a vacation in *eight* years, dammit! And I'll have another drink now that we've got that settled, if you please."

CHAPTER THREE

Lucy sat uncomfortably in the *Galileo's* ready room. She could almost feel the captain's eyes on the back of her neck, and she resisted the impulse to look over her shoulder with difficulty. She felt each of her twenty-five—almost twenty-six—years individually.

Twenty-four hours had now passed since the disaster at Camp David, and the full depth of her position hadn't revealed itself to her yet, though she had some suspicions. She doodled on another in a long chain of pieces of paper, seeing nothing and accomplishing less. Finally, she picked up her commlink.

"Communications, send messages to Captains Kane and Chapman. Have them meet me in the... my ready room as soon as possible, please." Captain Jerry Chapman had been her executive officer until she took over command of the *Galileo*.

As she waited for the two officers to arrive, Lucy tidied up her calculations onto a fresh sheet of paper.

She waved at the chairs in front of her as the two came in together and began without preamble. "The first thing I see is that if we don't do *something*, and do it fast, this whole thing is going to come unraveled. We need to get some momentum back, and we need to show our people that we can do it without Simon. *And* without Kitty. No one person is necessary to the continued existence of the Terran Alliance. Because

I'll tell you, if any one person truly *is* necessary, then we should all beam down right now and call it quits."

Marsha and Jerry started to speak at once, and Lucy held up her hand "One at a time, please."

Jerry was the first one to get a word in. "Can't you feel it, Lucy... uh, Captain? We can't end this. Not now. It's taken on a life of its own, and if we don't help it grow, especially now that the whole Earth knows, then we're doing the whole human race a disservice."

"This is a Captain's Call, Jerry. First names are allowed here," Lucy said. "How about you, Marsha? Let's have your opinion."

Marsha looked uncomfortable. "Well, I don't want to go back now, either. It's too much fun. And yes, I know it's going to get considerably less fun in the not-to-distant future, but sacrifices get made in the name of progress all the time. We have very concrete reminders of that with Simon dead and Kitty... whatever. I say keep on."

Lucy shifted uncomfortably in her chair. "Okay, here's the deal. I have three communiqués from the base captain and commanders essentially saying they'll support whatever decision I make. I have you, Marsha, standing right here yesterday asking what *you* could do to help. And you, Jerry, when I said you were the new captain of the *McCaffrey*, you said, 'Yes, ma'am, thank you, ma'am, I'll do the best I can, ma'am,' so I'm assuming I have your support as well. Do I, or don't I?"

Both captains nodded their agreement and Lucy said, "Very well. For the moment, construction of Taurus Base is on hold. We have two ships ready to be crewed now, and that will be our priority. The

McCaffrey and the *Heinlein* will both break orbit carrying as many extra personnel as possible without overtaxing the life support systems. I estimate you can carry an extra fifty people on each ship, especially if you use Marsha's new trick of short-jumping straight out to your destinations. The *Heinlein* will rendezvous with Orion and offload a skeleton crew to get the new ship back here to the *Galileo*. The *McCaffrey* will proceed to Gemini and do the same. Both ships will return straight here. Trials will come later.

"I want to maintain a one-week trip time back from the belt to get as much training into the new crew as possible. At least they'll be able to find their stations and quarters when they walk onto the ship. Marsha has worked out the micro-jump parameters, so I want her to download those to you, Jerry. Do that for the new ships when you get there and get back here. We'll do what we can on this end to have crew ready to fill out your rosters when you arrive."

She slid two folders across the table to the captains facing her. "These are the rosters for your ships—who you'll be keeping and who you'll be transferring to the *Arthur C. Clarke* and the *Andre Norton*. Inform your people and have them ready to break orbit right after the funerals day after tomorrow. Any questions?" she asked.

And, of course, there were. The new Captain Chapman was concerned with shipboard minutia.

"That's what you have an executive officer for. Remember how I'd delegate things to you? You need to learn that you can't have one-hundred-percent control of your ship, but you do need to have that kind of control over your officers and department heads. Your job is to tell people where to go and what to do, and look competent doing it. You also handle the big decisions, which gives you the big headaches. The best advice I can give you is to delegate as much as possible to people you trust. Simon once told me that if going to the captain with a problem is a traumatic experience, people will do their damnedest to solve it themselves. Let's keep them thinking like that. But the trick is not overdoing it. We can't have people doing something stupid because we fostered an image."

Marsha stopped doodling on the pad in front of her. "Okay, Lucy, I can see the rationale here. Seven days out to train a crew, a couple of days on-station, and micro-jump back. That's nine days for us. My question is what's the *Galileo* going to be doing?"

Lucy had unconsciously adopted one of Simon's gestures, which was to stare down at the tabletop while someone was speaking. She raised her eyes to Marsha's and said, "The *Galileo* is going to sit right here and train as many people as well as we can so we can crew those two ships. As for me, I'm going to carry on Simon's vision of getting bases for us, and I'm going to find out what happened down there."

"Are you sure that's wise, Lucy?" Marsha asked.

Lucy bristled. "Let me ask you something, Marsha. If I punched you in the nose, would it be wise to retaliate or let it go? If you let it go, what do you think I can do to you tomorrow? And the next day? Yes, I think it's wise. Now, I'll admit I'm not the most diplomatic person you'll ever meet. I believe in saying what I mean, and I don't believe in beating around the bush. I think that's the root cause of some of the worst things that have happened in human history—specifically, worrying something to death instead of getting the matter resolved.

"I've been watching the newscasts. Constant repetition of the same stuff all day long. It gets very boring. What I do get out of it is that the Senate and the House of Representatives are up in arms. Republicans and Democrats are unified on something for just about the first time in history. China, Russia, and Great Britain are screaming for an answer. *Everybody* is screaming for an answer. Nobody wants to lose their piece of the technological pie, and messages have been beamed at us from every satellite circling the globe, none of which I've bothered to answer. I'm gonna let 'em sit down there and stew for a while. What I see here is a televised funeral beamed down to every television on the planet. Until we do that, there will be no response to any overture from anyone on the surface. Then, and only then, do we begin any kind of negotiations.

"We're only going to be 'burying' eleven coffins. We all understand that. It's the symbolism I'm looking at here, for us as well as the people down there. I was having a problem deciding whether to launch them into the sun, into permanent orbit, or send them home. Home won out. Besides, it'll make a bigger spectacle, and Simon taught me that if something could serve two purposes... Anyway," she continued after a choked pause, "we load the coffins with something pyrotechnic and send them on long, shallow courses so everybody gets a good look. And those who matter won't miss the message that we can drop something anywhere we want. Anything else?"

With a strange look on her face, Marsha stood up and answered, "No, that just about covers it, I think, which leaves us with things to do. Jerry, why don't you come with me? I'll explain micro-jumping and get you a download for the *McCaffrey*."

The two captains headed off, discussing the esoterica of micro-jumps and the command of star ships.

Lucy took her own advice and delegated. She delegated Kitty's care to the doctor and engineers, the day-to-day running of the ship to her new executive officer, and preparations for the trips to Orion and Gemini to Marsha. This left her with time on her hands—time she wished she didn't have.

She wandered down the *Galileo's* corridors until she found herself at the sickbay. Not knowing quite why, she walked over to the... container... holding Kitty's body and stood there, looking into its cloudy interior.

"I don't know what you or Simon would do," she said, with a tinge of agony in her voice. "I only know what I *think* you would do. I think Simon would fight to get the embassies and get Taurus built, and you would have stood beside him every step of the way. All I can say is that I will continue that fight as long as I have breath in my body. I may not go about it at the same pace or in the same way, but it will get done.

"Now, I'm going to set up a funeral. I hope you approve." Lucy called Stephen to meet with her and the Chief Engineer on the projects deck, and with one last look at Kitty, she left the sickbay.

"What I want is a highly visible display," she said to the two men seated at the small table tucked away in one corner of the immense room. "We'll start with a ceremony here on the projects deck with as many people as possible, which will be broadcasted live to Earth. Then, the coffins will be launched in such a way that they traverse most of each time zone from north to south so more people get a chance to see it. There are four time zones across the US. Launch a coffin in each zone at ten p.m. local for best visual effect."

The engineer spoke up. "The launches themselves are no problem. Either move the ship or have Mambas haul them to the right places and release them at the right time. As far as the visual display is concerned, different materials give off different colors and break up differently. I can load each coffin with enough stuff that they'll burn for a while. We have the entire construction area to help with that. Don't worry. But you'd better not plan on having pallbearers. These things will be heavy, trust me."

Stephen had listened quietly to the exchange and finally asked, "Are you sure this is what you want to do?"

Lucy looked at him and said, "Stephen, if you or Gayle or anybody else who knows Simon... knew Simon... thinks that he wouldn't do this... if even one of you thinks that he wouldn't, tell me so, and I won't do it. And he would make the ceremony a live broadcast, just like I intend to do, don't you think?"

Stephen sat there and let the silence grow uncomfortably long.

"I'm going to take your lack of answer for agreement, Stephen. I have to. Now, there's something else I have to do, and that's organize the funeral. And I'm not what you could call good at public speaking. Either of you want my job?"

Both men, one twice her age, demurred.

"We are gathered here today to mourn the loss of eleven voices," Lucy said as she tore her eyes away from the somber crowd before her and looked down at two agonizing days' worth of notes. "Voices belonging to people we have come to respect, cherish, and even, to some extent, love. Eleven people whom we will never be able to turn to again to share good times or bad. Eleven people who have passed beyond the need for our help. These eleven people were taken from us maliciously—four by greedy men who sought to take what we were going to freely give to the people of Earth, and seven by unknowns from outside our solar system."

She stumbled through the worst twenty minutes of her life, talking about the four people killed in the fighting at Camp David and the seven others, saying something about each of their lives and detailing their deaths. The situation wasn't made easier by the fact that she had insisted on making this a live broadcast to the world below. She'd rehearsed it fifty times if she'd done it once, and she still felt like she had a mouthful of rocks. It wasn't until she began speaking of the future that she became a little more comfortable standing where she was.

"We are a young group," she said, "not quite three years old, so we don't have many traditions. Today we start one. These eleven martyrs," she hesitated after the word to give it more strength, "are returning to the planet of their birth as shining symbols of what men and women can achieve if given a free hand. We of the Terran Alliance urge you all over the world to join us now in paying homage to these fallen souls."

As Lucy spoke, she turned to watch the side doors of the projects deck slide open, leaving only the force fields between the mourners and the emptiness beyond. With Earth as a backdrop and eleven Mambas standing by, the eleven coffins were trundled to the force field where the internal capture fields picked them up one by one and gently slid them out to the waiting ships. Each Mamba moved forward and took charge of a coffin, then moved back into place. Turning in a synchronized movement, the eleven ships moved off into the night. As the door slid shut on the sight, Lucy turned back to the crowd of mourners before her.

"We invite the people of Earth to step outside in about ten minutes and look to the north. Mourn with us the passing of the sons and daughters of Earth and rejoice in their homecoming."

Lucy looked at the camera, positioned near the back of the crowd of mourners, without speaking for a long minute. "I'd like to end these services at this point by introducing Marsha Kane, Captain of the Terran Alliance Ship *Robert A. Heinlein*, and Jerry Chapman, Captain of the Terran Alliance Ship *Anne McCaffrey*."

Standing to one side, she beckoned to the two captains to come onto the dais. Marsha, looking like she'd like to be anywhere but in front of an entire planet, stepped forward. "Ladies, and gentlemen, I am Marsha Kane of the Terran Alliance. By unanimous consent of the ranking officers, we have promoted Lucy Grimes to the position and rank of First Captain of the Terran Alliance. This act places her in command of all Alliance forces and personnel, and grants her the power to make treaties with or war upon any group of her choosing." Turning to Lucy, she said, "Congratulations, First Captain." Nodding slightly for Jerry to follow her, she stepped off the dais and melted into the crowd.

Lucy stood for a long second, then spoke a final time into the camera. "Ladies and gentlemen, thank you for your time. Watch the skies, mourn their loss as we do, and good night."

The monitors in the ready room showed eleven streaks of light as eleven Mamba pilots reported missions accomplished.

"Well, that's that then. Time to be getting back into action," Lucy said.

"Before you do that, Lucy, you should think about something," Marsha said. "This is the captain's ready room, the captain of the *Galileo*, that is. And you aren't that person. We, that is the 'Advisory Council,' thought you should have more appropriate quarters, so we..."

Gayle broke her uncommon silence. "What Marsha is trying to say is that we have a surprise for you. Let's go for a walk, okay?"

Lucy followed curiously down the hall past the elevator and down deck three to an otherwise anonymous room. Then she saw a plaque affixed to the wall. Its two lines of print said simply, "Fleet Headquarters. Lucy Grimes, Commanding."

"No!" she exclaimed. "You're *not* doing this to me!"

Stephen, seemingly alarmed, said "Can we get out of the corridor? Let's go inside and talk about this rationally."

"Oh, talk we shall," Lucy vowed. "But rational? Someone else will be the judge of that."

Stepping through the door, she came to a complete stop. Standing up from behind a desk at one side of the room, Lt. Commander Kimura said, "Captain on deck!"

The only other door in the room opened, and a man she knew by sight walked in. "Commander Lloyd Pike, ma'am. Mamba pilot off the *Heinlein*. When Captain Kane put out the word that she was looking for staff officers for you, it turned out that I was the least unqualified." A crooked smile crossed his lips. "Or most qualified, or whatever. By virtue of my parents having money and flaunting it, I happen to have picked up a bit about how to anticipate the wishes and needs of others. Most often from the other side, I'll grant you, but then, I'll be back there someday."

"And that makes you my...?"

"Aide, ma'am."

Looking at Commander Kimura, Lucy asked, "And you?"

"Your personal secretary, ma'am. And I already have messages for you."

"Messages? Already?" Lucy was beginning to know what the term 'shell-shocked' meant.

"Yes, Ma'am," Kimura said. "The captain of Orion and the commanders of Gemini and Libra send their congratulations, as well as the captains of the *McCaffrey* and the *Heinlein*."

"Get Agent Daniels in here, Commander," Lucy said

self-consciously. She was still reeling from the shock of finding out what her new position entailed, and she smelled a rat. This trick smacked of Simon's doing, but he was dead, so she shifted her attention to Stephen.

He had a hand in this, she thought. *Could Simon have told him to engineer an outcome like this, if worse came to worst?*

Her consternation was at her new duties. As overall commander of three stations—very soon to be four—and three ships, she'd been removed from personal command of any particular vessel. Sure, if she wanted the *Galileo* to do something, it would get done but under the command of someone else. And the same held true of any ship in their slowly expanding fleet. And they gave her a staff? She also had a suite of rooms specially prepared as her personal quarters, along with a dining room big enough to serve as a banquet room, two aide's quarters, and a small gym.

I have an "aide," she thought. *And a valet, personal secretary, and two gophers! Well, if I'm in charge, I guess I'd better get at it.*

She picked up her commlink and said, "Commander Kimura, please call Dr. Walker and Captain Kane. I want to see them first. And find Agent Daniels."

Lucy read the paper in her hand for about the twentieth time. *They* tried *to think like lawyers, but they didn't take into account just how vindictive I can be.* The paper she perused held her operating instructions, so to speak. She could only be removed from office by a unanimous decision of all the captains, and she could appoint her advisers carte blanche.

This is where I got 'em, she thought.

She was jerked out of her reverie by the sound of her commlink.

"Ma'am, Dr. Walker and Captain Kane are here."

"Well, send them in." *God, don't let me come off as pompous*, she prayed. Unable to sit behind her desk, Lucy paced nervously.

"Do I ask, 'What's up, Lucy?' or do I say, 'Captain Kane reporting as ordered, ma'am,' Marsha quipped as she strode into the office, Stephen at her heels.

"I don't know, and right now I don't care, Marsha. I just wanted to let the two of you know how much 'help' you've given me recently."

Eyes darting in Stephen's direction, Marsha said, "That's nice of you to say, Lucy."

"The point I want to make is that I appreciate it so much that I want to do something for you in return."

Stephen's eyes narrowed at being included in Lucy's expansive wave. "What do you have in mind?"

"Well, this for example," she said, waving the paper she was still holding. "It says here '... no limitations on appointing advisers as deemed necessary by the First Captain.'" She sat down on one of the couches in the more informal area of the office. "I really think I have too much room here. I need to fill it with something. I know what! Advisers! Guess what, guys? You're appointed."

Stephen began to protest. "I have enough to do! It seems I've inherited some kind of 'senior scientist' status. People come to me to solve problems I'm not even associated with."

"And how do you handle things like that?" Lucy wanted to know.

"Well, usually I know who to turn the problem over to for the best results. I can only be in so many places."

"There you go! My new technical adviser!" Turning to Marsha, she asked sweetly, "And just how do you plan to weasel out of this? Let me guess. Senior line captain is best suited to advise from the command perspective?"

"Uh, something like that," Marsha said and looked down, an unreadable look on her face.

"Something like that," Lucy mimicked. "Sit down and talk to me. I want to send the *Heinlein* and the *McCaffrey* out to bring in the two new ships ASAP. I'm thinking micro-jumps both ways to shorten time, properly crew them, and send them out of here on their trials. Any objections?" When neither Stephen nor Marsha responded, she went on, "If both ships go out as stuffed as their environmental systems will handle, we can have four ships in orbit. Allowing two days to transfer crew and do a full systems check, we could accomplish that in about eight days. Comments?"

"That many people crammed into one ship will take some innovation. But if it's not for more than a week, I think we can handle it," Marsha said.

When he became the target of Lucy's cool gaze, Stephen said guardedly, "I don't see a *technical* reason not to. Actually, I really don't see *any* reason not to, but I'd like to know what you have planned for the *Galileo* while they're gone."

"Good. Marsha, tell Jerry to find a way to load an extra hundred aboard and you do the same. I want the *Heinlein* to go to Orion with your second in charge. Jerry goes to Gemini. You'll stay here and help me out as part of my new Advisory Council. See that both ships are under way within forty-eight hours, that is after getting the crews aboard and familiar with their duty stations, if possible. Okay?"

At Marsha's stunned nod, Lucy turned to Stephen. "The *Galileo* will sit right here bringing new volunteers aboard and getting them acquainted with living and working aboard ship. When the new ships arrive, I hope to have crews ready for each of them that will at least know their way around a spaceship."

"And..." Stephen prompted. "What about *you*? Are you planning to retaliate?"

"Retaliate? Who would I retaliate against? Whoever's responsible will have covered their tracks too well by now. I'd thought of moving our North American embassy to Canada. Kind of a snub at the U.S., don't you think? But I also realize the advantages of having a base in the greatest country in the free world. But the U.S. no longer speaks for us— that will be their punishment. I have a couple of thoughts on people to work out a proposal with the Swiss and others to work on someplace in a Far East country. Which one, I don't know yet. I'm going to let the U.S. stew for a while. For now, though, I'm going to look toward convincing the United Nations that it's best for all parties to work with us. Which is why I want to see agent Daniels, now."

Picking up her commlink, Lucy called Commander Kimura. "Do you have Agent Daniels for me, Commander?"

"Captain, it seems that Agent Daniels isn't aboard. I called both the *Heinlein* and the *McCaffrey*, and he also doesn't appear to be aboard either of those vessels."

After four days of intense discussion, Lucy's shuttle landed in Zurich. Chosen for this meeting due to their well-known neutrality, the Swiss had gone all out to make the Alliance delegation welcome. Security was tighter than she would have imagined, but never having been in a situation like this, she really had no frame of reference.

The crowd was unbelievable to a person who hadn't seen more than a few thousand at one time in her life. There must have been fifty thousand spectators on hand when her shuttle landed at the airport, accompanied by a four-ship flight of Mambas, the newly named Hawke Flight. It wasn't until twenty nerve-wracking minutes later that the near riot was under control.

"Ma'am, Zurich Tower reports all clear and requests that we expedite debarkation. Message ends, 'Welcome to Earth.'" The pilot fairly glowed with suppressed glee. "We got 'em!"

"Don't go jumping to conclusions, Lieutenant, but it *is* a good sign." Lucy stepped out of the shuttle with a feeling of dread. The last time this happened, people had died. But the attempt must be made. This time *she* was walking into the fire and taking with her the people she'd come to know and trust. Marsha, Stephen, and Gayle were along as the newly formed Fleet Advisory Council, and they were accompanied by half a dozen well-armed security personnel.

Flanked by her staff, Lucy walked toward the delegation waiting a safe distance from the shuttle. After the introductions, she was left standing with the assistant to the Secretary General of the United

Nations and Vice-chairman of the UN Security Council.

"Please permit me to welcome you to Earth, Captain Grimes. I am Heinrich Juergens, special attaché to the Secretary General. I apologize for our unseemly haste, but it would be better if we continued our introduction in a more... secure... location. The penthouse has been made available in one of Zurich's oldest and most prestigious hotels." He waved grandiloquently toward the waiting motorcade, and a bottleneck immediately presented itself. Separating Lucy from her security detail was out of the question.

Lucy felt utterly alone and stupid as she stood there and let her aide argue over *protocol*, for God's sake, with a total stranger as if she wasn't even there. Feeling like a chess piece, Lucy grimaced when her personal aide, Commander Pike, turned to her and asked, "Stephen and Gayle in the lead car, Marsha and myself in the rear, each with one guard, and yourself in the middle with the other four. Will that be acceptable, ma'am?"

Relegating each person to their place, the two men finally got the motorcade under way. The attaché himself rode with Lucy and her four guards as the trio of cars sped away from the airport. "I assure you, all three vehicles will stay together, and you'll be delivered to your hotel momentarily. The council will be in session at nine a.m. tomorrow morning and extends an invitation to attend."

"You appear to have things well in hand, Herr Juergens. I have every confidence that our stay here will be a pleasant one as long as we have you to look after the details." Lucy smiled at the slightly older man.

About Simon's age, actually, she thought. *And where does Mr. and Mrs. Grimes' little girl get off sounding that pompous?*

"Don't you get a feeling of sheer age here?" Lucy asked. "To think that this place is over three hundred years old... and look at the furniture! Antiques, all of it."

"And bugged to the hilt, too, I'll bet," added Lloyd Pike. "There will be two guards outside your room tonight and one inside." Forestalling any comment from Lucy, he went on, "I have it on good authority that if anything happens to you, my ass is grass. So much for a cushy assignment!"

The next morning, after a lavish extravaganza called breakfast and served by liveried footmen, the attaché was led into the room by Commander Kimura. "Ma'am, Special Attaché Juergens is here."

"I see that, Rukia. Thank you. Coffee, Herr Juergens?"

"Yes, thank you. Black, bitter." He looked toward Rukia as she left the room. "You aren't used to this are you, Captain? Or should I call you 'First Captain?'"

"Wha... what do you mean, Herr Juergens?" Lucy stammered.

"Being waited on. Having someone to do your bidding. Being in charge."

Praying that Rukia was just outside the open door, Lucy said, "A spy. I should have known. And 'captain' will do."

"Not at all, Captain. Just connections. We, that is,

the Security Council, know that you are Lucille Angelina Grimes, born of John and Darla Grimes of Cincinnati, Ohio, on the 12th of October 1988. Placed third in your last high school long jump, and just missed being on the honor roll. Satisfactory grades at Colorado State University until you dropped out. All of this is a matter of public record, Captain. And, of course, now you're the supreme commander of a group of people who have control of the most advanced technology in human history. Quite a jump, Captain."

"Quite a jump, yes, Herr Juergens," Lucy said as Rukia walked back in with two cups of coffee. Facing away from the diplomat, she raised her eyebrows questioningly. Lucy shook her head slightly. "But not what it seems," she continued as Rukia left the room. "Just a matter of being in the wrong place at the wrong time. After all, I'm not the one who *found* the ship, just one of the first volunteers. And I still don't appreciate being investigated."

"There's an old German saying, Captain, 'If not your enemies, then your friends.' It means that somebody is going to do it, so why *not* your friends? Besides, don't you think your own country has done much worse? And I'm not even counting that whole Camp David affair. Please excuse me if I offend you with the memories of recent losses."

"And *are* you my friend, Herr Juergens?" Lucy asked, pointedly ignoring the remarks about how her own country had treated her people.

"And why not, Captain? No matter today's outcome, I will still be somebody's attaché. But I was talking about your relative newness to... power... shall we say? And in reference to your subordinates, I was going to say that you looked uncomfortable with having servants. And that is surely what they are. I was going to offer you some advice..."

"Herr Juergens, advice I have coming out of my ears. But oddly, I still don't have enough. I would appreciate what you have to say."

"You are most gracious, Captain. I was going to say that you should let your people wait on you. They feel useful and happy, and *you* can get more done. I've seen this before. New leaders come before the council, and they don't know how to *appear* effective. Remember, in this line of work, appearances are *everything*. Accept your subordinates as if they are your due. Just don't treat them that way. There's a fine line there, and the best politicians learn it early."

"Politicians! I'm no politician. How dare you think that!"

Heinrich saw that he'd finally reached Lucy's core. That kind of anger ultimately signaled final acceptance. "I beg to differ, Captain. For just a moment, let your mind accept the premise that you *are* a politician. How did you arrive at that exalted status? By acclamation, of course. Your peers voted you into place. They *gave* you authority over them. And now you are here to speak before the United Nations Security Council. How is that possible for the daughter of John and Darla Grimes? Because she is the head of the most powerful yet smallest group of people ever to exist."

Heinrich stopped and took a sip from the dainty cup in his hand. "Some of the finest china in the world," he said admiringly, then returned to his original tack. "Accept it, Captain. Once you do, your life will be much less... stressful. I speak as one who has seen many of the leaders of the world pass by me. Even *I* am one of those people. The subordinates, that is. I have someone I answer to. So I have a unique perspective, don't you think? And as one of those subordinates, I can say that we truly thrive on it if treated properly. There are those who lead and those who follow. Fate decides which. And you, Captain, are one of the leaders, whether you like it or not."

During the attaché's impassioned speech, Lucy had laid her head back on the couch and closed her eyes. "Why should I believe you, Herr Juergens?" she asked.

"Because, Captain, once you've finished speaking before the Council, I'd like to apply to be your first volunteer after the embassy gets established here in Switzerland. I told you, I'm a follower, not a leader. And I would consider it a privilege to be attaché to the senior Terran Alliance officer."

"I'll think about it, Herr Juergens."

Better the spy you know than the one you don't. And I may get some use out of him.

Seeing the smile flicker across his face, Lucy remarked, "I may be from Ohio, Herr Juergens, but I am most certainly not from the sticks. I think you wanted me to see that smile, or I never would have. So what do you wish to say? And do me a favor, will you? Leave out the diplomatique. Just tell me in plain English."

"You think me a spy, and you think that in the knowing, you are safe. And now you will deny that, not wanting to be revealed to have such callous thoughts. But I warned you, I am adept at this business. It is to me what flying in space is to you. Here, *I* have an effect on the thin air of global politics.

I have seen many pass through these rooms, and in you I see promise. It is my desire that you appear confident and competent at tomorrow's council meeting, and more importantly, at the gala that will be sure to follow a successful conclusion of tomorrow's meeting."

"Gala? Maybe I *am* a country girl after all. Explain a gala, please."

"Held here in Zurich," Heinrich began, "it means royalty. A baron and a few earls, high-ranking members of society, higher-ranking members of various military organizations, some ambassadors, and just possibly, a few heads of state will be on hand to meet you and your staff. I realize that on the face of it, you think you won't be able to function in such an environment, but you can. Again, I have seen much, and you have the determination and stamina for it. The others will enjoy themselves. You'll be miserable, and that's because you care about the opinions of those around you. And you should. It does matter, but the difference is that the burden rests squarely on your shoulders, and you *want* to succeed."

Leaning back in his chair, Heinrich studied Lucy. "Have I frightened you? I have but told the truth, about you as well as your situation. And to ease your mind, I have the privilege of being assigned as your personal guide and liaison during your stay."

"Ter-*bloody*-rific," she muttered.

In a two-hundred-year-old building, the Security Council met in special session. Not normally the setting of such rarefied discussions, the building had been pressed into service so the council could meet in secret with Lucy. The secret was only to be kept from Joe Average, but nonetheless, there were several hundred people outside when her motorcade arrived.

Surrounded by guards and staff, Lucy walked the gauntlet of spectators from the limousine to the steps. When she slowed to answer a question from the crowd, Herr Juergens subtly pushed her forward.

"Not now, please. If you answer one question, you'll be here all day, and the Council is waiting."

Feeling put out by the incident, Lucy strode up the steps and into the darkened cavern of the foyer.

Commander Pike met her inside the entrance. "I took the liberty of going on ahead to check security," he said. "If you'll follow me, ma'am, there's a room prepared for you to wait in until the Council calls you. I've been assured that you won't have long to wait."

"That is most certainly the case, Commander," Juergens said. "If you'll excuse me, I must go inform the Council of your arrival."

Lucy stood in front of a gilt-edged mirror and examined her appearance. "Are you *sure* this is appropriate, Marsha?"

"Lucy, you need to put on a show here, style as well as substance. Your speech will be the substance, your appearance the style." Marsha stood behind her and tugged on the uniform jacket. "You look fine. This is what all the up-and-coming Terran Alliance officers will wear for dress occasions."

Designed by Gayle, the uniform each member of the party was wearing was basically the same as a duty uniform—a finer-quality material, of course, and fewer pockets as had been discussed once long ago. Lucy's golden captain's comets were now surrounded by a gold wreath, and the thin golden stripes up the legs of her pants were a direct steal from US military uniforms, as were the four stripes around the cuffs of her jacket.

"I feel like an attraction in a circus!"

Marsha looked herself over and swiped at a piece of lint. More understated, the other uniforms had less braid around the jacket cuffs, giving the visual impression that Lucy was in charge. *And it works to perfection*, Marsha thought.

Heinrich walked into the room in his Special Attaché persona. "First Captain, Captain, Commanders, if you will follow me, the Council requests your presence." He led them to an ordinary wooden door. "It is amazing to me how much of a symbol a door is," he mused aloud. "They can signify endings, as in 'closing the door on a chapter of your life,' or a beginning, as in 'opening a door on a bright new future.' I sincerely hope you and your people open it onto a bright future, First Captain. I offer this advice: on the other side of this door, speak only the truth as you see it. If you truly want a bright future, it cannot be built on lies and deception." He glanced at his watch and said, "And now your turn has come. Good luck." With the last word, he opened the door and stood aside.

Since the Security Council was not in its customary building, having come to Switzerland so as not to appear to snub their noses at the Alliance by making them meet on American soil, the four Alliance officers walked directly into the middle of the special session for which this meeting had been arranged. Their appearance was surely expected because Lucy heard not a sound as several hundred pairs of eyes examined her and her friends.

Looking around, Lucy located the chairman and broke the silence. "Sir, I am Lucy... Lucille Grimes, First Captain of the Terran Alliance, and I have come to you today to ask for your assistance."

The face of the man who answered her could have belonged to anybody's grandfather. The eyes belonged to... she didn't like where her thoughts were leading her and looked away from the eyes. The feeling of being ten years old again and sitting in the principal's office was so strong she almost laughed out loud.

"What would you have this Council do?" he asked, breaking the spell.

"All I ask is that you listen to what I have to say. If after that, if you have any questions, I and my colleagues will be ready to answer."

"I call for a voice-vote," the man announced loudly. "And in the interests of saving time, I ask only, does anyone vote against allowing First Captain Grimes to speak?"

When several seconds had passed in silence, he waved to the dais. "First Captain, you have the floor."

Lucy stepped onto the dais, turned to the assembled crowd, and faltered. The looks of interest, boredom, and amusement, she could take. It was the hostility she saw in some of the faces that caused her to hesitate.

Marsha caught her eye and crooked a finger, and when Lucy bent down, whispered, "Remember, they're as afraid of you as you are of them. Give 'em both barrels!"

Lucy took a deep breath and launched into her

prepared speech. "We stand, by purest luck, on the *real* last frontier. Once thought to be Alaska, then the ocean, and finally the moon, *space* is the true last frontier. And we have a chance to exploit our luck.

"By now, you all know how we came into possession of this marvelous ship," Talking about familiar things and ideas helped put an end to her nervousness, and she warmed to her subject. "You've all seen some of the things it, or its technology, can do—both good and bad. I stand before you today to ask for three embassies on Earth. The Terran Alliance promotes the same values that the United States of America and most other nations around the world today do—freedom from persecution of any kind, and equal opportunity for all regardless of race, gender, creed, or color. What we ask for are a few paltry acres of ground and the same basic liberties for our people that would be offered to *anyone* in a free world. What we offer is a bright new future—a future where everyone has enough to eat, a future where the power to heat a home in winter and cool it in summer will be available to all, and a future where pollutants in your air, water, and land will be things of the past.

"For three embassies on Earth, we offer all this. For the right to accept volunteers into the Alliance, we offer this. As a gesture of good faith, I have with me today the plans to construct a device that will convert any organic matter into food. This device is cheap, economical, and easy to build and operate. Before I leave today, I will also deliver two dozen *working* models of the device.

"Ladies and gentlemen, the Earth is getting crowded. The last major challenges have been met. Yes, there are a few left but not enough to occupy the hearts and minds of mankind's dreamers. These dreamers are the troublemakers of today because there's no place for their energy to be directed. Let it be directed up and out toward the stars. Isn't that what man has wanted since the days when he first stood outside a cave and looked up in wonder?

"Time grows short, ladies and gentlemen. Some of our people figure that the original owners of the *Galileo*, the ones we've been calling the 'Builders,' will come looking for her. She represents a major effort in construction and cost, or so we believe. They wouldn't let her go without at least trying to find out what happened to her and her crew. Sooner or later, they'll come here. When they do, we *must* be ready to repel, if necessary, any attempts to take this technology from us. We have no way of knowing how they'll view our usurpation of their technology. How will they react to 'the new kids on the block?' We don't know. So, we must be ready. To that end, we need volunteers in this bold venture into the future.

"A future I must remind you, that is not without risk. You've heard rumors of an attack, I'm sure. I can clear that up now. Our first base, called Orion, was attacked by unknown ships that used technology markedly different from that which we have acquired. This argues strongly for a *second* alien race in our galactic neighborhood. We lost ten people to the unprovoked attack but managed to repel it through the heroic efforts of our personnel. Later, we found another ship hiding in the asteroid belt. When approached, the vessel came out of hiding and began to fire on our craft—a fatal mistake as it turned out. No trace of the vessel was left, nor any of her crew, so we have no way to verify the race of her personnel. The result, though, is the same—no more attacks on Alliance property or personnel since then. That's not to say there will be no further attacks. We believe that the ship was an outrider or scout, if you will, and working alone. We also believe they had no time to get a message off to... wherever. What orders they were working under, we'll probably never know. But if that one vessel can find us, so can others... of both races. Our mission is clear—to build as many ships as possible and be prepared for any threat. To that end, I ask you again to grant us a charter that will let us recruit personnel, and at the same time, allow those personnel to return to Earth whenever they choose without fear of arrest, interrogation, or retribution.

"Thank you for your time. We are now at your disposal to answer any questions you may have."

For several seconds there was bedlam until the speakers sorted themselves out. The first intelligible question to arise was, "Why no weapons or propulsion technology?"

Marsha answered for the Alliance. "As far as propulsion is concerned, the facilities do not exist to manufacture our power sources on Earth. The matter we use comes directly from the corona of a sun, and we use an unmanned station to convert that material into matter and antimatter monopoles. Some of the scientists among you will recognize the fact that monopoles are just now being recognized as a theoretical possibility. If matter and antimatter come in contact with each other, you will have a situation much like Camp David. As for weapons technology, most of it is powered by the same basic principles that power our engines. And I have a question for this august body: Don't you have enough weapons, nuclear and otherwise, to destroy this planet several times over? What need do you have for more?"

An uncomfortable silence followed Marsha's questions. "I'm going to assume from your silence that you *don't* need better ways to kill yourselves. Next question."

"Georg Ustinov, Ukraine. Where do you propose to place your embassies?"

"That, Mr. Ustinov, is a good question. Our hopes are to get three countries to agree to host our embassies—the United States, for one. Even though there's considerable tension at the moment, it's admirably suited due to their location. As is Japan, if they will agree. But our first choice has always been Switzerland, a country known throughout the world for their neutrality. Next question."

A man at the back of the room stood up. "Willem Boch from South Africa, Captain. It has been my experience that nothing is ever free, especially those things that are touted as free. How much will this technology cost us?"

At a nod from Lucy, Stephen stood up to answer. "Commander Stephen Walker, Mr. Boch. I agree with you that all things come with strings attached, and the food processors do have a string. We will make available to all the nations of Earth complete plans for construction of these remarkable devices. They allow a ship in space to travel many lightyears without a lot of storage of bulk organic foodstuffs. Here on Earth, the system will prove itself in no time at all. Put organic material into one end, and food comes out the other. The unit is fully programmable, and drugs can be left off the menu so the unit won't get misused.

"But the same unit in a hospital, for example, can be programmed to produce the most important life-saving drugs ever imagined. It's programmability allows a unit in the hands of Hindus to produce food that isn't 'tainted,' while an identical but differently programmed unit will be busy turning out cheeseburgers. These units *are* free. We refuse to hold hunger over the heads of Earth's people. Remember, we are of Earth, too. The string attached to this item is that we will make occasional unannounced inspections of various sites to determine that everyone is benefiting equally. For example, we will not allow one person to control a unit and charge for the food that comes out of it. Maybe someday, when there's no more hunger, a chef can make a dish, program it into a processor, and sell what comes out to diners. *But not until every belly on the planet is full!*

"As for other items, if Earth has the technology to produce an item, we could outright sell the plans to you, and every nation gets a copy. For items that can't be produced on Earth, we'll lease the rights to use them and produce them for you. As Earth's technological level rises to meet the new items introduced, the number of things we produce will diminish.

"The prices will not be extravagant, but someone other than those of us standing here will have to hammer out the details. What dollar figure will apply, we have no way of knowing. Next question."

A woman stood up next. "Marta Koenig of Germany. I see that three of the four of you are female. Is this the norm among your population? And in a related question, who will be allowed to volunteer?"

Lucy responded to the question. "The disparity has been a subject among ourselves on occasion. To answer your question, both asked and alluded to, I can only say that the ratio of male to female officers is purely coincidental. To the best of my knowledge, the crew is pretty evenly split between male and female now. If one sex is more predominant, it would probably be males. To be honest, I've never really considered it before. One restriction will be enforced, however. No one who is presently under sentence or indictment of any kind or who is on the run from the law will be allowed to volunteer. All others are welcome to apply. We realize that our population will be growing at a very slow rate at first, so we won't be able to take many people at any one time. Some won't want to stay, preferring to return home. We are *not* going to bleed Earth dry of all her brilliant minds, ladies and gentlemen. On the contrary, we'll be enhancing Earth's database. Think about it for a minute. No matter what, for the next hundred years at the very least, everyone who signs on with us will come home for vacations, to visit friends, to attend family functions like family gatherings and burials, and to retire. The sum total of all that they learn about us and our technology will come home to Earth! This process allows everyone equal access to what we have at a rate that will let the planet progress without the massive disruptions that you will surely see in the short term. Next question."

"Jose Gallegos, Brazil. What 'massive disruptions' do you see from introducing your technology at this time?"

"A very good question, and from a direction that's

more pivotal than you might expect. Let's go back to the food processors for a moment. If you have those, then clearing all the land you do will become unnecessary, won't it? Less cleared land equals more forest to produce oxygen equals less ozone depletion. Another point—what happens when advanced solar technology is wedded to antigravity? Rather than let you think about it, let me tell you. Several industries will disappear, and some countries depend heavily, if not exclusively, on those industries.

"Advanced solar technology will provide electricity to power antigravity motors that can be applied to anything from personal transportation to home heating. There will no longer be a need for huge power-generating stations, oil production, gasoline manufacturing, natural gas distribution, automobile tire production, service stations, and a host of other industries that we haven't even thought about yet. And that's just from *two* innovations. Think about all the people out of work! Governments will be in chaos, and there will be rioting in the streets, *unless* preparations are made in advance and the technology is introduced slowly. Job retraining will have to be a governmental priority. And we will offer some form of assistance while the retraining takes place.

"There are so many things that impinge one on the other that no one person can say for sure just what will affect what. We realize that we will be the architects of much sorrow and heartache in the future, and we wish it wasn't so. But the *benefits* to all! We ask only that you think as hard as we are about what it can mean. Next question."

"Sonja Detweiler, Netherlands. It is assumed that

the vast majority of Alliance personnel are American. Why did you not turn this over to your government?"

Gayle stood up. "Captain? If I may? This is one that Stephen... Commander Walker and I, have discussed repeatedly."

"Go ahead, Commander."

"Well, Ms. Detweiler, what do you think would happen given the scope of the world's intelligence community? If we turned our find over to our government, there would *be* no ship. Specifically, in this day and age, another government would sooner or later find out about it and decide that the balance of power had changed. And not in their favor. What would the schoolyard bully do? Surely you've faced or seen a bully in action at some time in your life. He would launch a 'preemptive strike,' is what he would do. As a dear friend once put it, 'If I can't have it, you can't either.' So, no one nation can be allowed to have control of our find. 'How about turning it over to the United Nations, then?' you might ask next. Same thing applies. A very few nations would have control of something that would change the way we look at the universe, and that's not fair to all.

"We've come to see things differently, Ms. Detweiler. Perhaps I should invite you aboard the *Galileo* to see what we've seen—*that there are no boundary lines from space!* This planet is one delicately balanced biosphere. I think of it as one big family. We *must* get along or the structure is forever fractured. *That* is why we've taken the steps we have—to prevent the fracturing of our family. And it has cost us dearly. Those who gave their lives trying to protect the ship have become martyrs to the cause, so to speak. Simon was killed by greed. He was murdered on television in front of the whole world. And his wife is now held hostage to the very technology you wish to usurp.

"Hostage, you ask. How is that? Well, to tell the absolute truth, after three years, we're still learning about what we've acquired. Sometimes we get bit in the butt by the technology. Simon's wife..."

"That will be all, Commander," Lucy intervened. "I think we've covered the high points and should leave these good people to discuss what they've heard so far."

"One last question, if you please, Captain," came from an unidentified voice. "Who will get what as far as the technologies are concerned?"

"That one is simple. You, earthbound humanity, will decide just what it is you wish to introduce to the planetary economy. Once the decision has been made, we will provide that technology to *all* the nations of Earth, along with the identities of those who requested it.

"At this point, I feel that all that can be accomplished here today has been, and since we're living and working on another time schedule, I beg that you allow us to get some rest. Thank you for your time, ladies and gentlemen. We realize that you have gone to considerable extremes to be here today, and we appreciate it. We do think, however, that another venue would be better for further discussions, and we're open to suggestions to be considered at a later date. At this point though, it's time we depart."

CHAPTER FOUR

Sitting in the suite provided by the city of Zurich, Lucy finally had a chance to relax. She called the *Galileo* and ordered that the shuttle and flight of Mambas return to the ship. "There's no reason they should sit there and be targets," she asserted. "Besides, they won't be of any benefit if something should happen. And if we need to, we can beam in and out with no one the wiser."

Three times during the evening, her secretary, Commander Kimura, was approached by undersecretaries of the three countries that had been mentioned as possible bases for embassies. The United States, Japan, and Switzerland, all sent tacit, if not overt, approval of Lucy's proposal for embassy locations.

Lucy never saw these people. Herr Juergens advised against it.

"Protocol and appearances are everything, Madam Captain. And please, call me 'Heinrich.' The Security Council has granted you full ambassadorial status by allowing you to speak in front of them the way they did. And, as you're the highest-ranking person in your Alliance, you're the de facto head of state. It would not be seemly for you to meet with underlings."

The last visitor of the evening was a page who merely handed Commander Kimura an embossed envelope bearing Lucy's name and title. Obviously hand-printed by someone with a calligrapher's bent, it said simply, "Lucille Angelina Grimes, First Captain of the Terran Alliance."

"Lucille," she exclaimed in disgust. "If I didn't love my parents so much, I'd kill them for giving me that name! And does *everybody* know my middle name?" Turning the envelope over to open it, she found a wax seal on the back. "Heinrich, what do we have here?" Lucy asked.

Taking the envelope in one well-manicured hand, the attaché looked it over carefully and pronounced, "A significant honor for you, Madam Captain. The von Schlenker family crest is embossed on the front, and that crest is repeated in the wax on the back, which means the baron himself has extended this invitation."

"How do you know it's an invitation when you haven't even opened it?"

"The baron is famous for his galas, and this," he said, handing the invitation back to her, "is the standard form of invitation. Although, to honor you, he has addressed this one, himself. Protocol requires that your secretary respond to the RSVP that is surely included within the invitation. You should open it and find out when the event will take place."

Doing as Heinrich instructed gave her almost forty-eight hours to prepare for the gala. "I don't know what to do at a gala! I don't even know what a gala *is*!" she exclaimed. "I'm Lucy Grimes from Ohio!"

"You will circulate," Heinrich said. "You will be pleasant and mysterious as befits a visitor from outer space, and you will converse. You will eat little and drink less, and sometime during the evening you will be approached by the American ambassador, the Japanese ambassador, and the Swiss ambassador. These events are where most... deals... are solidified. And the Terran Alliance will make its official debut on the social scene.

"Madam Captain, if you'll forgive me for being forward, may I suggest something other than the uniform you wore today for a gala? Not to say there's anything wrong with your uniforms; there isn't. Simple black always makes a statement, and the name tag, the patches on the shoulder, and the rank insignia add authority. But you're going to a *gala*. It's light and airy. You want to present the glamorous side of your Terran Alliance."

"I have nothing to wear that could even remotely be considered glamorous!"

"I have some ideas in that department, Lucy," Gayle said. "Marsha and I discussed them when we were upgrading these outfits. We'll do some makeup to give your eyes a little mystery and enhance your cheekbones. Then, we'll do something simple yet elegant for your hair, and leave the evening attire to us. Suffice it to say that if you want glamour, silver and white should do the trick. And now, Herr Juergens," Gayle said, "if you'll excuse us for the evening, we girls need to talk clothes."

Juergens got up and walked over to the door. "Breakfast will be at nine in the morning. Shall I send a car around at about ten for a tour of the city?"

The next forty-eight hours were a nightmare for Lucy. Between the deliberate drop-ins by various ambassadors and the casual 'accidental' meetings in various public places, Lucy became superficially acquainted with several dozen of the ambassadors who'd found their way to Zurich. Between times, she was busy beaming back and forth between the *Galileo* and her suite being fitted for a gown made from scratch. "This... isn't... going... to... work! It isn't possible!" she complained

"It *will* work," Gayle said, "if you'll just hold still and let me get my job done! Stephen and Jerry were easy. All they needed were white pants, a white turtleneck, and a black dinner jacket. We added some silver piping for accent, and they were done. These new, lighter materials make things a snap. What *we* are going to have are dresses that have two skirts. The outer, longer one is almost floor length and can be removed and used as a wrap, leaving us with the inner one at about knee length or whatever length you want. We'll have a long-sleeved jacket with a scooped neckline that gives just the right emphasis to the cleavage, which always gets a man's attention. A silver braid on the sleeves and the Alliance logo on the left breast will fill out our outfits in pure white. Yours will be the same, but instead of just white, there will be a thousand little points of light picked up by the various kinds of illumination you're either under or passing by. Your dress will never be the same from one moment to the next. And your logo will be in the same shade of blue as your eyes. There's plenty of time!"

The Alliance team made quite a show as they exited their hotel's elevator. First out were two security personnel who looked around and then signaled Lucy forward. She made her way across the lobby slowly, as if measuring each step. The procession of four white-and-silver-clad officers, accompanied by Lloyd Pike in his formal blacks and six guards in their duty uniforms, caused all in the lobby, even those *used* to spectacle, to stop and stare. Heinrich Juergens waited by the main doors and watched the procession closely.

In much the same arrangement as the day before, Juergens ushered Lucy and Lloyd into the middle limousine and climbed in with them and three guards. A fourth sat in the front with the driver.

"Keep the window between us *down*, driver. Understand?" Lucy said.

Gayle and Stephen rode in the lead limo, and Marsha brought up the rear, each car having one guard assigned to it. The motorcade made its way through the city, the traffic, and the approaching dark until it left the city proper behind.

"The gala is being held at the ancestral home of Baron Manfred von Schlenker. A ten-minute ride will have us there," Juergens said.

The time passed quickly as Heinrich filled the two Alliance officers in on the do's and don'ts of meeting royalty. "Even a baron is jealous of his prerogatives. When you meet in the receiving line, introduce yourself first. Formally. Full name and title. He will then set the tone for any future conversations."

Shortly, the vehicles turned off the main road onto what was obviously, even in the dark, a well-manicured driveway that seemed to go on forever. Through the trees, Lucy could see a large lighted structure flickering in and out of view. One final turn of the tree-lined lane brought the building into clear view.

"It's a damned *castle!*"

"Indeed, Captain," Juergens responded. "It has been the von Schlenker family residence for over three hundred years. The outer battlements are still intact, even rebuilt in places, but the inner wall that enclosed the bailey was taken down about a hundred years ago to use for other buildings. The baron keeps a stable of some of the finest Arabian show horses in the world. And, of course, no castle is complete without its own set of ghosts."

"Have you ever seen one of them?"

"In truth, I have not, Captain. But I did once lose a silver cigarette case under mysterious circumstances some years ago. It was found some months later in a room that had, reportedly, not been opened for several years."

The motorcade pulled up in front of an impressive set of stairs. Several vans with imposing-looking antennae on them sat to one side, while reporters and their cameramen stood in a front of cordoned-off vehicles filming the entire scene and calling out questions. Liveried footmen hurried forward to open the doors of the three vehicles and recoiled in confusion as four women stepped out and began surveying the area.

Lloyd Pike joined the women and spoke quietly to the team leader. He leaned into the center limo and said "Captain, your gala awaits. You shall go on my arm, and Captain Miller will go with Commander Walker. Captain Kane can bring up the rear." This last was said as if some social gaffe had occurred.

Once the four officers had gathered, Juergens looked them over with a critical eye.

"Perfection," he said quietly. "And as one who's

been to many of these events, please trust me when I say that the lack of adornment or jewelry adds to the mystique. Now," he said briskly, turning to look Lucy in the eyes, "remember, among these people, image is everything." In a schoolmaster's cadence, he said, "Heads up, shoulders, back, and... chests out. Walk as if you own the ground beneath your feet. A regal step is *always* deferred to. If you act like a queen, you will be treated like a queen."

This solemnly delivered pronouncement was greeted with titters of laughter by Marsha and Gayle. "Oh, my! The Queen of Outer Space!"

A look of pained confusion on Heinrich's face prompted Lucy to say, "Private joke. Maybe I'll explain someday." To her companions she muttered, "Once more and you're dead."

Heinrich shrugged. "Go. Mingle. And remember—eat little, drink less."

One step ahead of everyone else, Lucy arrived at the top of the massive stone staircase in time to see yet another liveried man stepping out of a small stone gatehouse. "Invitation, please," the man ordered.

Lloyd quickly reached into his inside pocket, pulled out the embossed envelope, and handed it over. The gatekeeper glanced at the invitation and returned it to Lloyd. He then took a step forward, opened one of the huge doors, and with a courtly bow, pronounced, "By the baron's command, enter and be made welcome."

The group moved into a large anteroom that, despite all the stone, was still amazingly warm. Two liveried men stood guard at another set of doors directly across from them. The room was decorated with suits of armor, flags, and tapestries. Weapons adorned the walls, along with a few portraits, all of which should have been in a museum somewhere.

"I'll say this," Marsha commented, "the man sure knows how to set a mood."

"Well, ladies and gentlemen," Lucy said, "it looks like we're expected. Let's go to a party."

Lucy led her entourage across the foyer, and the footmen, acting as if their movements had been rehearsed a thousand times before, moved to open the double doors just as they arrived. Continuing into the next room, Lucy stopped, stunned. The scene before her was right out of a movie. The white marble staircase leading down to the ballroom floor, the pike-carrying footmen flanking the top and bottom of the staircase, and the fancifully dressed people circulating below could all have been provided by some movie company for atmosphere.

But this is no set, Lucy thought. *And I have to cope!*

Another hurdle to be passed stepped toward them from his position at the top of the stairs, hand out held. Lloyd, hesitating only slightly, handed over the invitation one more time. With a practiced movement, the gaudily dress man flipped the card from the envelope and read it. A small throat-clearing noise alerted the nearest footman, who banged his weapon on the stone floor three times. When the echoes stopped reverberating around the stone room, all eyes were on the group at the top of the stairs.

"Lady Lucille Angelina Grimes, First Captain of the Terran Alliance and party!" Stepping back into position, he gave a small surreptitious wave of his hand to indicate that the group should proceed down the staircase.

Leaving her bodyguards to follow from the rear for a change, Lucy started walking down the staircase one measured pace at a time. She now had a feeling of what a bug on a plate felt like. Every one of the hundreds of pairs of eyes were on her... again, bringing back the feeling of her visit to the Security Council. It hadn't seemed so... daunting... aboard the *Galileo* because she either knew everyone on board or had something in common with them. Here, though, the only sound was the tapping of the feet of her party as they moved down the staircase, at the bottom of which was a line of people staring at her expectantly.

Later, Lucy wouldn't be able to place name or title to any face she met in that line, with the exception of the last two. Baron and Baroness von Schlenker were dressed to match the room in which they stood. Louis XIV never dressed as well. The matching ermine-trimmed half-capes of the baronial couple were royal purple, and the clothing, while of the finest material, was cut in the style of the fourteenth century.

The baron was a huge bear of a man. Mutton-chop sideburns and a goatee stopped just short of being a full beard. A heavy gold chain with an equally heavy gold pendant hung from his neck, while every finger sported a ring with a different stone. Speaking a word or two to each of the apparent half-dozen children of the baron had given her enough practice that by the time she reached the man himself, and she was able to get through the ritual without stumbling.

"Lucille Grimes, First Captain of the Terran Alliance," she said, holding out her hand.

Rather than shaking her hand, the baron took it in both of his and, raising it to his lips, kissed it. "I am

Baron Manfred von Schlenker. And I am in your debt. To have three such beauteous women as yourselves grace my home is indeed an honor." In a stage whisper, he continued, "And it doesn't hurt that this is the first public appearance of the Alliance Commander. It is certainly the social coup of the century. Now, if you will forgive me, I have a few more guests to greet. Make yourselves welcome. I will come rescue you shortly, after some of these people have decided that you are real and don't bite."

Taking a risk, Lucy asked, "Who said I don't bite?" and got a muffled laugh in return.

As Lucy moved uncertainly away from the baron, nervously eyeing the people who were blatantly staring at her, she was intercepted by a waiter.

"Libation, Madam?" he asked.

Lucy started to reach for one of the delicate crystal flutes, but remembering Heinrich's admonition, said, "Not just yet, thank you."

The waiter stepped ever so slightly into her path and lowered his voice. "Perhaps Madam would be more amenable to ginger ale? It also gives one something to do with one's hands."

"Thank you," Lucy said. "Um, could you see to it that my friends are served the same? I would be most grateful."

"It would be my great pleasure, madam," the waiter said, turning the tray half-way around. Several glasses stood apart from the others on the tray. Lucy selected one and took an experimental sip. The waiter gave a small bow and turned away.

She turned around to examine the hall and the guests resplendent in their finery, coming face-to-face with an older lady dressed in a tweed suit and wearing enough pearls and diamonds to buy half of Cincinnati.

"Haw! First to meet 'cha, don't ya know!"

"Well, if that's supposed to be a feather in your cap, then congratulations. I'm Lucy Grimes, and you are...?"

"An American! I'd hoped that with the name 'Grimes' you might be a subject of the Queen. No matter. I'm Lady Olivia Harrington-Smythe." At the silence that met her pronouncement, she went on. "Wife of Sir Jonathan Harrington-Smythe, British Ambassador to the United Nations."

"I don't have time to keep up with politics, Mrs. Harrington-Smythe, so I apologize for not knowing who you are, but pleased to meet you nevertheless."

"That would be 'Lady' not 'Mrs.,'" the old woman corrected. "And since our dear friend the baron has conferred the title of 'Lady' on you, you'd be wise to use it at every occasion. Now, you simply must meet Birdie."

"Uh, Birdie?"

"My husband. Jonathan Birdwell Harrington-Smythe."

The next half hour was a blur to Lucy as she was towed from one small conversational group to another by the indomitable Lady Olivia, her guards never too close or too far away. She caught occasional glimpses of the other three members of her party, and each one was always surrounded by a wall of interested listeners. Her guards, on the other hand, seemed to have a no man's land around each of them as they jockeyed to keep her and the others in sight. Stephen and Gayle, never far from each other these days, were very animatedly explaining something to the group surrounding them, while Marsha was making motions with her hands that could only have something to do with piloting a Mamba.

Lucy took her fourth glass of ginger ale off a passing tray and turned back to another in a long series of banal discussions with woefully uninformed women and silently prayed, *Help me to endure, please!*

"It must be oh so exciting," one woman, a little younger than the rest, exclaimed, "to be flitting around outer space without the constraints of gravity."

Once again, Lucy had to disabuse someone of their notions. "I'm terribly sorry, ma'am, but we do have artificial gravity on all our major ships. Only the fighters don't have it because of their size. Walking around in our spaceships is just like walking around in this room. And I don't get to do much 'flitting.' I spend much of my day in a dreary office without even a window to break the monotony, signing forms and pushing papers from one stack to another. I think I'll have to do something about that window though." While not quite literally true, Lucy's explanation had portrayed a fairly accurate description of what her days were like now.

Finally, salvation appeared in the form of Baron von Schlenker himself. The portly man in the purple cape inserted himself into the small group around Lucy and exclaimed, "Ladies, ladies! My deepest apologies for this interruption, but I'm afraid I've been remiss in my duties as host, and I find that I must now spirit the good captain away from you." He lightly placed a hand on Lucy's elbow and said, "Lady Olivia, as always, it is a pleasure to have you in my home. I regret that we didn't get to speak more. Perhaps next time."

"I'll hold you to that, Freddie, I will. And you owe me for keeping her away from the riffraff."

"I owe you nothing for that, Olivia. You took that chore upon yourself, and gladly, from what I could see. Now, I'm afraid the captain and I must go."

"You'll wait a moment more, Freddie," Olivia said with a dismissive wave of her hand. "Lady Lucille, it has been my great pleasure to spend this last half hour with you. And I'm sure Birdie will agree with me when I say that if you're ever in England, you'll be welcome in our home—a delightful country estate. Not the dank and dreary pile of stone this is. Now, you go with the baron and relax. He's been declawed, and I promise you that if he does anything more than ogle your cleavage, his wife will hand him his head on a platter!"

Lady Olivia's laughter diminished as the Harrington-Smythe ship of state slowly made its way through the huge room, and Lucy turned back to the baron. "There goes an amazing woman," she said.

"She's a tough old bird," the baron said. "And sugar wouldn't melt in her mouth, but she knows her politics, and she has Lord Harrington-Smythe's ear. If *she* likes you, you've arrived."

The baron had begun to steer her across the crowded floor when she noticed she hadn't seen any of her party for the last little while. "Where are..."

"They're perfectly safe, my dear. I'm sure one of your security persons would have informed you if there was a problem. They've been hovering over the five of you so much that half the people here are calling them 'angels of death.' They're waiting for you in my study, along with several others who are anxious to make your acquaintance in more than just a social setting. So," he asked conversationally, "what did you think of Lady Olivia?"

"Well, I've already said she's an amazing woman. Surprisingly, I think I like her. And I think she fancies some distant relationship between us."

"Really?" the baron said incredulously. "Normally, she won't even recognize her own kin. How is that possible?"

"She heard my name was Grimes, which apparently isn't an uncommon name in Great Britain, I'm led to believe. But it just happens to be her great-great grandfather's name. That particular Grimes on her family tree apparently had a rather checkered past and disappeared not long after fathering her great-grandfather. Her oral family history has him being killed by someone or other for his misdeeds, but oddly enough, we Grimes' trace our heritage back to North Carolina at about the same time her ancestor disappeared. Our family history says he was hung as a horse thief. Coincidence, I'm sure, but they both have the first name of John. It would be interesting to be related to royalty, but the chances aren't good."

"You would only be related by marriage anyway, Captain. Lady Olivia, for all her pearls and diamonds, was a barmaid back in the 1940s when she met and married a young RAF pilot who'd had the great good fortune to survive the war. He came home, and on his father's death, ascended to the title of Lord Harrington-Smythe, Baron of Dunsmere. For many years, he was an influential member of the House of Parliament. Those years of selfless public service got him knighted to Lord and earned him the post of ambassadorship to the United Nations."

As the baron finished the recital of the life of Harrington-Smythe, they reached a small door artfully hidden by some potted plants and a suit of armor. The baron opened the door, and said, "My private study," ushering her in ahead of him with a slight bow.

Lucy stood and took in the whole room. The size of it was impressive. Oak beams crossed the ceiling some twenty feet up, barely visible in the dim light thrown by several strategically placed lamps in various nooks. The walls were lined with books, some of which had to be hundreds of years old. One wall had a fireplace big enough that it could be used to roast whole pigs, large ones. Above the mantle were two crossed pikes with pennants hanging from them, and as an integral part of the setting, a shield was hung in the upper portion of the "x" formed by the pikes.

The furniture was overstuffed, dark-leather couches and chairs that a person could sink into, accompanied by massive oak coffee tables and end tables, waxed to a glossy sheen and seeming to make the room seem a bit smaller by their sheer presence. And all of this was set off by Persian rugs scattered over the floor, their light color and sometimes whimsical designs serving to, somehow, tie the room into an aesthetically pleasing whole.

Four men sitting in the area fronting the unlit fireplace rose as one when Lucy entered the room. No one spoke until she'd finished her examination of the room.

As Lucy turned her attention to the four men, the baron swept past her and announced, "Gentlemen, I have managed to rescue our guest of honor from the clutches of the evil Lady Olivia." The good-natured laughter that followed this declaration only served to assure Lucy that she was skirting the edges of an inside joke. "Gentlemen, it gives me great pleasure to introduce you to Lady Lucille Grimes, First Captain of the Terran Alliance. Her companions you have already met."

Indicating each man in turn, the baron began introducing the strangers. "Lady Lucille, please allow me to introduce Ambassador Miyagishima of Japan, Ambassador William Hargrove of the United States, and Ambassador Hans Rennert of Switzerland. With us also is Lt. General James Crenshaw, who is the American President's adviser on matters... shall we say extraplanetary. And at the back of the room, speaking with your Commander Walker, is Colonel Jason Deering, United States Army. He belongs to one of your special intelligence services, I believe."

Lucy shook each man's hand as she was introduced but gave the colonel only a nod of her head since she was too far to shake hands. *Which suits me just fine. From the look on Stephen's face, I don't have enough disinfectant to get my hand clean with anyway.*

Lucy sat down facing the four men. She glanced first at the glass the baron set down beside her and then up at the baron.

"Any good host," he said haughtily, "keeps track of his guests. Ginger ale, Captain," he said with a smile.

"Thank you, baron," she said, "but now that it's time to talk business, I'd like to get a good scotch under my belt." Turning to the four men now seated across from her, she inquired, "To what do I owe the pleasure of this meeting, gentlemen?"

The Japanese ambassador spoke first. "I admit to being at a loss. I was under the impression that your title was 'First Captain,' but I have heard the baron refer to you as 'Lady' on several occasions, denoting royalty. Before we progress further, how do you wish to be addressed?"

Lucy smiled, the first real one since she'd arrived. "The 'Lady' part is a fabrication on the baron's part, I'm afraid. My rank is first captain, but 'captain' will suffice, Mr. Ambassador."

"Very well, Captain." The ambassador leaned forward and laid a rolled-up parchment scroll on the table between them. It turned slightly until it was stopped by the knot in the red ribbon tying it closed. "My government has instructed me to offer you the use of some two hundred acres of land about twenty miles from Tokyo with ocean access. We would be honored if you would accept the loan of this land for your Asian embassy and allow Japan to host you."

The Swiss ambassador also leaned forward and laid an identical parchment beside the first. "While we don't yet know where we would place such an embassy, the Swiss government would also be honored to accept an embassy from the Terran Alliance."

Lucy nodded her head as gravely and regally to the Swiss ambassador as she had to the Japanese. *I think I'm getting the hang of this! It's like acting— play the part and roll with the punches.*

She turned her attention to the American ambassador, who wilted after a few seconds under her frank stare. "I'm afraid I haven't been given instructions in that area as, uh, clear-cut as my fellow ambassadors," he stumbled. "There are matters, uh, details, rather, that need to be discussed before I can authorize..."

"Well," she said sweetly, "that's quite all right. I'm sure my good friend, the baron, can contact the Canadian and Mexican ambassadors for me. Both countries have qualities to recommend them, though I daresay I do like the thought of having an embassy near Cancun. How about you, Stephen? Wouldn't you like to get rid of some of that 'spaceship pallor'? Marsha? Gayle?"

The Special Assistant to the President finally decided to take over. "Ma'am, Captain, we're not saying there isn't a *possibility* of an embassy in the United States. To be perfectly honest with you, we're concerned with the thought of retaliation."

The look on Lucy's face was if she'd bitten into something extremely bitter. "That statement, Mr. Crenshaw, would, under normal conditions, make me run screaming from the room. And that would not be... appropriate... right now, would it? First, the 'perfectly honest' part, coming as it does from someone so closely allied to American political figures, is immediately suspect. Second, are you suggesting that we, that is, *I*, would be so petty as to retaliate against an entire country for the actions of a few? Especially when it's obvious that the few got their just desserts on the spot. And I'd like to know why you are sitting here instead of Mr. Galway. Did he survive the explosion?"

"President Drake didn't feel that Mr. Galway was the... appropriate person for this situation due to his previous involvement. It was decided at the highest level that you'd consider it an insult to have him present."

"Allow me to deliver a newsflash to you, Mr. Crenshaw," Lucy said, steel in her voice. "I have come to know John Galway, and while I don't know him *well*, at least I do *trust* him, which is more than I can say for you. And I want him back in the loop. Do I make myself clear, Mr. Crenshaw?"

"Perfectly, Captain."

"Very well, then. I expect to hear from him shortly. That being said, I believe our business is concluded for the time being. Mr. Miyagishima, Mr. Rennert, I wish to apologize for my behavior just now. I'm not used to dealing with matters of such a rarefied nature. The Mr. Galway we were just speaking of has accused me on more than one occasion of being more direct than he was used to. I think he said there was more give and take in situations like these, but I've never in my life had a use for being anything less than direct. It saves time, and everyone knows *exactly* what I mean." She let her gaze move over the people assembled in the room. "Now, before we conclude our business for the evening, is there anything else we need to cover?"

Immediately, Colonel Deering stood up. "Before I sign on with any of this, I need to be convinced that this is the way to go, *Captain*. Along with telling me, *and the world*, why a twenty-five-year-old *girl* gets to set policy that will affect a planet and its people for centuries to come." Deering's stance and total concentration on Lucy earned him the undivided attention of everyone in the room. And his baiting of her had more than one pistol in hand.

"Take a break, people!" Lucy stood up and glared

at everyone present. "Everyone is taking themselves way too seriously here. And that includes me, dammit. I'm going to answer the colonel's questions, but—surprise—*none* of you are going to like my answers. Sit *down*, Colonel," she ordered.

"First off, I don't *want* this job! But I have it, having been shanghaied by my *friends*," she said. "Colonel, I just lucked into this, if you can call it that. Someone else found the ship—someone your people murdered, by the way. I was among the first group to become volunteers. We all were, it seems," she said, waving at her party. "I just happened to be the second one to get a captaincy. The first was his wife, Kitty, who is now in what our engineers think is a recuperation tank aboard the *Galileo*. Since I was the ranking line officer, I was forced by my *peers* to take this position. What it amounts to is that I was left holding the bag."

Lucy shook her head as she glowered at the colonel and special assistant. "If we had turned the *Galileo* over to you, Colonel, not one soul on this planet outside of the military would see anything out of it for decades, if ever. And, there's another consideration. I've had this discussion with Galway, so I'm truly surprised that we have to go through it again.

"There is no way in *hell*, gentlemen, that something as enormous as the *Galileo* could remain a secret for long. Sooner or later—and we were betting on sooner—someone would find out and there would be consequences on a global scale."

The colonel settled into one of the massive, leather-covered chairs, and with every outward sign of confidence said, "Okay, *Captain*, enlighten us as to what those results would be."

"I'll be happy to, Colonel, but first, let me clear something up. I've given you and your rank every bit of civility I know how. If you ever speak to me in that tone of voice again, I'll take one of our lasers and make you wish you'd never seen me. Do I make myself clear?" She stalked over to her guards with her hand out, and one of them placed a pistol in her hand. She let it dangle, pointing at a sensitive part of his anatomy. By the time she had stopped talking she was bending over the chair, knowing her cleavage was revealed down to her bellybutton, but the colonel only had eyes for the gun in her hand.

"Yes, ma'am," he said apologetically enough that she almost believed he meant it. She handed the pistol back without looking at who it had come from and returned to her place in the room.

"I don't know how long you've been in the loop, Colonel," she continued, "but we've had a few years to consider the ramifications of our actions. Have you ever had to deal with a bully, Colonel?" Lucy's pacing had brought her back to the hapless officer again. "We give the ship to you and the balance of power changes. The whole planetary dynamic is thrown off. We give it to *anyone* and the balance changes. No one would let that government or entity alone. If they didn't get their share *immediately*, they'd do their best to see that no one got it. That would mean two things, Colonel—the end of the United States you swore to protect and the end of life on Earth as we know it."

All eyes followed Lucy as she left the colonel and began to pace the floor. "Colonel, before you could learn to operate the ships' defenses, how many countries would launch nuclear missiles to destroy the *Galileo* rather than let you have sole possession? At least three! And the result of that, Colonel?" Lucy said, badgering the older man. "After a world-wide nuclear exchange with no benefit in sight for anyone, Colonel, every political system on the planet would disintegrate almost overnight. Stock markets would plunge, making the crash of the last century look like a small dip. Every transportation line in the country would be broken, and no food would reach the millions of people stranded in the megacities like New York and San Francisco, just to name two. Greed and corruption would run rampant, and every nation on the planet would collapse under the weight of the political decadence that would remove all hope from the disillusioned masses. Around the world, assassinations would serve to destabilize any remaining solvent governments, leaving the wicked and the meek alike to fend for themselves.

"It's the scared little man who'd be blamed for the fall of civilization, Colonel, if there were any left to write the history books. But it would be the greed and fear of men like you who'd be the *real* root cause of the end of the world." Lucy looked down at the man in the chair with contempt. "As long as there's one person the planet who would try to make that scenario come to pass, we need people like you, Colonel, to remind us of what we *shouldn't* become. Even though I find that personally offensive, I can still recognize a fact when I see one. As you should, Colonel. And the basic fact is that we did right by keeping the *Galileo* out of governmental hands."

Heart racing at the thought of how she'd just spoken to a man twice her age and a representative of the most powerful country on the planet, she added almost pleadingly, "The only scenario that lets life as we know it go on is one in which no one finds out you have the ship. Think you can keep that big a secret, Colonel?"

"I don't know what would happen, Captain, and to tell the truth, I don't care. That's the job of the people appointed above me."

"Just doing your job, Colonel? Even somebody who follows orders blindly has a conscience. Somewhere deep down inside of you is a little place labeled 'right and wrong,' and I'm betting you're going to have to reevaluate some of your precepts. If you don't, then I feel sorry for you."

Changing tack fast enough to take everyone by surprise, Lucy turned to the seated ambassadors and said, "Gentlemen thank you for your time tonight. Remember, we need to have all three countries in agreement before we move into the first embassy. That having been said, can I have my secretary contact yours to make the proper arrangements?" Getting their instant agreement and business cards, she turned to the baron. "Sir, Your Grace, or Majesty, or Highness, or whatever, how do we get out of here without appearing abrupt to our newfound friends?"

The baron, a smile on his face, said, "Gentlemen, if you would be so kind, I have a private matter to discuss with the captain. I'd be most grateful if you'd avail yourselves of the hospitality of my home for a few minutes while we talk." He waved his hand toward the door and the five men headed out to mingle with the rest of the guests. "The rest of your party may stay as well, Captain.

"Mag-*nif*-icent!" he exclaimed. "Just the right

amount of wounded pride coupled with indignation and determination! You were a diplomat in another life! I'm sure of it." Waving the four friends to sit, he continued, "And from this day on you will call me 'Freddie!' After the way you handled yourself, I certainly don't want to be on the list of people who are *not* your friends!"

When the door closed on the departing men, the baron turned to Lucy and her friends. "I wasn't just making excuses when I told them I had a reason to speak to you alone." Lucy quirked an eyebrow and waited for the baron to continue. "While my government doesn't yet have an idea where your embassy should be, *I* do. Some years ago when my country hosted the Winter Olympic Games, I offered a portion of my lands to be used as housing for some of the athletes." Seeing that he had the attention of his guests, the baron leaned forward in his chair, elbows on knees and hands clasped in front of him. "Due to the political climate at the time, that housing was built with security foremost in the minds of the contractors and construction crews. Since those games, the complex has remained dormant. I'm thinking that the front half of the first floor could be used for offices, meeting rooms, or whatever you need them to be. The back half has a swimming pool and a gymnasium. There's another office on the second floor, with the third and fourth floors as living quarters for resident personnel."

"And how do you propose that we pay for this... largess, you offer, Freddie?" Lucy had imitated the baron's posture, giving him a view of the cleavage Lady Olivia had alluded to earlier, and smiled inwardly as his eyes strayed downward.

A supreme effort brought his eyes back to Lucy's. "The estate will cover the utilities, of course. But it would be bad form not to exact *some* form of payment. I suggest one dollar a year for each year the Terran Alliance is in residence. *And,*" he continued before anyone could react to the offer, "I'd like a ride in one of your marvelous spaceships. Of course, you'd be nearby to attend the occasional party we have here. Not too onerous a task, I think."

Lucy looked at her friends. "I think we could live with that arrangement, Freddie. I'm sure the Alliance would be able to put in an appearance at most of your functions. Of course, I, personally, won't be able to attend each one, but that won't be a problem, will it?"

"Of course not, Lady Lucille! I shall make the arrangements known to my government through our ambassador immediately. If they agree, we have a deal! Then, I'll arrange for you to take a tour of the facilities. You can make your final decision at that time. And for the balance of the evening, may I suggest that we rejoin the other guests? There are still many who wish to meet you."

Lucy stood and took the baron's gigantic hand in hers. "Yes, we should do that, shouldn't we?" She reached up and pulled his head down to her level, kissed him on the cheek, and said, "And, Freddie, please call me Lucy."

The big man, overcome with emotion, could only bow deeply as he opened the door and allowed the Alliance delegation to return to the gala.

FUGUE

Her world was a featureless void, and she inhabited her world neither thinking nor not thinking. Simple existence was more than enough effort for her. But slowly, after an indeterminate time that could have been days or millennia, a sense of self began to insert itself. With this sense of self came vague and formless... things...that she eventually decided were emotions... or possibly feelings. One thing her world didn't give her was certainty.

The elusiveness of these feelings, which stayed just on the edge of her perception, gave rise to an uneasiness and took away the comfort the formless void had fostered for so long. Eventually, one of those fleeting feelings got close enough to be grasped and held, to be studied and made a part of her. And when this had been accomplished, she recognized it. This ephemeral feeling was loss, and it brought with it such emptiness that she cried out in despair as much for the emptiness itself as for the fact that she didn't know what it was she had lost. Somewhere, something decided that she should sleep.

CHAPTER FIVE

Simon, sitting in a wheelchair in Father Timothy's office said, "All I know is that I need to get to Denver. With my wristband ruined, the quickest way I know is to get in touch with a... recruiter we have out there." He looked at the men in the room.

What a crowd, he thought. *A ghetto priest, a defrocked doctor, and a pawnbroker-slash-fence. And not one of them has a single reason to help me* or *a rogue FBI agent.*

Michael had returned to the mission within the forty-eight hours he'd hoped, wearing a worried look and carrying bearer bonds. "Fifty-six thousand dollars! And the reaction I got! They took forever to make all their tests and inquiries. So, what are you planning to do now?"

"Head west," Simon said. "Agent Daniels has offered to help me. Neither of us thinks we should take any kind of public transportation. I'm *supposed* to be dead, but my face has been shown so many times in the past few days that someone would be sure to recognize me. So, it's the lesser of two evils—a car. Know where we can buy one?"

As plans have a habit of doing, these grew. The brothers Jeffers had convinced themselves that they were coming along to volunteer. They'd been fans of science-fiction since they were kids and still enjoyed their old argument. "Of course you think a lightsaber is more elegant! You preferred armored knights before that. But look at the simplicity of a phaser!"

They laughed at their private joke while Simon and Daniels shook their heads.

"How about taking my Winnie?" Michael suggested "She's old, but I keep her up. Three days for my guy to get her out of storage and checked out. I can always fly out and drive her back... after. Brian said you need that long anyway before you're fit to travel. Sleeps six, so the four of you should have plenty of room." At Simon's lifted eyebrow, he exclaimed, "Hey! Some of us can't just get up and go traipsing around the country. But take the RV. That way, I'll be there in spirit."

That evening, Simon first watched Lucy's broadcast and then his own funeral. "It's spooky knowing that's supposed to be me," he said, staring up at the startlingly green trail left by the reentering coffin. "but now I have more questions than ever. If they think I'm dead, why isn't Kitty on the television? She was second in command. *She* should be First Captain." His mind tried desperately to skirt the possibility that the broken and battered Mamba the news report showed being carried back to space after the destruction of the shuttle had been piloted by Kitty. Or maybe she was in mourning. Somebody had to take over, but to not know for sure...

"And what is Lucy likely to do now? I'd just love to hear some of the meetings on the Hill," Roland said. "That's what's going to be on the mind of every person on the planet. You do know they are afraid of you, don't you? Because you have power they don't."

"Hell, even *I* don't know what she'll do!" Simon winced as he slapped the right arm of his chair and felt the vibrations all the way into his left shoulder and wrist. And the new cast made him feel clumsier than ever. "I thought she was pretty bright and a quick thinker, or I wouldn't have given her a ship in the first place. But she can be a little rash at times. All the more reason to get to Denver as soon as possible."

A pissed off, worried Simon was nearly impossible to be around, much less live with for any length of time. Kitty could have told his companions this, but they wouldn't have listened. Men tended toward being problem solvers, and Simon's attitude had become a problem. The fact that they couldn't remove the cause any more than he could didn't help either.

Simon worried about Kitty constantly. He wanted her to know he was still alive so she wouldn't worry. And, not incidentally, her knowing he was alive would result in his rescue. And rescue was just how he'd come to see it. Loner that he'd always been, it had been easy enough to conceive of leaving Earth and all that meant. He'd still be dependent on the planet of his birth for some time yet, but it really was only a matter of time.

His frustration was at his forced idleness and inability to do for himself. Having his left wrist in an inflatable cast meant he couldn't use a cane to get around while his leg healed. And he'd be confined to the vehicle during the entire trip.

He was pissed at the deaths of three people who'd trusted him and for whom he felt responsible. *Maybe more*, he thought as he remembered the pictures of four Mambas hauling a fifth back up to the *Galileo*. Simon blamed himself for their deaths, no matter that they were dead due to the ambush. *I should have considered the possibility. I should have made plans.*

Michael picked up the four men and drove them to his house in the suburbs so he wouldn't have to thread the big vehicle through city traffic any more than necessary.

A week had passed since Simon had been wounded, and he was able, for short periods of time, to hobble around without his chair. The able-bodied members of their small party moved supplies into the nearly-bus-sized rig prior to their departure as Simon looked on in frustration.

The Winnebago left the small community of Falls Church, Virginia, and headed west. The battered-looking RV with the cracked vinyl spare-tire cover proclaiming it to belonging to "The Reardon's," got onto the road four days after the funeral broadcast to Earth.

Simon slept through most of the days' drive, courtesy of Dr. Brian. "I just slipped a sedative in with his antibiotics. He needed the rest. He's on orals now, so it was easy."

"And not incidentally gave us a rest from his temper, too?" Father Timothy asked.

"Think what you want, big brother. He needed the rest, and it helped keep us sane. Besides," he said, glancing at his watch, "we'll be parked for the night soon, and he's due to wake up anyway. We'll have dinner, and then he'll go back to sleep and so can we. This has been a long day for all of us, and tomorrow is time enough for him to be staying up more. I've finally gotten the infection under control. All he needs now is time to let the damage heal."

Tuning the little TV to a local channel while they ate their Chinese meal that had been delivered, the four were treated to the next phase of Lucy's agenda. The news anchor said, "Due to the secretive nature of the dealings with the Terran Alliance, we were fortunate to have had a correspondent in Switzerland when word of the landing was released. Our Sarah Parker brings us the details."

The screen flickered and a young brunette stared out of the screen. "Thanks, Pete. I'm Sarah Parker, reporting from Zurich, Switzerland where we've been lucky enough to capture the landing of the Terran Alliance spacecraft on camera." The screen shifted to a view that was unmistakably an airport. "A shuttle that appears to be identical to the one destroyed at Camp David early last week is landing here in Zurich." the woman's voice said over the picture. "Also with the shuttle are four of the ships called Mambas, leaving me to wonder if they're the same four that hauled the damaged craft back to... wherever. They do appear different in that these four are painted with the image of some kind of bird."

The picture zoomed in to show a closeup of the lead Mamba landing between the camera and the shuttle. Just under the edge of the cockpit, a name could be seen—Dahlquist, Shirley, Commander. Emblazoned on the nose of her ship was the legend, "Red Shift."

The scene moved as the cameraman jockeyed to get a view of the occupants emerging from the shuttle.

"Rumors here are that the Terran Alliance has decided to take their case to the United Nations. In an apparent attempt to mollify the Alliance, the Security Council has agreed to meet on neutral ground and hear from the Alliance Commander, Lucy Grimes. We managed to get a shot of her party as they stepped onto the tarmac, preceded and followed by armed guards."

Simon named each one as they appeared. "Lucy, of course. And there's Marsha, along with Gayle and Stephen. I don't recognize any of the bodyguards. Not a sign of Kitty."

Simon seemed to live on an emotional rollercoaster over the following days. Father Timothy tried to help as best he could, but when all was said and done, it was truly up to Simon to get past those hurdles on his own. The continuing lack of any word about Kitty in the news stories that were constantly airing began to be a dull ache at the back of his mind as he continued to learn to cope with his disabilities. And those were lessening daily, with a corresponding improvement in attitude, both of which his companions enjoyed.

Scrupulously keeping within the speed limits so as not to arouse any more attention than necessary, the four men drove west at a sedate pace. The first night saw them at an RV camp in Indiana, the second somewhere in the Mississippi Valley, and the third found them on the Great Plains. As Simon continued to improve, he realized that moping and a foul temper weren't helping matters.

They all began to look forward to the nightly stops so they could catch up with what was going on with the Alliance. Every day it was someone new telling some audience what the Alliance was all about from someone else's viewpoint. Or reporting that the two ships that had sat in orbit with the *Galileo* were gone, expounding for hours on the significance of that fact. Simon laughed for the first time in a week when heard that the Alliance Commander had accepted "an invitation to a gala to be held in her honor at the castle of an expatriate German nobleman living in Switzerland." The reporter responsible for that particular piece of journalistic sleuthing was none other than Sarah Parker, who'd catapulted to international fame by being the only reporter with feet on the ground when the Alliance landed in Zurich.

"Personally, I think it's true," Simon asserted. "This Parker woman has had it right so far, and all I can say is that Lucy is going to kill me when she finds out I'm alive! She hates attention almost as much as Kitty." Simon bestowed his second smile on the three men he was traveling with. "And she said it would start at eight p.m., so that would be noon here. Let's stop for lunch and see what's on TV."

The past week hadn't been kind to Agent Daniels, either. As short a time as that was, it was all it'd taken to make a man who prided himself on his dedication, loyalty, and devotion to duty to begin to question his basic beliefs under the right circumstances. From his first impulsive act of shooting the soldier, Daniels had been in just as much turmoil as Simon had. The fact that it had been self-preservation was irrelevant to him. But having been conditioned by the military and later the FBI to endure long periods of solitude, the agent was more adept than most at keeping his quandary hidden from the others. Now, it seemed, it was time to make the final break.

"Agreed," he said. "There's a small town just down the road. But first, we need to talk. Or at least I do."

Brian, sitting behind the wheel, reached out and turned the radio off. "Revelation time, Roland?" he asked.

Father Timothy looked at the two men sitting at the small table. "You told us you two weren't partners before we left the mission. Something else on your mind?"

Daniels shook his head. "Not that. I never made any bones about who or what I was after Simon woke up. I just said we were partners then because I didn't feel the need to confuse the issue with facts. Now I do. I was on that shuttle escaping from the Alliance. They would have let me go anyway, but not with these." He pulled two disks out of his shirt pocket. "Or with this," he added, pulling the laser pistol out of the back of his belt and laying it on the table beside the disks.

"Once upon a time I believed in my country. I still do, I think. But after what happened at Camp David, I can't be a part of it. Those disks have all the information I could acquire on your propulsion and weapon's systems, as well as a lot of stuff you probably wouldn't have released to us for years, but we'd still have a leg up on most other countries. It contains deflector screens that would protect most major cities with just the power of any major hydroelectric dam. Think of it. And there's more. I'm not bragging, but I'm *good* at my job. And the gun was just because I'm a weapon's nut. You should see my collection someday.

"Back to the main issue. Yesterday, I called a friend, hoping to call in a favor. I didn't get it, by the way, but I got something better—or worse, depending on how you look at things. It appears I underestimated the owner of a certain cartage company. He called the police when he found his truck 'misplaced.' He wanted to be sure it hadn't been used in a crime, or so he told the police. They fingerprinted the truck and sent the prints to the National Crime Information Center, NCIC. That and some mysterious bloodstains on the passenger side have let the wrong authorities know that I'm back on Earth, and since I haven't checked in, there's a nationwide alert out for me. And because of the blood, Simon, too."

"I'd think," Father Timothy said, "that the word 'treason' would be bandied about in relation to both of you then."

"I'll go ya one better, Timmy," Brian said from the front of the Winnie. "These two would just disappear. No trials, no publicity. And since we just happen to be with 'em, we would disappear, too. Only difference is that they'd survive longer than we would. Both of *them* know something. We just came along for the ride, so to speak." Brian glanced into the rearview mirror at Daniels and waited for his response.

"What can I say after..." the agent said. "Look, the best thing we can do now is split up, and the town coming up is just as good a place as any to do it. We've got enough money to buy a car and go on to

Denver separately. Here's the address of the two men you need to find." At Simon's startled expression, Daniels shrugged. "I told you I was good at what I do. Besides, what if you hadn't woken up or something? Anyway, it's done."

The four men stopped on the outskirts of Salinas, Kansas, found a local channel carrying international news, and watched Lucy and her entourage emerge from a series of limousines and walk up the steps of a medieval castle.

Shaking his head, Simon could only ask no one in particular, "What is that woman up to?"

The morning after the gala, Lucy woke to a message light on her phone. She lay there staring at the sun shining off the western slopes of the Alps for several minutes, reveling in the clarity of the view. *They make the Rockies look like foothills*, she thought. *I'm ruined for life. This is the most gorgeous sight I've ever laid eyes on.* She drew as much strength from the panoramas she could, knowing what was coming. Having gone partying as the Terran Alliance in front of international television, she was going to have to keep up the persona.

While things seemed to have gone well to that point, she still felt like she was about to make a fool of herself at any moment. So far, everyone seemed to be taking the Alliance seriously, with the notable exception of a certain few.

She dreaded the thought of picking up the handset and letting the world know she was awake.

The second ring brought a response. "Good morning, Captain. It's 10 a.m., and you have messages waiting. Would you like the messages first, or breakfast?"

Lucy stared at the phone for a few seconds. Putting it back up to her ear, she said, "Uh, Commander Kimura?"

"Yes, ma'am?"

"Are any of the messages unable to wait for breakfast?"

"No, ma'am."

"Okay. Orange juice, wheat toast, strawberry jelly and half a grapefruit. With sugar. Real sugar, and butter, please."

"Yes, ma'am. About twenty minutes?"

"Uh, fine." At the extended silence that followed, she said, "Uh, that will be all, Commander."

"Yes, ma'am."

The line went dead, and Lucy stared in amazement at the phone. *I heard Simon tell Kitty once that if you act like you have the right, most people will go along with you. Damn if it doesn't work. I say having the goods to back it up helps, too.* Putting on the uniform that had mysteriously appeared while she showered, she blushed. *God! What did they think of that caterwauling I call singing?"*

Minutes later a knock at her door made her jump. "Come in."

"Breakfast, ma'am, and the local English newspaper." Setting the tray down on a centuries-old desk at the side of the room, Commander Kimura said, "After breakfast, there's a stack of messages on the desk in your office." One of the bedrooms in the three-bedroom suite had been converted to an office for Lucy the second day. The third bedroom was occupied by Commander Kimura, and at least one member of the security detail was awake at all times in the dayroom. Two more were on guard in the hallway at all times, too.

She took a drink of orange juice and sprayed half of it all over the paper. There she was in as close to living color as a newspaper could get. Right on the front page! Along with Marsha, Gayle, and Stephen, of course, but the article began with the letters AP, which stood for Associated Press, and they delivered their news all over the world.

What the hell are Mom and Dad gonna think of this?

The article covered the landing, the visit to the Security Council meeting, and of course, the gala. She continued to force a few more bites of toast down, but they began to feel like lead in the bottom of her stomach. Finally setting the tray and paper aside, she stood up, dusted herself off, and with a deep breath, opened the door.

Commander Kimura started to get up, but Lucy waved her back down. "Don't be doing that. Let's do away with as much protocol in private as possible, okay?"

"Yes, ma'am. You now have twenty-six messages on your desk. Fourteen of them are from ambassadors or representatives of various countries, arranged in order of who called first. The other twelve are television and news crews wanting an interview. They're all using the word 'exclusive' and offering obscene amounts of money."

"I don't want this kind of notoriety! Get Marsha in here. And Gayle. Tell them I want to see them for a late lunch, around one o'clock, probably after I talk to all of those government guys. And remind me to call home today, please. Right now, I'll go tackle those messages."

Having her secretary (still a freaky feeling) call each of the ambassadorial messages back, she spoke to each one personally, assuring most that they would all share equally in the distribution of technology, and assuring them that the larger nations would not set the agenda for what was released. They felt, as did the Alliance, that something other than weapons should be on the agenda for release. Then Lucy went through the stack from the media and finally settled on the woman who'd broken the story of their arrival. There was something about her...

Setting the last piece of paper down, she went out into the dayroom. She sat down in the ornate chair next to the desk and laughingly asked, "What's new?"

"Well," Commander Kimura said seriously, "more ambassadors, and now people wanting to sell things. One man wanted to sell us meteor insurance! Where do these people come from, and how do they get our number?

"Oh yeah, and then there're the groups that want to pay *us* to do something—carry a satellite into orbit, launch personal remains into the sun or orbit, build a space hotel as a resort, and provide shuttle service. Take 'em to the moon. Take 'em to Mars. Who knows what's next?"

"I sure don't! Let's get lunch and then I want you to set up an interview with this woman after I talk with Marsha and Gayle." She passed a piece of paper across the desk. "Sarah Parker. She's done the best job of reporting this so far, and she hasn't been pushy. Yet. Schedule her tonight. Here. Her and one cameraman. We'll have our own cameraman, as well, to prevent doctoring unless we allow the changes."

Gayle and Marsha walked in, and Lucy said, "We're about to have a lot of money coming in. There will be people who want us to do any number of things for them—hauling things into orbit, bringing things down, taking people here, taking them there, that sort of thing. Hell, we could license our technology rather than sell it or give it away. Even if all our power is free, we still have to have cash. Some, if not all, our people would like to be paid if possible, though I think a lot of 'em would stay on for free. Marsha, among other things, will you figure out a pay scale of some kind? Base it on the US military. We've taken so much else from them, why not more? You are hereby appointed to the position of Secretary of the Treasury, but that won't stop you from taking command of one of the ships due to arrive soon. I called the *Heinlein*. They have their skeleton crew aboard and are ready to micro-jump back. We'll have four more ships in orbit very shortly. I asked the *McCaffrey*, too, and they report almost ready.

"Oh, and one more thing. It's past time we had a lawyer—at *least* one. Gayle, you look into that for me, will you? Maybe you can find someone who grew up on science-fiction. Or maybe one of our crew has a relative somewhere willing to take on the job. Maybe Freddie, Baron von Schlenker, can be of some help in that area. Look into it and get back to me. No time limit, but soon."

"Commander Kimura?" the young woman asked suspiciously. "And just what are you a commander of?" She glared at the phone in her hand as if it had bitten her.

"Terran Alliance," the voice returned. "And my boss has ordered me to call you and tell you that you've been chosen for the exclusive interview you requested."

"Yeah, right. Who put you up to this?"

"Miss Parker, your last written message to the office of the First Captain used the phrase, 'I most anxiously await your response,' just before your signature. And your last call to this office, answered by me, by the way, was the third since 7 a.m."

"Tell me where and when." The reporter's voice immediately turned professional.

"Here. Two hours. You and one cameraman. We hold final rights over what goes out. That's not to say that you're restricted in your questions, just that we intend to make sure the reporting isn't biased."

Met at the hotel's main entrance, Sarah and her cameraman were hustled into an elevator and whisked to the penthouse level. Once there, they were led into two different rooms and thoroughly searched before being deposited in front of a desk behind which sat a small Asian woman.

"Uh, I was expecting..."

"To meet the Captain immediately? Oh, no! You're getting the grand tour, Miss Parker," Kimura said with a grin.

Nonplussed by the Alliance woman's response, Sarah tried to regain the initiative she felt she hadn't had since pulling up in front of the hotel. "I *really* don't appreciate the tactics your Amazons used on me and my cameraman," Sarah said. "You people invited us, remember?"

"And *your* people are responsible for the deaths of four of ours and dozens of your own, remember?" the secretary shot back. "To that end, we reserve the right to inspect all of your equipment before any of it's allowed around First Captain Grimes. Now, you've passed the first hurdle—getting your equipment in here. Do you want the interview, or do I call one of these others?" she asked, waving the stack of messages at the young woman.

"No!" the reporter said hastily. "I mean, I'll do the interview. What format do you want to use? Straight Q and A? Or informal chat? How much time can you give me? And where do you want to have it? And we haven't discussed your fee yet either."

Commander Kimura looked like she'd bitten into something sour. "I don't know enough about that to even comment. The captain said we should have the interview, and *before* it airs, your people can decide what it's worth to you. See? We can be pretty easy to deal with. As to your other questions, how about an informal chat? Do you have some questions ready? Need more time?" When the reporter shook her head, the commander went on. "As to the amount of time, the captain said as much as it takes. We may have to break for business matters, but we can always pick up where we left off. All in all, probably no more than a few hours. Is that agreeable to you?"

"Uh, yes. Certainly! That only leaves where to hold the interview and when."

"Well, here's where things could get a bit sticky. How do you feel about traveling?" Kimura asked, grinning mischievously.

Parker glanced at her cameraman. "It would depend on how far we have to go and how long it will take to get there, wouldn't it?"

Kimura said, "Well, how far? About, oh, I don't know, I'd guess around twelve thousand miles. And how long to get there? Less time than it would take you to get from this floor to the ground by elevator. Are you in?"

"In? In what?" the reporter asked as she glanced apprehensively at her partner. "How do we travel twelve thousand miles that fast?"

"With these," Kimura said, holding up two small disks. "We call them locator disks. You hold one and when I press the button on my wristband, we all beam out of here. Just like in the movies. We wind up on the *Galileo*. You've heard of her, haven't you?" She continued sarcastically. "The big one sitting up there in orbit? The one that started all this fuss in the first place?"

"Sarah," the man holding the camera said. "I think we're getting a chance no other team on the planet has a shot at. Take it! A Pulitzer for you, maybe. And look what it'll do for *my* career! Hey, lady," he said, changing his focus. "I can't speak for her, but I'm in. If she won't go, I'll do the interview myself!"

"Hey! Back off, Dwayne. Give a girl time to be stunned, will ya? Of course, I'll do it. How does this work, again?" she asked taking the disk from the other woman.

"Just hold it in your hand. Dwayne, make sure that anything you need is in your hands or strapped to your body. Otherwise, it, or parts of it, could be left behind. Here's your disk. Ready?"

"Wait! This is cool and all that, but why can't we

do the interview from here?" Sarah asked. "I mean, hell, I don't know *what* I mean."

"Well, to be perfectly honest with you, Miss Parker, Captain Grimes had some pressing business on board the *Galileo*. And while she wants to do the interview, the best place at this time would be aboard ship. I can't say any more than that right now."

"Okay. Do it before I change my... mind. Holy *shit!*" The reporter stood motionless in the confines of a hexagon on the floor of a metal-walled room. A console on the far side was operated by a young man in a uniform to match the one their host was wearing.

She watched as the Alliance Officer took a small device off her belt and spoke into it. "This is Kimura. I have the interview team with me."

Sarah heard the faint sound of a camcorder beginning to operate and turned to her partner. "Do you believe this shit?" she asked. Remembering the microphone in her hand, she moved away from the cameraman and posed in front of him. "This is Sarah Parker. I have the honor to be standing in the... where are we?"

"Transport Control."

"I have the honor to be standing in Transport Control aboard the spaceship *Galileo* about twelve thousand miles above the surface of the Earth. I am here today to interview the commander of the group that calls itself the Terran Alliance. It would seem that First Captain Grimes had duties that precluded an interview in Zurich at this time, so I and my cameraman have been...transported... aboard. With me now is Commander Kimura. Commander, just where are we aboard this ship, and when will we get to see the First Captain?" She moved the microphone toward the commander and waited for a reply.

"We're on deck seven, about three-quarters of the way back from the front of the vessel, which is about thirty-eight hundred feet long. We'll be going to deck eighteen, which is also known as the 'projects deck.' There, you'll be allowed to film a ceremony investing two of our officers with command of their new ships, and you'll be in time to see the ships arrive if we hurry. Your cameraman can continue filming as long as he likes. Follow me, please." Taking a headset from the ensign manning the transport console, she placed it on her head and led the way out of the room.

Keeping up a running commentary as they moved out of the room and down the corridor toward the elevator, Kimura said, "Part of the technology we have aboard is artificial gravity. Our scientists are still trying to work out the math, but it helps that we have the hardware to work with. Working models, so to speak. Knowing that something can be done helps with learning how to duplicate it, but it's still slow going. We don't want to get ahead of ourselves. Right now," she said as the elevator doors opened, "we're running at well over one hundred percent of crew complement because we'll be transferring personnel to the two new ships I mentioned. They'll arrive with skeleton crews aboard, and we'll transfer crew to each ship until they're fully crewed. Then we'll recrew the *Galileo* herself, and she can start on her next mission."

As the elevator moved downward, Sarah motioned Dwayne to turn off the camera. "Let's save storage where we can, okay?" Turning to their guide, she asked, "What's the next mission, Commander?"

"To build the fourth and final space dock. We have

the first three in operation now, and the fourth will be big enough to turn out ships the size of the one we're on now. It will take about a year to build as opposed to the six months or so for each of the other three."

The door slid into the wall, giving the trio a view of a huge open space filled with people in identical uniforms. Sarah heard the camera begin to whir behind her again and asked, "Most of the uniforms look the same. Are these people all crew of this ship? And what about the differences I see?"

"As I said, many of these people will be transferring to the two new ships arriving shortly. And yes, the uniforms are all the same. We call this particular uniform the duty uniform, and it's worn every day for most functions. You've seen the dress uniform when the shuttle landed in Zurich, as well as the fancy dress uniform worn to the baron's gala. The differences you see here today are primarily in the patches people wear on their shoulders. We have a few people aboard from each of the three space docks, some from each of the two active ships, and quite a few who will be moving to the two new ships. Plus, the *Galileo* crew have their own shoulder patch."

"And how will we see these ships arrive, Commander? Some type of screen or viewport?"

"No, Miss Parker, not quite. Come with me." Kimura led the two visitors through the crowd and over to a relatively clear area. She glanced at her watch and said, "Dwayne, you might want to get a shot of that wall." Pointing her arm in the direction she wanted him to aim his camera, she dropped her arm and waited.

"What are we going to see, Commander," Sarah asked at about the time that the entire section of wall began to retract. "Oh my God!" Sarah cried. "We're all going to die!"

"Relax, Miss Parker," Kimura said with a smile. "You've just been initiated. Almost everyone has the same reaction the first time. We're protected by force fields strong enough to stand up to a meteor impact yet selective enough to allow the passage of any material at the field operator's discretion." She pointed to a room raised above the main floor of the deck where some dozen people were doing arcane things to consoles the visitors couldn't see.

"And now, Dwayne, you will aim your camera about... there, shortly," she said pointing into space. "Look for four shapes. Another way to spot them is to look for stars that disappear and reappear. That would be a ship passing in front of them. Soon enough, you'll see the ships themselves. Unlike the *Galileo*, which is an uninspiring grey-metal color, the new ships have been subjected to an annealing process that makes them white. We wanted to do something to set ourselves apart from the Builders, which is what we call the original owners. Some of our Mamba pilots have started using the process to decorate their ships. Over there is one of the Hawke Flight ships."

Sarah and Dwayne looked in the direction indicated and saw a Mamba being swarmed over by a group of people. "What's going on? Repairs?"

"No. It's called 'nose art.' The main colors have already been added. What they're doing now is adding the pilot's handle and name on top of the hawk design." As Dwayne zoomed in on the ship sitting by itself at one end of the immense bay, he was able to make out the name "Avatar." Just under the clear cockpit was the name, "Randall, Velma, Commander."

Dwayne turned the camera toward Kimura. "Aren't you worried about the government finding out who your people are?"

"Not at all. At least for some of our people. We do ask before we reveal anyone's name. I understand that one of the requests is that we give a full list of the names of all our personnel. The official reason is that the United States wants to make sure none of our people are wanted for crimes on Earth. So far, that hasn't been a problem. Trust me, we don't have Elvis or Jimmy Hoffa on any of our ships or bases."

The commander cocked her head to one side as if listening to someone on her headset. "Now would be a good time to get over by the force field while you can still get a good shot," she said. "The *Heinlein* and the *McCaffrey* are about to arrive."

The reporter's and cameraman's feelings of being out of place grew as they moved through the crowd of identically clad people over to the edge of the deck. Sarah put her hand out and felt it collide with... something. "That's the force field," Kimura said. "It won't pass organic material unless the overrides in the control room allow it, and that doesn't happen often. Now, Dwayne, aim your camera there," she said pointing outwards.

At the same time that Dwayne was filming the arrival of the four ships, Lucy stepped up onto the dais and stood in front of her staff. "Good afternoon, ladies and gentlemen. I am First Captain Lucy Grimes. Quite a few of you don't know me yet. I hope to remedy that in the months to come, but for now, let me say that I'm glad you're here. Each and every one of you are here, I hope, because of your belief that mankind belongs in space as more than a visitor, but that's what the space stations of Earth provide—visitor status. The Alliance offers full residence as a separate and independent entity. Once, we thought we'd be an appendage of Earth, and that could still be true, but for the time being, we'll remain a unique and distinct entity. As more and more of our technology becomes a part of Earth's daily life, we'll become a greater part of Earth, lessening the distinction. And as more ships need crews, more volunteers will come up to join us, constantly changing our uniqueness in directions we can't yet imagine. But that will be a slow process— faster than if we'd turned this ship over to any one government, to be sure, but slow nonetheless. We hope to have as minimal an effect on the economy of the planet of our birth as possible while exporting the most technology we can.

"It will be up to all of us—Alliance members, as well as the people of Earth—to make sure that economic upheaval is minimized while progress is maximized. I realize these are platitudes, but they must be voiced for the benefit of all. We don't want to upset the applecart. It is, after all, our planet as well. We, all of us, have homes down there, as well as friends, lovers, pets, dreams, and aspirations for the future. Only a few of you standing here today will make the break that will turn you into true members of the Terran Alliance, real spacers. The rest of you will stay with us for a time and then go home.

"That split will be with our blessing. You'll take your memories with you, and more. Most of all, you'll take with you *information* that will eventually seep into Earth's database and enrich everyone. We encourage this. But that isn't why you're here today.

"You're here because of those." Lucy turned to look at what the cameraman had centered in his viewfinder—four gleaming white ships. "All four of those ships need crew, and a large portion of you will fill slots on board those ships. You'll become true spacemen! Buzz words, yes, but you've been aboard the *Galileo* training for two weeks now, most of you, and you *know* deep down that this isn't a game."

"Not once," she continued as Dwayne's camera panned through the crowd of rapt faces and up to hers, "have we made any claims that the adventure you are about to embark upon is anything but dangerous. Already, almost a dozen people have died. But that's true of any leap forward in human evolution. The deaths are deplored, but those who've passed on will not be forgotten. Their memories will sustain us in the dark of space when nothing else can."

Only the sound of air passing through the ductwork could be heard as Lucy stood silently before the multitude. She looked down on their faces and continued to speak. "I want to thank each and every one of you for being here today. Without you and the dreams you bring with you, we couldn't even begin to accomplish this great work. Those of you who'll be moving to the new ships already have your orders. Those of you who'll be staying with the *Galileo* will have a job bigger than any you've attempted so far—the building of Taurus Base. But now, it is my distinct pleasure to present to you the captains of our two newest ships."

Taking two steps toward the side of the dais, Lucy said, "By unanimous consent of the Fleet Advisory

Council, it has been decided that the captain of the Terran Alliance Ship *Arthur C. Clarke* will be Commander Gayle Miller. Commander Miller, front and center!"

The fact that she'd seen this same ceremony before as a participant did nothing to lessen the impact of the words. With a lump in her throat, Gayle took two hesitant steps up onto the dais and stood before Lucy. Marsha had stepped forward to stand beside the First Captain and held a black velvet box.

"Gayle Miller," Lucy intoned, "by the power vested in me by the Fleet Advisory Council, I hereby promote you to the rank of captain." Taking one of the gold comets from the box, she pinned it to her lapel. Repeating the task on the other lapel, she stepped back and saluted. "Congratulations, Captain Miller."

As a cheer went up throughout the deck, Gayle returned the salute. "It's also my pleasure," Lucy continued in a voice that cut through and silenced the cheering, "to present you with this plaque," she reached out and took a large object from another of her staff. "As Simon would say, 'Hang it in your reception area, Captain.' And I would like to say congratulations again. See me in my ready room afterward, please. For now, dismissed." She saluted Gayle again, winked, and said quietly, "The drinks are on you when time permits, Captain."

Lucy watched her new captain leave the dais with a bemused look on her face. Memories of first meeting Gayle surfaced, followed by dozens of memories from the past three years, and she had to mentally drag herself back to the present.

Even so, she thought, *she deserved to be a captain*

long before me.

She surreptitiously motioned Marsha back to her side as more memories threatened to sidetrack her, but she forced them back. "Commander Robert Greene, front and center," she commanded.

When the man she'd served with for the past three years stood before her, she said, "Again, by unanimous consent, the Fleet Advisory Council has approved your promotion to Captain of the Terran Alliance Ship *Isaac Asimov*. Congratulations, Robert. It couldn't happen to a more deserving person." She pinned his gold comets onto his lapels and transferred the brass plaque that was handed to her into his hands. "Hang it in your reception area, Captain, and good luck. Please see me in my ready room after the ceremony is over."

Lucy watched Robert descend the dais and stand beside Gayle. Looking back at the crowd of people before her, she said, "In accordance with traditions that started with the completion of Orion Base, I hereby declare a holiday! Well done to one and all. Tomorrow all hands will report to their assigned ships by 0800. Until then, all food processors have been reprogrammed to allow beer for all hands. Except," she had to yell above the clamor, "for those who have duty tonight. Sorry folks, it can't be helped. Dismissed!"

CHAPTER SIX

Pankatt Korchon, Kravar Sept-leader, strode down the corridors of the palatial estate followed by two escorts and the stink of his own fear. Quite often these peremptory summons resulted in the recipient's head being mounted on a pole outside the front gate until the skull gleamed white in the light.

The krath-hide vest he wore was decorated with his Honors and stained with the sweat the Korvil exuded when their fight-or-flight reflexes were in effect but couldn't be acted upon. So much time had passed, nearly a quarter-cycle now, since he'd filed the report, that he'd convinced himself there would be no reprisal. He should have known better. Even in the Korvil Hegemony, paperwork moved slowly. But no Korvil got elevated to the position of Sept-leader and then lost a ship, not without an accurate accounting. And as surely as big krath made little ones, he was here to be held accountable.

The corridor darkened as it narrowed down into the center of the complex. Angling down, it led to the ancestral caves that were the beginnings, or so thought some of the old greybeards, of his Lord. Each Lord had a similar place that embodied the beginnings of Korvil supremacy over the lower animals of their world. One of the great Plains Lords, it was said, had a palace made of carefully interlaced bokon trees that was over fifty generations old.

The corridor ended at the entrance to a huge, sand-floored room. Once a cave, the structure had been covered over by level after level of living and working spaces dedicated to the service and expansion of his Lord's influence. Here was the heart of Supreme Lord Marcad, Korvil's power—his throne room, the visible symbol of his Lord's exalted status.

Senses honed by fear, Pankatt felt his escorts move to block any possible retreat. Swallowing hard, he stepped onto the burning sand and strode toward the throne, dimly glimpsed in the distance. Lit only by torchlight, the shadows in the great chamber reached out for him and evoked ancestral memories that only served to strengthen the fight-or-flight reflex he was working desperately to subdue.

Alone, he approached his Lord's throne, his two escorts having remained at the entrance to the chamber. It wasn't until he neared the great seat that embodied Lord Marcad's supremacy that he realized it was empty. The dancing shadows had served to hide that fact until he was almost upon it. Glancing swiftly around, Pankatt could see nothing of his Lord. Only the precious varch furs draped carelessly over the arms, seat, and back of the great wooden chair gave evidence of his Lord's presence.

After what seemed like an interminable period of waiting, the Sept-leader began to move about the room slowly, no longer able to just wait for his fate to overtake him. Sniffing the air, he moved quietly past the fancifully carved pillars that supported the roof. Feeling the hot sand work its way up between the pads of his toes, he paid attention to the information his sensitive nose relayed to him. Something had been here recently, and it was *new*.

He found himself staring out over a large circular expanse. Here was where he'd given his life to the service of his Lord. This was only his second time to stand in a Pit of Justice. Legend said that opponents in the Pit could only speak the truth whether for good or ill. As he stared in fascination at the Pit, his imagination provided the sights and sounds of the combats that must have occurred there over the generations.

As he stood there, a sense of wrongness penetrated his forebrain, and he dropped back into the moment, the possible past already relegated to memory. At that instant, his lips skinned back from his teeth, his breath hissed in his throat, and he dropped into a battle crouch, reaching for the sword he'd been forced to leave with his escorts. He held the pose for several breaths as he slowly examined each object within his sight in the flickering light provide by the torches lining the Pit. Just as he began to relax from combat mode, thinking he must have been wrong, out of the gloom a sword flew through the air and landed at his feet.

"Take up the weapon Sept-leader," said the voice he'd only heard once before, on the day of his ascension to leader of his Sept. He had knelt in the sand before the very throne somewhere behind him and proclaimed loyalty to that voice. Sliding gracefully back into his battle crouch, his hand reached for the hilt of the sword. Not quite touching it, he surveyed the room again. All of his senses went into overdrive—his nose cataloging every stray scent, and his ears moving independently as they tuned in to even the faintest whisper of pads on the sand. The very fur on his body rose to feel for eddies in the air currents that passed over him, secondary lenses snapping into place over his eyes as he searched for even the slightest movement.

For all his keenness of sense, he couldn't place the source until one of the carven statues that lined the Pit moved.

"I have gifted you greatly, Sept-leader," the hulking figure said as it moved out into the center of the Pit. "Land, power, and females have I given to you, and Honors on your own merit as you moved up in my service. Of all my Sept-leaders, only you had the daring to take the position offered to you in the outer provinces. Your skill and bravery have brought wealth to your Lord and Honor to you." The huge figure paced back and forth in the great Pit, brandishing the huge torch held as if it were a twig. "Pick up the weapon, Sept-leader, and step into the Pit. I would question you."

The krath-hide vest darkened with his sweat, and Pankatt's hand slid smoothly onto the hilt of the sword as he sidled out into the expanse. Keeping the sword pointed at the ground, he waited. "If your opponent is the stronger, let him come to you," his teachers had said enough times that it had become ingrained. But the instinct to attack was just below the surface.

Stopping the requisite three paces away, Pankatt faced his Lord and benefactor. Going down one knee, the Sept-leader placed his head to the burning sand. Arms outstretched, he extended the sword. "As you command, my Lord, so must I obey," he recited the ritual words. "With the gift of this sword, I once again pledge my allegiance and dedicate myself to your service."

Hearing the great torch whistle through the air, he rolled to one side and into battle crouch as the fiery end of the torch slammed into the ground where his head had been but one second before.

"You prattle to me of loyalty?" the shambling figure roared. "I raise you above almost all others, and you repay me with incompetence!"

The great torch went flying into the shadows as the furious Lord moved in on his victim. "If you don't answer my questions to my satisfaction, I will rip off your arms and beat you to death with them! I will disperse your wives across the hegemony! I will eat your male cubs! Then I will replace you with someone who won't lose my property! Where... is... my... ship?

"Power I gave to you. Authority and responsibility I gave to you. And you were to use those things to protect the Korvil Hegemony. *My* Hegemony! A double handful of ships I gave you, and you lose one!"

"Sire! I but followed the procedure you set down. I sent in the reports on anomalous readings on the long-range scans from our outermost scouts. War Minister Darmag sent back instructions to dispatch ships into that area over your signature, Lord, to investigate. I sent out two teams of two, Lord— standard procedure when we approach the Shiravan colonies. Only one ship has appeared on scan, and that is *Fist of Vengeance*. Long-rang scans show her engine signature to be fluctuating, which is what is slowing her arrival. She was teamed with *Hunter's Luck*, but she arrives alone. Until she docks, I have no knowledge of any losses!"

"*Hunter's Luck* didn't have any problems with her

engines, Sept-leader, and she came all the way to Korvil to report directly to me. At first scent, according to the *Luck's* captain, the hunters had found a nest of Shiravi. But it would seem that what your patrol discovered was an entirely unexpected surprise. It would seem *this* colony was progressing in an unexpected direction. Rather than building a base for personnel, this bunch built defenses first! When your forces attacked, they had fighters to defend the nest. *Two* of your ships are lost, Sept-leader, but I will let you live. For the information we have uncovered is nearly unbelievable! Not one, but two new races! And they are working in unison to fortify a system using Shiravan technology. This means that we face an alliance composed of two races we've never scented before. What say you to that, Sept-leader?"

"I would say, Lord, that any further contact with these new aliens be made in force. They must be discouraged from having anything to do with the Shiravi. Keep one's enemies at each other's throats and they will be too busy to defend themselves in unison *or* separately. What do we know, Lord, of these new races, if one as unworthy as I may ask?"

"We know this, Sept-leader."

The monarch growled into the gloom, and immediately the sounds of approaching feet could be heard, along with the sound of something being dragged. From between the pillars, figures moved into the Pit. There were four in all, half-dragging two *things* with them. Aliens!

"Tell me what *you* think."

Pankatt walked up to the two creatures held up by the guards. They were both naked, so it was obvious that they were at least similar, but they were two totally different colors. The darker one was obviously male, but the other one was white and if it was a female, there was something wrong. Her teats looked to be full of milk, but she was unmistakably barren. He sniffed up and down their bodies, inhaling deeply.

"Lord, I have no explanation. They would appear to be of the same species but for their coloration. They smell akin to each other, but the female must be weak. She is milk-full but barren. And they have no hair to speak of except on top of their heads and between their legs. How is that a survival trait? Perhaps they are both diseased."

"It was my idea to have them dissected, Sept-leader. Perhaps we can learn something from their composition." The great monarch looked down appraisingly on the smaller beings.

"Yes, Lord. But if a humble servant may ask a question, could we not learn more from them alive? It would seem that great care should be taken to study all aspects of these new creatures. They can always be dissected later. I have to wonder how anything so defenseless can be formidable enough to destroy two ships though." He lifted the hand of the male and inspected it, then did the same with a foot. He repeated the process on the female, massaging her teats in wonder. The two beings just stood and allowed the indignities to occur. "They have no claws. He lifted the female's head by the hair on top of her head and pushed back her upper lip. "Flat teeth, not hunter's teeth, but they have hunter's eyes. And they are *soft*." He walked around behind the two beings and poked them in various places. "I don't understand how they survive. Perhaps they are pets?"

"Perhaps, Sept-leader. But they do make the same

kind of gabbling noises the krath-Shiravi make. Not that any of the crew of the *Luck* was ever able to understand a sound they made. Simple gestures, is all. The black one keeps putting its paw to its mouth. It is believed that this indicates hunger, but they cannot survive on real food. It seems that trail-paste is all they are able to absorb." Trail-paste, a high protein concentrate, was a blend of cooked meats and several things no proper Korvil would eat in its natural state—nuts, berries, and grains. These last ingredients served mostly to act as preservatives but also to add protein to the meats because, over time, they tended to lose their potency. All ships carried a quantity of it for emergencies. "Many things were tried before someone tried the paste. So, tell me Sept-leader," the huge being asked in more conversational tones, "what sector did you send the missing ships to explore?"

"Sector korvatch-nine, Lord. But the captains were given the standard instructions to follow their own instincts and expand their search as necessary, as well as to maintain communications silence. It's possible, Lord, that the other two ships could still be operational."

"*Not* possible," the hulking creature roared and made a lightning grab at the young Sept-leader, who barely managed to evade the stroke, feeling claws barely graze his throat. "At least not for one of the ships," he continued in more reasonable tones. "*Luck's* sensors detected an explosion consistent with our engine pods just before the final attack on the nest. Perhaps *one* still stalks prey but certainly not both."

The imposing figure moved ponderously around

the two aliens, scenting deeply of each and enjoying the fear-smell from the smaller white one more. "Perhaps, if we find their homeworld, they would make good prey—if not for us, then at least for our cubs. They really don't have much in the way of natural weaponry, do they?"

Pankatt barely managed to suppress a flinch as his Lord suddenly jumped in front of him and batted the forgotten sword aside as if it were a toy. "The ships I gifted you were among the best to come out of the Darmesh yards! And their crews were among the best in the entire fleet! I will not hear tales of engine disruptions or meteors or ineptitude on their part! We will send an expanded taskforce to search korvatch-nine. I want my ship found, do you understand, Sept-leader? Or word of its fate. And," he said, looking back at the two aliens still being held up by the guards, "I am going to gift you with these two pitiful specimens. *You* are now responsible for their care and maintenance. *You* are now responsible for wringing sense out of their gabbling noises. Return to your Sept, Pankatt Korchon, and know that you still have your life only by my pleasure and generosity. Guard well these two creatures, and report by fastest courier ship any progress in learning to communicate with them. That is all."

Pankatt bowed low before his Lord, exposing the back of his neck for several seconds, and when he raised his eyes back up from the floor, only the two soft creatures were left, lying on their sides in the sand.

The return to Kravarine was not without incident.

First taking their leashes in hand, Pankatt dragged his prisoners out of the Pit, out of the Palace, and into the streets of Darkoma. The capitol city of the Korvil Hegemony was only about two hundred thousand or so, and they were all Korvil. The lesson was that they had no chance of hiding.

Taking the simple expedient of just walking off holding their leashes, he left the decision of following or being dragged up to the aliens. This lesson was that obedience made their lives easier.

As he led the way to the city's markets, he used his communicator to speak to his First aboard *Predator's Claw*, the Kravar Sept, informing him of the impending arrival of unusual items for the ship's cargo hold. "No, I cannot say more. There are ears to hear, and the wrong inferences may be drawn. Consider the materials to be temporary additions to *Claw* for the duration of a mission assigned by Lord Korvil himself. That will be all."

Standing in the middle of nearly a hundred booths and stores, he faced the female and forced her eyes up to his. Using the simplest gestures he could think of, he finally got through to her the concept that she should choose foods for herself and the male. It was insanity, really, since Korvil females didn't have the mental acuity to understand more than the simplest of gestures. He smiled slightly as the pale-white, bare-skinned creature finally began to hesitantly move among the booths and stalls, searching each for foodstuffs that were compatible. Surprisingly, fruits, nuts and berries were high on her list of acceptable items. Each time she found an item, she would go to the male and offer him some. On some occasions he would agree, and others disagree, so she wasn't the final arbiter for the pair but perhaps the junior member.

Each time an item was agreed upon, Pankatt allowed each creature to eat some and ordered each proprietor to send cases of the item to the *Claw*. *Joruun will think I've gone crazy*, he thought. A smile crossed his face as he envisioned the First's reaction when he brought these two aboard. Finally, he intercepted the female as she tried to get the male's approval on some berries that were normally used as dyes. The look that crossed her face could have been confusion or anger.

I will have to learn their expressions. Sometimes it is wise to study your prey before attacking. The trick is in knowing when.

Making her understand that she should ask him for permission to have the food took some patience, but when she got it, he rejoiced inwardly. That was the third lesson—that they had food only by his pleasure. And they were trainable! If he could find their homeworld, the free labor alone would enormously enrich him. And if they made good prey, so much the better.

Indicating that the shopping spree was over, he headed out of the market, intending to look for a hire-vehicle to take them back to the *Claw*. Suddenly, the leash in his left hand tightened enough to spin him halfway around. The female had stopped at a stall, and when he looked at her, she pointed at a bolt of cloth on a table. He mimed that the cloth was not food and turned to go, pulling on her leash. When she resisted again, he sprang to her side, grabbed the longish hair on top of her head, and bent her backwards over his knee, holding her in place with his other hand on her belly. When she started to squirm, he unsheathed his claws just enough to break through the soft skin covering her and felt her grow still.

Pankatt pulled down hard enough on her head to bend her farther backwards, and a sound of pain escaped her lips, high-pitched enough to hurt his ears. When he saw the male begin to move toward him, he placed his teeth firmly on the female's throat and prepared to tear it out. Looking at the male, he saw him stop, stunned by the sight before him. Sinking to his knees, the creature almost seemed to *beg* him not to kill the female. He growled around the quivering flesh, stared at the kneeling male for a moment, and then removed his teeth. Some two dozen drops of blood stood out starkly on the pale white skin of her throat. He stood up, keeping his eyes on the alien male, and let the female drop heavily to the ground. When the male tried to go to her, Pankatt growled loud enough to stop him in his tracks. Finally, he signed that the male could approach the female. The fourth lesson was learned—that they had their lives only by his pleasure.

During the trip back to Kravarine, Pankatt ordered a pair of cells to be constructed and placed them in a room where the prisoners would be able to see each other through the clear plasticine substance used to form their box-like prisons. During the time it took to build these special cells, he left the creatures strictly alone, ordering that food be delivered twice daily and that no apparent notice be taken of them unless they attacked.

When the cells were ready, he went with four guards to the small lavatory that had been used to house the prisoners and immediately noticed the absence of any unpleasant odors except for the creatures themselves. Apparently, they'd figured out how to use the facilities for their own waste disposal, as well as any food residue. They'd also cleaned their furless skin to an unusual degree, and there was the smell of disinfectant about them. That boded well for their ability to learn, and he was encouraged about his plans for them.

Guards dragged the prisoners to their new cells, which were tall enough to stand upright and long enough to lay down in. The guards first placed the male in his cage, then the female. Their leashes were removed, and a punishment collar was locked about each neck. Both cells had a sleeping mat and elimination hole, and were cunningly designed so that the height could be lowered, forcing the occupant to crouch or sit. The length could also be shortened, forcing them to sleep erect, and the lights were left on at all times.

Pankatt remembered that the female had seemed to covet the cloth from the market almost as much as the food, and she'd been willing to suffer much to acquire it. Deciding this was a useful piece of information, he'd paid a handsome sum to have a bolt delivered along with the foodstuffs, a fact that he kept from the creatures for the time being. He surmised that the female wanted it for artificial coverings because of her furless skin.

After two more days of isolation, Pankatt decided it was time to begin lessons. He needed to learn the position of planetary defenses, major population centers, transportation systems, population levels, technology levels, etcetera. And the only way to learn was to teach them his language. The female was the logical choice. She seemed to defer to the male, but she also seemed the smarter of the two.

Several days of eating well and resting had restored much of the creatures' vitality. A report had been handed to him before the *Claw* departed Korvilene, stressing their robust condition. This was a significant improvement considering that their condition when he'd taken them aboard had been anything but "robust."

He entered the cell of the female and she shrank back into a corner. Pointing at the floor at his feet, he said, "Kneel here." When she refused to move, as he'd known she would, he showed her the small device in his hand. It had two buttons on the face of it. He pointed at one button and then pointed at her. Then he pressed it. She screamed in pain and grabbed the collar around her neck. He released the button and waited for her to recover. He then pointed at the second button and then at the male. Once again, he pressed the button, and the creature's scream of agony was barely audible through the two cell walls.

Holding the pain applicator in his left hand where the female could see it, he pointedly placed a finger on the male's button and again pointed at his feet. "Kneel here." This time she obeyed but stopped too far away. He pressed the button and listened to the scream. "Here!" he said, and she moved within easy reach. He put one hand on her shoulder, refusing to flinch at the feeling of bare flesh, and pressed down until she knelt. "Kneel!

The lessons continued all the way back to

Kravarine, alternating between the male and the female. Often, he would take one or the other around the ship, leashed, as he inspected or just socialized with the crew. Total immersion was the only way to learn his language in time to do him any good. The cell walls were too thick for them to communicate with each other without yelling, and that seemed to hurt their throats in an amazingly short time. He became confident that he'd be able to communicate with them much sooner than anyone would have imagined. Perhaps his Lord would even bestow another Honor upon him and his Sept.

Pankatt had leashed one creature to each side of his command chair and was directing the landing approach to Kravarine when the inconceivable occurred—Shiravan craft attacking! Nine craft sprang into position from behind Kravarine's one dismally small moon. Six of them targeted his two ships, and the others made strafing runs on the unsuspecting spaceport.

Within seconds, all his plans were in ruins. A hand apiece of The Korvils's finest raiders lay in ruins on his Sept-world! And the sister ship that had traveled with him from Korvilene was destroyed in the first moments of the attack, taking its attacker with it. Shiravan ships had never executed an effective defense, much less a coordinated attack! Not a command had escaped his lips, but the pilot immediately flipped the ship and dove for the surface.

Pankatt recognized his pilot's maneuver as one that used a gravity well to help accelerate a ship so that it could bypass a planet's defenses quicker. It could also be used, he knew, to help escape a superior force. Using the sling effect, he could effectively exit the gravity well anywhere he chose, and unless his enemies were *very* lucky, he'd escape to report this... abomination to Korvilene. Of course, he'd lose his head, but Honor dictated only one course.

The dive into the gravity well went smoothly—too smoothly, at first. He was treated to the sight of the main Sept-hall in ruins, along with the harem and nursery. He saw the spaceport demolished as well, along with virtually all of the infrastructure that had been built up over the past fifty cycles of occupation. It was then that the *Claw* shuddered. She rang like a bell, and the echoes reverberated within the hull for several seconds.

Half of all the consoles went dark, and the First said, "Report loss of drive power! Artificial gravity gone, life support gone. Minimal response to atmospheric controls. Abandon ship! All hands, abandon ship!"

Pankatt Korchon, Kravar Sept-leader, had not expected to reign at the ignominious end of his Sept's existence, but he had. Apparently, his was the only life pod to escape the *Claw* before a lucky shot by the cowardly Shiravi holed her drive room. He watched through the viewport as his First maneuvered the ship into the path of the attacker and accounted for a second enemy ship in its death throes. The explosion from that slammed the just-ejected life pod into the ground with enough force to stun the two Humanz he'd dragged along with him. If the krath-Shiravi had missed his pod's expulsion, and if he survived long enough, a ship would rescue him. If he could keep the Humanz alive as well, perhaps there was still a chance the Kravar Sept would not disappear into the mists. Honor could still accrue.

For hours he skulked toward the main Sept-hall, hoping to spot any sign of life. It could not be possible for the Shiravi scum to have destroyed his entire Sept! Almost as an afterthought, he dragged the two creatures with him, forcing them to hide whenever he sensed an overflight.

They appeared as he stood up to make the final dash to the main hall. He could see the entrance, cracked and broken, to the subterranean ways. There he would find safety from the abomination—krath-Shiravi who fought back and won! Four of the disgustingly red creatures blocked his path to the lower ways. He spun to go around them, only to find two more of the krath-Shiravi approaching from behind. He'd been herded!

The fury that overtook him at this realization wiped out generations of "civilized" conditioning. No longer able to consider the consequences of his actions, he screamed his rage and drove at the nearest opponent. With his legs pushing him forward at blinding speed, he almost reached the nearest creature before half a dozen beams of light ended his existence.

CHAPTER SEVEN

Rentec do' Verlas, Shiravan Spatial Affairs Minister, was on vacation in the Dukara Mountains when his communicator chimed. He set down the perlwood pole, an heirloom handed down from his father's father. Disgusted at the interruption, he walked away from the river's edge and picked up the offending piece of technology that kept him tied to his job.

I could easily do without this, he thought. *I spent three days doing everything Ramannie wanted to do, and finally I get some time to myself. By the Spirits of Space, I barely got the line wet!*

Forcing his voice into neutrality, the young minister picked up the device and spoke his name. "Minister," a voice responded, "this is Undersecretary Ralith. We seem to have a situation."

"And just exactly what kind of situation requires that you interrupt the first vacation I've taken in years?" do' Verla asked with a precise amount of irritation in his voice.

"Minister, I beg your indulgence, but I cannot answer that question at this time over an open channel. Your presence is required at the Ministry of Spatial Affairs at the earliest possible moment. Colonization Minister Foran concurs with the opinion that you should be apprised immediately."

"Can you give me any idea over an open line what this is all about?" do' Verlas pressed.

Several second passed before the undersecretary spoke. "It's *possible*, sir, that it has something to do with a returned patrol ship."

"You know where I am," Rentec said. "It will be several hours before I'll be able to make an appearance. All I can do to speed the process, I will do. Rentec do' Verlas, out." He threw the communicator back onto the seat of his floater and turned to Ramannie, who was sitting in the shade of a tem tree nearby. "I'm sorry, my dear, but it would seem that one of the perquisites of my job is interrupted vacationing. Someone has decided that my presence is required at the Ministry Building, and apparently Minister Foran agrees."

The gorgeous young woman turned her ruby gaze to the man who, just the night before, had asked her to become his consort. "And what could possibly be so urgent that they need to drag someone as important as the Minister for Spatial Affairs away from a well-deserved rest?" Ramannie asked, venom in her voice as she stroked his arm.

"Oh, I'm not so important as all that, Ramannie. Minister, yes. *Junior* minister, and only for Spatial Affairs. Not the most prestigious posting, love. But one does hope for promotions. Economics, finance, security, colonization, diplomatic minister—all of these are more important than my lowly posting."

"But, Rentec," Ramannie pointed out, "you are Minister for Spatial Affairs in an Expansionist government. You have the potential to become someone... formidable."

"True. I will admit that the potential does exist," Rentec acknowledged slowly. "But at this time, it is only potential, and I am only a junior minister. And I *will* come when Foran calls. If I want to keep my position and potential, I can do nothing else."

Loading his fishing gear and the remains of their picnic into the back of their vehicle, Rentec and Ramannie climbed into the floater and strapped in. Their return to the port city of Quillas required that they first drive back up the mountain to get to the main road. As they passed the lodge, Rentec called to request that their possessions be packed and sent to their homes in Quillas. While keeping the floater at its maximum height of about eight feet, he headed back at just under the legal limit. Refusing to activate his communicator on the drive back into the city, Rentec split his attention between keeping the little vehicle airborne and talking to his consort-to-be.

The tricky part about operating a repulson-powered personal vehicle was that errors tended to magnify themselves the faster one traveled, so compensating for such things as wind changes, turns, braking, and even elevation and terrain all had to be handled with infinite care. Almost as much care, in fact, as it took to keep Ramannie mollified. He finally managed to sidetrack her by opening a discussion about the upcoming meeting with his mother.

"Not meaning to brag," he said (meaning to ever so little), "but the women of the do' Verlas line have, for the last fifteen generations, been renowned for their matchmaking abilities. The ability seems to be passed on by the male but is seeded in the female line. That means that the first girl-child will have the same abilities as my mother and hers before her and so on. And they can tell who's meant for whom. Something about empathic awareness, I'm told."

Ramannie sat quietly for the rest of the ride.

She's afraid, Rentec thought. *And who wouldn't be, knowing that your fate is in the hand of someone you've never met.* For a do' Verlas woman to pronounce "nay" upon a union effectively ended it before it began.

Dusk was falling as Rentec and Ramannie approached the spaceport employee's housing complex.

"So, what's the big emergency?" she asked as they neared her building. "I've refrained from asking, but I'll find out, you know. I do work for Minister Foran, after all."

"The undersecretary couldn't tell me over an unsecured line, but he did let me know that it had something to do with a returning patrol. Just what, I'll know shortly."

"Could it be the one you and Minister Foran sent out the search mission for?" she asked suddenly interested.

"Oh, I doubt that, Ramannie. The only way it *could* be that would be if the *Dalgor Kreth* turned up back in Shiravan space on its own. Which I suppose is a possibility—remote, but a possibility. I think, though, that if that had been the case, the undersecretary would have just passed on the information without worrying about secure communications. And my presence wouldn't be so urgently required that we couldn't finish our vacation. This is something far graver, I believe."

Rentec's vehicle settled to the ground outside Ramannie's building, and she stepped out into the deepening gloom. "Well, I'm sure it's nothing so urgent that it should have taken you away from your vacation," she said. "No one with your level of responsibility can work day in and day out without relief. You should make them extend your vacation when you finish with this charade."

Agreeing to think about the situation, Rentec drove over to the Spatial Affairs building as soon as Ramannie was out of sight. *It's odd that the building is named after one of the more junior offices in it*, he mused for the thousandth time as he settled the vehicle into its place and hurried into the looming edifice.

Rentec arrived as full night fell, and he found the main building fully lit. More than just unusual, it was virtually unheard of to have so many people around at this time of the evening. Even more of a surprise were the checkpoints he'd to go through to get onto the Ministry grounds. On three separate occasions, he was stopped and his identification demanded. Upon identifying himself yet again when he actually entering the building, he was directed to a briefing room.

During his several Turnings as a minister, Rentec had never been in this particular briefing room. He found that it was more in the nature of an auditorium, with its raised stage and chairs rising up in tiers from the floor to the highest seats in the back.

The room was already crowded when he arrived. This time, rather than having his identity checked, he was merely asked for his name. Rentec watched the guard strike through his name and noticed that it was the last one on the list.

"Minister do' Verlas, you are the last to arrive," the guard said. "I've been instructed to inform Policy Minister sel Garian when the list has been completed so the briefing can begin. Please, make yourself comfortable."

Rentec found himself standing shoulder to shoulder with the Underminister of Defense, a distant cousin of his, Parlo do' Nallen. "This doesn't look like any briefing I've ever attended. It looks more like a..."

"A council of war?" cousin Parlo finished in a strained voice.

"So it would seem," Rentec noted. "We have Economics, Intelligence, Defense, Personnel, Finance, Supply, Military, and Spatial Affairs, and those are just the ones I can see right off. The last time we had this many ministers gathered together was just before my father's death. The discussion then was whether or not to send ships out to harass the Korvil as they've been harassing us for centuries."

"That was before my time, too," Parlo said. "But it's obvious you haven't heard. Where have you been?"

"On vacation in the Dukara Mountains," Rentec said sourly. "I asked Ramannie to be my consort. This is not an auspicious beginning for our life together. Heard what?"

"Ah! A betrothal trip! Did she accept? And is this Ramannie the same beautiful young thing I've seen you with over the last several months?"

"Yes, she did, and yes, she is," Rentec said lowering his voice. "And what haven't I heard?"

"You haven't heard that scout ships from one of the reprisal fleets finally located a Korvil raider's outpost," Parlo said with equal amounts of elation and fear in his voice. "You haven't heard that we ambushed two of their ships in space, destroyed almost a dozen more on the ground, and destroyed the entire compound. And when one kill-crazed survivor we believe to have been a Sept-leader tried to attack the ground troops, he was shot to death literally at the feet of the assault team. We have effectively declared open war on the Korvil Empire."

"Silence!" Rentec hissed, looking down at the stage. "There's sel Garian."

Minister sel Garian was famous. The entire sel Garian Clan were rabid Isolationists, with the exception of a very few who could afford to buck the clan system. Manura sel Garian was the most prominent of these. As Policy Minister, she was the matriarch's closest adviser. It was she who had led the fight to empower the Reprisal Fleets, and the council vote had gone her way by sheerest luck, one might think.

Rentec had his doubts about that though. The Shiravan colony-world, Harlo, had among its members relatives or offspring of many of the ministers who, for one reason or another, would abstain from voting in favor of a war. But the tensions were too high after the report of Harlo's capture by Korvil forces. And sel Garian had chosen the absolute perfect moment to call a vote on the Reprisal Fleets, winning only because of Harlo. His father had told him of that vote—of how the vote had been called for when word of the calamity reached the council, and of how, afterwards, there were those who wondered aloud at the timing of the release of the report and how sel Garian had refused to rise to the bait and challenge any of those who spoke out. sel Garian had been instrumental in crushing the Isolationist uprising some twenty turns earlier. Her brutal tactics during the suppression had earned her the title of "Butcher of Harasel," a label she never bristled at and never denied.

The wizened old woman walked out into the center of the stage and glared at the audience until silence reigned. "That's better," she grated harshly through the artificial larynx that was the legacy of her actions during the revolt. A fanatic from her own clan had tried to behead her during the last bloody hours of the uprising, only to fail because of his own mortal wounds at her hands. "There's no time for debate. No arguing, no finger pointing, and no name calling—just action. Each and every one of you are relevant to the effort we are about to embark upon. Everyone knows about the Reprisal Fleets, and now you can be told of the success of one of those fleets.

"Because of their hit-and-run tactics, it has until recently been virtually impossible to even *find* a Korvil outpost. Thanks in large part to the Ministry of Intelligence, and in some part to the Goddess of Luck, we recently located and identified one such base. We then planned and executed an assault upon that base, raider style. The Goddess of Luck flew with the women and ships of Second Fleet, and of the nine vessels involved in the attack, seven returned. We mourn the loss of the crews of the two ships and commiserate with their relatives and clans. Their names will be marked among those of Honored Ancestors in the Dusternas of each clan from this day forth.

"As I said, the Goddess of Luck rode with this fleet. Not only did seven ships and their crews survive, but we accrued an unexpected bonus. Along with the nearly one dozen ships caught on the ground, we caught two on approach vectors and destroyed them as well, but not without a cost. Both of those enemy ships managed to ram the nearest unfortunate ship and take it down with them. The bonus is that in the aftermath of the attack, while all the data were being reviewed, traces of a life pod ejecting from one of the inbound ships was detected.

"Teams were sent down to search the destroyed base and environs, and a survivor was found. Following their usual policy of fighting to the death, this one did so as well. And had it not been for the proper placement of personnel, he might have inflicted serious damage upon the landing team even though he was unarmed. We believe, from what little we know of Korvil hierarchy, that this individual was the equivalent of a clan mother. I believe from the few translations we have been able to obtain that the proper term is 'Sept-leader.' We also believe that this individual was responsible for the raids throughout the entire Parrasine sector." During the last minute of sel Garian's presentation, video from the ground teams flashed on the screen behind her, ending with the scorched Pankatt Korchon, last Kravar Sept-leader.

"The type of destruction," sel Garian continued when the screen went blank, "along with the debris from our two ships, will show quite clearly to the Korvil monarch that Shiravan ships were responsible for the destruction of the outpost. We expect the reprisals will be extremely unpleasant to all Shiravans everywhere. For over two hundred turns, the Shiravan response has been minimal. Defend, defend, defend. This way lies death through attrition. It has now become necessary to learn from our tormentors, and learn we shall. The crews of our three Reprisal Fleets that have been put into space over the past five turns will comprise the core of our new, revised fleet structure.

"While our ships are armed, they are neither as heavily armed as Korvil ships, nor do their crews have the accrued experience that winning battles brings. This will change. As time and material permit, ships will be brought back to Shiravi for refitting, but their crews will have to gain experience as they go. It's my hope that this briefing will have laid to rest many unsubstantiated rumors. Unfortunately, sometimes the truth can be worse than imagination. All ships and crews are hereby impressed into the service of the matriarch for the duration. All Shiravan personnel are requested to comply with new, soon-to-be-published rules that cover the hoarding of supplies and war-related material. All ministries will receive instructions on how their business is to be conducted as we go to a full-scale war footing. There will be no questions at this time. All questions can be submitted to the Policy Ministry. This meeting is concluded. I want the ministers, underministers, secretaries and undersecretaries of the following Ministries to remain behind for additional instructions: Intelligence, Defense, Finance, Commerce, Spatial Affairs, Colonization, and Production. That will be all."

When the room had been cleared of all but the seven dignitaries of each of the named ministries and their assistants, the little old woman motioned to have the doors locked by the remaining guards as they left the room. Rentec, still sitting at the back of the now nearly empty room, noticed the doors being locked and started to make a formal protest against the unusual nature of the action, but for some reason he decided to see where this particular turn of events led. All six of the other ministers protested the action, along with several underministers and a secretary or two. Rentec's cousin, Parlo, would have joined in voicing his objection as well but for Rentec's restraining hand.

"Just wait and see what happens. sel Garian wouldn't take this position if she didn't feel she had backing. If we oppose sel Garian, we oppose the matriarch, and I'm not prepared to do that."

The protests continued until the old woman raised the volume on her throat mike and grated, "Silence! Everyone move down to the first few rows."

Rentec watched his fellow ministers with something akin to amusement and waited while they complied with sel Garian's command. He looked back to the stage to find the Policy Minister staring directly at him, and he wished he could be anywhere but under her scrutiny. It reminded him too much of his mother's gaze the day he'd been sent home from Academy for playing a prank on a professor.

Turning the volume up even farther, sel Garian bellowed, "Silence!"

The walls shook, and Rentec could feel the sympathetic vibrations as they were transmitted from the walls, through the floor, and into the chair he sat in.

This time sel Garian got the silence she demanded. She turned the microphone down to a more reasonable level and waited, spearing each member of her audience with those angry red eyes. When she felt the silence had served its purpose, she said, "Everything that has gone before this point is for public consumption. It will be reported throughout the Polity in even more detail than you've heard tonight. What the general public *won't* know is what you are about to hear. This is a matter of the gravest importance, make no mistake about it. You will *not* reveal what you are about to be made privy to—not to your mothers, not your consorts, not your lovers. You will tell no one, and you will not discuss what you are about to hear and see with anyone who is not in this room right now, with the exception of the matriarch. The oaths of everyone in this room to the matriarch are invoked. Is this clear?"

It was if somehow sel Garian had disappeared from the stage and been replaced by a maddened vorloper, horns and all. The Ministers and secretaries closest to the stage moved back as if they thought she would reach out and shake the bones right out of their skins. Rentec saw the hand she snaked to the control box on her belt and only smiled at the next jolt she gave her audience. "I said, 'Is that clear?'"

Even expecting the subsonic pulse, Rentec began to sweat and nodded along with the rest, just to get on with hearing what she had to tell them next. "Each of you are here because your various ministries are so deeply involved, and discussion of the following information is forbidden outside of secure areas." Again, she stood in silence and let her last remarks sink in. "Now," she said sharply enough to make Rentec jump, "the item that is not for public consumption is this. In four hundred and fifty years in space, we've found only one other intelligent race—the Korvil."

"If you can call them intelligent," Parlo said quietly. "I, for one, think they operate mostly on instinct. And that knowledge can't be what is so secret. Everybody already knows it."

"Instinct doesn't allow you to devise new manufacturing processes to be able to reproduce stolen technology," Rentec countered quietly. "Nor does it allow you to innovate the kind of battle tactics we've had to deal with so far. In almost every encounter with the Korvil, we've lost because we didn't know what we were doing. The one major action we won—the one we just found out about—we won because we were somehow able to mount superior forces and catch them by surprise. Now be silent."

sel Garian waited patiently for the murmurs that followed her declaration to die down. "That statement has held true until recently," she continued. "We now have proof that there is another race out there somewhere."

Pandemonium broke out throughout the auditorium, and the old woman let it go on. Rentec sat silently.

His cousin asked, "Aren't you the least bit concerned?"

"I'm concerned that I won't get to hear what sel Garian has to say, cousin. Don't you think she'll have some kind of proof to back it up? She *has* to. Wait and listen."

"What is not for public consumption is the fact of the existence of these new aliens, and that two representatives of this race are on Shiravi now! At the time our forces killed the Sept-leader, he had with him, chained and leashed, two members of this new race—one male and one female. After much deliberation, the matriarch has decided that anyone, any race, that's an enemy to the Korvil can only be a friend to the Shiravi.

"The spirit of these two people—yes, I said *people*, for that is what they are even though they look different—the spirit of these two people is amazing. The first pictures we have of them show them dirty, emaciated, kept on the verge of starvation, beaten, and abused. The male, still chained, tried to fight off his rescuers until they made it clear to him that they meant no harm to him or the female. The two biggest problems faced by the members of the fleet were gaining their trust and finding the right food for them to eat."

sel Garian stood patiently while the ministers and secretaries spoke amongst themselves. Finally, the Minister of Commerce, a rabid Isolationist and distant cousin of sel Garian's, managed to get her attention. "Minister sel Parris," she said in recognition, granting him the right to speak.

Adopting a considerably more aggressive stance than polite Shiravan custom would normally dictate, the recognized minister asked, "What assurances do we have that these reports haven't been exaggerated and that these 'aliens' actually exist?"

The only sound in the room came from the air flowing into the room through the vents during the time sel Garian stared at sel Parris. By the time she finally responded to him, even the people from his own ministry had begun to physically distance themselves from him. "I would consider carefully any further words you might have for me, Minister. You are *dangerously* close to calling me a liar," she said as she stepped off the stage.

"No, Minister sel Garian, I'm not calling you a liar. I'm merely pointing out that you, like the rest of us, could be duped into *believing* a lie, which you could then pass on to us as truth. And believing it yourself, you could easily convince us."

"So you're saying that I'm not a liar?" sel Garian asked. "But rather that I'm gullible?"

"Minister, you twist my words," sel Parris protested.

"Minister, it is the *job* of people in our profession to twist words, thoughts, and ideas," sel Garian said chidingly. "Of course, I twist your words, just like you twist the words put into your ears by your superiors. The difference is, Minister, that the words are coming out of *your* mouth, and you should have better sense than to utter them in my presence. Here and now, we will deal with my 'gullibility,'" she said, looking sel Parris up and down. "First, the matriarch would not authorize the destruction of two vessels *and* their crews to maintain a fiction. Second, the visual details agree with the written reports in every detail. Third, cross-examination of every surviving member of that fleet agree with both the written and visual records. And concerning the two aliens that you wish to dismiss so handily, I'm here to tell you that they were not only rescued but survived to set foot on Shiravan soil. We have among us two representatives of a third sentient race. These two beings have been handled badly at the hands of the Korvil, and it is the matriarch's opinion, with which I concur, that once their rulers find out about their treatment at the hand of their captors, they will be no friend of the Korvil. There's an old maxim, Minister sel Parris, that you would do well to heed: 'He who would oppose your enemy should be cultivated as an ally.'"

"We still have no proof, Minister sel Garian," the Commerce Minister said, "of the existence of these future allies. And if they do exist, how do we know they *will* be allies?"

"We know they'll be allies, Minister sel Parris, because they were mistreated at Korvil hands, rescued by Shiravan forces, and so far, have been treated with the utmost respect and consideration. At this particular moment, we cannot converse with them beyond basic needs, but we'll remedy that situation in the near future. Now, as to their real or imagined existence..." sel Garian left the sentence unfinished, turned her back on the larger man, and stepped back up onto the stage. Thumbing her throat-mike to a new frequency, she gave a command unheard by the stunned ministry personnel. Seconds later, the door opened, and one of sel Garian's secretaries entered the auditorium, followed by an... alien! No! Two aliens!

Rentec was as stunned as the rest of the people in the room to see what came next. The first being to follow the secretary onto the stage was shorter than the Shiravan average by a noticeable amount, while the second was even shorter, and she was *white*. Her skin seemed to be bleached of almost all color, leaving only the vaguest tint of red to her complexion, and she had long brown fur growing from the top of her head. But the first! If he ever saw anything in his life that said 'alien,' it would be the taller of the two creatures now standing beside sel Garian. He—if it was a "he"—was black! He looked as if all the darkness of space had been condensed into one individual, and the fur on top of this one's head was short and composed of tiny ringlets pressed tightly against his skull. Both... *people...* seemed to be heavier across the chest than most Shiravans, possibly indicating a greater strength.

It seemed to be a night designed for pandemonium. The ministers and secretaries crowded around the stage, causing the two aliens to step back. sel Garian took one step forward, arms held out. "That's far enough! Minister sel Parris, step up here, please."

When the Isolationist Minister stood before sel Garian, she asked, "Please tell me now what you think of our 'fictitious' aliens."

"I... I have no response, Policy Minister."

"Of course, you don't. You haven't had your ears filled with the *wisdom* of your elders in Clan sel Parris. Nor will you! Knowledge of the existence of these two is restricted to the Reprisal Fleet that brought them in, the matriarch and her staff, and the people in this room. If this bit of information gets out, be sure that the matriarch will not be pleased, and I will track down the perpetrator. That would amount to treason and would be dealt with appropriately. This is only a temporary restriction until we can learn to speak more fluently with these people and learn something more of their culture and their race's intentions. Then more can be said. For the time being, these two will be removed to a safe haven and kept in seclusion for their own wellbeing."

She motioned for her secretary to take the two aliens out, and the unlikely trio made their way offstage. When the doors closed, sel Garian turned back to the assemblage. "Each Ministry will receive instructions in the coming days. For the time being, that will be all. And remember: Not. One. Word!"

CHAPTER EIGHT

Sarah and Dwayne were led on a whirlwind tour of the *Galileo,* showcasing her bridge, quarters, dining halls, gyms, factories, and engine room. "The captain thought your viewers would like a tour," Kimura said at the outset. "This may save you a question or two and will certainly do your careers a world of good. In about an hour, you'll be sitting down with Captain Grimes. How much space does your camera have, Dwayne?"

"About twelve hours' worth. I'm more concerned about batteries, though. I can only run for about three hours. What's that walled-off section down there?" Dwayne asked, pointing toward the bow.

Kimura looked forward and said, "Save ten minutes of battery power. You may get to see a game of Z-tag."

Explaining in a clear, concise manner could be an easy way to lose an audience, but not when one has a sense of humor and an infectious attitude, which Kimura had in spades. Between destinations on the tour, Sarah asked how she'd come to be aboard.

Looking distinctly uncomfortable, she said, "I am Rukia Kimura. I'm third-generation Japanese American, and I was expected to do something useful with my life, but this wasn't exactly the kind of thing we had in mind when I left for college." She looked up to see the camera pointed at her and didn't miss the red light on top. "Anyway, some friends of mine went to a science-fiction convention and disappeared. That would have been bad enough, but other friends told me *how* they disappeared. 'Beamed up!' they said,' but don't tell anyone.'

"Well, I didn't tell anyone, but still the police, the FBI, and people who never said *who* they worked for interviewed me. Then, about seven or eight months later, a couple of friends who'd disappeared showed back up with some *very* impressive evidence, so this time when they had a meeting, I went. I'll tell you right now, the first time you see a beam-in or beam-out is something you'll never forget!

"So, I've been aboard for about two years or a little more now. I'd like to take a vacation, ya know, but the higher-ups think most of us should wait until... wait a while and see how things develop. When we don't have to worry about being picked up by some government agency and grilled about what we know... Okay!" Kimura said with some relief, "Here's the engine room. Operating on principles just now being *thought* of on Earth, these engines can move a vehicle this size into what we call quantum space. A trip to Alpha Centauri would take a bit over four months each way. And contrary to popular opinion, there isn't that much time distortion—no double ages like in the old sci-fi novels, just a clean, relatively quick transition to another place at a high rate of speed..."

Finally! Sarah thought as she recognized the woman seated at the table in one of the dining halls aboard the massive ship. "I'm sorry I couldn't take the time any sooner, Miss Parker," Lucy said, standing up and gesturing to the chair opposite her. "Will this do? I hope Commander Kimura kept you entertained?"

"Uh, ladies? Can I get you to sit at nine and twelve instead of six and twelve? That way I can get you both in one shot without any cutting."

"If you have no objections, Captain," Sarah said, staring daggers at her cameraman.

"You'll thank me later, Sarah," Dwayne muttered.

"Um, thank you, and yes she did, Captain," Sarah said as she moved around the table. She didn't quite know how to take the young woman sitting across from her. Short, slim, and with a figure Sarah would have died for, the darkly pretty woman seemed both older and younger than she'd appeared when she stepped off the shuttle in Zurich.

I think she's actually younger *than I am! The aura of command seems to surround her, probably because so many people seem to defer to her*, Sarah thought.

At the same time, a redheaded woman came up to the table. "Would you care for refreshments, Miss Parker?"

Sarah glanced at the glass sitting in front of the woman she'd come to see.

"Ginger ale, Miss Parker. I find that it helps me focus."

"That will be fine," she said in a weak voice. Keeping the running camera ever in her mind, Sarah began before the redhead could come back with her drink. "Let's start with the basics, I guess. What do I call you?"

Waving her hand negligently, the other woman said, "If we were aboard a ship assigned to me, you would call me 'captain.' My *rank*, however, is First

Captain, and that would be appropriate, I think. But here and now, you can call me Lucy."

"Okay, Lucy, tell everybody out there how you got to be the head of the Terran Alliance."

"Let's see… How to make a long story short?" Lucy said speculatively. "I was among the first group to volunteer. There were thirty-five of us. When 'watch' schedules were being assigned, I was lucky enough to get third shift and be put in charge. You need to know that at that time, no one person knew any more about what we were doing than any other, so it was essentially luck that put me where I wound up. I got promoted to captain when the first two ships were commissioned, and when the captain, Simon Hawke at the time, and his wife Kitty were..." her voice cracked with emotion. "Well, I was the senior officer left, except for the base captain and commanders, and they refused to take the position. They're engineers, and we needed them where they were. So the other captains and Marsha Kane, who's captain of the *McCaffrey,* teamed up and shanghaied me into the job."

"What effects do you see as a result of releasing this technology to the general public?"

"There lies one of the biggest problems we have to face," Lucy said slowly. "You see, a lot of this stuff is so far ahead of Earth's technical level that it can't be reproduced on Earth, at least not until several levels of technological upgrades are made. But for the things we *can* do now, the results can be devastating. We hope to minimize the pain, of course, but whole technologies will give way to new ones. If this ship were to disappear tomorrow, do you think the world would go back to being the same? No. Just the absolute knowledge that there are other people out there will spur people on. The simple fact that something *can* be done will make people try to reproduce it. But what will happen to the people who get displaced? We don't want them to suffer. They have families to feed, lives to live, bills to pay. But change will inevitably occur.

"It's the short term we worry about, right now. What happens when hundreds of thousands of people are out of work? Economic devastation is what. We want to turn over technologies that will benefit the planet and see that people get retrained *before* they wind up out of work. Governments will have to help with that. Possibly a voluntary retraining program could help people get into the new technologies. Construction of the facilities to produce the new items, as well as removal of older buildings to make way for those new buildings, will be needed. We'll also be introducing ways to help end some of the pollution that's causing the greenhouse effects— cleaner fuel technologies, ones that don't need replacement as often as say, coal, or gasoline. And those are just two."

Caught unprepared for the next question by the implications of the previous one, Sarah, blurted out, "Who designed your uniforms?"

Oh, God! Sarah Parker, reporter for Interplanetary Fashion Review!

Lucy smiled. "Well, they were just supposed to be utilitarian, and for the most part, they've stayed that way. The short sleeved duty uniform you see on most of the crew grew out of that concept, as well as the longer, more formal dress uniform, of course. But I must admit that when we received our invitations to

Baron von Schlenker's gala, we were caught flatfooted. Here we were, finished with three space docks and ready to go build a fourth, and nothing to wear to something *really* fancy! The uniforms for the gala were mostly done on the spur of the moment."

Sarah picked up the amber-filled glass the redhead had put down in front of her during Lucy's last answer and took a sip. Clearing her throat, and asked, "Where do you get your recruits, Lucy, and what do you expect to happen to them when they go home?"

"More good questions, Miss Parker. They're tied together, by the way, and we see them as the second major obstacle. First, we have a few people who, for one reason or another, weren't able to sign on as active shipboard personnel and who still want to contribute. They've been acting as recruiters for us down below. Our extended absences caused a lot of problems at first, as you can imagine, since most people who want to believe just *can't* believe when someone says, 'Guess what? I've got a spaceship.'"

Sarah laughed out loud. "I can sympathize with them. I'm actually *sitting* here and I'm having trouble believing. So, how did you get around that situation?"

"Well, as I remember it, a bunch of us went to a sci-fi convention and there was a billboard mentioning a talk by a Dr. Stephen Walker about transporter technology in the modern age. It drew about forty people and we got shown transporter technology using Commander... Captain Miller as a first test subject. After that, he said, 'Guess what? We've got a spaceship.' A lot of us told Dr. Walker to put up or shut up and wound up going on our first beam-up. Some of the others came along because of Captain Miller. She's not the kind of woman you meet; she's the kind of woman you experience."

Sarah had settled down into "interview mode" and glanced down hastily at some of her scribbled notes. "And how do you see your people being treated when they choose to go home?"

"I'm sorry to say that I don't expect to be seeing them treated well at all, much less by their own government, which is primarily the United States. As yet, we haven't had the opportunity to recruit outside the U.S., so most of our people are Americans. I have been the target, albeit lightly, of some of our more... clandestine government agencies. I understand," Lucy said, holding up her hand, "that they're just doing their job, but their methods are born of fear, since they believe that what they can't control can harm them and must be feared. I see our people being picked up, interrogated, and kept under lock and key until they've had all their secrets 'squeezed' out of them. I see whole families being subjected to this same process just for being related to someone aboard an Alliance craft. Refusal to 'tell all' could result in charges of treason if the government really wanted to scare someone.

"It's the natural condition for a living creature to want to continue its existence, and a government is surely a living being. Never doubt that. Governments are born, they mature, they die. And they *will* reach out and hurt you if you hurt them. They'll try to attain whatever they need to stay afloat in the cesspool of politics they foster and swim in. They attain money, often underhandedly, and spend it, often foolishly. I call that living. And they *should* exist. In this day and age, almost every nation on Earth is full of ethnic diversity. Some like it, and some don't. In either case, there are laws to protect 'good' as it's defined by the inhabitants of a particular area. To enforce laws, you need police. To control the police, you need more laws and a government to watch over them. But to answer the question you asked, I see our people being treated poorly until we get some form of recognition that protects them. Whether you want to call them employees, volunteers, or citizens, they have the same basic rights as always, spelled out in one of the United States' most revered documents—the Bill of Rights."

"You've been out here for three years now. What prompts people to stay?"

Lucy's eyes drifted out of focus for a second. "Well, it sure isn't for the pay, I'll tell you that! What prompts them... us... to stay? Look around you! In three years, we've taken a derelict alien spaceship and learned how to use it well enough to begin to duplicate it! That doesn't mean we understand everything we do. We're just following directions, so to speak, but we learn more every day. Hell, I'll bet if you were to go home right now and ask, you'd find that a surprisingly high number of people don't know how a light bulb works and don't care enough to find out.

"But back to your question. A few go home, but we've managed to keep a fairly low profile."

"What do you plan to do with all the ships you're building?"

"We believe," Lucy said after several seconds' hesitation, "that the original owners will come looking for their ship eventually. If they want it back, they can have it. But if they don't want technological competition, there could be resistance, and we want to be able to handle that successfully. We've already made several modifications to their existing technology that the Builders apparently hadn't conceived of. For example, the force fields that got such a reaction out of you earlier."

"What do you mean?" Sarah asked, reddening visibly.

"When we got the ship, the entire cargo bay had to be depressurized to move cargo in and out of it. But after our engineers got through with the capture fields on the shuttles, we had force fields that could selectively pass objects through when needed. The Builders don't seem to be very innovative. It looks like they get something that works and just keep it. For example, they don't seem to have grasped the fine art of miniaturization, at least on a grand scale. By that I mean that they would make a... something... smaller to fit into a smaller space, like a shuttle, but leave it large on a ship like this one. Their use of what we call the 'capture field' is another example. It was only used on the shuttles and their fighters. (By the way, we've reworked their fighters into something bigger, faster, and far more deadly than they *ever* had.) We adapted the capture fields to be used inside the ship here in the cargo bay, and with minimal reconfiguring, turned it into the force field that not only surrounds the bay doors but the entire ship itself. And we've just figured out how to put partial shields on our fighters."

Sarah looked down at her notes for a few seconds and finally asked, "Do you intend to hold to the statement that your Captain Hawke made in relation to the disbursement of technology to Earth?"

Expecting this question, Lucy had a reply ready

instantly. "New administration, new policy. I'm sure the governments down below will recognize that fact. They won't like it, but they'll get used to it. Basically, the result will be the same. Earth will get a technological upgrade at the end-user stage, and the Terran Alliance gets cash or concessions. Call it licensing fees if you want, or whatever. The good thing is that we have no place to spend the money except on Earth, so it all comes home sooner or later."

"Are you worried about spies or industrial espionage?"

"Of course, we are. We're taking what measures we can to minimize the losses, but remember that once we part with a particular item, it's out there. We can't call it back. And if *we* can see implications in a piece of equipment beyond the obvious, don't you think someone will come up with an idea we missed? Actually, industrial espionage will cost us, but that will only be money. The only restrictions, remember, are on weapons and propulsion technology. And the propulsion technology is only restricted because it requires a *lot* of vacuum and zero gravity, access to a sun's corona, and the ability to make monopoles, some of which are antimatter. Do you really want another Camp David to happen somewhere on Earth? I think not. And as far as weapons are concerned, it will take the output of one of those sets of monopoles to power weapons as powerful as we have. And that begs the eternal question: aren't there enough nuclear weapons on Earth right now to wipe it out several times over? What would we need stronger weapons *for*?"

Sarah looked up to see a man pulling his finger across his throat. "I assume that means you have to go, Captain?" she asked, indicating the man.

"I'm afraid it does, Miss Parker," Lucy replied. "I believe I have a staff meeting with my two newest captains."

"One last question, if you would, First Captain," the reporter begged. "I'll make it an easy one, I promise."

"The only 'easy' question was about the uniforms," Lucy retorted. "But I think I'm up to the challenge. Go ahead."

"How does your family feel about this development in your life?"

Momentarily stunned by the change of direction, Lucy sat there, mouth open, until she closed it with a snap. "Of all the questions you could have asked, Miss Parker, that's the one I least expected to hear." A smile crossed her face. "Actually, it *is* the last question, isn't it?" she asked, head cocked slightly. "Okay, I'm from the upper mid-west, I guess you'd call it. Middle-class family, middle-class values. My family wasn't easy to convince and still aren't really, but once they see this, there won't be any doubt, will there? My mom has her pottery classes and bridge club and can't understand any of this, and my dad is an electrical engineer and *won't* believe it. I have one brother and no sisters to shock with the news, and I have no idea about aunts, uncles or cousins."

Sarah turned to face the camera squarely. "There you have it, ladies and gentlemen. The first unrehearsed interview with First Captain Lucy Grimes, the leader of the Terran Alliance. I'm Sarah Parker, reporting from the starship *Galileo* somewhere in Earth orbit."

Simon and Daniels left Salinas, Kansas in a car older than a lot of the members of the Terran Alliance, while the brothers Jeffers followed at a discreet distance in the RV. The old green Impala was chosen because it had a rebuilt engine theoretically capable of reaching Denver and a CB radio to keep in touch with the Winnie.

Keeping to a sedate sixty-eight miles per hour, the old Chevy led the RV by about three miles. "We'll have to shorten the distance once we reach the mountains," Simon said into the microphone. He leaned back on the cracked-vinyl seat and looked at the mountain chain growing in the distance.

I've flown a Mamba through the asteroid belt, and I still feel a sense of awe at the sight, he thought.

It was discovered that the Chevy had a tendency to overheat when it had to climb, so Simon and Daniels spent a lot of the next morning and early afternoons sitting in pullouts alongside the road. It worked out well, actually, since the Winnebago needed to climb in a lower, slower gear anyway.

"My guess would be thermostat," Daniels said, "since we aren't losing coolant."

It was during the third such stop that the luck that had been following Simon seemed to vanish. Pretending to be tourists while the car cooled off, the two men would stand and gaze at the view in a near-companionable silence, more often than not.

The two men watched as a Colorado Highway Patrol car pulled into the rest stop and cruised slowly past the scattering of parked cars and pickups.

"Well, what do you think? Are we on his agenda?"

The lone officer didn't seem to pay any special

attention to the old Chevy as he passed. They watched him turn his car off, speak into his microphone for a few seconds, and get out.

Simon heaved an audible sigh of relief when the patrolman headed in the direction of the restrooms. "That's the kind of reaction that gets people arrested, Simon," Daniels said. "Let's get to the car. Now."

"What's the hurry? He went to pee."

"It's glaringly obvious that you've never had a major run-in with the law," Daniels noted. "First, he didn't lock the doors on his cruiser. Second, he wasn't moving like a man on *that* particular mission. He was moving like he wanted someone to *think* he had to pee. Third, he never looked at any of the cars or people he passed. Ever seen a police officer who didn't make eye contact with at least a few individuals? Entirely too forced. Let's go."

Simon managed to hobble to the passenger door and get settled as Daniels started the engine. "Temp is still too high. Call Brian and tell him we need a pickup, quick,"

Simon keyed the mike. "Stargazer to Sawbones. Pass the next rest stop and pick us up just past the abandoned vehicle. Acknowledge."

"Will do, Stargazer. What's up?"

"I hope it's nothing. If we have company, just pass on by. You have an assignment. I'll say goodbye, now, just in case. Do not respond. Stargazer clear."

Daniels had the old car out of the parking space and headed for the entrance ramp to the highway when flashing lights pulled into the rest area behind them. "Company, Simon. And it isn't good," Daniels said as he took his eyes off the mirror and slowly accelerated. "We keep up appearances until they force us to do something. It's barely possible that it's not us... *shit!"*

The expletive was the first one Simon had ever heard Daniels utter. *That's a bad sign*, he thought. He hung the microphone back on the hook and turned the radio off while changing channels at random as a second set of lights came in from the wrong direction of the ramp. Daniels slammed on the brakes, and the old car nosed down and slid to a silent halt.

At least the salesman didn't lie about the brakes, Simon thought incongruously.

He looked over his shoulder as the second vehicle also slid to a stop, leaving inches between the two vehicles. Bad sign number three appeared in the form of officer number one. Simon was staring down a barrel big enough to drive a Volkswagen through.

"Step out of your vehicle with your hands up!" Came over a loudspeaker in the rear car.

"Suggestions?" Simon asked.

"Yeah, right," Daniels growled. "Just do what they say, and let me do the talking. Maybe I can get us out of this. I hope."

One hand up and outside the car, Daniels loudly announced, "Coming out, officers. Federal agent! Don't shoot."

"Step clear of the car, *Agent*, and keep your hands in the air. And your friend, too. Move!"

"No friend of mine, officer. Just a hitchhiker. And he's injured. Cut him some slack getting out of the car. Bum leg and arm in a cast."

"My, my. Aren't you the humanitarian? Don't lie to me!" the first officer said "We have descriptions of you from back at the car lot in Salinas. You shouldn't walk onto a lot and pay cash, mister. At least not in consecutive hundreds. Some people get nervous enough to report it. Now turn around. If you *are* a Federal agent, you know all about assuming the position. Do it!"

Simon struggled out of the passenger side and kept his right arm up. "Hey, guys. Busted arm, here. And a bad leg. Doing the best I can." He watched as the officer frisked Daniels and came up with a wad of cash, his badge and a stun gun.

"Not like anything I've ever seen," the officer said. Simon could see the name "Reynolds" on the silver nameplate the officer wore. Then he felt himself being pushed into the side of the car, his legs forcibly spread, and hands patting him down.

"This one's clean."

"Well, well. Looks like we hit the jackpot, boys," Reynolds said "This badge says we have FBI Agent Roland Daniels with us. And isn't that the name that came in on the fax a couple of days ago? Cuff 'em, and let's get out of here."

While getting their rights read to them and settling into the back of one of the cruisers, Simon saw the RV pull in and stop in the section for larger vehicles. Deliberately keeping his eyes on the seat in front of him, he waited until the three-car convoy moved out of the parking area with Daniels in the lead vehicle.

Looks like splitting up was a bad idea, he thought. At least Brian and Timothy got away. *Unless*, he felt the blood drain from his face, *they're being followed separately.*

The only words spoken on the drive into Denver were from the patrolman reporting in on his radio.

"Oh, Christ!" Brian exclaimed as he pulled the RV to a spot across the parking lot from the confrontation. "What'll we do? Hey! Roland left that laser of his with us. We could shoot out their tires..."

"Brian! Don't take the Lord's name in vain!" Father Timothy said angrily. "And will you listen to yourself? Shoot out the tires? How about shooting out the radios as well? Then shoot the officers, because they'll surely have figured out who's shooting at them by then. And if *they* don't shoot us, they'll tell every other policeman in the country. How far are you willing to go to carry out an assault?

"I don't like what I'm seeing either, but they aren't being mistreated. Those men are only doing their jobs as they see them. They have orders to follow. And when you think about it, we do, too, in a way. The best way we can help them is to get word to their people. And that gun is our ticket to proving our story, so *don't* go playing with it. It's not a toy lightsaber, you know."

Pushing the RV to its limits, Brian managed to keep the police convoy in sight until they turned off at a small town and into what appeared to be a county jail. A plan had formed over the last hour on the road, and it was immediately implemented. Realizing that Simon and Roland probably wouldn't be moved again for a while, they took a page from Daniels' own book and drove to a used car dealer.

Driving their new acquisition to a motel, they temporarily mothballed the RV and settled in to implement the second part of the plan they'd formed—contacting the Colliers or the Brandts.

It wasn't the contacting that was the problem, they found, it was the convincing, which was going to be no easy task. They parked their late-model Mercury in front of the two-story Aurora home and knocked on the door.

"How many times do we have to tell you people? We have no idea where Ted is. And why do you want him, anyway?" the obviously distraught woman cried.

Affecting the fatherly demeanor that usually helped when he needed to calm one of his parishioners, Father Timothy said, "Ma'am, we aren't lookin' to do the boy any harm. And who might have been here before us?"

"Who? How about first we had the police at our door, then there was that newspaperman from Billings, the FBI was here, the military, Federal Marshalls, and I don't know who else. We've had our phone bugged and our house under surveillance, and we get followed everywhere we go. I guess they think Ted or Alice will contact us sooner or later. Who are you?"

"I'm Father Timothy Jeffers, ma'am, and this is my brother, Doctor Brian Jeffers. I give you my word that we're not associated with any of the people who've been here before."

Ted's mother was the one to hit the nail on the head. "So how did you get our address then?"

"Ma'am," the priest said, "we are... associated with a friend of Ted's. He told us to look Ted up if there was... trouble."

Ted's father chose that moment to join the conversation. "Listen, mister, or Father, or whatever. We don't know where Ted is. He and the kids and his wife seem to have disappeared, and we aren't happy about it, even less happy than the government agencies that keep showing up here. We've told them everything we know in hopes of finding them. They have the best chance, after all, with all their manpower. We've told them about our lake cabin, his favorite hangouts, even his friends—a large number of whom seem to have disappeared, too. Personally, I think they've gotten themselves involved with some kind of cult."

"Harry, some of those people said he was working with that bunch of space people we've been seeing on TV, remember?"

"Yes, Glenda, I know. But Ted's too smart to fall for that nonsense. I can't see anybody falling for it for long. It has to be some kind of scam." Turning back to the two men at his door, the elder Brandt said, "And I sure as hell don't want to get involved with the kind of things that trouble a *priest!* Just go away and leave us alone. We have enough problems of our own right now, and you're upsetting my wife."

"I'm having trouble with the coincidence here," Brian said on the way back to their motel. "First Simon and Daniels get arrested, then we find out that one of the two people we're supposed to contact is in hiding from our own government. All of a sudden, this adventure doesn't seem like so much fun."

"I'm not too happy myself," Father Timothy said. "We either get through to Collier's parents, or we have to wait until the first embassy opens since we don't stand much chance of intercepting any of Simon's people. I'm hoping a more direct approach to the Colliers might work."

"Mr. Collier, I'd like five minutes of your time to tell you a story. If at the end of that time, you tell us to leave, we'll leave instantly and you won't see us again. You have my word." Brian spoke first and waited for a response.

"Five minutes, huh? By the clock, Mr. Jeffers. And a word of warning—your 'story' will have to be a real beaut to get past five minutes." The elder Collier, grey-haired and pony-tailed, made a point of setting a digital alarm. "You may begin."

"My name is Brian Jeffers, and this is my brother, Timothy. He's a priest who runs a rescue mission in Washington, D.C. I help out there when I can. About two weeks ago we met two very interesting individuals..."

"Interesting story, gentlemen, but I'd really need proof, and I can't see you coming up with that." The old hippie sat back in his chair long after the five-minute deadline had passed. "Besides, I still haven't said that I know how to get in touch with Jim or Babs or that I believe they could be connected with this Alliance of yours."

"I think I have something your son would recognize, even if you wouldn't, sir," Brian said. "You give it to him and let him decide if we're worth the risk. Here's our number at the motel. And here's the proof."

In a move almost as old as firearms themselves, Brian reached into his coat and pulled the laser pistol out. The elder Collier's eyes started to widen in alarm, but the expression turned to one of wonder when Brian handed the weapon to him butt-first. "That, Mr. Collier, is a working laser pistol. We don't know how much of a charge it has left, but go ahead and prove it to yourself. Is there anything in this room you'd like to see gone?"

"I'll go along with the gag. That old doorstop over there." Collier aimed the gun at a small cast-iron cow beside the door. "Always did hate that thing. Okay, how do you fire it?"

"Just tighten your grip. No recoil. Hope you're serious about the cow."

The old man's expression said, "Yeah, right," better than words could ever do as he re-sighted on the doorstop. Two seconds later it had changed to one of stunned amazement.

Father Timothy stood up. "Mr. Collier, quite a few people's destinies are now literally in your hands. I know you don't want the responsibility, but you have it nonetheless. If you do as we ask, lives will change, and if you don't do as we ask, other lives will change. We deeply regret laying this at your feet, but if you can believe our story, you'll see that we had no choice. We'll wait for a call. But please impress on everyone involved that time is truly critical. If Simon gets moved out of state before someone up there knows he's here, he could be kept hidden forever. Once he's proved to be alive, he can be rescued. But first, word needs to reach the Alliance. Thank you for listening, sir. Keep the gun to show to your son, if you see him. Good evening."

The priest sputtered angrily, "What were you doing with that gun, Brian?"

"What? Don't be stupid, big brother. Roland gave it to me so we'd have the proof we need. He had Simon, and we needed the gun. Besides, you *know*

I've had it ever since they arrested Roland and Simon."

"You're right. But with everything going on, I forgot, and it caught me by surprise."

"Besides," Brian said, "Roland said to use it this way. You did good to pick up on leaving it there. Now it's out of our hands, too. If we get caught, nobody gets the technology. That's another reason he gave it to me. And he was proved right, wasn't he?"

The priest shrugged. "It would appear that Agent Daniels knew what he was doing." He leaned over the table and brushed the remains of dinner aside. "But I hate waiting. So, what's next? If I'm going on telephone duty, I need reading material."

"No problem, Timmy. I saw a used bookstore about a block down. But if we got Collier convinced, I'm betting you won't get very far into a book before we're moving. Tomorrow will have to do, though," Brian said as he looked at his watch. "No reputable bookstore will be open this late."

"Come on, Timmy, rise and shine!" Brian walked into the motel room accompanied by several hundred pounds of very bright sunshine and the sound of the door hitting the wall. "I brought a newspaper, and it's time to go get breakfast."

"Okay, okay," groused the priest. "I never was very fond of cheerful early risers when I was growing up, and they're even more irritating now. How are things going down the street?" he asked, referring to the police station where they'd last seen Simon and Daniels being unloaded.

"So far, there doesn't seem to be any more traffic

than usual... although I wouldn't know what's 'usual' for a police station."

The two brothers spent the day taking turns waiting for the phone to ring. Boredom-prevention techniques included watching anemic television, reading, and getting outside the four walls for a while.

The newspaper brought them no closer to answers, of course, but it did leave them with more questions. The smaller headlines of interest to the two brothers varied wildly from stories about FBI agents searching the Metro area for "suspected terrorists," a pro-Alliance editorial, letters to the editor both pro and con, an article in what was apparently a series by a Ted Kammerman of the Billings Gazette, now being picked up by the Associated Press and United Press International, pointing out the correlation between the large number of missing persons from Denver and surrounding areas and a significant number of missing scientists from back East, and the revelation of some of the names of Alliance personnel, most of whom had ties to the Denver area in one way or another. One article mentioned the U.S. Government probe into the whereabouts of the two "terrorists." Another quoted a local astronomer saying that there were now *five* ships in orbit, and another talked about a shuttle launch to the International Space Station that would have the *Discovery* passing almost directly beneath the five orbiting objects.

It was getting outside that proved most effective for the two brothers. Evening saw Brian walking back into the room after an unusually long absence, and the look on his brother's face made him ask, "Still no word, huh?"

Timothy shook his head. "Not a word. What took

you so long?"

"Oh, I took a walk down to the station to see what was going on. There seems to be a little more traffic than yesterday. All unmarked cars."

As Timothy looked away from the TV screen, Brian put a finger to his lips in a shushing motion and handed him a much-folded piece of paper. Opening it, he found two things—that the handwriting was very unlike Brian's and that there was a small hand-drawn map attached to the main note. Glancing at the map, he detached it and set it aside. The body of the note read like something out of a cheap thriller.

"You're being followed," the note said. "It's possible that your room is bugged. Read this note, then destroy it."

Turning the paper over, he read instructions for a meeting, although with whom was not clearly stated. They were to drive so far north on such and such street, turn right, go so far, turn left, etc. The final destination appeared to be about a mile from the motel. Arrival time was to be 8 p.m., and they were to "make sure the priest drives."

Timothy got up, went into the bathroom, and before closing the door, made tearing motions at Brian, who just nodded.

"Just some guy!" Brian said defensively when pressed again about where the note had come from. "I was in the bookstore, and he asked me if I was Jeffers and then handed me the note. By the time I knew what it was, he'd gone. And I didn't know I was going to be quizzed like this!"

"Well, the note was right about one thing—we're

being followed by a beat-up old Ford," Timothy said. "But whoever wrote that note knows that and still gave directions and a time, so what next?"

"'Next' is a right at the next corner and pull over on the right. And the Ford just broke down. See the lights keep dimming? And it's blocking the street, too."

Timothy pulled the car up to the curb just outside the circle of light thrown by the corner streetlamp, and as he was shutting the unfamiliar vehicle down, the passenger door opened.

"You guys the Jeffers brothers?" a gruff voice demanded out of the darkness.

"Yes, we are," Brian answered. "Are you the man we're supposed to meet?"

"You Brian?" the man demanded.

"Yes, I am," Brian said testily. "Why?"

"You need to go back to the bookstore and ask for a first edition of *An Occurrence at Owl Creek Bridge* by Ambrose Bierce. And I'm just your stand-in."

"My stand-in for what?"

"For the merry little chase we're about to lead the Feds on."

With a dismissive wave of his hand, Timothy said, "That's not necessary. Their attempt at camouflage backfired. They were in an old Ford and it broke down a little ways back."

"Shows what you know, Father." The man slid into the seat vacated by Brian. "That was our car acting as a blocker. Now drive before they get past."

"I thought we were both going to see Collier," Timothy said. "I don't like splitting up like this."

"Can't be helped. You both know the same things, according to the colonel, so you and I will make the

Feds think what we want them to. You hungry? I know a decent place, and we won't have to worry about traffic. Turn left at the next light."

As the sedan moved through the intersection, Timothy saw that the man bore a striking resemblance to Brian and was dressed essentially the same. When he commented on this coincidence to the man sitting beside him, the response was, "The colonel started looking for ringers for you two. He found me first, and we had to move fast to get me in place."

"Wait a minute here. I've got all kinds of questions. Who's this 'colonel?' And how did Brian get the note? Who are you? And... I don't know."

"I'll tell ya what I can over dinner, which is on me, by the way," the man said conversationally as they trolled through the parking lot toward the restaurant. "Turn in right up here. As for who I am... since I'm supposed to be your brother, call me Brian. Let the rest wait until we get settled." He stopped long enough in the lobby to make a quick phone call that seemed to consist of just the name of the restaurant. "Now we'll have another car on us when we leave so we can switch back. So, why don't you answer a question for me? How is your brother going to get Captain Grimes to believe him?"

"He's going to ask her a question," Timothy said. "Something about one of her teachers, I believe. We have no idea what it means. 'Have you thanked Professor Weston, lately?' is what we're supposed to say."

In a portion of Brian's life that had surprises thrown

at him almost daily, this day looked like it was going to take the award. It had seemed like one continual surprise from the time he'd entered the bookstore until now.

First, the dark and musty bookstore made him think of the proprietor as some wizened little old man with glasses perched on his nose, and what he found at the back of the overflowing maze was a sweet young thing of no more than twenty.

Second, when he asked for a first edition of Ambrose Bierce's *An Occurrence at Owl Creek Bridge,* her eyebrows made a serious attempt to connect with her hairline. He'd never heard of Ambrose Bierce and had no idea why an "occurrence" at a place called Owl Creek Bridge should have any relevance to anything.

Third, she immediately began to lead him farther back into the dark warren of the store. He was momentarily blinded when she stopped in front of and then opened a narrow door between the floor-to-ceiling shelves. The light that enveloped him was florescent and of almost daylight intensity, coming from a thoroughly modern room. Chrome, glass and leather seemed to predominate.

Fourth, she led him into the room and picked up a small disk from among several laying on a side table. Handing the disk to him, she pushed a button on the wristband he hadn't known she was wearing.

The room fading out around him seemed like some special effect in a movie. And the fading in of a totally new scene—a metal-walled room with a console off to one side manned by a youngish man in a black shirt—also surprised him just a bit. Brian lost track of the surprise numbers as he realized that the black shirt was part of a uniform, and that he'd seen pictures of that same uniform on television.

"Uh, exactly where are we?" he asked the young woman who'd taken his wrist and was pulling him away from a hexagonal spot marked on the floor.

She plucked the disk from his unresponsive hand and said, "We're aboard the *Galileo*, sir, and you're here to see Captain Grimes, aren't you?"

"Well, y-yes," he stuttered. "But I didn't expect..."

The woman laughed. Somehow, Brian felt it wasn't so much at him as it was at his response, so he didn't take offense. "I have to get back down. Someone has to run the bookstore. It's been nice to meet you, sir." To the man at the console she said, "Could you call an escort for this gentleman, Crewman, and send me back to my original position?"

Brian watched as she walked back into one of the four hexes on the floor and disappeared in a cloud of blue sparks. His eyes were drawn to the ceiling as a faint glow vanished and he noticed four corresponding hexes there. Brian closed his mouth with an almost audible snap and came back to some level of reality when heard the man at the console say, "Sir? Your escort will be here shortly."

"Uh, thank you, uh..."

"Crewman Jakes, sir."

"Uh, yes, Crewman Jakes. Can I ask you a question, Crewman?" Brian asked.

"As long as it doesn't violate security. That's something they've been pushing pretty hard around here lately."

"How long have you been aboard?"

"About two weeks, sir. I volunteered right after... you know, Camp David." Brian could hear a capital "v" in the young man's voice.

"How do you like it here?"

"It's not what I expected, sir. I mean it *is* a spaceship and all, but we aren't doing anything really different yet, you know? I mean we don't go flying from planet to planet, or meeting aliens, or anything, like in the movies. We're supposed to leave orbit soon and go build a fourth space dock in the asteroid belt. I'm already learning to be a CP driver. That's a construction pod. Once a part of a dock has been built here on the *Galileo*, I get to move it into place and lock it down. Now, *that's* cool! I've already been outside in one, just to learn how to maneuver, ya know?"

Brian could hear the excitement building in the crewman's voice as he told of the experience.

They were interrupted by the arrival of another member of the crew entering the room.

"Dr. Jeffers? Would you come with me, please?" Brian noticed a patch on the left shoulder of the newcomer's uniform that said "Mamba Pilot." Also in evidence was the laser pistol strapped to the man's waist. If he hadn't held one in his hands himself, he never would have known exactly what kind of weapon it was.

"Where are you taking me?" Brian asked

"To see the First Captain, of course. That *is* what you wanted, isn't it, sir? Her office is on a different deck."

Brian followed the crewman down a crowded, metal-walled corridor and up in an elevator, equally crowded. *Kinda like a hive*, he thought, *with all the people running around on unknown missions dressed alike and acting so serious. Or, more like some giant machine going about the business of replicating itself.*

The areas he'd passed through so far seemed to be mainly living quarters. So many people! He wondered how they kept from killing each other. His escort finally stopped in front of a door with a brass plaque at one side.

"Fleet Headquarters," he read. "First Captain Lucy Grimes, Commanding."

Pressing a button below the plaque, the escort said, "Lt. Commander Trent reporting. I have a visitor for the captain."

The door slid silently open, and the man gestured for Brian to enter first. The room he walked into was about as ordinary as any secretary's office could be except for the metal walls and lack of windows.

"Welcome aboard the *Galileo*, Mr. Jeffers. Please have a seat. You'll be able to go in momentarily."

While it seemed that the woman was busily shuffling papers around and making occasional notes, it also seemed he was under her constant scrutiny.

And who can blame 'em, after what happened to their boss. And here I am, telling 'em he's not really dead.

Brian stared around the office. He saw a coffee table covered with magazines—none old he noticed—flowers in vases, all freshly cut, and pictures on the walls. All pretty prosaic, until looking at the pictures more closely. He got up and went over to look at them. He recognized a Mamba in flight from the telecasts, but the backdrop was blackest space with a rock in the near background. *An asteroid!* he realized. He saw what could only be the *Galileo* in another picture, and in another, three ships together—the *Galileo* with two others and Earth in the background. The small brass plaque beneath it read: *Galileo, Heinlein* and *McCaffrey* in Earth orbit. All of them appeared to be authentic photographs.

Brian turned around when he heard the secretary speak.

"Follow me, please." The Asian-looking woman got up and led him into another room. Furnished on the lines of a conference room, it had a long, narrow table capable of seating at least fifteen people with chairs to match, five of which were already filled, and more of the same type of photographs that had been in the secretary's office.

Somewhat surprised to find five people waiting when he entered the room, Brian hesitated a second.

"Please Dr. Jeffers. Have a seat. I'm Lucy Grimes, and with me today are Captains Kane of the *McCaffrey*, Miller of the *Clarke*, and Greene of the *Niven*. Also present is Commander Walker of our Science Division. You've already met Commander Kimura, who'll be recording this session. I understand you have a most... original story to tell us. Please. Go ahead."

The group he faced didn't project optimism so much as a polite willingness to listen to his story. He sat in the chair indicated and reached out, picking up the glass sitting in front of him.

"I don't know where to start except at what was the beginning for me." He took a sip from the glass, relieved to find that it was just water, and set it down with deliberate care as he ordered his thoughts. "It was evening on July 28th when my brother called and told me he had a patient filled with bullet holes..."

"Well," Robert Greene said after Brian finished his story. "That's quite a tale, Dr. Jeffers. It ties everything up into a nice neat package and even explains the pistol. But it doesn't convince me that someone like Daniels would go against a lifetime of training and conditioning on such short notice. The dilemma would paralyze most people."

"I say let's go for it," Gayle said excitedly. "It's just the thing Simon would do! He's a target, so he can't travel openly. He can't get to Europe where Lucy has been. And he can't openly approach someone in the United States until we can get an embassy open. He knows Brandt and Collier, of course, so naturally he'd go there."

Stephen looked up from the sheet of notes and doodles he'd been playing with. "Simon was... is... nothing if not daring. And inventive. It's the correlation between coincidence and Daniels that keeps getting in my way though. There are just too many of them. It was coincidence that he chose that particular time to stow away, and he just happened to have stolen a laser, and just happened to exit the craft right before it was destroyed. He happened to stop to see if Simon was alive and then just happened to find your brother's mission, Mr. Jeffers. You see where I'm headed with this? Or do I need to continue?"

Marsha spoke into the angry silence that followed. "Stephen, we all know how close you were to Simon. And you, too, Gayle. You were his friend from *way* before. But, guys, we've all seen the videos. I don't buy this hiding-in-the-smoke nonsense. It's too convenient. Somebody wants to use these two," she said, gesturing angrily in Brian's direction, "as some kind of smokescreen to get next to us. Look, you all saw the video. Kitty blew that shuttle and half of Camp David into their component atoms. And Simon went up with it, along with three others."

In other times and places, the look on Lucy's face would have been called the "thousand-yard stare," and it burned a hole through Brian as she turned in his direction. "Well, I want to thank each of you for your opinions. I hate decisions like this. I swear to God that if Simon were alive, I'd kill him for dumping this on me, but I don't see any choice."

Commander Kimura drew all eyes when she stood up and spoke. "I beg your pardon, First Captain, but I think there's a voice not represented here. Captain Hawke, Kitty, that is, has just as much at stake, even more, than the rest of you. I know how she felt about Agent Daniels and since so much of your decision is based on your opinions of him, you should hear hers. I was there when Captain Kitty met with Agent Daniels during her recovery from her... breakdown after finding the alien ship. After their meeting, she told me he was an honorable man working for the wrong side. She said she felt that he would be the kind of person she could come to like under the right circumstances. And I think saving her husband's life qualifies, if he truly did save it. I agree that there's reason for doubting the whole story at present, but there are also reasons to believe that it happened exactly as Dr. Jeffers said. Coincidences *do* happen. Look at the finding of the *Galileo* herself. Could Simon, Kitty, and Gayle have come into possession of her without the greatest of coincidences? The coincidences we're discussing here pale in comparison," she said, waving a hand in Brian's direction. "Don't judge a book by its cover, as an old saying goes. Just because he's an agent of a government doesn't mean he doesn't have a heart or principles. Governments are made up of people, both good and bad. Aren't we, here, right now, a government of a kind? Are we bad people? *Must* Agent Daniels be a bad person because he works for a government? For Captain Kitty's sake, if no other reason, you need to check this out."

Lucy listened without comment all the while Commander Kimura spoke. A thoughtful look stayed on her face as she asked, "Does anyone have anything else to say?" Heads shook and fingers twiddled until Brian hesitantly lifted his hand. "Yes, Dr. Jeffers?"

"Simon, that is, Captain Hawke, knew this would be the probable reaction. During his... less depressed... moments, we talked. Mostly he did. The man can spin a good yarn, that's for sure. Anyway, he said that if nobody believed me, as was likely to happen, I was to ask Captain Grimes a question. As I understand it, Simon meant the question to be the key here, not the answer."

"Well, what's the question?" Robert asked with exasperation.

Ignoring the taciturn young man sitting almost across from him, Brian looked to the head of the table at the woman who'd said relatively little during the entire meeting. "Captain Grimes, the question is, 'When was the last time you thanked Professor Weston?'"

A confused look settled onto Lucy's face, and the newly promoted Captain Greene spoke into the silence. "What the hell kind of question is that? Every one of us who've revealed ourselves, and probably quite a few who haven't, have already been investigated by the government, and I'll bet they know everything about us down to the brand of diapers we wore."

Lucy's eyes twitched left and right as though she were reading a book while her mind processed the question. "Let me think a minute, Robert," she said as she tried to put two people together from two totally disparate portions of her life. The silence seemed to go on forever, but it couldn't have been more than thirty seconds before she exclaimed, "Oh... my... God!" A blush started on her cheeks, spread quickly across her face, and down her neck.

At the chorus of startled exclamations that followed her own, Lucy said, "I had to put together how it would be possible for Simon to have known anything at all about Professor Weston. There's only one instance I can remember that I mentioned his name in Simon's presence. And as embarrassing moments in my life go, that particular event was one of the most embarrassing. You were there, Robert. As a matter of fact, the whole thing was *your* fault! You were the one who figured out that we could turn the gravity off on deck eighteen. And do you remember what I said that day, floating in midair along with everyone else?"

Greene shook his head in bafflement. "I remember the day well, as well as the event, but I don't remember what you said."

"Of course, you don't. It wasn't an embarrassing moment for you. But it was for me, and I still recall the day *very* vividly. To this day, I don't know which of Newton's laws it was, but I do remember that for every action there is an equal and opposite reaction. Which meant, Robert, that I started by taking off my shoes one at a time and throwing them away from me so I would move toward the gravity-control panel. But it wasn't enough. By the time I reached the panel, I wasn't dressed for a public viewing unless it was in the centerfold of Playboy, remember?"

"I confess that I don't remember, Lucy," Robert said.

"Well, as I said, there are parts I remember *very* clearly, and I definitely remember this. I said, 'Thank you, Professor Weston!' That means, ladies and gentlemen, at least as far as I'm concerned, Simon Hawke is alive!"

CHAPTER NINE

"We ran the prints through NCIC, sir, and it seems that we really do have Agent Daniels in custody in Aurora, Colorado," the earnest-looking young man said. His short hair and conservatively cut dark suit made him look like he'd been stamped from the same mold as the other man in the room. "And it looks like the man arrested with him is Simon Hawke."

The man behind the desk had a sleepy look on his face, and Richard Stanton had worked long hours to be able to adopt that look when he needed it. Most people would either underestimate him because of it or think he just wasn't listening. Either one was a plus in his line of work. "Name sounds familiar. Wait a minute. You don't mean the guy from the damned Alliance, do you, Agent Wilson? The one who went up with Camp David?

"Yes, sir, I do. It seems he didn't die after all. I recommend that we get a team out to Colorado and get them both back here where we can keep a close eye on them."

"Who knows they're out there?" Stanton asked.

"Well, sir, there are a few, it seems. I would guess all the members of the Aurora Police Department know, since we put out that notice to be on the lookout for Daniels. Then there are the ones here who took the call about their arrest, and the agent who passed the information to me. And of course, you, sir,"

Agent Wilson said. "I don't have a specific number though."

"Our people here, I'm not worried about. Get word to that police department that they're to keep this under wraps. It already had a security tag on it, but it has just become a matter of *national* security, and if one word gets out, people are going to be shoveling shit with their bare hands for life. Do I make myself clear?"

"Yes, sir!"

"And we won't move either of them right now. Get an interrogation team out there to find out what the hell is going on with Daniels. And see what they can sweat out of Hawke while they're at it. Anything else?"

"Just one other thing, sir. It appears that Hawke is wounded. The arrest report details that he has a severe limp, his wrist in a cast, his arm in a sling, and a scalp wound."

"That's consistent with what we've been able to piece together from that cluster-fuck Anderson set up at Camp David. And find out who's been giving him medical attention, too. We have enough traitors in our midst. Get a move on, Agent. Pick your team and be there yesterday. Got it?"

"Yes, sir, Director," was the only response as he moved through the door.

Once Lucy committed herself to the possibility that Simon was alive, she wasted no time setting up a way to get him back. "And we'll bring Daniels with him. I want answers, and he seems to be right in the middle of the whole thing."

An extended interrogation of Brian resulted in finding out, among other things, the true extent of Simon's injuries.

"So, who did the patch job on Simon?" Robert asked.

"I've already told you. I did," Brian said, exasperation shortening his tone. "I got a call at about eight p.m. on the twenty-eighth. When I got there, I pulled a bullet out of his left thigh, patched his left shoulder—the round missed all major blood vessels, thank God—set his wrist, and cleaned up his scalp wound. I set up antibiotic therapy for the infection that was beginning to set in and helped him get past the shock and back on his feet. I played nursemaid for him all the way out here. And I figured out for myself that he wasn't who Daniels said he was. It was a military 7.62 mm round that I pulled out of his leg. The only rounds of that kind that had been fired recently had been at Camp David that morning, and that fit in with the look of the wound and the beginnings of the infection. Roland finally told us to keep us quiet. Hell, he had to trust *someone*."

Stephen, always invited to any Captain's Call, asked, "How did those two get picked up and not you two?"

"Simon and Roland concocted the idea to split into two groups, saying that way we had a better chance of getting in touch with you." He shrugged, hands out, palms up. "Bad luck, I guess. Or good detective work by the bad guys. I don't know."

Mustafa Morgan, the *Galileo's* newest captain, broke in. "There's a problem with your story, *Mister* Jeffers. What doctor in Washington, D.C. makes house calls?"

"I lost my license to practice medicine. I was caught prescribing medications that I shouldn't have for patients who were terminal. My conscience didn't have a choice. The Board didn't either. So, I work for my brother on occasion when the need is desperate. Look," Brian said finally, "I've been straight with you guys. Time will prove me right. My brother walked away from his position with the Church and came along because he's as much of a visionary as I am. As you people are for that matter. Timothy fancies himself as the first missionary on the Last Frontier. Surely you have people aboard your ships who feel a need for church services?"

"Well, yes," Gayle answered, looking around the table. "There are unofficial services held that aren't of any specific faith, led by whoever wants to get up and say a prayer or sing a hymn, but we don't have anything structured."

"I get the impression from Simon that you're short of qualified doctors, too," Brian said. "And I think we could both contribute a lot if you'd let us."

"Mr. Jeffers... Doctor," Lucy corrected herself as she stood up and walked down the length of the table, "I realize that you have questions, too, but now isn't the time for us to get into long answers. It appears we have a rescue to set up. Please accept my apologies and a rain check for you and your brother to visit after this is over. And you can sign on if you still want to, of course." Lucy shook Brian's hand and said, "It's the least we can do if your information turns out to be good." She turned to Kimura. "Please see that Doctor Jeffers gets a wristband, Commander. Level five, if you would. And see that he gets back to Earth." Dismissing him from her mind, Lucy got back to the Captain's Call.

"She's not that abrupt, usually," Kimura apologized as she led her charge down the hall. "She has a lot on her mind of late, and now this. You realize that this is almost as new to us as it is to you? We've only been out here for about three years, and she's been in charge for less than two weeks. Is it any surprise that she should feel overwhelmed?"

"You're preaching to the choir, Commander. I've had a lot of my own preconceived notions challenged a lot more recently than yours. What's this about a 'level five wristband?'"

Kimura answered as she led him into a room a short way down the corridor from the briefing room. "It's a communicator, basically, a very simple one at level five. It will allow us to send a low-level charge through your wrist, a tingle, so to speak, and get your attention. Sit here," she said, motioning to a chair positioned beside a small box on a table. "Put your hand in here," she continued as she set a series of controls on the front of the machine. "When you feel the tingle, you'll press the red button to let us know you're in a secure location to be beamed up. If you're not near a secure location, press the blue button. If it's an Emergency, you'll get a sharper tingle."

"Suppose I press the red button without getting a signal?"

"It had better be important. Level five means that you'll be met by armed security."

"Trust me, Commander, I don't want to have to test that statement. But I have another question."

"Ask me on the way to Transport Control. You can

remove your arm now." The commander inspected the wristband circling Brian's wrist. "It appears to be in order. Follow me, please." As she led Brian down the corridor to the elevator, she asked over her shoulder, "What was your question?"

"I see that you folks have set yourselves up on a military basis. I'm not objecting to that, don't get me wrong," Brian said sincerely, "but I want to know how you keep all these people in line. I mean, it's not like you have the authority to punish people. What happens if somebody says, 'I don't feel like swabbing the deck today'?"

Kimura was silent as the elevator descended to the transporter level. "Two things keep people in line," she said as she led him down an identical corridor. "One is the ship itself. I mean, look around you. What would you give to live and work here?"

"I really don't know," he retorted. "All *I've* seen are an elevator and a couple of metal-walled corridors. I'll admit the beam-up effect is a good one, but give me a break, okay? Disney World can do just as good."

"Point taken," Kimura conceded. "I'll make you a promise. When you return, I'll personally give you a tour of the ship. Another part of the answer is 'location,' if this isn't a 'special effect,' of course. Look around you. We've spent an enormous effort in the asteroid belt, for Christ's sake, to build three space docks, and we're going out to build a fourth as soon as we get this new mess straightened out. It's not the weightlessness of the International Space Station, but the futuristic artificial gravity of the movies. It's not a baby step out into the cold, hard universe, but seven-league boots with which we can stride from star to star. The final part of your answer is that anyone who, for whatever reason, doesn't want to be here can go home. And if they didn't follow the rules that come down from on high, they'd be banished forever to that tiny, crowded, overheated mud ball down there. Each and every person who signs on knows that up front. Some just don't sign on, and others find out that we mean business. But those cases are rare. It takes a very adventurous spirit to even contemplate the *existence* of a group like this one, much less take a chance on coming up here, until recently, that is. Would you take a chance on being kicked out with no chance of returning? I don't think so, and neither do several thousand others."

"Do you have the concept of 'illegal orders'?" Brian said as they approached the door marked Transport Control.

"Of course. I can't give you an order to kill someone, for example," Kimura explained. "If I did, the trouble would land on my shoulders. I have a responsibility to you as a 'superior officer,' just as you have one to me as a crewman. Here we are. Dr. Jeffers. It's been a pleasure to meet you," she said, shaking his hand. "I hope to see you again soon. And I do hope your information about Simon pans out. For Captain Kitty's sake. For all of us."

Lucy was only marginally aware of Brian and Kimura leaving the room as she let her mind move onto another level. "We need someone who knows Aurora. Fortunately, a lot of our volunteers come from the Denver area, so we shouldn't have too much trouble in that department. Get our sensors trained on the police station as soon as we have it positively identified and see if we can locate Simon and Daniels. They would probably be in one of the more secure areas of the building, and for the most part, alone. I expect that sooner or later, FBI agents will arrive to interrogate Daniels if Dr. Jeffers' story is true, or pin a medal on him if it isn't. In either event, they're probably in one of the most secure areas, and I want to be able to snatch Simon and Daniels as soon as possible.

"Marsha, your job is to locate anyone who's familiar with the Aurora police station. Gayle, downside reconnaissance will be your job since you have the least exposure. Our one exposure in Switzerland shouldn't get you recognized in street clothes. Stephen, you're on the technical aspect of things. See what our sensors can make of the interiors of the buildings and the movements of people inside them. Draft whoever you need. Just get results! As soon as Rukia gets back from getting Jeffers home, she, and Lloyd, and I will be returning to Zurich to find out what the Security Council has to say. I also want to know what the Swiss have to say about setting up an embassy. I think we'll pass on having all three countries in agreement before setting up the first one.

"I'm really looking forward to Simon's return, assuming he's alive, of course. I'll take *great* pleasure in turning this mess back over to him. In the meantime, remember that the next mission for the *Galileo* is the building of Taurus Base. That means, ladies and gentlemen, that once we leave orbit, and we *will* leave soon, we'll be dependent on our shuttles for space-to-ground support. I'll probably be transferring my—or more appropriately, Simon's—flag to *Niven*. Sorry, Robert. Your ship will be staying in orbit to give weight to our presence here for a while. Once other ships roll off the line, your shuttles will be required to act as ferries to bring the new crews aboard. Once the *Galileo* finishes her job building Taurus Base, I plan to have her spend most of her time here freeing the *Niven* up for other duties.

"Specifically, I want the *Niven* to be one of the first ships to leave Earth space and actually begin to explore the surrounding stars I remember Simon and Kitty talking about in three-ship groups—two cruisers and a carrier. That will be the first thing to come out of Taurus Base if I can convince Simon to do it. Two ships with ten Mambas each and a carrier with forty more would make a pretty formidable taskforce. I think a supply ship would be a good idea as well, so four ships in all for our first foray into interstellar space. Is that a good enough carrot to dangle in front of you to keep you in good spirits, Robert?"

"I'll say! What kind of timeframe do you have in mind…"

Brian beamed back down into the same room he'd left and saw the same young woman sitting in a chair, reading a book.

"Maybe I'm just not on the right wavelength," she said, "but this Ambrose Bierce thing is a bit overrated for my taste. What do you think?"

"I'd never heard of him before, so I have no opinion the subject," Brian responded distractedly. "How do I get back in touch with my brother?"

"In such a hurry! Let me make a phone call." The young woman punched a number into a cell phone beside her and waited for a few seconds. Without speaking a word, she shut the unit down and said, "Go out front and wait. A blue car will be along to pick you up and deliver you to your brother. I'll really be glad when all this cloak-and-dagger stuff isn't necessary anymore, even if it *is* kind of fun. Stop in sometime when you aren't looking for anything in particular, Mr. Jeffers."

"Okay, Brian, give," Timothy said as Brian slipped into the seat vacated by his impostor. "By the way, we had dinner while you were gone. I didn't think it would look good if 'we' had dinner again, so I brought you this. He handed over a Styrofoam container.

"Well, long story short," Brian replied, "I got beamed aboard a spaceship. I think it was their *Galileo*. Neat thing, that. It felt like one long mild electric shock. Anyway, I was led down a long metal-walled corridor, up an elevator, along another corridor, and got interrogated. Then I got returned the same way I arrived. It's the details that make the story interesting though."

After relating his part of the adventure, Timothy took a turn. "Mine isn't nearly so involved. Actually, I did have dinner with a relatively good replica of you. I found out that there are about a thousand people who, for one reason or another, can't go on active-duty positions at this time. They've formed what they call the 'Terran Alliance Underground,' and do things like what happened tonight. Your double says they've about mined the Denver area out of recruit material, so they're looking at other cities to recruit from if the embassy idea doesn't fly."

Dressed in a conservatively cut three-piece suit, Baron von Schlenker appeared to be the consummate businessman that he, in fact, was. "I only play dress-up for some of our galas, not all of them," he responded to Lucy's compliments on his appearance. "My dear wife says that I'll never grow up. But you *did* see that she out-dressed any of our guests that night, didn't you?"

"Yes, Freddie, I did. But don't you dare tell her I said so. I'd just have to call you a liar to your face. I make it a rule not to upset the woman of the castle," Lucy quipped as she followed the baron on a tour of the now-furnished building he'd donated to the Alliance. "How did you get this done so fast? Everything was dust, cobwebs, and bare floors four days ago!"

"It helps to live in a country that still believes in royalty and having the word 'baron' in front of your name. It also helps to have money and contacts." The baron waved his hand dismissively. "This was nothing."

"It still costs money, Freddie, and I don't know how we'll repay you, or when," Lucy said. "As much as we *do* have, money isn't one of the things we're rolling in."

"I won't lie to you, Lady Lucille. This did cost a bit but not more than I can afford. Even Margit agreed that the money was well spent." A glint appeared in the old baron's eye. "There *is* a way you can repay us though. Both of us would like to visit your marvelous ship, the *Galileo*, is it? Then, of course there's the first year's rent on the property. I think we agreed on one dollar, yes? That would be in cash, of course, for which you would get a receipt. The estate will foot the bills for the utilities. And don't think we'll be getting nothing out of this. The publicity alone will be worth all the expense. At this early stage of the game, who can say where the financial trails may lead? And that doesn't even begin to include the prestige, and yes, the notoriety, which will accrue just by being associated with you."

"Notoriety can be a two-edged sword, Freddie. Someone predicted that the flow would reverse after a time. When the governments of the world finally figure out that they can't bully us into giving out technology we don't want to part with, they'll turn mean. Things like illegal arrests and secret interrogations will begin to happen. Star chambers, if you will, and possibly worse. Everybody wants a new weapon to wave in the face of everybody else. Some of the stuff we'll release can be converted to weapons, but that's true of a lot of things. A clever person took two sticks and some string and made a weapon that killed at a distance. What do you think clever people can do with matter-conversion technology? Or antigravity? Or some of the more advanced solar technology? Energy storage devices?

"It's going to be bad enough when people start going out of business because of the new technologies. We want to minimize that by releasing things slowly, but some won't be able to cope with even that, and it will add to the ranks of unemployed. Children will grow up with the newer technologies, and they'll be more comfortable than the older generations. Look at what happened when kids got hold of computers. We figure it will take a full generation before everything's integrated—say twenty-five years, maybe more. But we hope that, before then, *we* can become an integrated part of Earth society. That way, the whole planet will get the benefit of technology that will take us to the stars as a race rather than individuals."

The baron led Lucy through a door on the second floor of the building. "This I envision as your secretary's office," he said striding across the room. Without pausing, he opened another door. "And here's what I had in mind for you, my dear Lucy." With a grand flourish and a bow, he waved her into the spacious office.

"This is...is..." Lucy's voice trailed off as she took in the scene—huge oak desk, upholstered chair, and an entire wall of glass that gave a view of the Alps that was "to die for." Several chairs, somewhat less grand, faced the desk, while across the room a grouping of chairs and a couch gave a more informal place to relax, all fitting beautifully around the fireplace found in almost any space this large.

"I thought to put a few pictures on the walls just to liven them up but decided to let you do that for yourself," the baron said expansively. "I have several paintings that would go nicely in here. Several of the old masters come to mind, but you'd probably like something more in keeping with the, shall we say, futuristic aspect of your Alliance. Allow me to work with an idea that just came to mind. If you don't like it, you can change it."

"Agreed," Lucy answered. "And thank you for

what you've done so far, which brings up another point I've had rolling around in my head. I think we need a lawyer—attorney, barrister, whatever they're called. Maybe more than one. Someone we can trust to look after Alliance interests on Earth and keep things from getting all balled up. We don't need to see any revenue from licensing rights or outright sales of technology getting held up in the courts, and someone's bound to try at some point. It would be better to be prepared for attacks of those kind just as much as overt physical assaults, don't you think?"

"You are wise beyond your years, Lady Lucille. It would be wise indeed, and I have just the group for you. Incidentally, three of the partners in this group have already approached me for invitations to the next gala in hopes of meeting you. And the fourth! He has threatened to *sue* me for not inviting him to the last one! Each has children who would do well to get some discipline from some branch of military training, and your Alliance would serve admirably, I think. It certainly wouldn't hurt to entertain the idea, my dear."

"I think that's a remarkable idea, Freddie. There are complications I can't discuss just yet, but I'd certainly be willing to meet with these gentlemen. And that brings me to another thought. I've come to the conclusion that we need somebody to represent us before the Security Council and possibly the world. It's obvious to me that no one I know of is well enough versed in international matters to handle things without ruffling a *lot* of feathers. I want you to take on the job for us, and I have no idea how to go about asking except straight out. Will you do it? And speaking of leverage, has your government accepted us using this building as our official embassy?"

"Not yet," the Baron admitted, "but it will surely happen. There's too much to gain not to. It's my opinion that my government will wait to see what the Council does. Everything is contingent on that. And I'm honored that you would think of my poor, humble self to represent you. I accept."

"You see, Freddie," Lucy said, sinking into the overstuffed chair, "that's why you'd be perfect for the job. I've only known you for a short while, but I would call you neither poor nor humble. You *almost* made me believe you, though," she said with a laugh. "Now, how about that visit to the *Galileo* you asked for? Let me give you the full tour. If you're going to speak for us, you should know what you're talking about."

An hour after sending the baroness back to the castle, Lucy summoned her staff to a Captain's Call. "Ladies and gentlemen, allow me to present Baron Manfred von Schlenker," she said as soon as the last person was seated. "He has agreed to be our representative to the United Nations and to assist in acquiring a very prestigious law firm to take any cases that might arise wherein we need a defense. He's our newest volunteer, so to speak. As such, I believe he needs to know something about how we operate. He no doubt believes that everything we do is exciting..."

Laughter rolled around the table, stopping her for a few seconds.

"*But,*" she went on, throwing enough emphasis into that one word to silence the room, "I have some serious news. As you know, we're in communication with two men in the Denver area who help us get our volunteers. They've informed me that several of our recruits have been identified and have had their families picked up for 'questioning.' Since I made my name and face public, I checked on my folks. They've been picked up, too, as have Marsha's and Jerry's. My first reaction was disbelief, then anger, and I'm sure everyone affected feels the same. After talking with the baron, I feel that we have several ways to go with our responses. If I have to use world opinion, I surely will. The baron was quick to point out that America wouldn't like the 'what goes around, comes around' approach, as they've so often yelled about human rights violations in other countries. Laying it right on their own doorstep would be a bit much to take. Immediately after this meeting, I'll be getting in touch with Brandon Galway. I imagine an earful to him will get to the president in a hurry. I ask each of you to remain calm and let us try to get the problem resolved. And we won't be leaving orbit until it *is* resolved."

Standing at the head of the table, Lucy unconsciously leaned all of her weight onto her arms, hands splayed out before her. Looking around, she said, "Now to smaller things. First, a job for Rukia. As soon as we are finished here," she said, turning to her, "get in touch with Victor McCord on Libra. Tell him we need another name for commander of Taurus Base ASAP. Someone willing to go out with us on this trip. I plan to have the *Galileo* break orbit as soon as we get our little problems solved, and I'd like to have someone he trusts to take charge of the construction phase. Second," she continued, turning to Robert. "I need to get my offices moved from here to the *Niven*. Commander Kimura and Lieutenant Ross will assist you in getting that done. I'll be beaming down to talk to our dear friend Galway about Simon and Daniels. I've already started the process to put a bug in the Security Council's ear about it."

She went on to explain Baron von Schlenker's new role in Alliance affairs in more detail. "Next is Galway, and after that, if I have to, I'll go to our pet reporter and give her the dirt so she can tell the world how our own country is jailing our family members *again* in an attempt to coerce us."

"Since you're going to talk to Galway, Lucy," Marsha said, "give him a message from me personally, will you? Tell him that pissed off isn't even *close* to how I feel right now, and the more I think about it the madder I get! Make sure he understands that!"

Lucy looked at Marsha in sympathy. "I'll tell him, all right—for you, for myself, and everybody else affected by this stupidity now and in the future. This is exactly what we *should* have expected, but idealists all, we thought we were past this pettiness. There should *be* no impact on our families. Especially, not in *America*, for Christ's sake and I will make that plain in no uncertain terms!"

It was a fine, clear August morning when Lucy beamed into an alley not far from Union Station. She walked a short distance to a bank of pay phones and dialed Galway's private number. The phone went unanswered on the third ring, and she was about to hang up when she heard the click of a completed connection. "Galway."

"Lucy Grimes, here, Mr. Galway. We need to talk."

"Ever the blunt one, aren't you, First Captain? I can play that game, too. Name the place and I'll be there. If it's urgent, make it someplace close, would you?"

"Just sit tight and give me your address. I have a package I believe you should see. I'm having it delivered to you."

Giving a suite number in the Department of Labor Building, Galway said, "It's the best I can do on short notice. I understand I have you to thank for my reactivation."

"Anything is possible, Mr. Galway. I'll call back after you receive the package." She hung up the phone and called another number. "This is Grimes. You can send the package out now." After giving the messenger service the address she'd gotten from Galway, she was told it would be about an hour before the package reached its destination.

With an hour to kill, Lucy strolled out of the Station and up to the first taxi in line at the stand. "Air and Space Museum," she said after a short hesitation. As many times as Lucy had been in Washington, D.C., she'd never been to see any of the sights or memorials that dotted the cityscape. This one was of particular interest to her since she'd been aviation crazy from her earliest memories. While other girls had been playing with Barbie dolls, Lucy had models of P-51 Mustangs and lunar landers hanging from her ceiling.

Maybe one day we'll be in here, too, she thought as the cab pulled up at the entrance.

The hour came and went as Lucy wandered

through the exhibits. The Spirit of St. Louis was gazed at in wonder and a Mercury space capsule with awe, while a mockup of the first space station brought chuckles. Finally, she wandered over to the phones and called Galway's number, amazed that she now knew it by heart.

"Your package arrived two hours ago. I was beginning to think something had happened to you. It's about time for lunch and I've been here since six-thirty. Can I buy you a cup of coffee and a bite?" Galway said.

"Sorry 'bout that, Mr. Galway. I got wrapped up in some of the exhibits in the museum I'm in. How about I buy? Have you had a chance to look at the package yet?"

"I'll be happy with any arrangement as long as my stomach quits having this relationship with my backbone. And yes, I have. I've seen something like it before. The former president had a similar one, along with a letter in his office some time back, I believe," Galway said.

"True enough. Bring it with you to the Air and Space Museum. I don't need to tell you to come alone, do I?"

"No, you don't, Lucy. Can I call you Lucy? You got me back in the loop. I'm not going to repay that with some kind of double cross. I will say that I'm going to let my boss in on what's up, though. *Without* the specifics, like where we're meeting. If I remember correctly, it wouldn't do much good anyway, would it?"

"No, it wouldn't," Lucy said with a chuckle. "Be prepared for a short trip, though, and this time you won't need a bag. You'll be back in time for dinner, I promise. Twenty minutes? Thirty?"

"Twenty should do it, I think," Galway said.

Lucy stood near the entrance and watched as the taxi pulled up to the curb. When Galway got out, she strode out of the building and stood against the wall with every appearance of nonchalance. As Galway started to enter the building after paying off the cabby, she said quietly, "I forgive you, Mr. Galway. The last time we met I was in uniform. Unfortunately, I have to wear civilian clothes as a disguise."

"This is an improvement, so 'unfortunately' isn't a word I would choose," he said appearing only slightly startled. "Black really isn't your color."

"But I've become used to it after so long. Let's walk. Do you have the disk with you?"

"Yes," he said simply, sliding it partway out of his shirt pocket. "What is it?"

"It's a locator disk. We use it to beam people up who don't have one of these." Lucy said as she showed him the wristband that circled her left wrist. "At the moment the one you have is 'slaved' to my wristband. If you don't let go of it, you'll disappear from here and reappear on the *Galileo* when I signal for a pickup. Want to go for a ride?"

"As long as we get to have lunch. I'm free until I report back. How does it work?"

"Like so many things aboard the *Galileo*, we don't know. As Simon once said, we're in the position of a caveman in middle ages Europe. We can learn to *use* the technology and even duplicate it with the help of the ship itself, but much of it we just can't understand yet. Could that caveman have understood ships and sails and compasses and such? Well, we can't understand how the computers work because they're a protein gel, nor can we understand antigravity, artificial gravity, or any number of other things. But we *have* learned how to use them."

The older man and young woman made an unlikely pair as they strolled along at a sedate pace. "Do you mind causing a stir, Mr. Galway?" Lucy asked innocently.

"What kind of stir?"

"There are a few people who'd see us as we beam out, and I imagine some of them would find it necessary to report it to someone. Of course, if you've explained things to your boss, it won't go past him, and he'll have things under control by the time you get back. Wanna live dangerously?"

"What the hell. I've been out of the field for quite a while now. Let's do it. How about getting back?"

"The disk is also a tracking device. When you said you had it in your office, we used it to get a lock. Now we can send you straight back there. No fuss, no muss. Good enough?"

"Sneaky. Deal. Let's do it."

"And a sense of adventure, too. I like men like that. Stand still. It's easier that way." Lucy pressed the button on her wristband, and three people walking toward them stopped in amazement as the two people vanished in clouds of blue sparks.

"Welcome aboard the *Galileo*, Mr. Galway. I'll take responsibility for the visitor, Lieutenant," she said to the woman standing at the transport console. "You said something about lunch. Shall we?" She led him out the door and down a corridor brimming with people. Finally reaching the elevator, she said, "We'll eat in the officer's mess on level three, I think. Then a tour of the ship. In between times I have some things

I need to talk to you about, things you probably need to bring to your boss's attention. At least let him know that *we* know."

"Like what?"

"Like, for instance, we know that Simon Hawke is alive and in custody. We want him back immediately, of course."

"*What?*" Galway yelped. Lucy was glad they were alone in an elevator. "That's not possible. We have footage from three different angles. They all show him being shot, damn it all. I wish I could change that, but it's true. Somebody's blowing smoke up your... skirts," he finished lamely.

"We have good intelligence that he's alive and in detention in Aurora, Colorado, along with Agent Daniels of the FBI. Remember him? We want them freed and returned to us."

"If it's true, and I'm not about to admit that it is at this point, I can't guarantee that we can give you Daniels. Why do you want him anyway?"

"He has questions to answer in the matter of three of our members," Lucy stated unequivocally, "and he *will* be turned over to us one way or another. I promise not to let him get hurt, Mr. Galway."

The elevator doors opened, and Lucy led him down another corridor. This one was wider, but still just as busy, it seemed. Shocked as he was at the news, Galway couldn't help but stare at everything they passed. After three years of hearing about the ship that had taken on a near-mythic quality among the intelligence community, he was walking her decks. "So where are we going, First Captain?" he asked, trying to hide his eagerness with formality.

"You know, I really don't like that title. Most

people around here just call me Captain anyway. But you can call me Lucy for any informal occasion. Besides, if Simon is alive, I'll be going back to captain sooner or later."

"I'd like that, Lucy. And you can call me Brandon."

"Okay, Brandon, I will. As for your question, I thought to show you some of the *Galileo* in hopes of catching you off guard and giving away something I could use to get Simon free. You're either way too good at what you do, or you really are as surprised as you act. Either way, I lose. For now. Here we are, officer's mess."

Lucy and Galway walked onto the bridge following a leisurely lunch and interrupted a discussion between Robert Greene and Mustafa Morgan, the *Galileo's* Captain. "Hello, Robert, 'Stafa. I thought I'd chaperon our guest through a short tour of the ship. Brandon Galway, meet Captains Robert Greene of the *Niven* and Mustafa Morgan of the *Galileo*. Mr. Galway is associated with the Office of the President and could be a great help if we don't alienate him, so let's play nice, okay? So what did we interrupt?"

"I was just filling Captain Morgan in on your transfer to the *Niven*, Captain," Robert said. "He was of the opinion that there wasn't enough space for your suite until I explained the restructuring."

"You could enlighten me, too, Robert," Lucy said, sitting down at the navigator's station. "I've heard about it but haven't been filled in on all the details. That's what happens when someone takes over without a full briefing. So much gets lost that the replacement has to work with incomplete data. I'm going to make sure that never happens again, trust me. Once Simon is back in charge, he's going to keep his successor up to date if I have anything to say about it. Have a seat, Mr. Galway." Lucy waved her hand at the station next to hers. "Don't worry. All controls are offline when we're at standby."

"I was just explaining that the ceilings have been lowered," Robert said, uneasy in the presence of Galway, "which gives us an entire extra deck that the *Heinlein* and the *McCaffrey* don't have, so there won't be any trouble fitting your staff into place. As it stands, we have you just about completely moved out of the *Galileo* already. Actually, there will be even more room than you have now, ma'am. And there are other... modifications that I'll brief you on later." He shot a meaningful look in Galway's direction. "As an extra bonus, Captain Gardner sent along a special gift. It seems that he anticipated the loss of the transporter when the *Galileo* is off building Taurus Base, so he sent you a redesigned shuttle. Its crew complement is four and has been specifically designed for passenger service. It seats one hundred and twenty, so it won't take too many trips to get a crew of new arrivals aboard, once we can land openly, that is."

"That was very thoughtful of him," Lucy said, pointedly ignoring the sarcasm. I'll have to send him a thank-you note. Who's going that way next?"

"I think Marsha is, ma'am. She's supposed to stop at Vesta and see what progress the machines we left behind have made. It should be almost completely hollow by now, we think."

"Wait a minute!" Galway groused. "I know a little bit about our solar system. I have to now, thanks to you folks. And I know that *Vesta* is one of the biggest asteroids in the belt. Are you saying that you've *hollowed it out?* What on Earth...what the hell *for?*"

"Why, Brandon, we need a space station, too," Lucy said coyly. "And since we operate at a greater distance from Earth than NASA's astronauts, we need a base farther out. It seemed perfect, except that it was solid rock, so we set some machines to hollowing it out a year or so back. The *Galileo* will probably go there and outfit it before returning to Earth orbit permanently."

"Why would she come to Earth orbit permanently?"

"Once the major construction jobs are done, what do you think we should do with her, Mr. Galway?" Captain Morgan asked. "*We* thought to use her as a staging area for the new ships being built. And training areas, of course. Volunteers can beam aboard and train for however long it takes before being transferred to a new ship. It will work for personnel transfers, too. People getting tired of space or just wanting a vacation need to be replaced. Consider it a waystation between Earth and the rest of the galaxy."

"Captains, I'm sure you have a lot more to discuss. I'll take Mr. Galway on the rest of his tour and then send him home. What corner of the *Niven* do you have me tucked into, Robert?" Lucy asked, standing up and effectively ending the conversation.

"Just beam into the reception area, ma'am. Your Lieutenant Ross will be a comm call away."

The three men got through the ritual of handshakes and unmeant pleasantries, and Lucy led Galway off the bridge.

"Well! I'm glad to be out of that testosterone storm. First, how about a visit to the flight deck? I believe we have a Mamba or two for you to see."

Lucy stood with Galway in Transport Control after sending the technician out and said, "I have one other thing to bring to your attention, Brandon. We *know* that some of our relatives are being detained for no other reason than that they are related to us. Mine are among them, and so are two of my captains', and it's all I can do to keep a lid on the... level of emotional stability around here. If this situation doesn't rectify itself immediately, I will not be responsible for the consequences. I don't want to bandy around the word 'mutiny,' but I can't be everywhere at once, know what I mean? You tell that to your bosses, Brandon, and make sure they get the *full* impact of what it could mean to push us. Remember Lake Burgess? Now, none of us are angry at you, personally. Just don't let us find out that you had anything to do with this one!" Leaving the threat hanging, she called the technician back in to send Galway down to Earth.

As soon as Galway disappeared, she beamed over to the *Niven*, commed her aide, Lt. Diana Ross, and walked around the reception area while she waited.

"Welcome aboard the *Niven*, Captain."

She turned toward the speaker. Diana Ross, half of a pair of twins, had been appointed her aide when she was first promoted to First Captain. The young lieutenant, along with Commander Kimura, worked hard to keep her boss from having to deal with the minutia that would take her mind away from the necessary work of keeping the dream of the Alliance on track.

"Thank you, Diana," Lucy said to the flame-haired

woman. "I understand you know where our quarters are."

"Yes, ma'am. Follow me. And you have a communiqué from Commander Pike in Zurich. It's marked 'urgent.'"

"No rest for the wicked," Lucy sighed. "But I haven't had *time* to be wicked, so I don't know why fate is landing so hard on me."

The grumbling was good-natured, but Lieutenant Ross knew the sentiment behind it was no less valid for all that.

Lucy strode through the door marked with the now-familiar plaque beside it and couldn't repress the shudder she felt every time she read it. Turning her attention away from her own discomfiture, she looked around the room. A desk to one side was occupied by Commander Kimura, who stood guard over the doorway to her private office. There were chairs lined up along the opposite wall, fronted by a low table that was covered in the magazine effluvia that always occupied level spaces in waiting rooms. There were pictures on the walls, and a waist-high pedestal holding a single, head-sized rock in one corner caught her eye.

"It looks good, Rukia," she said to the woman behind the desk. "Takes talent to do this on such short notice. Diana, take the rest of the day off, and Rukia, you will too, as soon as you bring me up to speed on the rest of my day. And why do we have a rock on a pedestal in the waiting room?"

Her secretary blushed. "I, uh, found it among your personal possessions when we moved you over here, Captain, and I remembered something you said about the first thing you retrieved when you started flying missions during the construction of Libra. I thought it fitting to have it in the anteroom. If I'm out of line, ma'am..."

"No, you're not, Rukia," Lucy hastened to reassure her. "I'd actually forgot about that thing. It does fit."

Kimura relaxed slightly. "Thank you, ma'am. And if you don't mind, both Diana and I would like to stick around."

"But I do mind, Commander," Lucy shot back. "If as you say, I only have one appointment today, I think I can handle it myself. And if you haven't noticed, I have only one secretary and one aide. I hereby declare August 9th to be the First Interstellar Aides and Secretaries Day, so you can't be here. Out!"

Lucy stood there, trying her damnedest to look imposing, and pointed at the door. Only after the door had closed on the two young women did she drop her arm and walk into her office. *Huh!* She thought. *I wish everything went that smoothly.*

She opened the door to her office and looked around at the bare walls and desk heaped with papers. *I don't think people will ever get away from the need for keeping records on paper. Look at how much paper gets used in a "computerized" office downside.*

Lucy sat down in the chair and picked up the paper that lay centered in the small, bare space directly in front of the chair. "To: First Captain Grimes, *Niven.* From: Commander Lloyd Pike, Zurich," she read. "After returning from a Security Council meeting, Baron von Schlenker requests the pleasure of your company at his castle. He has left transportation standing by for your use. Come soonest."

Shaking her head, Lucy beamed over to the *Galileo*. "Send me to the Zurich coordinates, would you, Ensign?" Lucy asked the technician on duty. She beamed into the hotel suite and was immediately met by Crewman Wilson, one of the two men assigned as gopher and guard for her Zurich staff members. "Where is Commander Pike, Crewman?" she demanded.

"Uh, he's asleep, ma'am. It's the middle of the night here."

"Oh." Chagrined by her oversight, Lucy said, "Ask him to contact me as soon as he's up and ready for business." The man nodded, and before he could answer verbally, she beamed out.

Roland Daniels occupied one of ten cells set in two rows at the back of the third floor of the Jefferson County Sheriff's Office in Aurora, Colorado. Simon occupied one of the four-foot-wide, seven-foot-deep cells in the opposite row. By common consent, neither man had spoken to the other since their arrest—Simon because he wasn't sure what to say and Daniels because he was pretty sure anything they said would be recorded.

Daniels watched the potbellied, cherub-faced deputy with interest as he walked down the center of the corridor between the two rows of cells. Up until then, the only time a deputy had walked down this particular aisle, he'd been pushing a cart containing meals. So far, three such trips had been made.

This time the deputy stopped in front of Daniels' cell and said, "Turn around. Back up to the bars."

Daniels was eager to find out what was next on the

agenda but unwilling to let anyone know about that eagerness, so he feigned apprehension as he complied with the deputy's command. "Don't get bent all out of shape there, Mr. FBI man," the deputy said sarcastically. "I'm just taking you to see some friends of yours. And don't try anything funny. You've got three steel doors and several of my friends to get through. I don't think even *you* can do that right now."

Daniels was pushed through the door at the end of the hallway where he found three more uniformed men waiting for him. Equipped with leg shackles and waist chains, two of them wasted no time getting him trussed while the third kept a pistol trained on him at all times.

Eagerness to get to the next phase of what awaited him couldn't completely banish his qualms at being on the other side of the handcuff key for the first time in his life, and Roland Daniels felt the full weight of the chains as he was led into the quintessential interrogation room—steel door with tiny, barred window, grey walls, floor and ceiling, grey metal chairs, grey metal table and one-way mirror. The deputies pushed him into one of the chairs and chained him to it while cherub-face left. The next five minutes dragged on interminably, but finally Cherub-face returned leading two men.

Daniels took one look at the three-piece suits and said, "Well, it took you long enough. I would have thought you'd have been a little more anxious to talk to me. So, who are you guys with?"

The older of the two men looked at the deputies and said, "Out."

Cherub-face replied, "Sir! Our orders are to keep this prisoner under surveillance as long as he is out of his cell."

In a voice that would do a drill sergeant proud, the older man said, "There's only one door in or out of this room, *deputy*. And unless you have an ultra-top-secret security clearance, you will guard him from the *other side of the door!* This matter is classified so secret that if you were to find out what's going on, we'd have to kill you, do you understand?"

Cherub-face stammered his understanding and led his fellow deputies out of the room, leaving the three men alone. "Oh, and deputy, don't even *try* to use the surveillance room," the man said, referring to the darkened room behind the mirrored wall. "One of our people is there now."

When the door closed behind the four deputies, the younger man said, "Can you believe these rubes? Thinking they can barge into things that don't concern them?"

"Lighten up on the deputy, will you?" Daniels demanded. "After all, they did capture me and Hawke. All you guys did was put out a bulletin." He couldn't resist the barb even though he knew it would cost him.

"Listen, Agent Daniels, I'm going to extend professional courtesy to you, one government agent to another, okay?" the younger suit said. "We know you spent almost a year aboard their main ship, and we need to know what you know." He pulled out a pack of cigarettes, flipped one out with a practiced hand, and offered it to Daniels

Shaking his head in refusal, Daniels said, "No, thanks. Nasty habit. So, you're the good cop. Let's just skip the pleasantries. What do you want to know? What kind of weapons they have? I don't know, beyond their antimatter torpedoes, and those are pretty good, don't you think? They have a *very* effective method of keeping prying eyes out of secure locations. How many are there? Several thousand, at the very least, and growing daily. What are their goals? So far, I think they've laid all their cards on the table. Do you have any reason to doubt them? Other than your innate paranoia, that is."

Older suit spoke up. "You realize that you're in violation of your oath of allegiance to your government, don't you? We can hold you until you're old and grey, and no one will ever know."

"Okay, so you're the bad cop. Haven't you guys figured out that I don't have anything to tell you?"

"Give it a rest, Agent," the younger man said, "we're not the bad guys here. You and your friend upstairs are. There's a serious situation here, and we need to resolve it. We *have* to know what they're capable of and what they'll do. An unknown group as powerful as these people must be evaluated in the context of global politics. There are too many variables, and we need to get a handle on them. You were sent there for that specific purpose. Of course, we realize you were *requested* by Hawke. What we'd like to know is just what, exactly, did you do to impress them that much?"

"Impress them?" Daniels laughed at the younger agent. "Sometimes pissing someone off can get you the same results. It's the in-between that can get you killed."

"Is that a threat?"

"No. Just an observation made from many years in the business."

"You were supposed to report in when you got

back, Agent Daniels," the older man stated. "We had no way of knowing when you'd show up, but then we find your fingerprints on a stolen vehicle in the D.C. Metro area. Imagine our surprise! Your superiors *and* mine have been waiting very impatiently for the information you have, and you decide to disappear? *Not* an option, Agent," he said leaning over the seated prisoner. "We have complete access to your files. You were the first FBI agent in the western United States to be liaison to an ALERT team, the first agent to get close to one of the principals in the situation, and the first agent to get aboard one of their vessels. And you were supposed to report your findings to your superiors in Washington. Then you don't report in. Of *course,* we put a bulletin out on you! So, what are you going to tell us that will help to get you out of the shit pile you've fallen into?"

Daniels smiled. "You've just given yourselves away. DIA, right? Has to be, actually. They're the only ones outside the few FBI agents acting as liaison to local law enforcement that know about the ALERT teams."

Daniels and the two agents were alluding to the several teams of experts who'd been put together and kept as special units since the crash of an alleged unidentified craft in the New Mexico desert in the late forties. The acronym stood for "Alien Landing, Emergency Response, Tactical," and the teams were scattered around the United States and the world to be able to respond at a moment's notice to any alien incursion into U.S. Airspace or to try to recover alien technology. The purported objective of these teams was the capture of an intact ship for study, and Daniels was not only a sidewise member of one of these teams, but he'd been aboard one of the ships. The powers-that-be couldn't let him slip out of their grasp, and they couldn't let him keep his knowledge to himself. From his lofty vantage point of a dozen years' service in the FBI, Daniels knew what was ahead. Not from personal experience, but from rumor. "Just remember, guys, I've had the same training as you have at resisting interrogation. Anything you get from me will be highly suspect and unreliable."

"We'll keep that in mind, Agent, but we'll go ahead just the same." The older man spoke with finality. He walked over to the door and banged on it. When cherub-face opened the door, he said, "Take him back to his cell. We'll arrange transport for him and his accomplice. You are to keep quiet about what's going on in here, understand? Not one word to anybody, or you'll live to regret it, deputy." Turning to his partner, he said, "Let's go. Time to report in."

Baron Manfred von Schlenker stood on the battlements of a castle that had once hosted Hannibal on his trek across the Alps. For four and a half centuries, the castle had been the main western protection for the town, and later city for Zurich. Now, the many-times modified bastion guarded only one man's wealth and position in the rarefied world of sociopolitical, jet-setting movers and shakers.

The baron leaned against a crenellation that had once protected the castle's archers from invaders below and now graced the three-by-five postcards in the gift shop open on the first floor from nine to five, five days a week. Deplorable as that was, the baron decided long ago that if tourists were going to show up on his property anyway, he might as well make something out of the situation. Now the grounds were littered with signs directing tourists to the tours, (three daily at nine, noon, and three), dungeons (mostly fake), and the gift shop (filled entirely with cheap souvenirs).

Easily accessible from only one side, the castle looked down on the intersection of two valleys. The other three sides provided, he believed, the most spectacular views of the Alps and Alpine valleys in all of Switzerland. It also provided a view of the land he'd "rented" to the Terran Alliance.

Gazing down at the complex in the heavily forested valley below, he replayed the day's events in his mind. Seemingly unaware of the lengthening shadows that swallowed first the lowest depths of the valley below and then the upper reaches of the hills, he didn't move until the sun turned the snow-capped peaks carmine with its final rays.

The old man groaned as he stood erect, feeling every one of his seventy-two years. Every year the Alpine cold seemed to settle deeper into his bones, and this August night promised more of the same. He slowly moved back into the recesses of the castle and down to the library, mercifully warmed by the modern heating system situated on the other side of the wall and hidden in the labyrinthine bowels of a false dungeon. The disparity often amused the old man but never more so than on that night.

Labeled as a hopeless progressive by even his closest friends, he enjoyed the anachronistic picture he presented to the world by residing in the family castle while capitalizing on its image. The heating system was just one of the innovations he'd introduced. Modern lighting and electricity-generating systems, as well as shortwave radios to keep in touch with the world in the event of necessity, alarms, and intercoms were either well hidden or displayed surreptitiously, as was the fluorescent lighting.

Tonight, he smiled slightly as his mind calculated possible futures and poured a brandy for himself and another for the woman sitting in front of the fire. "Margit, love, I feel my time upon me," he said as he slowly settled into his favorite chair.

"Hush, husband. You're not ready for the midden yet. You have many years yet to irritate me."

"I don't mean tonight, woman, but don't be surprised if it should happen. I saw the count today."

Long thought to be haunted, the castle had a reputation for being home to Count Ludwig von Strassenweg, hung by the troops of Hannibal on their march. Refusing the immense army passage across his lands, the troops simply wrapped a chain around his neck and lowered him over the walls for all to see. Not surprisingly, they had no trouble gaining passage across lands not their own for quite some time after that. Now, his spirit wandered the halls and was seen by one person or another from time to time. Local folklore had it that if one were to see the count three times, their death was upon them. This sighting was the baron's second encounter with the shade.

Used to her husband's moods, Margit sat quietly, waiting for Manfred to speak what was on his mind. The brandy would loosen his tongue in time.

Setting the snifter down on the table between the two chairs, the baron picked up a small round disk that lay next to his humidor of Cuban cigars.

Machined to an exact circle with a dime-sized button on top, the burnished metal of the disk shone faintly in the firelight. The baron turned the device over in his hands and said, "The Security Council found in favor of the Alliance today."

When he didn't go on, Margit resorted to prompting. "And..."

"They have drafted a resolution declaring the Terran Alliance to be an 'independent power' and referred the matter on to the World Court, saying that the matter is now one of acceptance by each individual government. They also said that the Alliance has shown 'admirable restraint' in the wake of the incident at Camp David. In the matter of whether Simon Hawke is alive or not, an inquiry has been sent to the U.S. State Department requesting any and all information in the matter. I believe that's the first time in history that such a body has made a demand of this nature of the United States concerning one of their own citizens. I look forward to seeing their reaction since they've so often done the same to others. The Chinese, in particular, will have a field day with this."

The grey-haired woman took a sip from the snifter she'd been warming between her hands, first inhaling the aroma deep into her lungs, then exhaling completely before allowing the burgundy liquid to pass her lips. After this little steadying ceremony, she asked, "And this affects us how?"

"Both the Japanese government and our own have formally notified the Alliance of their intentions to allow embassies on their soil. Note the word 'embassies.' Ours has agreed to my suggestion to rent part of our property to them. Restrictions will be imposed on the number of travelers at any one time, and they'll have to have appropriate lodging and such things as that. Details only. Things for politicians to wrangle over. All in all, though, it's what the Americans would call a 'done deal.'"

"And how is it that you're in possession of all this information at such an early date in the proceedings, husband?"

"Why, you have the honor of being in the presence of the official spokesman for the Terran Alliance, a position I took after the last visit from the delightful Captain Grimes." The baron smiled at his wife. "You know how I like to be at the center of things, which is why I say that I feel that my time is coming on. I've long believed that the future holds more good than ill, and for most of my life, I've been able to envision that future. Now, though, a future I never imagined has landed in our laps with considerable force, and I can no longer see what's ahead. Too large a leap, now, for me to envision." A wry smile passed over his face. "And I will never know the fullness of what help I create. Do you see where my thoughts wander, love? And why I say my time is coming?"

"I do, my love. And I tell you now that you may not see the fullness, but you'll surely help an infant through its first growing pains and be the happier for it when you see the count for the third time."

"Indeed," the old man said. "Indeed."

"I *do* hope Captain Grimes has the strength for what lies ahead of her." Margit looked at her husband. "Have you warned her about the future?"

"Of course not," the baron said, snorting. "Sometimes the best way to shape events is to do nothing. Do you think the girl would go ahead with this idea of a 'Terran Alliance' if she knew the trouble that lies ahead? I think not. I think she'd hesitate, as would almost every person on the planet. Which is where one of the biggest mistakes lies. But she has one thing in common with all those people—she'll try her damnedest to bear up under the burden once it's been shouldered. The human spirit at its best, my dear. The willingness to carry forward with all of one's strength as long as there's a worthwhile goal in sight."

The companionable silence of almost fifty years of marriage settled on the darkening library, and the warm glow from the fireplace finally gave way to errant embers chasing themselves among the cooling ashes.

"Why do you not tell them tonight, Manfred? Surely Captain Grimes is anxious to find out the results."

"Tomorrow is soon enough. Let's enjoy the knowledge that our actions have helped change the destiny of a world. Tonight is the last night of an era. Gloat, my dear. Even Hannibal didn't have the effect on the world that we'll have. We won't even get a footnote in the history books, but we'll know, and that's enough, I think."

CHAPTER TEN

Still stunned by the sight that had awaited her when she beamed into the hotel in Zurich, Lucy paced the length of her office while she waited for the baron to arrive. The sheer volume of people camped outside the hotel entrance was overwhelming, though not as many as had been at the airport. There wasn't enough room in the streets for that, but the police had retreated into the lobby of the ancient stone structure, managing to keep out all but the most persistent reporters. Those few who were resourceful enough to get past the first line of defense were carted off to jail. The Commissioner of Police had said that since the jail wasn't big enough to hold all the influx, only the worst were being held, more as a deterrent to others than any real hope of stemming the tide of humanity that had descended on his town.

Even through the double-paned glass and stone walls, Lucy heard the murmur of the crowd as they hoped to get a glimpse of... anything.

"Don't go out on the balcony," Commander Pike warned. "Even if you had anything to say to them, you'd never be heard over the noise."

Lucy stared down at the sight. Interspersed throughout the crowd were dozens of camera crews—some filming the building, some the crowd, and some just waiting. Also visible were signs and banners both accepting and condemning the Alliance.

"Welcome to Earth," read one sign, ignoring the fact that the Alliance personnel were *from* Earth. "Return from whence you came," was another, ignoring the same fact.

Heart pounding and face drained of blood, Lucy flopped into a chair. "What have I gotten myself into? I can't face all those people!"

Lloyd Pike peeked around a curtain edge. "You don't *have* to face all those people, Captain. That's what you have staff for. And even we don't have to face all of them. Some reporters will be satisfied to get a statement from anyone in uniform. We'll set up a press conference for them. The rest will be refused admittance. Most of those will shake out into a few categories—volunteer candidates, glad-handers, and denouncers. We'll have the embassy handle those, but we do need to find people to fill those positions. The embassies will operate as public relations, as well as screening out most of the troublemakers. And we can hand out daily press releases to anyone -interested."

Lucy had only a few minutes for reflection before Commander Kimura stuck her head into the room. "Captain, the baron and baroness have arrived and are on the way up."

The announcement eased some of the tension in Lucy's neck and shoulders. "Show them right in, please." Shock after shock to a person's system could cause premature aging, and Lucy felt like she was a hundred years old as she hauled herself up out of her chair. "Diana, bring another setting for the baroness, please," she said and busied herself moving a few items around on her desk until she heard the outer door open.

A murmur of voices preceded the trio into the

room. "Simon will be pleased, baron," Lucy said, smiling broadly. "I truly think he will. Please sit down. Coffee?" When both guests nodded their assent, she motioned for Diana to serve.

Thirteen days had passed since the "Debacle at Camp David," as the news was now calling it. And the fact that so many had died was still causing Lucy grief—the four from the Alliance, three if Simon really was alive, and the dozens from the U.S. military, not to mention the civilian representatives of various nations on hand to meet Simon. And of course, the vice-president. And yet, almost all the things Simon and Kitty had worked for were coming to pass. It was the speed that was dizzying.

These thoughts chased the smile from her face, and the baroness noticed. "What causes you such discomfort, Lady Lucille? You've won much this day, I think."

Lucy looked down into her coffee and swirled the liquid around. "It's the cost, Your Grace. So many died when it wasn't necessary."

"Who says it wasn't necessary, Captain?" The older woman leaned forward and carefully placed the coffee cup on the table between them. "I'm not trying to belittle any of the people who died on either side that day, Captain. Each person was important to someone. But at times like these it sometimes takes a... galvanizing action to get Joe Common off his couch and away from his comforts. Manfred and I have seen two such events in the recent past. First was the ship being found, and the second was that most unfortunate event at Camp David. Both of those events are tied directly to you, Captain, and unfortunately, that makes you a focus. Now, things are going to start happening around you."

"I hope you mean the Terran Alliance when you say 'you,' Your Grace," Lucy protested. "Because when Simon comes back aboard..."

"Stop right there!" The baroness seemed to puff up to twice her not inconsiderable size. "First, we will dispense with the 'Your Grace' nonsense. You call my husband Freddie, and you can call me Maggie. And I'll call you Lucy, in informal settings of course."

"Second," interrupted the baron, "is the fact that it was *you* who spoke to the ambassadors from several nations in my library just four days ago. And it was *you* who stood before a special session of the United Nations Security Council just two days before that. *Your* face is the one being shown on television and magazines."

"Magazines!" The blood drained from Lucy's face for the second time in one morning. Had she not already been sitting, she would have fallen down. "What magazines?" The same feeling settled into the pit of her stomach that had been there the day she'd learned of the loss of Simon and Kitty, and the fact that she recognized the feeling as fear didn't help.

The baron handed her two publications, and her face leapt out at her from the glossy cover of Time. Obviously a still taken from one of her transmissions, it was undeniably her. The other was a different matter entirely. She stared in horror at the cover of a supermarket tabloid, seeing herself in front of a fanciful spaceship with a headline that read, "Space Aliens Arrive to Eat Your Young!"

"The world now perceives you as the head of this organization, Lucy," the baron said gently, "for good or ill. I remember the pictures of Simon getting off that shuttle, shown so many times. Mostly, though, for me, and I'm sure most of humanity, his face—his persona if you will—has been overshadowed by the carnage that followed. I'm afraid he'll become associated with those images, and he'll forever be scarred by the stigma of being 'that poor guy,' or some such equally unflattering thought.

"You, on the other hand," he continued, "have appeared as the voice of reason, not to mention having renewed promises to the world about the dispensation of your technology. Did you know that the food processors that were first shown and then given away have become indispensable in most third-world countries already? Any place there's a natural disaster, the processors arrive and fresh food and water appear as if by magic, thanks to the largess of the Terran Alliance. Whether you know it or not, you've already saved many more lives than were lost at Camp David, and one day the world *will* remember. I'm afraid that, to all intents and purposes, *you* are the head of your Alliance, Lucy, with all the good and ill that goes with it."

Lucy's mouth moved but no sound came out. Commander Kimura managed to look unimpressed. Lieutenant Ross and the baron grinned as the turn of events made itself clear to Lucy.

The baroness looked concerned. "Are you going to be all right, my dear?"

Lucy finally got enough air into her lungs to spare for talking. "I... I think so. This can't be real. What will Simon think? Freddie, Your Gr... Maggie, I'm sorry, but I need to think... I think." Her voice trailed off. "Commander, uh, Kimura will see that you get home. If you'll forgive me?"

Before leaving, the baron placed the two magazines on Lucy's desk, and she quickly forgot about them as her mind turned over the possible futures. Behind her, Lieutenant Ross's face was split by a grin that, fortunately, Lucy never saw.

Director Stanton heard the frustration in his agent's voice.

"Sir, we can't keep this quiet forever. Too many people already know, and it *will* leak, sooner rather than later. We need to get these two back to a secure location."

Ever mindful of his own years as a field operative, Richard Stanton chose his words with care. "I appreciate the input from someone on the scene, Agent Wilson, but we've come under a certain amount of... pressure here. Somehow, the State Department has become aware of your packages, one in particular. It's imperative that they be delivered without undue attention. Therefore, you will keep them under wraps until further notice. Is that clear?"

"Yes, sir," The answer was squeezed out from between thinned lips as Agent Wilson's white-knuckled hand threatened to crush the handset.

"You have the resources of an entire ALERT team at your disposal, Agent. Use them. Find a safe house if you think that's what's necessary. All you need to do is stay low-profile for a few days. Get me a number and I'll call you as soon as I can."

"It's been two days!" Gayle yelled. "Don't we have

anything to go on?"

"Yes, we do, Gayle, so settle down a bit."

The four Firsters and the first group of about forty second-wavers had become the cadre around which all else was being built. As two members of that group, Gayle and Lucy had grown close over the past few years, close enough that Lucy recognized the frustration flowing out of the diminutive woman. Gayle finally quit pacing and sat down in a chair while Lucy perched on the arm of another opposite her distraught friend.

"I told you we found out we have an 'in' with the Aurora PD—a young patrolman. Apparently, he's been to a couple of Brandt and Collier's meetings but didn't get recruited out of sheer bad luck. Or, in this case, good luck. He actually leaked the information to some of Brandt's people that the government had a high security prisoner they claimed was Simon *before* Dr. Jeffers did. But not by much."

Lucy got up and began walking in circles. "Now you've got me pacing, damn it!" Stopping in front of Gayle, she sat down on the edge of the coffee table. "They just moved faster than we did. We're new at this, Gayle, so they have the advantage. But they have to come out sometime. Brandt says his guy inside the station claims they're going to fly 'em out in the next few days. We need to watch the airport. Collier can get people in there to keep watch on all the private and leased aircraft. Do you want in?"

"Want in? Hell, yes, I want in. I've got to do something to help." The little blonde's smile was strained as she gestured expansively. "I find it ironic that we have all this shit and none of it will do us any good."

"Oh, ye of little faith!" Lucy said with a feral grin. She walked around behind Gayle and laid her left hand on Gayle's right shoulder. Waving her right hand dramatically, she said, "Imagine if you will, a clear August morning. A small private plane leaves a crowded airport and heads east over the Great Plains. About an hour into the flight..."

Three years of building contacts allowed Tim Brandt to be at the Denver International Airport the morning a black limousine stopped at the county jail and then headed in his direction. Luck allowed him to masquerade as the anonymous baggage handler who just happened to look over as two orange-jump-suited figures were hustled aboard a particular jet. Speaking quietly into a two-way radio, he reported to Gayle, who called Lucy aboard the *Galileo*. The result of that call almost wrecked the Lear jet as it neared the Mississippi River.

Lucy had been waiting for Brandt's call. She'd put everything else into the hands of her staff and worked solely on the preparations for the rescue mission, and she'd nearly gone crazy in the interim. Everything hinged on Brandt's inside man being real, and too much was riding on it for Lucy to be comfortable. Tiger and Cheetah Flights were standing by. Hawke Flight, with a temporary addition to bring it up to full strength, was also on standby. Each flight was on an eight-hour rotation so no one crew would be too tired to fly the ultimate mission. The *Galileo's* command shuttle was also pressed into service, with three crews on rotation. The entire mission could have ships en route to Earth on a mere ten minutes' notice.

Lucy kept herself apprised of every aspect of the situation that she could. Keeping in touch with baron von Schlenker kept her up to speed on what was happening with the U.S. State Department. So far, nothing. No group or Agency claimed to know anything about Simon or Agent Daniels. Families of Alliance personnel were being released as quietly as they'd been rounded up. Her hurried trip downside assured her that her parents were fine, although a full explanation, as well as effusive apologies, were required before she was allowed to leave the house.

August 13th dawned clear and crisp over Denver as a three-vehicle convoy rolled through the airport gates and into a restricted area that led directly up to a plane set apart from the others on the tarmac.

"Status?" Agent Wilson demanded after he stretched his six-foot-four frame back into shape after the ride.

"Fuel tanks are topped off, flight plan filed, all systems green, sir. We're ready to move," the pilot responded.

"No signs of anything out of the ordinary," the head of the ALERT team's security detachment said. "No one has been near this plane since we set down except us and the refueling truck, and the plane was buttoned up at the time. We've just finished a sweep for bugs or intruders. Negative on both counts."

"Very good, Agent Davis. Transfer the prisoners immediately." To the pilot he said, "Start her up and notify the tower. I want us wheels up within the half hour, understand? If they give you any trouble about cutting the line, just invoke national security. If they still give you trouble, call me."

Agent Wilson didn't need to be called. He sat in the passenger compartment and stared at his prisoners as he slammed back his third cup of coffee. Daniels, still dressed in the orange jumpsuit provided by the Aurora PD, elected not to notice as Wilson moved around the cabin. Simon, dressed similarly, followed suit.

The modified Lear jet flew east at a respectable percentage of the speed of sound. Federal black-budget appropriations had provided Agent Wilson and his ALERT team with the funds to revamp the craft after it had been confiscated in a drug sting. Engines built to military specifications, allowed the refurbished jet to take off or land at the smallest airports. They also allowed a higher cruising speed, of which the pilot was taking full advantage.

About six hundred miles into the flight, the pilot, a veteran of the 1980s Latin American drug wars, sat bolt-upright as the speeding jet was slammed by a gigantic fist. Being seated at the front of the aircraft was the only thing that allowed him to get any kind of assessment of his predicament. From the corner of his eye, he'd seen... something pass his windows, headed east at a speed that was quite literally impossible for any type of craft he was familiar with.

"Unidentified aircraft! You are interfering with official United States business! Veer off! I say, veer off!"

The order to veer off was totally unnecessary as the vessel had disappeared into the distance. Still, he had to say something. "St. Louis Control, this is Flight seven-one-seven out of Denver. I wish to report a craft headed east after passing my position.

Approximate speed..."

Agent Wilson landed in the co-pilot's seat, making violent slashing motions across his throat. When the pilot let go of the transmit button, Wilson said, "You will call no more attention to this flight. Is that clear? Say whatever you have to, but get those people off the air. Now!"

"Uh, St. Louis Control, this is Flight seven-one-seven. The object headed east appears to have been a meteor. Sorry, guys," the pilot finished lamely.

"Just as well, seven-one-seven, we have nothing showing on our screens here." Enduring the good-natured ribbing that inevitably followed, the pilot glowered at Agent Wilson.

"I don't care how pissed you are. This mission stays..."

The pilot suddenly rolled the ship to starboard and dove for the ground. "Anyone not strapped in better get that way fast! We've got company!"

"What the fuck are you talking about?" Wilson screamed. "What company?"

The pilot, all blood drained from his face, stared out the front of the cockpit and asked, "How can it do that?"

Wilson's eyes followed the pilot's, and his mind seemed to freeze. After a few seconds that felt like an eternity, he looked down at the instrument panel. The pilot noticed and said, "Six hundred and fifty miles an hour. And *he's* doing it backwards!"

Lucy strode into the *Galileo's* Flight Control and tersely demanded, "Update?"

Andrew Belkin, Chief of Flight Services and de

facto head of all flight operations, answered, "We just got word of their takeoff, ma'am. Since we had no way to tell until they were airborne, we were waiting to see which planes went where. My bet was on the fastest eastbound craft headed on the most direct route to the Washington area. I won the pool when this one," he said, pointing at an eastbound blip, "transmitted a message ending with Wilson's name."

Alerted to her own brusqueness by Chief Belkin's tone of voice, Lucy softened her approach. "Sorry, Chief. Just on edge, I guess. Good work."

The chief said, "That's your pigeon, Captain." He pointed at a blip headed east appreciably faster than some of the others headed the same way. "Has to be. Larger engines. Probably military grade. Just gotta get there, ASAP."

Lucy's heart was in her throat. What if they were wrong? She stared at the offending light as it mocked her. "Captain? Your orders?"

Lucy's thoughts went to the pilots sitting in their crafts, waiting to launch. "Chief," she said in resignation, "if you're wrong, I'll be in *such* deep shit..." Taking a deep breath, she said, "Begin the operation, Chief. You have control."

Instantly, the ex-traffic controller said, "Tiger Flight, Cheetah Flight, Hawke Flight, launch, launch, launch. Recon One, launch, launch, launch." Lucy shivered as possible outcomes ran through her head.

The five pilots of Tiger Flight had lost the toss and would stay in reserve, along with Hawke Flight, while Cheetah Flight would take the brunt of any response that might be mounted against the rescue mission. Recon One was the *Galileo's* command shuttle and would be overseeing the operation, as well as handling the transfer of Simon and Daniels. Jamming all local radio signals would be part of Recon One's responsibility as well. Since the Mambas' communications system operated on another level of the radiated spectrum, their signals wouldn't be affected.

The five pilots of Cheetah Flight, like their counterparts in Tiger, were veterans of the battle in the asteroid belt. The destruction of the alien ship not long after Orion Base had gone online had provided them with the mystique of "combat experience," so Captain Chapman offered their services to the mission.

Cheetah Flight, winners of the coin toss, climbed into their ships and, in concert with Recon One, launched from the projects deck where they'd been waiting. Tiger Flight, designated as blockers and backup, launched immediately afterward and formed on the rest of the ships.

Marsha Kane sat at the comm console of Recon One. "Okay, people, you've studied the satellite maps, and all the data has been loaded into your onboard computers. Tiger Flight, move out. One and Two, you are east and west traffic-blockers respectively. Three, Four and Five, you are assigned to aerial interdiction of any traffic not designated as 'target.'"

The pilot managed to stabilize his craft about two thousand feet lower than it had started out. The complaints were just starting to come in from the rear of the plane, as well as frantic inquiries from St. Louis ground control.

Shutting off the distractions of ground control was

but the flick of a switch. Silencing the distractions from the rear took little more. "Quiet down! Strap in and shut up!" Shutting off the intercom, he turned to the ashen-faced agent. "You fill me in on what I'm facing up here, and you'll do it now, Wilson! I swear, I'll put this bird on the ground so fast it'll make your head spin. Literally!"

"That's 'Agent' Wilson to you, and everything is on a need-to-know basis."

"Look," the pilot said in exasperation, "I've got a pretty good idea that thing was one of those Mambas." At the agent's expression, the pilot laughed. "Don't even go there! I watch television, *Wilson*, and this plane is headed down. Now. No way I can out-fly one of those. Son of a bitch!"

Although just as abrupt, this dive was more or less controlled from the start and smoothed out quicker than the last. "Well, now we know they can *hover* at ten thousand feet! Or should I just forget that?"

"We've known since Camp David that they can hover," Wilson said sheepishly. "We just didn't extrapolate it to this altitude."

Marsha ordered Recon One to take position behind their target and assigned three of Cheetah Flight to take position to either side and above the eastbound jet so they could be seen by the occupants. "Agent Wilson, this is Captain Kane of the Terran Alliance. You are ordered to land your craft immediately. There has been a seven-mile section of Interstate 70 interdicted for this purpose just east of Kingdom City, Missouri. The only way to make the landing is to begin immediately. If you do not reduce speed and begin your descent voluntarily, we will force you down. Safer all the way around if you just follow instruction."

The remaining two ships of Cheetah Flight ranged ahead of the jet, positioned to block any anticipated move to escape. Hovering in the jet's path had worked twice so far, and Marsha decided to keep with the moves that worked. When her comm tech reported that Agent Wilson was trying to radio for help, she smiled. "Agent Wilson, you are not able to transmit more than five feet beyond the outer skin of your craft, except to me, so save your breath and put that plane on the deck. Now!"

The pilot of the portside Mamba reported that he'd made eye contact with the pilot and seen several faces staring out the windows in the passenger compartment. The pilot on the starboard side reported much the same.

"Agent Wilson, we have you surrounded." *Oh, God, how trite can I be?* Marsha thought. "Last chance to comply willingly."

She released the breath she didn't know she'd been holding when the plane abruptly slowed. "Uh, Captain Kane, this is the pilot requesting more specific instructions for landing."

"You've been flying east following Interstate 70 for some time now. There has been a seven-mile stretch of highway cleared for your landing. All air and ground traffic will be interdicted. I have two flights of Mambas with me, plus the full resources of a command shuttle. It may not mean much to you, but Agent Wilson can tell you that there was only one flight at Camp David, and look how one-sided that turned out to be. If you don't begin your descent now, you will find yourself faced with more obstacles. Do I make myself clear?"

"Clear as a bell, Captain. Beginning descent now."

"Agent Wilson, I know you're still listening. No tricks and you and your people will all walk away from this. All we want are our people—Simon Hawke and Agent Roland Daniels."

"Agent Daniels belongs to us," Wilson said, "and he goes back with us. There is no debate on the subject."

"You're right about that, Agent Wilson, there will be no debate," Marsha returned, guessing at the owner of the new voice. "We are responsible for Agent Daniels' safety since he was assigned to us as special liaison by the president, who, I might add, is your superior. We will see to his safety and his return to the FBI. I suggest that since you're outgunned and outmaneuvered, you should back off."

Marsha watched as the jet began a steep descent, veering slightly to line up with the ribbon of asphalt that was Interstate 70. "Tiger Flight, heads up. Target has just gone below radar screen. Expect company," she said, switching tactical frequencies. "Pilot, you'll see a line of vehicles stopped on the Interstate by one of my Mambas. Touch down just past that point."

"Roger, Captain."

"Mission Leader, this is Cheetah Three. There seems to be a serious disagreement going on in the cockpit."

"Put the gun away, Wilson," Agent Davis said wearily. "You know as well as I do that I'm the only pilot aboard. Shooting me will deny them their people, true, but it'll kill you, too. Kinda like cutting off your nose to spite your face, don't you think?"

Agent Wilson reluctantly put his weapon away and keyed the microphone in his headset. "Okay, Kane, you get what you want. We're landing. I need assurances that my people won't be hurt." Marsha heard the fury in Agent Wilson's voice as the plane floated over the Mamba that was blocking the eastbound lanes and watched in satisfaction as the landing gear locked into place.

"You have the assurance of an officer in the Terran Alliance. What more do you need?"

"This craft is on U.S. Government business, Kane. You realize that you can and will be charged with air piracy? You're in violation of dozens of FAA rules and regulations. You're in violation of United States laws governing overflights by non-American craft, and you're dangerously close to being charged with terrorism. Desist immediately and I'll forget any of this happened."

Marsha considered for a moment, then answered, "As far as rules and regulations of the Federal Aviation Administration are concerned... I really don't care. As far as United States laws concerning overflights... I don't care. And I don't for one minute believe that you'll forget any of this for any reason, Agent Wilson. But you do have a point about piracy and terrorism, which may not be all that valid when all we're doing is retrieving our... property. Maybe we should discuss the laws concerning the illegal detention of citizens of the United States and their lack of legal representation. Then again, maybe not. I'm a lot more direct than that, Agent Wilson. I leave those things to the people trained to handle them. Of course, doing so would bring your operation to light, and you don't want that, do you?" Marsha asked without inflection. She continued more briskly, "Enough talk. I've already demonstrated that I can force you down. Give up, Agent Wilson. You're faced with superior firepower and superior numbers. No one will fault you for saving your people, if not your mission."

The jet's wheels touched the pavement, and the vehicle slowed to a halt in the middle of the flat Missouri plains where no aircraft had a right to be. The three Mambas hovered at cockpit level while the shuttle landed on the highway facing the nose of the plane.

Marsha began juggling various radio calls as the confrontation progressed. As she was about to ask for a report from Tiger Flight, she heard, "Mission Leader, this is Tiger One. On station blocking eastbound traffic. Tiger Two reports on station blocking westbound traffic. I'm facing some very amazed and upset individuals here. Three, Four and Five report on station as aerial cover. No inbound traffic on radar."

"Affirmative, Tiger One. Hold position until further notice. Mission Leader out." Switching frequencies again, she called, "Cheetah One and Two, you are released from blocker duty. Assist Tiger Flight in air and ground interdiction. Mission Leader out."

Switching frequencies yet again, she called the downed jet. "Agent Wilson."

"What?" came the surly response.

"Don't take it so hard, Agent Wilson. You did your job quite well considering your circumstances and opposition. Now break loose with my people."

While waiting for a response from the jet, Marsha smiled at the situation. There sat a sleek, gleaming jet that relied on its streamlining as much as its engines to get speed but was relegated to operations within the atmosphere, and it faced a squat, ugly shuttle that relied solely on the force of its power-plant for speed and was more at home outside the atmosphere than inside.

After several minutes had passed with no visible response from the jet, Marsha said, "We've got the firepower, but time is actually on their side. It's time to push some buttons."

She put on a headset and tied herself into the comm net through the console she'd been monitoring and told the navigator to keep her informed if he picked anything up on the radar. "It won't be long, guaranteed, before we have company. When that beauty went off the radar screens, you can bet that alarms went off all over the place."

Marsha strode to the back of the cargo compartment, marveling at the versatility of the vessels. The first ones had been a cockpit and engine room and a whole lot of empty in between. This one had been specially modified with the primary mission of carrying passengers from ground to orbit and back. It was more like a troop shuttle at the moment, she thought as she looked at the armed men grouped near the hatches, waiting for orders.

When news of the impending rescue mission had become public knowledge among Alliance personnel, the number of volunteers had been staggering, coming as it did from four active warships and the *Galileo*. Marsha had expected to see a trickle of people show up, but so many had that she'd had her pick of seasoned, combat-capable personnel, and she'd used some of them to turn the extras away. And since it had been determined that there'd be a ground force of only ten men, there was a lot of excess.

One of the things that had struck Marsha as curious was the large number of second- and third-generation volunteers there were. After just over four years, the *Galileo's* first crew, some nine hundred plus, were scattered among four vessels and three space docks, with the remainder being new members. The disparity in numbers shouldn't have come as a surprise, but it did anyway.

After as short a time as four years, patterns had begun to emerge—habits, customs. Finding things to call "traditions" became a way to tie everyone together, and Marsha was not unaware of the fact that the newer volunteers looked upon anyone from the "First Crew" with something akin to hero worship. Older crew spoke to newer about Firsters almost with awe, and it eventually got back to those being gossiped about, which fact Marsha wasn't above using at a time like this. Uncomfortable as it made her, she'd used her status as a Firster to call in volunteers for this mission.

She stood amongst the results of her choosing, all seconds and thirds, and cringed inside as thoughts of pep rallies not so far past filled her head. "Okay, people, this is above and beyond. I want you all to know I appreciate it," she said. "You all have your instructions. Following orders is what this is all about at the moment, but I trust each of you to use your own discretion as the situation warrants, or you wouldn't be here. Just be ready to back up your decision if you have to!"

Chief among those she'd chosen for this mission was one who caused her great concern—Bobby Lee Remmick. A onetime boyfriend and lover of Marsha's, and a three-year veteran of the Atlanta Police Department, Bobby had been recruited in the second wave. Marsha had returned to her hometown at her uncle's insistence to reassure her mother that she was all right and to explain the situation in person. "You owe your mama that much," her uncle had said.

How he'd found out she was home, Bobby Lee never said, but he arrived on her front porch in time to hear most of her explanation to her mom through an open window before he pounded on the door.

"Remember Collin Harper," he said after the shock of seeing him had worn off.

"None of these people are crazy, Bobby Lee. None of 'em are obsessed with me, and where would they kidnap me *to*, out there?" she retorted, her mind ranging back seven years to her senior year in high school when she was kidnapped by a deranged classmate on the night of her prom. Bobby Lee had been instrumental in the search that finally freed her from the nightmare. "But if you want to sign on, I won't tell you not to," she said, placing a hand on his chest.

Those three years in the Atlanta PD had earned Bobby Lee his position as head of the ground forces that would be deployed against the jet after it landed.

"But I was just a beat cop!" he'd protested.

"Which is more than any other volunteer we have at the moment," Marsha had said with finality. "Besides, I'd like someone I know and trust working with me on this."

Shaking herself free of her reverie, she said formally, "Deploy your forces, Commander Remmick," as she opened the hatches and watched them form the now-familiar ramps on each side of the shuttle. "Last time was a place of *their* choosing. This time it's ours. Then, they were in a superior position, they thought, and had surprise on their side. This time, they have no backup and we hold the high ground, so to speak. I'm not saying this will go like clockwork, but what plan ever does? Truth is, we don't know what's inside that plane, and it's time we found out."

Lt. Commander Bobby Lee Remmick saluted and said, "Deploy troops, aye, ma'am," the smile on his face not detracting from the seriousness of his voice. "A team out the port side, B team out the starboard side. If it moves, just pin it down unless it starts shooting. Don't forget, you have three Mambas for aerial support. Teamwork, people, teamwork. Keep to your assigned frequencies and no idle chatter! Move out."

Once both teams had reported back that all was secure, Bobby Lee led Marsha out onto the highway where she could see the jet's cockpit. Marsha thought it the height of overkill to have ten Mambas and twelve laser-armed people on hand to accomplish this mission, but it had been mandated by the captain.

Going with the orders she'd been given as Mission Leader, she used what she had. "Five minutes on the ground, people," she said on her all-frequency band. "Look around you, Agent Wilson," she said, switching back to the jet's frequency and overhearing the end of a transmission.

"…ayday, Mayday. This is U.S. Government flight seven-one-seven out of Denver International Airport.

We have been forced down on Interstate 70 just west of St. Louis by an overwhelming force of Terran Alliance craft. Immediate assistance required."

Smiling, Marsha said, "Remember, Agent Wilson, I'm the only one who can hear you. Now. We have things to discuss. Are you going to come out and play?"

"I'm not saying I have what you want, but if I did and gave it to you, what assurances do I have that nothing happens to my people?"

"As I said before, the assurances of an officer of the Terran Alliance, assuming that none of your people try anything stupid. Beyond that, you have no assurances at all, Agent Wilson," Marsha said sweetly. "No more assurances than we had at Camp David. Trust has to begin somewhere. We gave ours at Camp David, and I think it's your turn. Now, here's the best deal you're going to get all day—you turn Captain Hawke and Special Liaison Daniels over to us, and you and your people will walk away from here with all the information you've already acquired. Don't do as I ask, and I'll be forced to start carving parts off that government property parked in front of my shuttle." Marsha heard a beep in her headset calling for her attention. "You've got three minutes to think it over, Agent."

Glancing down at the comm panel strapped to her waist, Marsha pressed a button. *We're going to have to do something to make this more convenient. Maybe something with the circuitry built into the shirt, comm panel on the sleeve?*

"Mission Leader," she said.

"Ma'am this is Blocker West. I have a Highway Patrol officer here, lights flashing. He has a bullhorn, and he's ordering me to leave."

"Just don't let him past your position, Blocker West. Take out the car if you have to, but do not under any circumstances cause harm to anyone. We'll have this wrapped up soon. Mission Leader, out."

Turning back to the jet, Marsha said, "Agent Wilson, this is Captain Kane. You know, a girl's reputation rests on how well she keeps her word. Please don't make me start slicing parts off your pretty little airplane."

Marsha's innate sense of politeness made her wait a whole ten seconds before she began to carry out her threat. She drew the pistol strapped to her thigh, and said, "The first thing I'm going to do is destroy your cockpit's airtight integrity. I suggest that you clear your people out of there."

Having great power thrust upon one can be a heady thing, even when they're expecting it to happen. Even though Marsha had commanded a starship for over two years, the experience of having control over the lives of people who had not freely given themselves into Alliance service was new to her. The fact that she perceived this particular bunch to be adversaries made the feeling all the sweeter since she knew the capabilities of her team to be vastly superior to those ranged against her at the moment.

Commanding weapons that had only been dreamed of in science-fiction and ships that until then would have been reported as UFOs, Marsha laughed at the absurdity of it all, breaking the spell that had been stealing over her. She lowered her weapon back to her side. "I'll tell ya what, Agent Wilson," she said playfully. "You're getting one final chance before I start taking your plane apart around you. I swear, I'll peel it like a banana."

As she raised her arm again, a face appeared at the pilot's windshield. "Hold on! Hold on! One of your people is in need of medical attention *not* caused by us. We have an emergency escape chute at the back of the plane. With him injured, that's the safest way off at the moment. Is that agreeable?"

"All the way up to the point where you think you can get away with pulling a fast one, Agent Wilson. Go ahead and deploy the chute." She hadn't realized how high her tension level was until the rear hatch popped open a crack and she jumped about three inches straight up.

When her nervous system recovered from the adrenaline jolt, she realized that Bobby Lee was standing beside her, muttering into his headset. She pressed a button on her comm panel and listened as he gave instructions to his two teams. She felt his hand on her arm as he pulled her back and to one side.

As she started to protest, he said, "From here on, you're out of the line of fire from that hatch." She watched as the two teams moved into positions, covering all possible exits from the plane, pistols constantly moving back and forth. Two members of A team stood ready to catch anyone coming down the still undeployed chute, weapons holstered.

"Let's just add a little intimidation to the mix, shall we?" Marsha muttered to herself. She ordered Cheetah One and Two to hover at hatch level and report on what they could see inside the plane once the hatch was fully opened. She had chosen Cheetah Flight for the express reason that each member knew both Simon and Daniels by sight, thereby staving off the possibility that Wilson would get away with trying to pull a fast one on them.

Neither pilot reported anything untoward from their admittedly limited vantage points, and when nothing else happened, she called Wilson. "Having a change of heart in there, Agent?"

"I just don't want my people killed for no good reason."

"No more than I do mine, Agent. Which of my people is uninjured?"

"That would be Agent Daniels."

"Well, let me make a suggestion. How about you have him open that rear hatch the rest of the way, and quickly? He knows us and knows we won't hurt him. Let him lower Captain Hawke down the chute and then slide down himself. We go away; you go away. We get our people, you get all that information we mentioned earlier. Time's almost up." Twenty seconds went by, and just as she reached for her comm panel, Agent Wilson's voice grated in her ear.

"Okay, you've got a deal." Marsha felt a bit irritated at the fact that even though she'd unfailingly used his title, he hadn't had the courtesy to return the favor even once.

"Two minutes and they'll be coming out, Kane."

Bobby Lee had been listening from his own headset and began issuing orders to his teams. Her position, which had been dictated by Bobby Lee, may have restricted her vision of the interior of the plane, but she was able to see the hatch swing fully open and heard at the same time, "Mission Leader, Cheetah One. Confirm Agent Daniels aboard." Immediately afterward, the blazing yellow emergency chute cascaded away from the body of the plane and hit the ground with a resounding smack.

Glancing at her watch, Marsha said, "Nine minutes and counting, people."

Bobby Lee followed that with, "Heads up A team and B team. Things get tight from here. I don't want the wrong people shot."

"Tick, tick, tick, Agent Wilson. I don't pilot conventional aircraft. What's that little thingee sticking off the wing there?" Marsha asked. When a pale and worried face appeared at the windshield, she pointed at a small protuberance on one wing.

After a five-second pause, Agent Davis said, "that's the airspeed indicator."

"Will the plane fly without it?"

"Yes, but landing becomes harder when I don't know my airspeed," the pilot answered. "Why?"

Marsha calmly pulled her pistol back out of the holster and, taking careful aim, neatly sliced the indicated piece off the wing. "Your time is up, Agent Wilson. Get my people off that plane, now!"

"Mission Leader, Cheetah One. Confirm Simon! Repeat, confirm Simon! He is standing at the hatch. He appears to need the assistance of Agent Daniels to stand up."

"Very good, Agent Wilson. Now get them on the ground or I won't ask before I slice something else off your plane. And have the decency to look me in the eye when you talk to me!"

A total of ten minutes had passed. Simon and Daniels were at the hatch, and Agent Wilson glared out of the cockpit window at Marsha. "Don't worry, Agent Wilson. I'm not going to shoot you. But I don't want to deprive you of the pleasure of seeing what I do to your aircraft. That way you'll be able to give a full report on the capabilities of my *side arm*. More information for your bosses, right?"

"All right, I'm sending them down the chute now." The anger in his voice was mirrored by the venomous look he gave her.

She answered back, "Keep your microphone open. I want to hear the orders as they're issued."

She watched his head turn toward the back of the plane. "Okay, Simkin. Let 'em go." Turning back to Marsha he asked, "Are you satisfied?"

"I won't be *satisfied* until they're safely aboard my shuttle. But I'm getting there."

"Mission Leader, Cheetah Two. Daniels is helping Simon to sit down in the doorway of the plane. Looks like he's getting ready to slide!"

Simon, grinning broadly at the two Mambas in front of him, half-turned to Daniels, reached up, got a handful of orange jumpsuit, and kicked out, sliding out of the hatch and down the chute while dragging Daniels along with him.

"Keep alert, people! Now's the time for something to happen!" Bobby Lee said into his headset. "Patterson, Jordan, get Simon out of the line of fire!" Two members of the A team moved forward to help untangle the knot of arms and legs that had landed at the bottom of the chute, and the four men moved into the questionable refuge of the jet's landing gear.

"I heard 'em just before they brought me to the door," Simon said by way of explanation. "The plan was for you to push me out, and they were set to grab you and button up. I think Wilson planned to try to take off. Can't guess what he'll try now."

Simon slumped against one of his rescuers just as Bobby Lee yelled, "Gun!" and fired his laser through the rear hatch, raining molten metal down on an agent squirming his way into firing position. With a yell, the man jerked back into the darkened interior of the plane.

Reacting to a noise behind him, Daniels grabbed the laser off the hip of the man in front of him and spun around on one knee, fell backwards, released the safety and fired in one motion. A nine-millimeter pistol and hand fell to the ground from an open belly hatch.

"Captain!" Bobby Lee yelled loud enough to be heard inside the open hatch. "Two attempts to ambush us! All bets are off! A team, B team, if it moves, shoot it!"

Daniels tapped the crewman he had relieved of his weapon on the shoulder. When the crewman turned to Daniels, he handed the man his pistol butt-first and said, "You provide cover. I'll take Simon's bad side. We should head for the shuttle."

The four men began to shuffle in the direction of the grounded shuttle.

Bobby Lee, seeing the progress of the four men under the jet, said, "Prepare to pull back as soon as Simon is aboard."

Marsha said into her headset, "You want to play rough, Wilson? I can play rough. We can chop that plane up as easily as your agent. Fortunately, a laser cauterizes as it cuts." Not sounding too concerned, she added, "Your agent should live."

Changing frequencies, Marsha said, "Thirteen minutes on the ground. All Mambas form up on the shuttle. Blockers break off and form up. We lift in two! Bobby Lee, Simon is on the ramp. Get your people aboard!"

Trying to listen to all frequencies at once proved impossible, so Marsha finally cut out all but Recon One and Bobby Lee. Hearing her navigator report incoming aircraft arriving in three minutes, she laughed nervously and replied, "Commander Graham, I want this ship ready to lift on a five-second notice."

"Been there since we grounded, ma'am. Give the word and we're airborne," came the reply.

Men began to run past her position on the ramp. "Loadmaster! What's our status?"

"We're at minus two, Captain," Chief Hargrove told his niece. "As soon as you and Commander Remmick get off that damn ramp, we can button up and move."

As Bobby Lee backed up the ramp, pistol trained on the cockpit of the jet, Marsha called, "Cheetah One, prepare to launch special weapon." Calling the jet, she said, "I told you that if you played nice, I'd let your people walk away from this. Well, you sure as hell didn't play fair, but I'm going to let you walk away anyway. But only that, *Wilson*." Leaving the perplexed agent in the circuit, she said, "Cheetah One, on my command you will fire on the jet."

Acknowledgment of orders and a shriek of protest hit her ears at the same instant. Bobby Lee backed across the threshold, and she hit the button that closed the ramps, calmly saying, "Fire."

To observers on the ground, the black apparition called a Mamba was seen to hover a moment longer than its companions, lazily turn away, point its nose at the sky and accelerate with heart-stopping suddenness. What those observers also saw was the jet begin to sparkle, apparently of its own accord. Then a series of electrical discharges began flowing down the length of the plane from nose to tail, until, after about thirty seconds, they faded into nothingness.

"Commander Graham, you are on notice!" She began a five-second countdown, with the ramps closing off the outside light on "three," sealing tight on "two," status lights turning green on "one," and the world seeming to back away from the viewport on "zero."

Marsha looked at the group of people surrounding Simon and hit her all-ships frequency. "Tiger and Cheetah Flights, thank you for your help, and my compliments to Captain Chapman. You are cleared to return to base." Two more calls to make. "Kane to Flight Operations. Mission accomplished. Recon One returning to base." One more call. "Commander Graham, the ship is yours. Please take us home."

Barely listening to the responses from her calls, she stood behind the two medics checking Simon over. *Out of the frying pan and into the fire!* she thought. Taking a deep breath, she placed a hand on the shoulder of the nearest medic. She caught the motion of the man looking up at the edge of her vision, but her attention was drawn to Simon, sitting so unnaturally still in the chair.

Clad in a blaze-orange jumpsuit, he was at least twenty pounds thinner and, obvious even to her, near the edge of exhaustion. His left wrist injury, in a cast and strapped to his chest, was apparent. Not so apparent was the hair growing back on the left side of his head just over the ear. Closer examination under the lowered lights of the passenger compartment showed a livid, razor-thin scar trying to hide among the regrowth. And if memory served her, he'd come aboard limping with the assistance of two men, one of whom was Daniels.

With images of Kitty's automated crypt in her mind, Marsha asked quietly, "How is he? Will he be all right?"

Simon sighed, rolled his head with great effort in the direction of Marsha's voice, and opened his eyes. "I'll be fine. Thanks for the lift."

"Well, I won't say 'it was nothing, Captain, but at least no one got killed this time." Realizing her mistake, she reddened in embarrassment. "I'm sorry, Simon. I didn't mean to imply..."

Simon raised his right hand a fraction, and a small smile lifted one corner of his mouth. "I know *exactly* what you meant, Marsha. No offense taken. And you and your team deserve applause for what appeared from my position to be a relatively flawless operation. Take it from me—when you *do* let the shit hit the fan, and you will eventually, you'll be your own worst critic." His voice trailed off for a moment. "There's only one way to live with your mistakes, Captain, and that is to learn something from them. To let it have been for nothing, *there* is the crime."

Simon's eyes closed and Marsha had to lean closer to hear his next words. "And if no one got killed, you're going to have to explain your use of the words 'special weapon' and 'fire.' But let's do that later. Tell me how bad she's hurt, Marsha." The request seemed to come from a different man—one so devoid of hope that she had to look into his eyes to reassure herself that it was still *him*.

"Uh, it was my understanding that you'd been out of touch since Camp David, Simon," she stalled.

"How did you know…?"

"You can't love and live with someone for almost seventeen years and not get to know them, Marsha," Simon cajoled. "That woman would have moved heaven and earth for me, just as I would for her. If she's not here, it means she *can't* be here. It's married logic. And since you won't look me in the eyes or talk about it, it must be bad."

Marsha took a deep breath and fought the panic that threatened to silence her. "I really wanted to be a coward and pass this off onto somebody else, Simon, but you need to know before you get back. You must have seen the news footage of what happened at Camp David…"

CHAPTER ELEVEN

It would be four more days before the *Galileo* left orbit. Simon's collapse upon entering the sickbay and finally finding out the true extent of Kitty's injuries was just one of the many things Lucy had to confront. In this, at least, she wasn't alone. Gayle and Stephen flanked her during an arduous hour that couldn't be allowed to wait for him to recover. She came away from the session drained, relieved, and at the same time, frustrated.

Taking advantage of the fact that all ships' captains were in orbit, Lucy said, "Rukia, please let the other captains know that they're expected at a Captain's Call. My quarters, one hour. Stephen, you're invited to attend as well. Might as well get the show on the road, I'd say."

With none of the three base captains able to give any input on such short notice, Lucy felt a little less sure of herself as she spoke to the assembled group. Gayle was there, sitting with Stephen, a little apart from Marsha, Robert Greene, Jerry Chapman, and Mustafa Morgan, still new to his position as Captain of the *Galileo*. Noticeably absent was Simon since he was undergoing psychiatric evaluation. Each captain had his or her second in command along, except Mustafa, who'd brought his weapons officer. Lucy had Commander Kimura seconding her.

"I want to thank you all for coming," Lucy said as

she paced the length of her briefing room. "It's going to get harder to have a full Captain's Call without really good scheduling after this, I think," she said lightly, then turned serious. "Before the virus wiped the *Galileo's* memory, Stephen and some of his people were able to figure out that it would be at least five years, if we were lucky, before the Builders would come looking for their ship. Four of those years are gone, and we still need to build the fourth base. I'm glad Simon got back when he did, but he's not in any shape to turn this zoo back over to him, so I'll still have to make the hard choices. The timetable says we can dispense with the *Galileo's* presence long enough for her to get the fourth base built. And I have to decide what to do with a certain FBI agent, as well as Simon and Kitty.

"Kitty stays aboard the *Galileo*," she stated flatly, "for obvious reasons. Dr. Penn isn't willing to try to remove her from the chamber at this time. Simon will go along, of course, and recuperate, hopefully regaining his former... spirit.

"Mustafa, you will have two new members added to your permanent staff. Father Jeffers and Dr. Jeffers. Lack of current medical credentials notwithstanding, Dr. Penn has signed off on Dr. Jeffers' ability to do his job. Speaking of doing a job, how long will it take you to get crewed and under way?"

"Three days if we do the job right," Mustafa said, glancing down at the stack of papers in front of him. "Still want us to make the rounds?"

"Definitely," Lucy said "Here's a list of personnel. Get with Brandt and Collier on who to pick up. After you get the specifics out of the way, fill out the rest of your roster with regular volunteers. Just figuring out who to send where and who you need to pick up was a nightmare! We'll be opening a new department very soon. We need a personnel department *desperately*. Keeping track of who's who and where they are is going to be a full-time job for several somebodies."

While Commander Kimura murmured a note into a small recorder, Mustafa scribbled a note on the back of the papers Lucy handed him, turned to his weapons officer, and said, "Get these to the Exec." Grinning at the faces staring at him as he turned back to the group, 'Stafa said, "Expected the order to load up, but I didn't expect the lists." He glanced at his watch dramatically. "Your orders should be going into effect as we speak, First Captain. My Exec can get things started."

Hearing the military nickname for a second in command brought Lucy up short. The increasingly martial attitude of the infant culture that was growing up around the *Galileo* had little to do with starting off using rank to denote degrees of position. That was only a simple way to tell who was in charge. Nor was it a matter of "let's all pull together in a dangerous environment."

She recognized it for what it was, for it affected her, too. It was pride. It was the little kid inside saying, "See what I can do!" It was us against them. It was the same thing that had affected the young United States over two hundred years before. It was nationalism. There were some who didn't like that aspect of the Alliance and wanted to go home—one of the reasons the *Galileo* was going to make all the stops on the way out.

Lucy said, "Good." She stopped pacing and looked at the group. "Mustafa already knows about item one, so this is for the rest of you. The *Galileo's* engineers have documented a very slight but disturbing fluctuation in her power output, and peak demand times are being met with increasing difficulty. Apparently, this is normal with matter/antimatter power generation. The supply isn't endless, and we're fortunate to find out the easy way. I'd hate to have a ship run out of gas out in the middle of a big, empty… someplace. Have your chief engineers implement programs to monitor the situation on each ship and integrate them into normal watch rotations. The *Galileo* will have a three-day layover at Orion to have her monopoles replaced and then continue on to Gemini and Libra."

Gayle broke in. "What about the rest of us?"

"Don't be so anxious, Gayle. I've got something for you to do, too," Lucy said. Kimura, knowing what was coming since she'd been used as a sounding board for the scheme that was about to be proposed, put down her recorder and watched with interest. "There's still the matter of who attacked Orion, remember? Were they associated with the ship the *Heinlein* and the *McCaffrey* killed? Are either of those two associated with the Builders? We could be dealing with *three* alien races, out here people, none of whom may like *us* being here. And at least one of 'em knows where we are."

Lucy looked uncomfortable. "You three will start playing war games, and as we get new ships, they'll join in as well. Figure out amongst yourselves who can help devise strategies that will work in space. We humans are really good at exterminating things on our own world—to the point that many species have gone extinct—but on our world we're working with only two dimensions. We're stepping onto a whole other playground, boys and girls, and if we don't learn real quick, we're gonna get our collective asses handed to us."

Jerry Chapman, after conferring with his exec, said, "Someone could get hurt. A lot of someones."

"I imagine," Robert Greene said, "that we'll be using weapons with reduced power like the demo flights a few weeks back."

"Right," Lucy said, glad to go anywhere else than there. "And we *won't* be using the new plasma discharge weapon on each other. Too expensive." The new weapon, a prototype, had been mounted on Cheetah One to test against drones. "Marsha, I can't guess what prompted you to use it against a grounded craft. I'm glad you waited, I guess, but it was already down!"

"He pissed me off," she muttered.

Lucy missed the comment but not the reaction to it. She glared at Robert and Gayle as they fought to hold in their laughter. "And you'll get your share, Robert. I've decided that the *Niven* may not be permanently in orbit, especially if the climate downside continues to improve. I could just move my whole staff into the complex on Fre… Baron von Schlenker's estate. Actually, we could start to call it the Terran Alliance Embassy, move out of that hotel, and let Zurich get back to normal. I'm sure the mayor and chief of police would appreciate it. I'd like to see it up and running within the month. Then, after the other three finish their first set of games, they can rendezvous with the *Galileo*, pick up the returnees, and come back to Earth orbit. One of them will relieve you and you can go play interstellar cowboys and aliens, or whatever is socially relevant. I imagine Gayle would like to rest her crew first.

"And remember that new ships will be joining the party pretty soon, so they'll have to be crewed up as we go along." Lucy finally ran down and sank into a chair.

"And what will the Alliance presence be doing on Earth while all of us are away?" came from Jerry Chapman's exec.

"Murillo, right? Arthur? Like to be called Art?" At his nod, Lucy said, "The Alliance presence will be doing three things. One, our stated goal of recruiting volunteers. Two, keeping our word on another goal, specifically the release of technology to Earth. And three, public relations. We need to keep these people's good will. This is our home, too, after all. They are our families. They are our past and our future."

"How can they be our future?" Marsha asked. "We're trying to leave them behind, aren't we?"

Stephen spoke for the first time "On an individual level, that could be the case, Marsha. But look at the two groups. One has too many people now and needs someplace to put the 'extras.' And one needs the extras. And not just the extras. How about a technological base that is comprised of an entire *planet*? How many ships could we turn out with that behind us?" Stephen went into lecture mode. "It's truly a symbiotic relationship. They need us to get out into the universe, and we need their industrial base, after we help them upgrade it, and of course, their manpower to do so."

"Another point," Lucy said. "Some of us don't get to see our friends out on the bases all that often. That will change with regular stops to resupply, both them and us, or just visit so we don't get tired of the same old faces. Did you know that all three bases are operating at higher-than-expected rates? Records I found in Simon's desk detail conversations with Adam, Victor and Daniel," she said, naming the base captain and commanders, "concerning the stockpiling of dozens of extra Mambas and hundreds of missiles *at each base!* Obviously, he wasn't planning to get sidetracked, so he saw no need to keep others informed of the details. Apparently, each base is mining through a very concentrated cluster at about the same rate. Couple that with the innovation of smaller, more powerful warheads, and you have a very potent combination. And all of this without getting behind with ship production."

Stephen said, "Daniel was the first one to put it together. Of course, he had the 'advantage' of having to rebuild a portion of his own base before he could get back to business. Not only can each base handle its own repairs, it can handle add-ons. Without slowing production, they've managed to increase their capacity and size."

"Yes," Lucy said from the comfort of her chair, "but the problem is that without additional personnel, as well as replacements for those who wish to return to Earth, they won't be able to keep up that pace, so the *Galileo* is going out crammed with as many as we can get aboard. Once, it took a week to get to the belt, but now that we can micro-jump, we're talking hours, a day at most, so overcrowding is going to be something we really won't have to consider."

Lucy's anger boiled just beneath the surface. She'd been wrangling with the baron and Lloyd Pike for an hour.

"You *can't* say you're sorry," Freddie said. "It amounts to an admission of guilt, and unless you honestly feel you did something to apologize *for*..."

"He's right, ma'am," Lloyd said. "And the only thing you can do from that point is go into the reparation phase."

"Okay," Lucy said, frustrated at the prohibition. "How about, 'I regret the'..."

"No, no," the old baron said. "Using 'I' makes you specifically responsible. You must spread out the guilt. Say 'The Terran Alliance regrets...'"

Gritting her teeth at the restrictions placed on her, she said, "Which of you am I going to have to strangle first?" The time spent trying to compose a proper response to the U.S. State Department's strongly worded protest had worn Lucy down. "They can say 'unspeakable act' and 'piratical actions' and *I* have to watch what I say?"

"Their plane, their airspace, their casualties. I'm afraid you *do* have to watch what you say, my dear," Maggie said as she breezed into the room. "I'm off, Freddie, my Love. I simply must meet with that dreary Countess van Kirkendahl. Some fundraiser or other. You know the countess."

The baron's wife picked at an imaginary piece of lint on her immaculate tweed suit and walked over to Lucy's side when she saw the discomfiture of her guest. "Try this: 'The Terran Alliance deplores the necessity of interfering with Flight seven-one-seven, caused by the illegal nature of the arrest and the childish attempt at clandestine interrogation of one of our people and an American citizen for who's safety we had accepted responsibility.' That should defuse the situation, or more likely muddle it enough to put an end to it for all intents and purposes."

"That, ladies and gentlemen," the baron avowed, "is why I married her! So insightful, so incisive, so beautiful!"

"Hush, you old faker," Maggie admonished her husband. Turning back to Lucy, she said, "Have Agent Daniels deliver it to the State Department on his return to the United States, and include a statement like, 'We wish to commend Agent Daniels for his quick thinking and decisive actions in the matter of saving the life of Captain Simon Hawke and for his selfless attempt to help Captain Hawke regain contact with Terran Alliance personnel.'" With an airy wave of her hand, Margit, Countess von Schlenker, sailed out of the room without a backward glance.

Finding no need to change a word of what the woman had said, the three confederates leaned over the huge old desk and plugged the appropriate phrases into the document they were drafting. "I'll get it copied and see how Agent Daniels feels about delivering it," Lucy said with a sigh of relief.

"Ma'am," Commander Pike said, "I can be back with a clean copy in about half an hour. If you wish, I can brief Agent Daniels myself and bring him with me when I return."

"Okay, Lloyd," she replied, standing up and massaging a kink out of her back. "Meet us at the... embassy. Freddie said he had something to show me?" She turned the statement into a question as she took the baron's crooked arm, letting him lead her from the room. Behind her, Lloyd Pike disappeared in a shower of blue sparks, and the butler shook his head in wonderment.

"You're going to have to get used to traveling like a normal human being again, Lucy," the baron said as he handed her into his Rolls Royce. "Take us to the main building, please, Viktor."

"Very well, sir," was the only response from the liveried man behind the wheel.

"Not much will surprise Viktor," the baron said as the vehicle eased away from the curb. He turned to find Lucy running her hand over the surface of the sensuously soft leather covering the seats of the luxury vehicle. "Ostentatious, I know," he said. "And I wouldn't keep it if I didn't need to keep up appearances. Now, I'm afraid I need to broach an unpleasant subject."

Lucy's hand froze on the leather, and she looked into the baron's eyes. "That means I've done something wrong."

"More to the point, you've done something irreversible without letting me know in advance. Not that you should have to do so on most matters," he demurred with one hand up, "but when you make a move as drastic as interfering with government airplanes of foreign powers *in their own airspace,* you *need* to let me know as much in advance as possible."

"Spin-doctoring?" Lucy asked

"That or distancing myself from the situation. I am the Terran Alliance's *ambassador*, Lucy. One instance like this can be explained away or swept under the rug," he said. "Two or three cannot."

"I'll keep that in mind, Freddie," Lucy said contritely. "My dad used to have a saying about being painted with the same brush. It means you could catch hell just for being associated with the Alliance if we do too much that is out of step with what's considered proper conduct."

"You have an instinctive grasp of the situation, Lady Lucille," the baron said suavely. "I'm sure the matter won't need to be discussed again. Ah, here we are." The Silver Cloud pulled up at the curb, having bypassed the oversized parking lot, and the baron, at his debonair best, handed Lucy out of the car.

They stood for a moment gazing at the gold-tinted glass front of the building. The words 'Terran Alliance' were hung over the door in block letters. "We need to design a logo or something, don't we?" Lucy asked *sotto voce*.

Set back from the curb about seventy feet, the building shone in the evening sunlight. Walking up the two flights of widely spaced shallow steps, Lucy moved toward the doors in a daze. The baron opened the door with a flourish and Lucy stepped into the cool interior, freezing in astonishment.

The lobby floor, once covered in a neutral grey, was now covered in a light-absorbing black, relieved here and there by specks of color highlighted by the recessed lights shining down from the black ceiling. Silver accented the doorway and edges of tables, as well as the receptionist's desk.

Two sets of painters were busily covering the left and right sides of the room in murals directed by one man standing in the geometric center of the lobby. "No! No!" he said with all the feeling of a frustrated perfectionist. "You must make it *live!* It's the Horsehead *Nebula*, you cretins! Yes!" he said to the team working on the other side of the room. "The depth! You make it come alive! This is truly the Milky Way!"

"Karl," the baron said with mock seriousness, "the next set of painters is coming out of your pocket. Allow me to present First Captain Lucille Grimes of the Terran Alliance. Lady Lucille, Herr Doktor Karl Mensing, chief astronomer of the Royal Observatory in Stockholm."

"I want to thank you, Herr Doktor, for your time and effort here," Lucy said, sticking her hand out to shake his. "The murals are magnificent! And the rest of the décor!"

"They will be when these paint splatterers learn to follow directions," he said quietly, referring to the walls. "Pfffft! The rest, it just made sense." The monocled astronomer took Lucy's proffered hand, and instead of shaking it, turned it slightly and pulled it toward him, kissing the back of it, which caused Lucy to redden.

Lips on the back of her hand, the Doktor's eyes caught Lucy's blush. "You will have to learn to accept common courtesy with grace, First Captain."

"In the circles I'm comfortable in, a handshake is very common, Herr Doktor, but I find this most appealing."

Before the interchange could founder embarrassingly, the baron said, "First Captain, if you wish, we can continue the tour?"

"By all means, Your Grace, let's," Lucy replied.

The rest of the tour was of more prosaic surroundings—offices and storerooms, lavatories and living quarters.

"Some of your personnel will be day labor and some will be embassy staff," the baron said. "You'll need to be able to distinguish between the two, as well as visitors and unauthorized persons."

Lucy smiled. "Remember our tech advantage? Our wristband will be the deciding factor. There are a few items that will be left behind when the *Galileo* leaves orbit tomorrow." Her smile grew wider. "Simon, when he was fit, said you should never have just one motive for an action. We'll be sending down several of our computers to run the three embassies, defensive equipment, a few trinkets to impress the natives, and three of our wristband machines. We'll have the new shuttle Victor sent us from Libra to transport people to orbit, as well as the normal complement that would be aboard a ship of the *Niven's* class."

The baron stopped in front of an immense oak door bearing a plaque that read simply, "Lucille Grimes, First Captain, Terran Alliance." It was with the gallantry found only among continental Europeans that he said, "First Captain, your business offices. I've taken liberties, of course. You're welcome to make any changes you desire, and I won't be offended."

Lucy walked into what, under other circumstances, would have been any other secretary's office found anywhere, but the differences jumped out at once. While a normal office would have been a bright color, this room mirrored the lobby with its dedication to the black and silver motif. Three of the walls bore pictures of various astronomical phenomena, illuminated by cleverly hidden lights. The overstuffed black leather couch was accompanied by four black leather chairs, all of which surrounded a massive black coffee table. All six pieces were chased in what appeared to be pure silver and standing on the same style carpet that was found in the lobby. Off to one side was a black, silver-bordered pedestal bearing a small grey rock. The various black items seemed to complement each other, some gloss, some matte, while others were either hard or, in the case of the couch and chairs, soft. "I see you've been in collusion with Commander Kimura," Lucy observed, staring at the small asteroid.

"My transgressions will become even more apparent momentarily, I'm afraid," the old man said with a huge grin and no hint of remorse. "If you would, please?" he asked with a flowing gesture toward another door. Lucy, fearing another shock would finish her off, opened the door.

The normality she walked into was almost as much of a shock as all the surprises leading up to this moment. It appeared that her office aboard the *Niven* had been sent down *in toto*. The walls surrounding the desk and models of the various ships were different, though. A shimmering grey paint covered three of the walls, and the fourth was hidden by black floor-to-ceiling silver-chased drapes. Fanciful renditions of sights found around the solar system graced the walls. Lucy looked at the small brass plaque beneath one of the paintings: "Saturn's Rings Seen from the Surface of Its Moon, Titan." The signature in the lower righthand corner simply said, "Bonestell."

"Is this..."

"An original?" Freddie asked. "Yes, it is. I've had

it and several others in my collection for years. I couldn't think of a better place to display them. Can you?"

"Uh, no," Lucy responded lamely as she sank into the familiar chair behind the plain grey desk.

"I would suggest that you get a more prestigious desk and chair. I have a desk in mind—nineteenth century, I believe—that would be the antithesis of the rest of this entire building. It would draw attention to the person behind it. But the chair—lumbar support, three-way massage, heated, and adjustable to almost any position! Worthy of your inestimable self, my dear."

"Let me think about it, okay?" Lucy said vaguely. "This is beginning to snowball, and I have no idea where it will lead."

August 17th was clear and cold in Zurich, Switzerland. Lucy Grimes, First Captain of the Terran Alliance, became the de facto head of the Alliance delegation to the planet Earth when the *Galileo* headed out into the depths of space to rendezvous with Orion Base. Observatories around the globe reported that fact, as well as the fact that three of the four ships in the Alliance arsenal left as well.

Before the huge ship moved out, several deliveries were beamed down to the embassy. Three of the organic computers, one for each embassy, crate after crate of support equipment, satellite uplinks, prototypes of various items that should be of interest to scientists and military types as well, and dozens of boxes with attached contents lists began to pile up in some of the second-floor offices. Larger items, such as the three antigrav ground cars and the generators for the defense grids, along with all the associated hardware, had been shipped down by shuttle the day before.

Two Mambas sat in the parking lot beside the three Terran Alliance "automobiles," lending a lethal air to the otherwise peaceful scene they inhabited. Off to one side, on an expanse of grass that had been used as a picnic area, sat the personnel shuttle sent to Earth from Orion Base. The sight reminded Lucy that she'd be returning to Earth in the not-to-distant future. One of the people sent out on the *Galileo* was her replacement.

Dozens of volunteers from the recently commissioned *Niven* moved crates from one place to another, kept track of Alliance message traffic on communications equipment that had been classified as secret as the weapons technology, and in general, began to make the building feel lived in.

Technicians were in the process of setting up the defense grid when Lucy walked into the basement room that had been co-opted as the main computer room on her first inspection tour of the premises since personnel had begun to arrive.

The *Niven's* chief engineer looked up at her entrance. "Glad you stopped in, ma'am. It'll save me a trip to report," he said. "Six more hours, maybe eight, and we'll have the equipment installed. Then we can bring down the power core and energize this beast."

Lucy nodded her approval. "Thanks, Chief. I appreciate your team's efforts. How are you going to get the core down here?"

"In pieces," he said with a grin. "First will be the

core itself. Its force fields have been reconfigured to minimum tolerances and will fit in the freight elevator. The other equipment can come down in bits and be assembled as we go. Once the core is actually in place," he said, pointing at a bare space in one corner of the room, "it won't take us more than four or five hours to have the grid up and functional."

The core would provide all the power the embassy would need for the next several years and was just as secret as the comm units. If it weren't for the fact that the defense grids wouldn't work without the immense power output of the core, it wouldn't have been necessary to bring it along. One function of the computer would be to monitor the force fields holding the monopoles in place and adjust them automatically.

FUGUE

Another endless time passed and she neither knew nor cared how long that time was while she struggled to fill the Emptiness that had arrived when she re-integrated Loss into her being. She reached out to the other things that floated within her perception but beyond her grasp, fearful of what they might bring her, yet more afraid of feeling so Empty.

Fear of the Emptiness within her turned into Hatred, and she began to plot ways to trick the things into coming into her reach. She would look where they weren't as she strode through the void and then make a darting leap in the direction of the things. More often than not, they eluded her grasp, but occasionally she was able to lay hands one and draw it in to make it a part of her.

Time after time these things, these feeling*s*, these *emotions,* brought with them a degree of pain—not pain in the physical sense, for she had no physical body, she felt, but pain in the mental sense. Pain that took a brain and ripped it apart cell by cell, synapse by synapse, reveling in the discomfort It produced in Its victim.

Gradually, after several eternities, her efforts began to pay off. Now it wasn't just a sense of self. It was more than just, "I am." Faces appeared in the formlessness of her world, faces to which she could put names. Names that brought comfort. One such face was "dad." Another was "mom."

With these faces came the first kernel of what was becoming a growing sense of self. A sense of... identity.

CHAPTER TWELVE

Marcad Korvil, supreme ruler of the Korvil Hegemony, strode around the circumference of his family's Pit of Justice, stopping at each of the fancifully carved pillars to offer his respects to the ancestor within. Beyond mere structural support, each pillar was a tomb holding the stripped and cleaned bones of an honored ancestor. Inset into the upper reaches of each pillar was the skull of the resident ancestor, some so old that they'd begun to decay in the hot, humid atmosphere of the cavern that surrounded the Pit. Recent technological advances had allowed the skulls to be treated for the prevention of any further deterioration.

He stopped before the tomb of the father of his father's father, *The* Korvil, as he had come to be known, and studied again the life and accomplishments of the occupant. This one had risen to racial primacy through trial by combat, thereby giving the family name to the whole race, as well as the planet.

This communion with his ancestors was supposed to help him achieve, if not wisdom, at least balance. A full cycle had gone by since Marcad had given in to the urge to spare the life of Pankatt Korchon, his liegeman—twice the time he'd expected to wait before hearing back.

Deceit, even treachery, he expected. After all, had

they not been racial attributes of the Korvil since time immemorial? But so was obedience to one's Lord. It had been so since the earliest Memories. Cooperation had been a necessity on the young, volcanic world of Korvilene, called something else all those thousands of cycles before. Loners died out, while cooperative groups just hung on at first and finally grew to planetary dominance, with power residing in the smartest, strongest, or luckiest.

Power changed hands most often in the early days through trial by combat. Lately, it had tended to lie in family lines. Marcad's great-great-grandfather had stepped back into the race, so to speak, when, dissatisfied with his lot, he challenged *his* Lord to a trial by combat. Winning that combat led to Marcad's dilemma now. Each Korvil since *The* Korvil had pushed the race into the expansion that kept them bumping into the krath-Shiravi at every turn. Needing the space and being able to use the same worlds produced one of the sparks that kept the fires burning between the two races. Another spark was the drive to dominate that had not yet had time to mellow in the young Korvil race.

A large part of the inability of the Shiravi to interact peacefully with the Korvil was the problem with actually *hearing* Korvil words. In main part, it could be said that the concept of the Korvil as a race, the Korvil as an individual, and the Korvil as a ruler sounded the same to Shiravan ears, and this problem lent itself to all other aspects of the Korvil language as well.

The Korvil culture was at a more basic stage of its evolution and hadn't developed the "shades of grey" that the more advanced Shiravan culture had, so the concept of "me/mine" ran head on into "let's talk about it," with the result that the more restrained Shiravans had been caught off guard and had stayed there for almost three hundred cycles.

Fearing a power shift based on knowledge of the "human" captives, Marcad sent scout ships out to the farthest reaches of his empire to demand whatever information Korchon might have wrung out of the Humanz. Another half-cycle went by before the ships returned to report the news of Korchon's demise, along with his entire Sept, as well as the loss of the Humanz, bringing on the barely controllable urge to smash the perpetrators of such a heinous act.

So it was that Marcad had wound up in the depths of his palace, communing with the dead instead of marching out to exterminate the krath-Shiravi. For it was surely they who had done this to *his* subjects, *his* ships, *his* Honor. With the return of the fleet to Korvilene, he had in his hands indisputable and disturbing proof of the power of the krath-Shiravi.

The fact that the original sin—the massacre of the first Shiravan ship to land on his world and theft of their ship—rested on Korvil shoulders was lost on Marcad. They had occurred long before *The* Korvil had won the right to rule in personal combat lifetimes before. And *had* he known, it would have made no difference, for to the Korvil, all things belonged to the Korvil.

The major problem Marcad faced was not *whether* to attack but *when*. Since the inception of the Korvil space program, most manufacturing had been at the freighter and cruiser level. A few mid-sized vessels had been constructed, but not enough to even begin to think about attacking the fixed defenses the krath-

Shiravi had around their major population centers. And it took an entire hunter pack to take out one of their mid-sized defense crafts. That was why, even though able to take more damage than a Shiravan craft, there was some attrition in the Korvil fleet. It was for this reason that most of the Korvil objectives centered around lone ships traveling known lanes or new colonies on the outskirts of Shiravan space that hadn't had time to build their defenses.

Another problem was deciding how to respond and with what degree of aggression. Some response must be immediate, of course, to keep the enemy from gaining any more of an advantage than they already had.

The normal state of affairs for a Korvil, when attacked, was to fight to the death. That seemed to be the case in this instance, anyway. Conversations with Darmag, the Korvilene War Minister, had accounted for all of Pankatt Korchon's ships, grounded and in space at the time of the attack. It appeared that only two of his ships had been crewed, and it was surmised that the attack had taken place on Korchon's return to Kravarine after his interview with Marcad. The wreckage indicated that, while the krath-Shiravi had had superior numbers and possibly the advantage of surprise, the two active ships had each managed to attain Honor by taking their attackers with them. The laxity of having no ships on patrol could almost be forgiven since the krath-Shiravi had never mounted a more than ineffectual defense, much less an effective attack of their own. Most losses taken by the Korvil had been attributed to luck as much by the Shiravi as the Korvil.

The Korvil had operated with numerous smaller

ships in hunter packs and minimal support as Tradition and Honor dictated for so long that it was almost impossible to conceive of a different way of fighting. But a different way would have to be devised to teach the krath-Shiravi that they could not attack the Korvil with impunity.

In order to combat larger vessels with heavier weapons and a significantly increased aggressiveness, new ships were going to have to be designed and built. Nothing would please Marcad more than to rid the universe of the species that had visited this ignominy upon his people, his Honor. But even a cornered krath was a danger to unprepared hunters. And for *this* hunt, much preparation needed to be made in advance.

CHAPTER THIRTEEN

The days that followed sel Garian's revelations had left Rentec frustrated to the point of exasperation. His inability to talk to anyone about the meeting, along with the daily notices from various ministries concerning what *his* particular ministry was supposed to do, had drained him, not to mention Ramannie's endless questioning.

Telling Ramannie that the information was classified only served to infuriate her since she was running into the same lack of information in Minister Foran's office. What little he was able to tell her had already been public knowledge even before Rentec had visited her apartment the next day.

"I want to know what went on behind those closed doors!" she exclaimed. "If it's causing you this much discomfort, you should share it. 'Two to bear a burden halves the work,' you know."

"Don't mouth platitudes at me today," he demanded. "I don't want to be on the receiving end of one of sel Garian's purges. When the time is right, all will be revealed. Until then, isn't it enough that we are at *war* with the Korvil?"

The war footing the matriarch had embarked all of Shiravi on impacted the life of Rentec do' Verlas in four distinct ways. The first was that his relationship with Ramannie had cooled noticeably since the secrecy order. The second was that his ministry was catapulted into the forefront of the activities to prepare for a war no one had expected to be declared for many years to come. The third was related to the first. His visit to the do' Verlas estates had been postponed. And the fourth lay in wait, marking time until it could manifest itself properly. Not only was the war taking up his time, but with Ramannie on the outs with him, it was not a propitious moment to have his mother engage in a matrimonial reading for the two of them. Emotion was so much a part of the reading that any discord was able to throw off the results.

Following sel Garian's announcements, Rentec had become uncomfortably aware that ministers who hadn't given him more than a polite nod in the past were now trying to curry his favor. The experience was unnerving, to say the least, for the most junior Shiravan minister. Sitting in Minister Foran's office, he said as much over a glass of that worthy's more esoteric vintage.

"I have people from every ministry but yours, Intelligence and Military pounding on my doors day and night, Minister!"

"Of course, you do! You are now one of the most preeminent persons on the planet after the matriarch and sel Garian. You are the one with the information about which ships are where, what they're carrying, how they're armed, who crews them, and how they're trained," the older minister said, ticking off points on his fingers. "Colonization is at a standstill, so I have no reason to search you out. Military and Defense have their own ships and agendas, and they're tied to Intelligence by cords too strong to break. I've often thought that it would be simpler to have them under one central command structure, but too many ministers would balk at having that much power in one person's hands. Also, several would lose their jobs entirely and actually have to find work or return to the family compound. This would be a good time to initiate a new attempt at doing so, though. It would speed up reaction times to any attacks."

Rentec spent his days in a seemingly perpetual fog while barely managing to accomplish the nearly endless tasks appointed to his office. Disruptions, one after another, cropped up often enough to make him wary of walking into his office each morning. The sound of his comm unit caused him to sweat each time heard it in the middle of the night, and he began to noticeably lose weight in just the first week after sel Garian's bombshell.

Halfway through the third week of the Korvil War, a harried Rentec arrived at his offices to find workmen scurrying around, moving things without apparent rhyme or reason. "What's going on here and who authorized this?" he asked furiously, grabbing the arm of a passing worker.

Immediately, a burly man who was directing the operation interposed himself between the two. "Minister do' Verlas, I'm Building Superintendent Darvel," he said soothingly. "My staff and I are only following the orders handed down to us last week." The subtle emphasis on the last two words were not lost on Rentec. "Surely you were informed of the move?"

Rentec took the paper offered to him by Darvel

and scanned it quickly. Halfway through the work order, he stopped. "This *must* be a mistake! My ministry doesn't need the space indicated here. And on the *top floor!* What is being done with Minister Foran's staff?"

"Minister," the man said quietly, "I realize that you may not have had time to read all of your correspondence, but it may simplify things if you look at the signature at the bottom of the order."

Rentec's eyes widened in shock at the name scrawled across the bottom of the page. In the distinctive blue ink used only by the matriarch's staff was the phrase, "For the Matriarch, sel Garian."

Befuddled by lack of rest and one too many surprises, Rentec allowed the work order to be gently pulled from his numb fingers. His eyes strayed to a workman carrying a box labeled with writing of his own. He followed the man to the back of the floor and into a freight elevator that he half remembered led to Mondel Foran's Ministry of Colonization. Standing in an uncomfortable silence, he felt the floor press against his feet as the elevator moved upward, and he swayed in compensation. When the door opened, it was onto a scene he could not have imagined. The room, once sparsely furnished with a half dozen desks, one of which had been Ramannie's, was now crowded almost to overflowing with desks, computers, filing cabinets, and people.

He stepped hesitantly out of the freight elevator into semi-organized madness. The workman he'd ridden up with carried the box into the room, and Rentec slowly moved in the same general direction. Not one face was familiar to him as he desperately searched for someone he recognized. His staff had consisted of a private secretary, four general secretaries, and a pair of runners. Here were no less than thirty persons, all moving about as if each errand was of the utmost importance. Deducting the obvious workers who were just moving things from one place to another still left him with over twenty to contend with.

His eyes finally stopped on a young woman who appeared to be giving instructions to anyone who came within range. At the same time, she spied him, finished giving instructions to the woman before her, and headed his way. "Minister! I was expecting you to use the public transport or your private lift! Please! Follow me. I'll show you to your office." The poise with which she carried herself made him wonder why someone as competent as she appeared to be was directing the reassignment of a junior minister like himself.

The woman led him through a maze of desks to an aisle that led down the center of the room, which led to an office he'd visited many times before. The differences this time were stunning. He entered, expecting to find his friend and mentor, Mondel Foran, sitting at his desk as usual, perhaps reading the latest directive from Polity Headquarters. Instead, he found that all of his possessions used to personalize his own office were now placed tastefully around the room.

"I hope you approve of what I've done with your furnishings, sir," the woman said deferentially.

"Everything seems to be quite... all right..." Rentec turned from his inspection of the room and stared at the woman standing quietly just inside the door. "I am at a total loss here. And you seem to have me at a disadvantage, ther'a?" he asked, using the formal designation for a woman of unknown status.

"Maratai kep Parrasine, Minister. At your service."

Rentec fell into his chair in shock. The kep Parrasine clan was among the oldest and most revered clans on Shiravi. It was Kerel kep Parrasine who'd postulated theories that led to the construction of artificial monopoles. Later, it was his grandson, Mordas kep Parrasine, who'd constructed the first converters that allowed the power from matter/antimatter to be channeled into power generators that could accelerate a vessel into what scientists called "second-space." This had led to the colonization of a large portion of nearby space until running into the Korvil Empire some two hundred and fifty years ago, known then as the Tarkah Empire for reasons still not known to the Shiravi. A kep Parrasine stood beside Manura sel Garian at Harusel and had an entire sector of space named after him, and another was second only to sel Garian on the matriarch's staff.

The woman sat gracefully in a chair at the side of the desk and looked critically around the room. "Uncluttered, functional without being pretentious. It becomes you, Minister do' Verlas. I could be comfortable here."

Rentec, desperately trying to find a proper response, looked around the room as well. "Thank you, Doma kep Parrasine," he said, switching from equals mode of address to junior-to-senior. "But someone else put all this here."

"Nonsense! I supervised the entire move. Everything is as it was in your old office," she said authoritatively.

"Please, Doma," Rentec begged. "This is all... I mean, I don't understand. I've tried to do the best I could, of course, under the circumstances, but..."

"There are those who use the intelligence of those around them to their best advantage. For reasons of their own, they see in you one who can be of great help in advancing the cause of the matriarch. There are also those, Minister do' Verlas, who see in you the potential that was seen in your father before you. If I may suggest, you should read the correspondence on your desk. I've taken the liberty of sorting it into descending order of importance." kep Parrasine stood up and walked toward the door. "I've also taken the liberty of reprogramming your comm unit with all the codes you'll need to reach me or anyone else you should think necessary. Call me if you have any questions, sir. Your office should settle into proper operating mode by this time tomorrow. Now, I have other matters to attend to. If you will excuse me?"

Rentec nodded in shock and watched as kep Parrasine pulled the door closed. Several seconds went by before he looked down at the stack of messages on his desk. The first was in the same conspicuous blue ink that sel Garian was fond of using—so fond, in fact, that it had become her personal trademark. Fear slowed his hand as it reached out of its own accord and picked up the single piece of paper. He read, "Minister do' Verlas, at your convenience, please contact my office and arrange an appointment. For the Matriarch, sel Garian."

Hand shaking, Rentec set the paper down as if it were about to explode and reached for the comm unit sitting at one side of his desk. Running through the menu, he found that kep Parrasine was indeed right. Any number he might possibly need was already programmed into it, including the matriarch's personal number!

Scrolling down until he found sel Garian's name, he pressed the button and expected that he would be shuffled through several layers of bureaucrats before getting to speak to the infamous Policy Minister. Nothing could have surprised him more than to hear her distinctive voice answer.

"I... I'm sorry, Minister sel Garian. I expected to get a secretary. I was to make an appointment."

"Why not now?" the mechanical voice grated. "You have the time."

Rentec felt as if he'd stepped into a thitura's nest. The six-legged creature was the size of a small house pet, but the venom of this tenacious pest was almost always fatal, and it never attacked directly, coming at its victims from unexpected directions until either it or its target was dead. And he'd voluntarily walked in there!

Sweat beaded on his forehead as the little old woman read aloud from a paper on her desk. "do' Verlas. Mother: Kirel, of the kep' Ligera clan. Father: Tira do' Verlas, Minister for Spatial Affairs before you. 'Highly intelligent and capable but unmotivated unless challenged,' it says in your secondary school transcripts. We'll see what we can do about your motivation, young Rentec. And you *will* rise to the challenge. Of that I am certain."

Frozen in place by the carnelian gaze of the second-most powerful woman in the Shiravan Polity,

Rentec could only fight to keep his breathing as even as possible. *Don't let your enemies see your fear*, he remembered his father telling him on more than one occasion. *They will use it to break you*. Buoyed up by the thought of his father's advice, gone now for over three turnings, Rentec's chest eased slightly and he looked back, outwardly calm, into eyes whose depths he couldn't fathom.

"It had been decided," sel Garian said after a short pause, "that one of the things needed in this war is a more youthful viewpoint. Another is a spirit of adventure that seems to be sadly lacking in most Shiravans these days. It's most surprising to me to find that combination in a male. But we *are* speaking of the do' Verlas line. If we wish to win this war rather than become slaves to the Korvil, daring action must be taken." She stared at the young man who was squirming in the chair before her. "It has therefore been decided that you will be transported to the summer estate of the matriarch, there to become an adviser in matters that require a more youthful frame of mind." The words seemed to be forced out of the woman's mouth by someone else. "You will be expected to arrive no later than one week from today. Will that give you enough time to set your ministry in order and appoint a new underminister with more youthfulness and vision?"

"Of course, Minister sel Garian. May I ask what criteria other than youthfulness and vision are required? And from where may I choose a new underminister?"

"The decisions will be yours alone, young Rentec," he was told. "You may choose anyone you wish. The matriarch and I will be watching to see how you handle this assignment, and I believe we will all learn much. Now. I have many cords to pull this day. Go. Be inventive." She waved a hand at the door, and Rentec stood to leave. "Oh, and do' Verlas."

"Yes, Minister?"

"I would advise you to be more diligent about reading the correspondence that is sent to your office. Someone goes to the trouble to send it. It is rude to ignore it, don't you think?"

"Yes, Minister." Heart pounding, Rentec closed the door on her brooding gaze, feeling as if he'd barely escaped with his life.

On the other side of the door, the little old woman recognized a pivotal moment for the entire Shiravan race, her nervousness betrayed by one claw-like finger tapping a steady beat.

"It would seem, cousin," Pardo do' Nallen said admiringly as he looked around the new office, "that this war has done well by you already. Rumor has it that your star is rising rather quickly."

"Remember," Rentec said with asperity, "fast-rising stars burn hotter, and hotter stars have shorter lives."

Catching the temper of Rentec's last statement, Parlo chose to ignore it. "So, cousin, what did you have in mind when you invited me here? Knowing you, it wasn't to show off your new decor."

"Are you happy in your post at Defense, Parlo? Do you have enough to keep you busy?"

"Strange questions, Rennie," Parlo returned, using Rentec's childhood nickname. "Why do you ask?" The caution in his voice was mirrored by the narrowing of his eyes.

"What would you say about moving from Defense to Spatial Affairs? I realize that now wouldn't be a good time to change ministries under normal conditions, but these aren't normal times. We haven't spoken since sel Garian's announcement," Rentec said, alluding to the deeper nature of the revelations of that night, "and I was wondering if you'd be willing to move over here as my underminister."

"Are you serious? Of course, I would! But it would mean that I'd have to move into Quillas proper," Parlo mused aloud. "That could pose a problem. Living space is at a premium, right now, you know."

"I believe I can get around that, Parlo. All you need to do is agree to the transfer, and the position is yours." Rentec slid a piece of paper across the desk. "Sign at the bottom and my secretary will take care of all the necessities, including finding you an apartment befitting your new position nearby."

As Parlo reached for a stylus to affix his signature to the document, he said, "You had this ready in advance, Rennie. How did you know I would agree?"

"I didn't, cousin. You were just the first one I asked," Smiling sheepishly, he pulled a slim stack of papers out of a drawer. "Seven other names were under consideration. You do need to know that as underminister you'll have to fill in for me when my duties take me away from Quillas, which, as it happens, will be almost immediately and quite often."

"Sounds quite sinister, but I'll take the gamble. You have yourself a new underminister," Parlo said, signing the document on the table before him.

Rentec smiled slightly in remembrance of his

recent conversation with sel Garian. "Sinister could be a very apt word, cousin." He picked up his comm unit. "Doma kep Parrasine, would you come in here for a moment?"

"kep Parrasine? As your personal secretary? What are you hiding from…?" Parlo choked off the sentence as the woman walked through the door.

"Yes, Minister?"

"If you would be so kind, Doma, I need this forwarded to the Ministry of Defense," Rentec said, handing her the signed document. "Also, would you see about finding an appropriate apartment for our new underminister?"

"At once, Minister," she said deferentially. Turning to Parlo, she said, "Welcome to the Ministry of Spatial Affairs Underminister do' Nallen."

The lack of stature of the Ministry of Spatial Affairs in the past had kept Rentec from having a reason to visit or be invited to any of the matriarch's personal holdings. Now, with the ascendancy of his ministry, Rentec was treated as if he'd been a visitor for turns. A full day before the deadline imposed by sel Garian, Rentec took a private suborbital reserved for his ministry's use to the matriarch's summer estate halfway around the planet from Quillas. He'd argued as violently as possible to keep the suggested retinue down to a size that wouldn't embarrass him, but kep Parrasine's eyes bored into him with a focused look.

"You'll need to make an impression when you arrive, Minister," she said not unreasonably.

It is apparent to me, at least, he said to himself stepping onto the tarmac after the half-hour flight, *that I've* already *made an impression in some corner or other.*

After a week of dealing with kep Parrasine, his perverse nature came to a head. "I'm not at all sure that I care to have been thrust into the spotlight like this."

"It is the matriarch's opinion that you, Minister do' Verlas, are the proper person at the proper time to make a difference in the course of our history. It is not for you to gainsay her."

"Was it the matriarch's decision or sel Garian's?" he retorted with a vigor that was not his normal manner. "My 'youth' is not necessarily an advantage here, you know."

"Again, that is not your decision to make, Minister," kep Parrasine put a less than subtle emphasis on his title.

He fumed silently as he watched a valet, secretary, two runners, and baggage handlers deplane after him and kep Parrasine. "You will be happy to know that after this excursion, you won't have to deal with a kep Parrasine again for a while, Minister, since I'll be staying here after your visit. I'm not unaware," she added tartly, "that I, as well as the rest of my family, are held in less than the highest esteem by some because of our military, and that causes unease amongst many Shiravans. You'd be well advised, also, Minister, to keep in mind the fact that at this time in our history, we need a militancy that has been absent for more generations than I, personally, care to count. People like sel Garian are needed to deliver our entire race from the ignominy of slavery to the Korvil—that is, the survivors, at least. And much as you'd wish it otherwise, you are one of those who will stand beside a kep Parrasine *and* a sel Garian to deliver our people from that fate. Now, Minister, put on a less antagonistic face, if you please. We are about to be in the presence of those who will report every word to the matriarch."

"As if *you* won't?" Rentec's perversity kept surprising even himself.

"Be careful, Minister. Even my patience has limits," kep Parrasine warned.

The ride from the landing field to the matriarch's personal summer holdings went past some of the most beautiful sugar-sand beaches on the planet, and Rentec marveled at the sight. The Stala Mountains ran almost a thousand miles north to south, bordering those beaches until they doglegged west, leaving a fertile plain which the des' Harras clan had held title to for over two thousand turns. It was here that the matriarch chose to settle in the summer to avoid the heat that afflicted Quillas City.

Rounding the final bend in the mountain range, Rentec saw for the first time the shimmering buildings constructed of the fabled gava stone mined only in the Stalas. The operation had made the des' Harras clan rich many times over in the past millennia, and the reason was most obvious here. The last rays of the westering sun illuminated the scene, causing the buildings to glow with an internal light all their own—the property of gava stone that made it the most expensive and sought-after building material on Shiravi. Gava stone was highly prized for its reaction to light and heat. A single stone, big enough to be set into a ring or pendant for a man or woman, could cost a week's pay, a sculpture, or a king's ransom, and here was an entire *city* of the stuff.

Rentec's suborbital grounded at a private landing field not far from the glowing, fanciful structures, and he self-consciously led the group of people with him (at kep Parrasine's nearly subvocal direction) toward the waiting transport. Seating himself, Rentec looked out a window toward the ship and saw the baggage module being transferred to the transport. Glancing out the other side of the vehicle, he saw the city shimmering in the distance, situated to catch the full effect of the setting sun.

Rentec found himself in a suite of rooms with a valet arranging his clothes, his discomfiture growing with each passing moment. "Leave. Now." he said irritably. He wandered around the suite aimlessly, wishing Ramannie were there for him to talk to. The reason for their spat was now forgotten, a thing of the past, and his feeling of isolation continued to grow until a chime sounded, calling him to the door.

The liveried attendant showed no surprise when Rentec opened the door. "The matriarch's compliments, Minister do' Verlas, and would you attend her at your earliest convenience?"

"Would now be an inopportune moment, ther'a?" he asked, adopting the informal mode of address.

"Your request has been anticipated, Minister," the woman said, "and the matriarch awaits your arrival."

"Very well, ther'a. If you would be so kind as to lead the way?"

Apprehension growing with each step, Rentec copied the sedate pace of the attendant as she led him without interruption past several obvious guard stations into the private apartments of the matriarch.

An interminable wait followed as she disappeared to inform the Shiravan ruler of his presence.

Rentec truly hadn't known what to expect, but the last thing he *did* expect was to find Linnas des' Harras, Matriarch of the Shiravan Polity, sitting on the floor giving a language lesson to one of the aliens—the shorter female he surmised from his one look weeks earlier.

"Rentec do' Verlas, Minister for Spatial Affairs," the attendant said formally.

"Come," the woman on the floor said without preamble. "Sit here and help me, Minister do' Verlas." She patted the floor beside her. "I wish to introduce you to Maggie Spencer. We seem to be having some difficulty with our language lessons, as usual. Perhaps you might be able to help?"

Rentec sat down slowly beside the leader of the entire Shiravan Polity and asked, "If I may, Your Grace, what are you trying to teach... her?"

"'Her' is proper, I think. I do believe her to be the female. I want her to learn that this," she said, setting a cup of water down on the floor, "is called a 'cup,' but we seem to be running into a barrier."

He picked up the cup and looked at the alien long and thoughtfully. The long, yellowish fur on her head was disconcerting, as were her features, but he could see the intelligence behind the eyes. A vivid blue, they were causing him to stare unabashedly.

"I had the same reaction," the matriarch said. "Not a proper color for eyes at all."

Rentec continued to study the alien female. She had two eyes on the front of the head, indicating predatory ancestry, ears on each side providing directional hearing, a single nose in the proper place but deformed into a lump, along with a mouthful of teeth that indicated an omnivorous heritage—not altogether unlike his own race. Physical differences could be attributed to different evolutionary tracks, but all in all, the similarities were enough to make him think the problems were not insurmountable.

"How are you describing this, Your Grace?" he asked holding the cup out to his ruler.

"I set it on the floor and say 'cup,' of course."

"I see several things that one not familiar with our language could imagine from your actions, Your Grace," Rentec started.

"Name two," she challenged him.

"The idea of 'cup' versus the idea of 'water' for starters," he said. "Then there's the concept of 'place on floor' or 'place *cup* on floor.' May I?"

"By all means, do."

Rentec looked at the alien and poured the water onto the floor. He reached out and patted the wet spot with one hand, saying, "Water." Holding the cup up at eye level, he tapped it with a finger. "Cup," he said distinctly.

The alien watched this process with intense scrutiny. She reached out and took the cup from Rentec. "Water," she said. The sound was not intelligible, but the action that followed certainly was. She raised the cup to her lips and mimed drinking.

The elder woman, just entering her seventh decade, clapped her hands in joy as if a small child had just said her first word. "I think she and her mate, if that's what he is to her, are afraid of us. We've been able to learn their names, but that's about all, with the exception of basic concepts like 'cold' and 'hungry.' 'Water' is the first word either of them has learned."

Rentec picked up a towel lying to the side and began to absentmindedly mop up the spilled water. "If I'd been taken from my people and subjected to the kind of treatment that led up to the condition we found them in, I'd be wary of strangers, myself, Your Grace."

"And how would you suggest we proceed from here, Minister?"

The feeling of traversing a narrow, lipless bridge over a deep chasm while blindfolded came to Rentec. "You ask me, You Grace? I've barely had time to get used to the fact that these aliens exist."

"Yes, I ask you, Minister," Linnas des' Harras said regally. "Of all the people at the meeting where Policy Minister sel Garian introduced these beings, only you made comments that showed your grasp of alien mentalities. I will grant you," the woman went on, "that your comments were about the Korvil, but if you can make those assessments about a race with whom we've had so little contact, then you should be of immeasurable use to us now."

Rentec looked at her sharply. His comments that night had been for his cousin and not much above a whisper.

At the mention of the Korvil, the alien woman jumped up and began to speak for the first time since Rentec had walked into the room. Nothing was understandable, of course, except for the word 'Korvil,' but it was obvious she was agitated.

"Perhaps, Your Grace, we should try to reassure ther'a Spencer that we are truly friends. How are they housed?"

"Housed?" she asked. "In a private apartment down the hall where they won't be disturbed."

"And doubtless they are under constant surveillance?" Rentec asked.

"Of course," Linnas retorted. "For their own protection, of course. Where are you going with this, Minister?"

Rentec hesitated. "I realize I may be overstepping my bounds, Your Grace, but if we want to win their trust—and, through them, the trust of their entire race at some time in the future—we need to give them some measure of respect, the same respect we'd give to any member of our own society. First, all surveillance devices should be removed from their private quarters. Second, it's time for all of Shiravi to learn of their existence. This will make it easier for them to be accepted by our people when we start taking them around our world and showing them what we have to offer." As an afterthought, he said, "And someone should start to learn *their* language."

Linnas des' Harras stood up and started pacing the room, constantly being followed, Rentec noticed, by the eyes of the alien woman. "Why?" she asked after a time.

Startled from his circumspect study of the alien, Rentec asked, "Why, what, Your Grace?"

"Why all of it, Minister? Except the privacy part. That I can understand, and it shall be as you say." She turned to an inconspicuous young woman at the side of the room. "Sitha, you will see to the removal of all surveillance devices in the private apartment of our guests immediately." Anticipating the question that was to come next, she said, "Of course, you'll leave all exterior devices in place."

"Yes, Your Grace. *Right* now?" the woman asked with concern in her voice.

"Yes, right now. I'm sure Minister do' Verlas and I can take care of ourselves while you get the process started." The matriarch turned back to Rentec. "Now, continue, Minister. The question was, 'Why?'"

"These are matters of policy better left to those who are wiser than I, Your Grace, but it seems to me that our people should know that there's another race out there with as much reason to hate the Korvil as we have. It will give them a new spirit, I think. I hear the talk when the secretaries think I'm not there. If their conversations are any indication of the populace at large, we don't have a lot of support for this war. Allies would make all the difference in the world."

"Continue, Minister. I would hear more," des' Harras urged.

"Consider their side of things, Your Grace. We are the second race these people have seen. And in both cases, they are caged. Our cage is plusher, I would think, than that of the Korvil, but in my estimation, a jail is a jail no matter how well appointed." Rentec stopped for a time to marshal his thoughts. "Allowing them access to our world and people is a way to show they aren't captives, and that we have nothing to hide. And finally, Your Grace, to have someone learn their language would be a sign of respect. Of course, they should learn ours. There are only two of them, right? Much easier for them to learn ours than to have a translator around all the time. But again, it seems to me—who knows nothing of these things—that it would be possible to gain valuable insights into these people if we knew how they spoke. Hasn't the same been said of the Korvil? Learn to think in their language and you learn to understand the people."

The young woman chose this time to return to the

room. "The devices are being removed as we speak, Your Grace."

"Thank you, Sitha. Would you escort our guest back to her room? I would speak privately with Minister do' Verlas."

Motioning Rentec to a pair of chairs on a balcony overlooking the plains, Linnas des' Harras poured a sweet wine into two subtly carved kemwood cups. "How is your mother these days, Minister?"

"My mother, Your Grace?" he asked, surprised by the change of subject. "She's fine. Recovered from the surgeries and beginning to get back to work. She only spent a few weeks in a healing chamber. Still mourning my father, of course."

"As do we all mourn the tragedy. A voice was stilled well before its time, and it was a loss to all Shiravi. When next you speak to Tira, tell her that her absence has been noted, and I would enjoy the pleasure of her company should she ever choose to visit here again."

"Again? I hadn't known she'd ever visited here, Your Grace," Rentec said with confusion.

"Your father was a frequent visitor here, and he often brought Tira along with him. You take after him in many ways, not the least of which is your outspoken manner."

Rentec blushed. "My mother says the same thing, Your Grace."

"Still a woman of infinite insight, I see. And what will become of your consort-to-be now that her ministry post has been dissolved?"

"Ra—Ramannie?" Rentec stammered. "She has no close family, Your Grace, merely her clan affiliations. I had thought to move her out to the family holdings until our matrimonial. It seems a perfect solution."

"Perfect to a *male*, young Rentec. How about to Ramannie and especially to your mother? No matter. It is a time when we must all make sacrifices."

Rentec would have reason to remember that phrase in the days to come.

"Now, if you will forgive me," Linnas said, draining her small cup. "I have one other interview before my day ends. Please make my home yours for the night. Sitha, if you would, please?"

After Rentec was led away by the attendant, Linnas stared out over the darkening plains of her ancestral home for a time before speaking to the figure standing in the shadows behind her. "Well, come and sit and tell me what you think," she ordered.

"I think you will do what you will do, as ever, Linnas," grated the mechanical voice of sel Garian, "and only historians will be able to call you fool or savant."

"It is my job to see that we *have* historians, Manura," she replied quietly.

CHAPTER FOURTEEN

Lucy Grimes sat watching the morning sunlight wash over a bare desk in her office at the Terran Alliance Embassy, Zurich, wondering what to do next. With a staff of four in the outer office and some forty other personnel from the *Niven* acting as temporary building staff, she still felt lonelier than she had in a long time.

It has to be because Galileo is gone, she thought, *along with the* Niven's *sister ships and almost everybody I've come to care about.*

Comm calls were possible, of course, but when it took a message minutes to reach its destination and the same length of time to return, gossiping was an exercise in futility. Add to that the Alliance's still uncertain status with the U.S., where it wasn't exactly advisable to travel at present, and the feeling of isolation fed upon itself. Lucy wasn't unaware of what she called the "incongruous irony" of her situation. She'd made three trips to the asteroid belt and helped build humanity's first three deep-space installations, and the fact was that she felt trapped in one of Earth's most beautiful countries.

She looked down at the barren desktop and muttered, "If I don't find something to do, I'm going to go crazy. And the *Galileo* hasn't been gone a good hour yet." Reaching a decision, she called in Rukia Kimura and Lloyd Pike. "As soon as our phone lines are up and running, we're going to be swamped with calls twenty-four hours a day. First, we're only going to be taking calls for twelve or fourteen of those hours, like any other business. Second, I want an after-hours message put on the phone lines directing people to call back the next business day. Come up with something appropriate and get it set up, will you?

"That's the easy one," she said as she plopped a stack of folders down on the desk. "Here are the complete lists of all personnel aboard all four ships. The bases will send their info as soon as they get it compiled. We need to get all this entered into the computer. We've got name, home address, education, shipboard job, *which* ship, interests, and special knowledge on each person we've recruited. You two know this. You filled out one of these, just like I did."

Rukia screwed up her elfin features and reached for the stack of folders. "Well, I guess this is my job," she said. "It'll give me something to do, and it *is* the work of a secretary."

"You're right about it being the work of a secretary, which I don't consider you to be. Not for a minute. Official title, yes, and you've served in that capacity so far, but I have more in mind for you than that. Right now, pick out a few people and get them started on this, then get back here. You may wish for something as simple as data entry before this day is over."

She watched Rukia leave and turned to Lloyd. "You're my aide because you've had more experience out in the real world than a lot of us. What do you know about hiring people for sensitive jobs?"

Lloyd hesitated for a few seconds. "My father was a contractor for the government for several years. We produced some equipment for Gulf Storm. I'm still not sure what they were, but I do remember that he needed to hire people with a reasonable certainty that they weren't flakes or totally inept. There was a test he brought home." He took a deep breath and let it out slowly. "I wish I'd known I was going to be asked questions like this," he said with a weak grin. "I'd have paid more attention. As it was, I took the test, along with about twenty of Dad's most trusted and well-known employees. To see if the test was valid, you know? It was a kind of word-association thing, like 'which of these words does not fit with the rest?' and you get four or five to choose from. Pretty good results as I remember."

"Good! That's just what I want," Lucy said. "Get with Baron von Schlenker and see if you can locate one. If it goes to things like reliability, aptitude, and things like that, I want it. I think it'll be necessary for you, me, and Rukia to do the initial testing and evaluations, so I want to practice on our people here, like your dad did. We need to get managerial and secretarial types to man the embassies first. *Then* we can look to filling shipboard slots. We've got about a week before I expect to be doing those first tests for real. We've got all those reporters out there to spread the word for us about the tests, plus our pet reporter, Sarah Parker."

"We're going to be up to our asses in people," Lloyd predicted. "We need to make sure that when the report of this hits the news, people are told in no uncertain terms that the trip is at their own expense, as well as their accommodations and meals. We aren't footing the bill for that, and the Swiss won't take kindly to a shitload of indigents wandering around one of their tourist attractions. Also, let 'em know that we're just taking *applications*, not accepting volunteers."

Lucy looked speculatively at Lloyd. This was the first time she'd heard a curse word come out of his mouth. As a matter of fact, there was a rumor that he didn't know how to use a contraction, and here he was, cussing *and* contracting! *Dear god, there's hope for this guy yet!*

"We should probably have some kind of press release made up," Lucy said, "stating those facts in detail and stressing the fact that there will be no shipboard assignments for some time. We can probably farm that out to Parker to be disseminated to the world at large and have copies for anyone who comes through the door.

"Oh, yeah! Here's another one!" Lucy exclaimed. "Project Vesta is nearing completion—at least the hollowing-out process. We're going to need people to man *that*, too. There'll be deep-space observatories, zero-g experimentation, a supply depot, a rest and relaxation center, a real home office (if we decide to do that), and so much more. I envision it as a home-away-from-home for those who, for whatever reason, want off the ships for a while but still want to serve the Alliance in space. I asked Marsha to stop by and check on the progress so we can get a better idea when we can get started on the interior construction. My idea was to have the *Galileo* construct another habitat with construction module immediately after finishing Taurus. And using Taurus to help build it will cut down the construction time. The *Galileo* can tow it into position, leave it and a crew there, and return to Earth. It'll add a bit to her away time, but it really should be worth the effort."

Lloyd built on the preceding ideas. "How about a daily press release? Or not so much a press release but a jobs list. When we have a new ship about to arrive, we could put out a list that says we need one ship's captain, four cooks, and so forth. We could have a section that never changes much, like scientists and janitors, and one that reflects whatever we need at the moment."

Weeks turned into months. Mid-November arrived and gripped Switzerland in one of the coldest winters in history. A massive low-pressure system stalled over the area, held in place by the sheer mass of the mountain range it had run into.

Lucy drove her skimmer, as they were now referred to, into the brightly lit, heated garage and left the depressingly overcast afternoon behind her. Elation banished her unconscious irritation at the lack of sunlight as soon as she settled the antigrav auto in its space.

She commed Rukia and Lloyd. "Meet me in my office in ten minutes, please."

She hadn't expected either of them to be readily available this late in the day. The embassy had settled into a routine that had finally begun to feel normal. Lucy, Rukia and Lloyd only fielded the most persistent or high-ranking callers these days. The volunteer staff, mostly locals now, went home at five p.m., at which time visitors and applicants were turned away at the main gate. This left the building sparsely tenanted, sounds echoing eerily through the darkened rooms and corridors.

Her meeting at Freddie's had gone on longer than expected, but then, so many of them did these days. Still, she walked into her office smiling. What would stuffy Lloyd think of her coming in reeking of wine? The truth was, she'd stumbled while accepting a glass for a toast and spilled her glass all over herself and the Japanese Ambassador.

Not one of my better moments, she thought, her smile fading a bit.

She plopped into a chair and looked at her two friends, crooked grin still in place.

"Okay, Luce," Rukia asked, "what do you know that we don't?" Rukia Kimura had learned to read her boss pretty well over the last several months, but this was just too obvious.

"First, let's recap the dailies, Okay? Fill me in."

"Now? I was just going to dinner! Oh, all right." Her pique at not first hearing Lucy's news passed, and Rukia said, "All three bases report everything on schedule and even a little bit ahead. Seems like the infusion of some new people and the removal of some unhappy ones has caused a production increase. Mambas and torpedoes are being built right alongside whichever ship is in the yard. With the addition of extra *Sundivers*, courtesy of Adam Gardner out on Gemini, we have power cores and missile heads to spare. The *Galileo* reports that the construction of Taurus is a bit ahead of schedule. Their *Sundiver* returned, and they're ready to power up the habitat section, and the *Galileo* has taken on new power cores. Kitty's condition appears unchanged, but Dr. Jeffers says Simon's mental state is slowly improving. He's never personally seen a depression that deep, and can't predict the progress in any case." She shrugged her shoulders and sighed. "Simon blames himself for Kitty's condition, you know."

"Yes, but true or not, he's got to learn to live with it."

"I don't know how I'd handle something like that, or even if I *could* handle it. Let him alone, you two," Lloyd said caustically. "If he comes around, great. If not, you're doing fine."

"Don't be such a kiss-ass, Lloyd," Rukia said. Lately, there'd been no love lost between her two senior staffers.

"I'm not a kiss-ass, and I resent you saying so. She *is* doing fine. So what if it hasn't been just exactly like you think Simon would have done it? The result is still the same."

Lucy stepped in to separate the two. "Don't make me pull this car over!" Her comment was ludicrous enough to get through to the two antagonists. "Good. Now that I have your attention," she said, "it's time for my news." She felt the quivering tension in the air and savored it for a moment. "It will be announced at Baron von Schlenker's soiree later tonight, but I thought you'd like to know first." After torturing them for a few more moments, she said, "We got the Japanese embassy!"

Astonishment washed over Lloyd's and Rukia's faces "God! What did you promise 'em?" Lloyd asked.

"Plastics," Lucy said simply. It turned out that one of the things no one had ever thought of was what the Japanese wanted to produce. And, upon reflection, it made perfect sense. A plastic that was almost as tough as steel, lightweight, durable, almost impervious to damage, and extremely heat- and cold-resistant had been used aboard ship to make seat cushions, tabletop covers and balloons for Z-tag. The Japanese took one look at it and saw the potential inherent in such a substance for use in everyday life. Of course, they were already involved in the processes of miniaturization in almost all parts of the Alliance.

She'd been looking for a trade with the Japanese. They had, after all, provided a nice place not far from Tokyo Bay for the embassy site and then proceeded to build an embassy building that was loosely modeled on the Swiss building but with a flavor to it that allowed it to fit into the existing architectural styles around it. Giving them the plastics concessions should allow her to ask another favor. It had been determined long ago that the Builders hadn't gone in for miniaturization. Now was a good time to upgrade some of their own technology by melding it with Earth-based advances.

Information flows both ways, she thought.

"That's not so bad." Rukia said. "We can still use the antigrav with the Germans, right?"

"No, I was going to use that to mollify the Americans," Lucy said with a sigh.

"But the Germans were expecting that," Lloyd said, confusion in his voice.

"But they'll be satisfied with the superconductor technology," Lucy said wearily. "Just like the Chinese will take the solar cell technology. The British will get something else, and everybody gets a piece of the pie," she finished sarcastically. "Somebody shoot me. I've turned into a fucking politician!"

Uneasy laughter at this pronouncement was

interrupted by Lucy's valet, Lt. Diana Ross. "Ma'am, you asked to be reminded that the baron's car will be here in one hour."

"Thanks, Diana," she said, standing. "Out of the frying pan and into the fire, and all that stuff."

"Wait a minute! What about the Japanese embassy? Are there any details?" Lloyd asked.

"Oh, yes." Lucy stopped before heading to her bedroom door. "News. We leave for Tokyo in three days." She looked at Rukia, "Will that leave you enough time to get us packed and ready for a week or so?"

"With Diana's help, no problem at all," Rukia replied, nonplussed. "Who's going?"

"You, me, and Lloyd for sure. I figured on a few others for effect and a couple of Mambas with their pilots, of course—all armed. And later, a core staff of engineers." The policy of going armed outside the embassy grounds had evolved over the past few months as Alliance personnel increasingly found themselves accosted on city streets and in shops. Having their weapons visibly strapped to their thighs tended to keep away all but the most persistent. Japanese officialdom had balked at that particular proviso but backed down when Lucy made it clear that it was a safety issue and not a matter for negotiation.

"What about me?" Lloyd asked. "Surely you've got something more in mind."

"Oh, indeed, I do," Lucy said, the smile finally coming back to her face. "Ladies, meet the new temporary head of the Alliance Embassy, Zurich."

Emotions flowed across his face almost too fast to follow. "You can't... I'm not..." he sputtered.

"You can and you will, Lloyd," she said authoritatively. "And that's what you get for laughing at me when Freddie explained *my* situation!" Having accomplished half of her admittedly childish payback plan, she pulled the door closed behind her as she headed for the shower.

Lloyd stared at the door. "She had her back to me, and I only *smiled!* How did she know?" He turned on Kimura. "You told her, didn't you?"

"Hell, no! I was grinning so hard my face hurt! Ratting you out would have been implicating me, you idiot. Besides, I didn't think of it," she finished lamely. "Oh, shit. If this is what she does to you, what's going to happen to me?"

"Like you're so much better than me," Lloyd groused. "She probably didn't see you, or she'd have found a way to get to you, too!"

Baron Manfred von Schlenker's long black example of extravagant decadence pulled up at nine o'clock to carry Lucy to the castle. Tonight's soiree had no special theme, but Lucy wore her ball gown anyway. For some reason she couldn't get the thought of Cinderella out of her mind, and she smiled to herself. Maggie had commented that the white material gave her a more vibrant look than her customary duty blacks, and that the gold highlights complemented her hair. *Whatever* that *means,* she thought on the short ride to the castle.

The intervening three months since the opening of the Zurich Embassy had dulled the immediacy of news about Alliance activities on Earth. Volunteer applicants walked into the Alliance building daily and came back out, volunteer employees worked there daily and went home at night, and crewmembers from the various ships in orbit came and went in the streets of Zurich. Alliance personnel occasionally visited a nearby ski lodge for a day on the slopes. Of course, the media had now spoken to almost all the family members of all Alliance members.

Since crew lists had been published with the nearly unanimous approval of all Alliance personnel (this was one thing Lucy refused to dictate), every talk show host, news commentator, and radio personality were trying to get the "true story." The media had finally been saturated with Alliance news, and only things of real importance reached the nightly news shows.

Tonight would be one of those nights. Freddie had given her a guest roster before she'd left earlier in the day. It included the Japanese Ambassador to Switzerland (with whom she still felt uncomfortable after the toast incident), a dozen wealthy businessmen from around the world, and a smattering of officials from some of the major nations. Chief among those on the list were Virgil Collins from the U.S. State Department and a name she recognized—Brandon Galway listed, she noticed with amusement, as the representative of the Deputy Minister of the Interior.

Can you be arrested for impersonating a politician? Probably. But they'd send you to the loony bin instead of jail. She giggled at her joke and stepped out as the chauffeur opened the door to the flashes of cameras and the shouting of questions, which she no longer heard.

No longer a novice at these kinds of entrances,

Lucy waved to the crowds on both sides as she marched up the steps. There would be the obligatory photo op after the "beautiful people" had finished with her.

Lucy had lost track of the times she'd traveled these steps now and had come to know the footmen by name. "Good evening, Georg. How's your father?"

"Just fine, Lady Lucille. Looking forward to summer. Claims he can feel the cold in his bones, but he won't let us move him. Obstinate, as usual."

"Sometimes parents can be that way, Georg. If he starts to hurt badly enough, he'll move," she predicted.

She moved across the foyer and onto the balcony serving the main floor. Hello, Robert," she said to the pike man at the top of the stairs, and then, "Good evening, Thom," to the pike man who announced visitors.

"Good evening, Lady Lucille," came back in stereo.

"If you would be so good as to announce me, Thom?"

Lucy began the walk down the stairs that let everyone gawk at whomever the newcomer happened to be.

Like a fly on a plate, she thought behind the phony smile plastered on her face. *Why didn't I bring someone else with me? 'Cause I'm stupid, that's why!*

She spent the next ten minutes saying generic nothings to people she'd never meet again. After a time, she made her way to the side of the room where Freddie, whom she hadn't seen since she reached the bottom of the stairs, waved her over.

"Gentlemen, allow me present Lady Lucille

Grimes, First Captain of The Terran Alliance. Captain Grimes, Mr. Lee and a few of his associates. I beg your indulgence, but I have someone I must see right away."

The baron seemed as if he was asking permission to leave, but he was gone before Lucy could even raise a hand in what could be construed as dismissal. She turned back to the Texan, slightly annoyed. "Let me guess, you want to pay for the right to get first crack at some of our technology, correct, Mr. Lee, is it?"

"Yes, ma'am, Aaron Bidwell Lee of the Virginia Lees." At her raised eyebrow, he added, "Our particular branch of the family found it advantageous to relocate for a time after the War. (He pronounced it Waw-wuh, and his inflection left no doubt to which Waw-wuh he was referring.) We moved to Pennsylvania because our politics didn't coincide with the rest of the family's. That's where we got into oil. Then we moved on down into Texas at the turn of the century where we've been in the same business for the last hundred years," he said proudly.

"And just how can I help you, Mr. Lee?" she asked more tartly than she would have liked.

"Well, now, ma'am, I'm sure you've been approached every way there is, but we have to make our pitch so to speak," Lee said. "My friends and I want to say that we are perfectly willing to pay whatever we must to get the rights to produce some of your technology for Earthly things. I know I'm not saying it right, but we've never really had to consider this scenario have we, boys?

"The truth of the matter is that rumors are flying faster than a hummingbird about the fact that oil will very soon become a thing of the past, and we want in on the ground floor of whatever is going to replace it. Here's the thing," he said, apparently the spokesman for the group, "we want to get in on this antigravity stuff. Since the oil market is going into the toilet, we need to produce something that will keep us afloat in a changing world, and antigravity looks like it could be the Microsoft of the twenty-first century. Yes, of course there's money in it, for us and for your Alliance, Captain," he said speaking so fast that his accent all but disappeared. "Remember, money isn't a bad thing if you have enough of it."

"I believe you're getting ahead of yourself, Mr. Lee," Lucy said. "We still haven't come to a firm agreement with most of the major governments of the world on just what to release and to whom, especially the United States. We still haven't forgiven you for three murders, an abduction, and the loss of Captain Katherine Hawke, who's still encased in some kind of suspended animation."

"Perhaps that's because some people are too shortsighted to see what it will take to get this project moving so the most people benefit while the least suffer, First Captain Grimes," said a voice from behind her.

She turned halfway around to the speaker. "And you have the answer to this Gordian Knot, Mr....?"

"Collins, First Captain. Virgil Collins, U.S. State Department. And this is my associate—"

"Brandon Galway," Lucy finished in time with Collins. "We've met. I see you've been promoted to the Interior, Brandon. Congratulations."

"Here today, gone tomorrow," Brandon demurred. "I hear good things about you, too, Lucy."

"Then you aren't hearing them from American sources!" Nervous laughter rolled through the group. "Brandon and I are friendly adversaries, gentlemen. Don't let us ruin your night." She turned back to the newcomer. "Since you made your statement in front of these gentlemen, Mr. Collins, I assume they'd be welcome at a private discussion in the baron's study? There's no need not to be comfortable while we bounce this around."

When Collins nodded his agreement, Lucy led the group to the understated door that opened onto the baron's library. Causing no end of ruffled feathers, she stood to one side, holding the door open while the group passed within. Before doing so herself, she looked out at the crowd. Freddie, regaling a group of women, gave a small thumbs-up at her, and she pulled the door closed.

"Brandon, would you be kind enough to pour drinks for us? Make mine scotch. I'm not driving tonight," Lucy said as she entered the group of men trying to sort themselves into chairs. The jockeying for an advantageous position was almost comical to watch, especially since she herself hadn't landed anywhere yet.

"See here, First Captain!" Collins exclaimed in disapproval.

"All right, Mr. Collins, since we don't seem to have any servants around us and you don't want me ordering Brandon around, how about you doing it for him?" Lucy asked as she slipped into what had become her favorite chair in the room. Positioned so that it afforded a nice view of the Alps during the daylight hours, it also allowed its occupant to see almost the entire room at a glance, and it was also sink-up-to-your-eyeballs comfortable.

"No, no," he demurred. "Just not used to having someone else order my staff around, is all."

Hiding the ghost of a smile behind her hand, Lucy said, "I believe you'll find several kinds of spirits on the sideboard, Brandon. And the baron serves some of the finest coffee in the world. At least, that's what this country girl from Ohio thinks."

"So, Mr. Collins," she asked politely, "just what did you mean by your statements out on the ballroom floor?"

"I think Mr. Lee would be better able to answer that one, First Captain. After all, it was his idea in the first place."

"Just 'captain' will do in private, Mr. Collins. But how about you go first. After all it was you who opened your mouth to try to salvage the situation."

"Captain," Lee said smoothly, "it really would save more time if I started this off as Mr. Collins is only slightly briefed on the situation. The way *we* see it is that you should have local people, that is non-governmental persons, doing the actual production of the items, whatever they are. We, the locals, already have the supply lines in place and the distribution network to send finished goods off to whatever markets *you* choose. If you make the government do it, any government, they would have to build all the infrastructure again. Sure, the government has those things in place now, but they're geared to military matters. This is directly in the private sector's province."

"How so?" Lucy asked, nodding at Brandon as he handed her a cut-glass container with at least two fingers of amber liquid.

"All I can say at the moment, not knowing what the project would be, is that if you gave us an item to build and the plans to build it, we could start the process, sometimes the same day. We'd just make a call to our suppliers and the material would be on the way. The problem is if, and when, we have to retool a plant or build an entirely new structure. At that point, the government would guarantee ridiculously low loans to get us set up," Lee said, looking at Collins for confirmation.

Lucy, seeing him nod, motioned for Lee to continue. "All of this would employ the same people we've used all along until we get to new production. More jobs there. The new plants go online. More jobs there. We produce a new widget or whatever to replace an old one, and you have new jobs coexisting beside old ones. And since the older widgets are no longer useful, there would be less call for them and their makers would be transferred over to the new item, providing a steady labor pool for the steadily increasing new widget market. Minimal loss of jobs, minimal impact to the economy. Very little cash outlay for the government, and they get their cut right off the top in taxes."

"Sounds good on the face of it, Mr. Lee, but I'll have to run it past a few people who know how to find loopholes in such things."

Brandon, finished with his drink chore, sat down with a beer and said, "You should look at this proposal real close, Lucy. It's one of the better ideas to come down the pipe. Most of the others are top heavy in favor of the government concerned."

Collins, trying to appear on top of things but getting further behind all the time, said, "If it means anything, Captain, Mr. Galway here is one of the initial proponents of this plan."

"I'll take it under advisement, Mr. Collins, I promise. The disbursement of technology is one of our primary goals here, along with not inconveniencing anyone any more than necessary."

"Can we inquire as to what other things concern you, Captain?" Lee asked. "Maybe we can help—a mutual assistance pact, so to speak."

"Well," Lucy said speculatively, "we're going to have three ships in orbit in about three months. That's another, oh, twelve hundred personnel we're going to need. A few months after that, Taurus Base as we call it, comes online. That's another thousand or so there. And, of course, there's Project Vesta. An unknown number will be needed to fill that one out, and it won't be in the hundreds, I assure you." She appeared to think for a few seconds. "Most of our problems are personnel-related, Mr. Lee, but I believe we'll have that wrapped up shortly. You've heard, I'm sure, that the Alliance has an announcement to make?" At Lee's nod, Lucy went on. "Find a comfortable spot, gentlemen. In about an hour, all will be made clear."

The meeting broke up, and Lucy made her way back to the main ballroom. She wandered around for a time, talking quietly with one person then another, waiting for the hour to end. She ran into Galway on the way to the top of the staircase. "Sure it's a good idea to be seen with the enemy, Brandon?" Lucy gibed.

"I'll take my chances. I've already been painted with the same brush once, so a second time can't be that much worse. What's the big announcement? I surely can't tell anyone in time to derail anything."

"Even if you're wearing a wire, what's ten minutes?' she said and shrugged. "I'm going to announce, with the Japanese ambassador standing beside me, that the final hurdles to building a Japanese embassy near Tokyo have been removed. I'll be going to Japan in about three days to inspect the site. Then, we'll have another source of volunteers for those new ships I told you about a while ago. And none of those volunteers are going to be American. That's because, of course," Lucy said biting off each word, "your people won't get off their collective asses. The future is about to leave America behind, Brandon. Acting now will put an end to that prophecy. Don't wait too long."

Not waiting for a response, she continued up the staircase. His expression thoughtful, Brandon watched her until the huge doors boomed shut between them.

The press conference went as such things always did. Standing on the courtyard steps so the cameras could get good shots, the Japanese ambassador stood beside Lucy and agreed with every word she said about the new embassy in Tokyo. He then, along with her, answered questions for about ten minutes before backing away from the small stage, leaving her to face the crowd alone, Lucy had become an expert at these functions, and they no longer terrified her like they once had. She chose which questions to answer fully and which to answer with more fluff than substance. Finally, she called a halt to the session, pleading exhaustion, and escaped into the safety of Freddie's castle.

An hour later, back at the embassy after her final goodbyes of the night, Lucy slipped out of her clothes and into the bed she'd waited for all day. Turning the lights down, she gazed at the stars and let the view lull her to sleep.

Lucy gazed out over the expanse of water dotted with the colorful sails of hundreds of boats. Pleasure craft, fishing vessels, and merchant ships vied for the same space, and Lucy marveled at the fact that so few collisions occurred. February had brought them to Tokyo, and three new ships were in Earth's orbit. Two of the ships, named the *Andre Norton* and the *Isaac Asimov,* finished off the list of names Simon had come up with, so Lucy had decided on *Shasta* for the third.

"Because I like the name, that's why!"

Rukia had merely asked how she'd arrived at the name, and the vehement response had momentarily stunned her.

Lucy sat for half a minute more and then turned to Rukia. "Sorry. So much on my mind right now that having to pick ships' names seems like a petty thing to blow up over."

"It's because of the Americans, isn't it?"

"Yes, it is," Lucy admitted. "But how did you know?"

"You set it up so that I read every piece of mail that comes in here and also every radio communication. I know the Americans have finally given approval for an embassy, so I also know you'll be leaving soon," Rukia said. "It's nerves, of course. It's a big step. *The* big step as far as the rest of the world is concerned. Once America buys into the embassy notion, it's as good as written in stone. I guess you're leaving me in charge of this embassy?"

"I had that in mind, yes," Lucy admitted. "If you've figured that out, then you're the right person for the job."

"I'd have had to be blind *not* to have figured it out, Luce. With all the 'go here' and 'meet this person' going on, everyone saw that you were grooming me for the spot. Besides, I saw what you did to Lloyd, so it made sense. Tell me, how *did* you know we were laughing at you that day? Lloyd pointed it out that you had your back turned to us and couldn't possibly have seen us."

"If I tell you," Lucy said lazily, "it'll ruin my mystique! Lucy Grimes, mind reader extraordinaire." She changed the subject. "You know I'm leaving tomorrow."

"Yes, I know," Rukia said, letting some of her temper show, "I need to tell you that even though I *look* Japanese and have a Japanese name, I really don't understand the Japanese. I was raised in California, for Christ's sake! How am I supposed to get along with these people?"

"Use common sense. You know as much as I do about the day-to-day functioning of this embassy now. So what if you aren't familiar with the culture. No one *expects* you to be. Get a cultural attaché to help smooth out the bumps. I'm sure Mr. Karagawa would be happy to assist you," Lucy said, referring to a persistent gentleman who had, from almost the first day, tried everything in his power to get Rukia to go out with him.

"He's entirely too persistent for my taste. When I

tell someone no, I expect to be listened to. It must be that horrid Western upbringing of mine." Her comment fairly dripped with sarcasm. "And if you don't tell me how you know we laughed at you, I'll...I'll…"

"What?"

"Quit!"

"You wouldn't do that after all we've been through," Lucy said with conviction.

"Try me."

"Okay, *geez!* A girl can't even have any fun," Lucy said, pouting at her friend. "You two were so busy laughing at me that you must not have noticed the mirror at the side of the room. But *I* saw it, and I saw the two of you. And I vowed to get even. Laugh at my discomfort at being thrust into the spotlight, will ya? Well, what goes around, comes around. Your turn, only *I* won't laugh. Didn't with Lloyd, and I won't with you."

Just a small lie, for as soon as Rukia walked out of the office, laugh she did.

Lucy's shuttle landed in the *Arthur C. Clarke's* bay, and she strode about halfway down the ramp and stopped. A small band was playing something martial off to one side, something vaguely familiar but nothing she could put a name to. "Permission to come aboard?" she asked formally of the commander standing at the foot of the ramp.

"Granted, ma'am, and welcome aboard the *Clarke*. The captain's compliments, and would you care to join her in her ready room?" came out of the mouth of the officious-sounding young man who wore a set of duty blacks that looked as if they'd been tailored to fit.

"Delighted, Commander. Lead the way." Lucy knew that she could teach this one a thing or two about his own ship but passed up the chance to bring him down a peg or two.

The fresh-faced commander knocked on a door with a brass plaque reading: Gayle Miller, Captain, *TAS Arthur C. Clarke*, Commanding. Hearing a muffled voice from inside that he translated as, "Come in," the young man did just that, stopping in the doorway and effectively blocking it. "Ma'am, First Captain Grimes."

"Send her in, Charley, and for God's sake quit blocking the door for superior officers. It's rude and could turn you into a *lieutenant* commander in no time flat."

Lucy closed the door on the startled face of the commander and looked at Gayle. "Who is *that*?"

"Someone entirely too serious for his own good. I think he'll make a good tactical officer though, if I can only get some of the spit and polish off him. Got good marks on all of the tests we could devise, some of which he helped develop, so things are suspect there. But he's coming along. Got great marks on games theory and something called chaos theory. Just needs to get over himself." The two women hugged and sat down. "So, to what do I owe the pleasure?"

"Well, I've come to steal some of your people. The American Embassy has been approved..."

"Congratulations!"

"Thanks, but the problem is that I don't have enough trained, trustworthy staff to set the place up properly. I took all I could from the *Niven,* but they're now stretched between Zurich and Tokyo. A couple of dozen bodies are all I need, and I can get you good replacements from the tests we're administering. I need experienced engineers to oversee the installation of the power core and security screen, and a few bodyguards. I haven't needed those since Zurich, but Lloyd and Rukia insist that I have them. Mother hens, both."

"Well I, for one, agree with 'em. Do you really trust that bunch of..." Gayle stumbled to a halt, at a loss for words.

"Okay. Okay," Lucy said, picking another subject. "How's Simon doing?"

Gayle, who'd just come from the *Galileo*, said, "He's doing okay. Seems more like himself all the time. There's just this... shadow, ya know? Like a cloud he can't get out from under. I came back by way of Vesta. Thought you'd like to know."

"What?"

"All the machines are idle. Took a shuttle into the thing. Job's done. Completely hollowed out and ready for the next step."

"Good. We should get the *Galileo* to build a habitat and factory section and tow it to Vesta. Crew that and start laying grav lines. Then we get the interior aired up and we're on our way. The rest of the construction can go at our leisure. Oh, there is one other thing."

"Yes?" Gayle asked expectantly.

"The band. It's embarrassing, Gayle! I mean, I agree with the symbolism, and thanks for the thought, but save it for special occasions, okay?"

"Special occasions?" Gayle was all innocence. "Do you mean to say that the commanding officer of the Terran Alliance visiting one-seventh of her battle fleet isn't a special occasion?"

Commander Diana Ross, newly promoted, walked into the room carrying a stack of papers. Appointed to be Lucy's personal secretary after the promotion of Rukia Kimura to head of the embassy in Japan and overly conscious of the new insignia on her collar, she set the papers down on Lucy's desk. Still uncomfortable with the familiarity to which she was now entitled, Diana, said, "This is the first batch, uh, Lucy. I've flagged the ones that look most promising in blue and the least in green."

Lucy stared out the window at the San Mateo Mountains as the map on her wall called them, and asked, "How many good ones, Diana?"

"Out of over four hundred applications, we have about two hundred sixty-five, ma'am."

"That takes us over the top for the first ship, but keep the interviews going," Lucy said absently as she watched the sun set behind the mountains. "Call up the first crew and have them report for their initial introduction class. Let Security know we'll be having arrivals and give them a list of names. Get housekeeping to assign quarters and notify the mess halls to begin to expect an increase at the tables. Tell all the other acceptable applicants that they're in the 'keep a bag packed' file."

The three ships in orbit awaiting crews preyed upon Lucy's mind. Two months had passed since skeleton crews had delivered them to Earth orbit, and still they sat with only skeleton crews. She had envisioned these three ships as examples of what the Terran Alliance really stood for. Crewed with a truly international mix, these ships needed to get under way as soon as possible. The sticking point was the damned Americans. It had taken Congress months to decide to cede even a small portion of the New Mexico desert to the Alliance, and still more months—meanwhile, the Japanese embassy had taken off like a bat out of hell—for the infrastructure to be set in place and become operational, and none of it would have been possible if it hadn't been for the surprise that arrived on her doorstep three days after the embassy opened. Lucy stared out the window and wondered if the U.S. could have picked a *worse* place to cede them. She doodled in the ever-present dust that seeped through every possible crack in the ancient buildings of the old army post.

Her introspection was thankfully disturbed by the phone ringing. The guard at the front gate was calling to say that an unusual convoy had come to "enlist." When Lucy asked what was so unusual about this particular group of people, she was told that all of them claimed to be friends of Simon. Intrigued, she told the guard she'd be right out, grabbed Diana and two guards, and headed for the gate in her skimmer. After a long conversation with the leader of the group, a Sergeant Mike Abernathy, Lucy provisionally agreed to allow them inside the complex. "I'll have to speak to Simon first to confirm your identities," she said.

"Abernathy?" Simon asked when Lucy's message brought him to the *Galileo's* comm center. "Yeah, I remember him and most of the other names you read off. Platoon mates of mine from my tour in the Army. You want some way to know that he is who he says he is? Okay. Ask him why his nickname was 'Double Cross.' If he blushes, he's the right guy. And don't ask. Maybe someday I'll tell you the story. And anybody *he* vouches for is okay, too. Why not use 'em to help set up a functioning base? You're going to have more people than you know what to do with running around all over the place shortly. Let them handle security and train the new security personnel. Tell him I'll see him in about six months, and if he doesn't behave, I'll tell everybody how he got the nickname."

She sat behind a grey, military-style desk some thirty miles north of a New Mexican town called Truth or Consequences and started to wade through the stack of blue-flagged papers Diana had deposited on her desk. Her desire to see the personnel mix as equal as possible was what'd been holding her up. Her original thought, seeing these papers, was that one ship could be up and running, but then she thought of all the applicants in Japan. A simple call to Rukia Kimura might just get *two* of them out of orbit and into training mode.

Lt. Commander Thomas Breen, second-wave volunteer, rode down to Earth in the shuttle, orders in hand. His surprise at being called to the First Captain's office in New Mexico had been complete. Serving as the weapons officer aboard the *Galileo*, he'd been pleased to be off Earth and away from the stifling family life he'd endured prior to his enlistment in the Alliance. But it was the wording of the invitation to Alliance Headquarters that baffled him. "Captain Grimes requests the pleasure of your company," was not a phrase that engendered worry. "At your convenience" also gave the impression that the invitation was less than urgent. The problem was that, until he received the summons, Thomas had only met the First Captain once before, and he'd been sure she hadn't taken much notice of him.

A redhead led the small crowd into a room and handed her clipboard to a waiting ensign wearing a shoulder patch that read "Alliance Training Command." The ensign immediately left via a second door, and the redhead, Diana, walked down the aisle between the two groups of chairs, stopping at a podium at the front of the room. She turned to face the expectant assemblage, waving expansively at the chairs.

"Please take a seat wherever you feel comfortable." She began as soon as the last person got settled. "Thank you all for being here."

"As if we were given a choice!" came from the right side of the room.

Diana turned to the speaker. "Lt. Commander Mark Grant, isn't it?" At the speaker's startled nod, she looked down at her podium "Born and raised in Joplin, Missouri. Never missed a day of school, straight As in every subject all the way up to college, which you got into two years early by jumping two grades. Five years studying physics at Cal Tech where you finished up with a short string of degrees at twenty-one. Very impressive. You've distinguished yourself in the position of science office aboard the *McCaffrey* over the past year." She looked the young man up and down. "You also got high marks on the tests everyone's been required to take recently. Unfortunately, they didn't cover manners or patience. If they had, you'd probably have failed." She looked at the rest of the room so they'd know they were included in the next statement. "Those tests, along with the bios we asked you to fill out at the same time, are the reason you're here today. Any of you are free to leave at any time—back to your assignments or back to your homes, whichever you want. Or," she said, turning to the uncomfortable young man, "you can pipe down and listen to what I have to say first, *then* get huffy and leave. I don't really care."

After a short silence to let her heart rate slow down to something approaching normal, Diana said, "Ladies and gentlemen, among other things, I'm the personal secretary to First Captain Grimes, who'll be stopping by momentarily to speak to you. I have the privilege of giving you the good news now so less time will be spent once the First Captain arrives. You've been selected out of four ships, three bases, and the newest recruits from our new Japanese embassy to be the nuclei for the command crews of the three new ships we have in orbit right now."

The bomb thus dropped, Diana waited for their reactions. It had been a matter of intense debate at all levels as to who would get the coveted bridge positions, and stunned amazement was the first reaction, while elation and suspicion followed close behind. The meetings between each ship's captain had only served to fuel the debates, but until now, not one word of those decisions had been leaked. Lucy had spoken personally with each ship captain and lengthily with the base commanders about the top scorers on the affected ships and bases, and she'd finally chosen the first four positions for each ship. In a fit of pique at the wasted time, she'd fleshed out an idea about a selections board to handle the process. The handwritten notes in an old-fashioned notebook soothed her somehow, as if committing an idea to paper gave her a purpose, a goal.

Lucy entered the room by way of a side door before anyone had time to begin questioning Diana, and Lt. Commander Grant, first to spot her, jumped to his feet and said, "Captain on deck!"

Inwardly, Lucy shivered. *Will I ever get used to this?* Outwardly calm, she stepped up to the podium and said, "Thank you, Diana." Turning to the small group of people standing at attention before her, she said, "Ladies and gentlemen, at ease. Please be seated."

Diana made her way to the side of the room, and Lucy looked at each face for a moment as they settled back into their seats. Their expressions ranged from bewildered to wary and guarded. "First, thank you for coming on such short notice. I realize you've just had a shock to your systems. Believe it or not, I do keep up with what is going on among the crews. The information you've just received has been the topic of open debate for weeks now. But once you've heard what I have to say, I think you'll agree that it was time well spent."

Lucy stepped out from behind the lectern and began to pace slowly, in time with her words. "We are entering, after a little more than four years, a new phase in the life of the Terran Alliance. We've finally been accepted as members of the international community, and with the opening of this embassy, our status is virtually locked in stone. It's for that reason that you're here. Since we now have the ability to recruit from all the major countries on Earth, and most of the others as well, it's time to put our principles into practice. You know that we've had three ships sitting idle in orbit for two months now, and there are more coming as soon as the bases get them completed. We've been waiting until enough people qualified under the guidelines we've developed to begin filling out crews. As of last week, we have enough to fill the command roster of two of those ships completely, as well as enough crewmembers to fill out the empty berths, and the next isn't far behind.

"Over the next few days, I'll be having talks with each of you individually and then as collective command teams. That will be followed, in about a week, by actually moving aboard your respective ships. Prior to that, you'll be getting to know your new crews and the instructors who'll be working with you and your people until you're ready to take on your individual assignments.

"At present, this embassy has about six hundred people in residence. Some of those are slated as crew, and more will be arriving all the time. Others are here to provide services for the people passing through. We have cooks, janitors, guards, radio operators, admin personnel, and so much more. We have a small, very new, very fragile community of constantly changing people here, and most of the folks working in the ground slots expect to be promoted to ships as they become available. That's why you won't make the mistake of pissing *any*one off. It's all too easy to have one of the people assigned to a ship you'll be on. The way things stand right now, each new ship's crew will be composed of fifty percent experienced personnel and fifty percent taken from the three embassies, about half of whom will have some limited Alliance experience from serving in the embassies."

Lucy glanced at her watch. "I wish I could give you more time right now, but I have to see a delegation from one of the nearby towns to assure them that our ships don't pose a radiation hazard to them or their children and cattle." A round of laughter passed through the room, and she smiled wryly. "I'll be happy to change places with any one of you. Just let me know!" She nodded at Diana and stepped away from the podium. "Diana will give you your housing assignments and keep you informed of meetings and classes."

Taking this as her signal, Diana stood up straight and said, "Ten-hut!" The dozen people jumped to their feet with such alacrity that she was glad of the time spent saying that one word to a hapless saguaro cactus growing out of a sand dune behind the barracks she lived in. As soon as Lucy left the room, Diana said, "At ease and be seated, people."

Almost as one, the twelve people sat down, and Diana walked back to the podium. She reached down to a small shelf under the stand and brought out a small stack of papers, which she handed to Lt. Commander Grant, saying, "Make sure everyone has one, please." To the group as a whole, she said, "These are the do's and don'ts. Things like *do* pay attention to your instructors and other personnel assigned to give you support. *Don't* get drunk. No fighting. No sneaking off embassy grounds, primarily for your own protection. It's twenty miles to the nearest town and quite a few critters out there would consider any of you food. Mostly common sense, but you never know, right? Also, mealtimes are listed, as well as class schedules. We now have a few people who've generously volunteered their time to help you adjust to your new positions. They are your instructors, and you won't give them any lip, will you, Commander Grant?"

As laughter rang through the group, Diana walked to the door. "Follow me back to the bus, please." She stepped into the hall, and the ensign she'd handed her clipboard to returned it. "Thank you, Ensign."

The young woman sketched a salute, turned, and hurried back the way she'd come as the group climbed into the bus painted in a color known as olive drab.

Diana let the bunch get settled into their seats on the bus and spoke to the driver. "Quad C, please, Mickey."

"Righto, Miss!"

Diana swayed and grabbed a pole as the bus got under way. "Mickey worked here during the seventies before they decommissioned the base. His grandson joined up, so he decided to see what all the fuss was about and stayed on. When we need to move large groups of people, we call on Mickey." She glanced at her watch as the bus glided to a halt. "It's getting on toward dinnertime here, so once you get settled into your quarters, your barracks monitors will show you to the mess hall." She saw the strange look on a few faces. "Don't worry. The food is better than the name makes it sound."

Two crewmen, one wearing a *McCaffrey* patch and the other a *Niven*, waited for the newcomers to step down off the bus. When the semi-organized gaggle quit milling around, Diana stepped over to the two crewmen, turned to face her charges, and said, "Ensigns Collins and Matthews will take things from here. Ladies go with Collins, gentlemen with Matthews. In case you get lost, ladies, your barracks is C1, and the men's is C2. Tomorrow will be a busy day, ladies and gentlemen, so please take time to read page one of your handouts. And make sure you've left nothing on the bus."

Diana and the dull green bus disappeared around the corner of the quad with a grinding of gears.

One of the women, glancing through her handout, asked, "What's this six o'clock in the morning shit? Reveille? Make our beds? What is this? Boot camp?"

Ensign Collins glanced at her companion and said, "Essentially, yes, ma'am, it is, with a little bit of officer candidate school thrown in for good measure. There's a lot to go through if you want to get your ships under way in the shortest time possible. So, we all need to get started early, and in some cases, work late. Truthfully, the sooner you get started, the sooner you get out of this heat. Now, if the women will follow me, I'll get you settled in your new quarters. Gentlemen, if you'll follow Ensign Matthews, he'll do the same for you. Meet back here," she checked her watch, "in about half an hour and we'll show you how to get to the mess hall. Remember your housing assignments and look on the corner of your building if you get lost." Turning, she pointed out big block letters that read "C1." Saying nothing further, she started off toward the building indicated, leaving the five women in the group to gather their bags and follow her.

The two groups followed their assigned barracks monitor, put their few possessions away, trooped over to the mess hall, and went through the basic military procedure that had worked for so many millions of soldiers from all nationalities over the years: they stood in line until someone asked for proof that they were authorized to eat in that particular facility. In this case, that just meant showing their wristbands to a scanner at the door.

They made their way through the cafeteria-style service and sat down at two adjoining tables to eat and discuss the day's events. The complainer, Lt. Commander Anna Zandt off the *Niven*, said, "Can you believe it? They can cram up to forty people into those rundown buildings. And the facilities! Communal showers, and stalls all lined up in a row while people run around outside 'em taking care of... business? And we have to keep those places clean! Mops, buckets, brooms and stuff, and all before 'formation.'" She was referring to the gathering of all personnel for the day's duty assignments before first mess. "I've got a good mind to go back to the *Niven* and let the bunch of you rot here!"

Thomas looked up from the mass-produced meatloaf and mashed potatoes in front of him and said, "I'll bet if you do that, you'll never rise higher than you are right now, Zandt," he said, looking at her name tag. "Just what *was* your job on the *Niven*?"

"Nav officer," she said uncertainly. "Do you really think so?"

Tom finished his mouthful and chased it down with the iced tea in front of him. "As a matter of fact,

I do. Look at the way things are shaping up. First, we were accepted willy-nilly and plugged into slots for OJT. Now, we have these tests and personal histories to fill out. And from what I hear, all new volunteers are taking the same tests *before* acceptance now. For Christ's sake! Those tests *determine* acceptance! And now, we're dumped on an old military base to train. And things are being run a lot more militarily, which, to my way of thinking, is necessary. We have too many people to just say, 'Do whatever, whenever,' so we have to get regimented. Eventually, we're going to have instructors who've actually served out there training the upcoming classes. Right now, I'll bet we just have something like professional motivators or efficiency experts giving general advice. Make the best of it. This could be a turning point for those of us who want to stay with the Alliance." With this pronouncement, he turned his attention back to his plate and tuned his fellow diners out.

An hour later, the twelve candidates, still talking over coffee, had long since pushed the two tables together. So far, they'd used military rank freely, not thinking about the eventual consequences, but the almost certainly fortuitous happenstance of getting a military base handed to the Alliance for an embassy rubbed their noses in the fact that sometime in the *very* near future, a real decision needed to be made. Their surroundings and circumstances told them as surely as words what none of them had really believed until now: that they were truly a part of an organization at odds with the government they'd grown up thinking of as generally kind and benevolent. It was the lure of all their dreams that had masked the problem until then. After all, what sci-fi buff could actually have passed up a chance to become a crewmember of a *spaceship?*

Shirley Dahlquist, the gold stars of a full commander on her collar, spoke for the first time since they'd gotten off the shuttle. "You guys realize that this is for keeps, don't you?"

Sarcasm dripping from his voice, Mark Grant said, "So the great Commander Dahlquist speaks! Please! Bestow your wisdom on us lowly mortals."

Looking through the place Grant sat, Shirley said, "Bite me, pest."

"Lighten up, Grant. You don't have any reason to talk to her that way," Thomas said, trying to settle things down. "She's not only a full commander, but she's a Firster, as well. And if anyone at this table has a right to speak and be listened to, it's *her*."

"Well, I just don't like it when someone gets ahead just because they're lucky," Grant said weakly.

"Luck!" Anna Zandt exclaimed. "How far back are you gonna take that one, you idiot? How about as far back as the luck that let the Hawkes get hold of the *Galileo* in the first place? Or the luck that let them get the good people to crew her the first time? Which, by the way, just happened to include Shirley. Or the luck that let *you*," the word dripped with all the sarcasm Grant had used, "be in the right place for the second wave? You coulda been left out of that for any number of reasons. I'm guessing you've about used up your luck. I'll be surprised if you're lucky enough to get through whatever they have planned for us." After a few seconds, she said sheepishly, "I guess that goes for me, too."

Thomas, wanting to hear what Shirley had to say, asked, "What did you mean by 'for keeps'

Commander?"

"First, for now, let's drop the 'commander' stuff, okay? Call me Shirley. And I meant that what's happening here is a full split with the United States. We're talking *embassies*, for crying out loud. Who has embassies? Okay, if it hasn't sunk in yet, I'll tell you. We're talking *countries*, people. What we're doing is in effect becoming members of a foreign country. Do you want to give up citizenship in the United States? Most of you have folks here, and you're going to need a visa to go anywhere outside the embassy compounds before long." Not one to indulge in unnecessary scare tactics, Shirley did her best to shock her companions into at least considering her words.

"Yes, I got lucky enough to be what some of you call a Firster. I was also lucky enough, if you want to call it that, to be involved with the destruction of that alien spaceship that was most likely involved in the attack on Orion. And, I'll tell you something else: I don't have a problem joining up as a full Alliance member. I expect there to be an oath of allegiance in the near future. I'm going to take it without any hesitation because I've already done my soul searching. You people would probably be wise to start considering the idea yourselves. You'll give up a lot, but look at what you'll be giving the human race in the long run." She stood up and drained the last of her coffee. "Think *hard*, people. It's going to be really difficult to change your minds no matter which choice you make." She picked up her dishes without another word, walked over to set them inside the passthrough window for the kitchen staff to take care of, and walked out without a backward glance.

Grant, still a little taken aback by Shirley's words, looked at Thomas. "So, what do you plan to do, Breen?"

"First, I plan to follow Shirley's example and stick to first names, *Mark*. And second, while the idea she put on the table isn't exactly new to me, I'm going to give it a whole lot of serious thought over the next few days. I really don't care why you feel the way you do about her, but she's still right, and we need to take her advice into consideration." He looked at the four remaining women at the tables. "You guys, especially, should think real hard about those things. Surely, you've noticed that we have an uneven amount of men and women in the top slots. Why that is, is a mystery to me, but it does say that things are stacked slightly in your favor. Simon took care of the first appointments, and then Lucy took over. Now I hear there's a selections board being set up to handle promotions and appointments to various posts, not to mention a personnel department. I guess we're getting so big that one or two people can't keep up with it anymore."

Silence reigned as words warred with each other to escape.

"Whatever. I think Shirley's right. We're gonna have to make a choice soon—stay and become Alliance citizens with all that implies or drop out now and spend God knows how long being debriefed by various factions of our own governments. Me, I'm going to see which way the wind blows for the next little while." Thomas looked at the remaining candidates and waited. When the only response was an uneasy silence, he cleared his part of the table and followed Shirley out of the building.

Lucy was in a position many wished they could try to survive—having more money than she'd ever imagined could exist. Earnest money, or good faith money, began rolling into Alliance accounts that had been set up for just that purpose. Lucy had organized a group to start handing over specs on various pieces of technology, with her as final arbiter of any deals. To keep things fair, she'd given some advance notice to those who were going to have to completely retool their factories, but that was the only concession she'd been willing to make.

Polling her people and their families, she got the names of several psychologists and psychiatrists and called them personally about their availability to help with the selection process. "More in the line of helping them to understand adjusting to the level of responsibility they're about to have pushed on 'em," she said to one of her contacts.

Games theorists arrived to help set up simulations for potential pilots, navigators, gunners, helmsmen and all the other jobs that required their services. They began arriving at about the same time as the shuttle flights from Zurich and Tokyo began. Those classes and the command lectures were almost all the training available downside, so trips to whichever ships were in orbit were arranged to give recruits hands-on experience that virtually guaranteed they wouldn't be wasting the instructors' time and Alliance funds.

After two days of interviewing the first group of recruits, Lucy felt like her head was going to explode. The sun had long since set behind the mountains, and

Diana brought her a glass of water and two Tylenol. "God, I'm glad that's over. I swear, one way or another the personnel department is going to have a new department called a selections board!" She slumped down into the rusty brown couch left behind by the last base commander and put her feet up on the scuffed, scavenged coffee table. "So, what's on tomorrow's agenda?" she asked after the water had rinsed the desert out of her mouth. No matter how well she closed the windows, the sand always found a way to get in.

"Tomorrow?" Diana parroted, all innocence. "I do believe you have tomorrow free."

"Free? What about that Ladies Civic Committee from Truth or Consequences? Complaining about the increase in traffic or something, wasn't it?"

"All taken care of," Diana said firmly. "Rukia invited them here this morning while you were busy and pointed out that their proximity to the embassy was going to be a boon to the entire community—restaurants, souvenir shops, barbers, grocery stores. Everybody is going to make money from this, and not just from our own people, either. There will soon be the biggest influx of people since the gold rush. Certainly, the city itself will profit, from the taxes if nothing else. Then I reminded them about the increase in traffic fines and what that would do for the city coffers, and they left thanking us for being here," she said quietly.

"What about those eco-people? I've got to tell them something..."

Diana held her hand up. "Done yesterday. I told 'em we're not going to be doing any desert training and would pretty much stay behind our little fence.

That seemed to stop them dead in their tracks. Actually," Diana said, forestalling anything more from Lucy, "you've got the next three days free, boss."

The familiarity raised Lucy's eyebrows. "Since when did you start listening to Rukia, and what do you have up your sleeve?"

"Well, actually, I did talk to Rukia last week. I think it was when you were interviewing those shrinks. We exchanged notes on you, so to speak, and decided you need a vacation."

"Oh, you did, did you? And did you decide what *kind* of vacation I was going to take, too?"

"Well, we noticed that you're almost the only person who hasn't taken time off to go home and visit family now that we're back on Earth. So, we got it arranged for you to leave here tomorrow morning and fly to Cincinnati to spend a couple of days at home soaking up family vibes, you know? And sleeping in your old bed. I know from Rukia that you've spoken to your folks a few times since we started the embassies, but you haven't been home. It's time, boss. You owe it to yourself and your family."

Lucy sat quietly for a time. "Seems like I taught you too well, girl." She shook her head. "And I'm sure you know how I'm going to fly to Ohio, spend my free time, and get back?"

"Of course." Innocence ran rampant through the room. "You'll climb into a Mamba, fly to Cincinnati, meet your folks and fly back three days later."

"'Climb into a Mamba,' huh? Are you aware of things like flight plans?"

"Yes, ma'am, I am," Diana said stiffly. "You have to file one upon departure, which you can do with our own control tower here. Then, when you reach

Cincinnati, they'll pick you up on their radar and request identification. You tell 'em 'First Captain Grimes, Terran Alliance, requests permission to land,' and you'll be added to the landing pattern."

"And just how do you know all this?"

"Brandon told me, ma'am."

"Brandon? You're on a first name basis with Agent Galway? Since when?"

"Since I called him last week."

"*You* called *him*?"

"Yes, ma'am."

"What about?

"About your vacation, ma'am."

Lucy finally recognized Diana's retreat into formality and apologized. "I'm sorry, Di. Really, I am. Tired, I guess. And a real good reason for that time off, huh?" she asked sheepishly.

"Pretty much. You know, your folks would probably love to see their kid climb out of a Mamba. I'll bet you could have quite a reception if just your old friends were aware of your arrival."

"I'll bet you've taken care of that, too, right?" Lucy said with a small grin.

Diana smiled. "I asked your folks to tell anyone they trusted not to spill it to reporters. Cincinnati Traffic Control was spoken to by Galway. They should keep quiet, too. It'll slip out somehow, but you should only wind up with local news if you're lucky."

"Won't someone get pissed about that?" Lucy asked.

"Probably only reporters, since Agent Galway is handling security from that end. But if we don't say anything, they can't get mad until after the fact, and then you'll be gone. Plus, the *Heinlein* will have you under surveillance the whole time. And you do have your wristband. You can't beam out of course, because you wouldn't want to leave your Mamba behind, but you sure can call for help."

"Okay," Lucy said with a smile. "You've covered all the bases, I guess. So, who have you spoken to besides Galway?"

"Oh, just Greater Cincinnati International Airport's control tower. They'll be expecting to hear from you. Did you know it's actually in Kentucky? Of course, you did," Diana yammered on, showing her nervousness. "And I spoke to your folks, of course. Called 'em to let 'em know your arrival time, and they'll be there to meet you."

Lucy's silence stretched out and Diana finally asked, "Did I do wrong?"

"No!" Lucy announced with enthusiasm. "It's just that I haven't seen them since this started. My little brother will be, oh, almost twenty by now. I've managed to get a call in every now and then, but the opportunity to go home just hasn't presented itself. I guess I've got some fences to mend and some explaining to do, huh?"

Diana smiled at the mental picture of the leader of the Terran Alliance getting called on the carpet and chewed out.

"Yeah, I guess. You know, you could call now and be home in time for dinner. One word of advice though. Once you get near Cincinnati, Brandon says you should slow down to the same speeds as other aircraft. And be sure your transponder is on. You know how tight U.S. security is these days."

"You're right about that," Lucy said. "And, Diana?"

"Yes, ma'am?"
"Thanks."

CHAPTER FIFTEEN

Lucy's natural exuberance at being back in the cockpit of a Mamba was tinged with worry at her family's reaction to her absence, return, and situation, so she herded the machine northwest at a speed only slightly 'faster than most military jets. America's state-of-the-art craft was the F-15, also known as the Eagle. It flew in excess of Mach two (upper limit classified), and at will, her Mamba could leave an Eagle in the dust. The high speed reduced her travel time, and her passage through a number of radar nets produced enough radio chatter that she didn't have time to get a full case of nerves before she finally heard, "Unidentified aircraft, this is Cincinnati International Control. Please state your identity and destination."

Lucy squirmed upright in her seat, removed the ship from autopilot and answered, "Cincinnati Control, this is First Captain Grimes, piloting Alliance Flight One, requesting permission to land at GCIA."

After a brief pause, a new voice spoke to her. "Alliance Flight One, welcome to Greater Cincinnati airspace. Permission granted. Do you have special landing requirements, and what is your fuel situation?"

"My fuel situation is fine. I guess you guys would say 'nominal' or something like that. I can go into your holding pattern and stay there all day if I have to.

As to my landing requirements, this ship has full VTOL capabilities, and I only need a space about two hundred feet long and two hundred wide."

"Very well, Alliance One, reduce your speed to two-five-oh and your altitude to four thousand. On my mark, come to a heading of oh-three-oh."

"Uh, what's your name, guy? We need to talk. Oh, yeah. Speed two-five-oh, I think, and altitude about four thousand."

The voice came back. "Uh, I'm Carson Gamble, First Captain. How can I help you?"

"Here's the thing, Mr. Gamble. This ship isn't really built to fly in this environment. It's built for... a bit farther out, so it doesn't have the kind of instrumentation to let me follow all of your instructions as given. You're going to have to say things like 'a little lower' or 'a lot slower.' And I can hover at need. This ship will actually move backwards if necessary. And I'd appreciate it if you could have a mobile ladder available. This thing has a pretty big first step."

"I have a suggestion, First Captain. First, I need you to cut your altitude by about half, please, and slow down a bit. Turn slightly to your left... there! Hold that heading for now. The suggestion—I can have a security car with its light bar lit up on the runway in about three minutes. Land behind him and taxi to a gate."

"Counter-suggestion, Mr. Gamble. Have the car be in the middle of the space you want my ship to sit in for the next three days. As I get ready to land, the car moves, and I set down. There's a defense shield around this ship that will damage anything that isn't ground or concrete. By the way, do you know anything about whether or not my family has arrived?"

"Uh," the voice said, "yes?" The last word had a questioning note in it. "There's someone here who'd like to speak to you, First Captain. Reduce your altitude by another half, please, and bear a little to your right. There."

Lucy could still hear the open channel to Gamble, but another voice spoke to her. "Morning, Lucy."

"Brandon Galway! Your name was being bandied about just yesterday. What are you doing in Cincinnati?" *As if I didn't know!* she thought.

"Well, it just so happens that you are a *Seriously* Important Person right now, and I was sent to coordinate things with the various agencies that have been alerted to see to your protection and keep the peace. It's not like an announcement was made of your arrival, but there was no effort to conceal it either. We'll just see to it that your visit has a minimum of, shall we say, disturbances? And if you don't mind, I'd like to join the welcoming committee."

"Well, thank you, Brandon. I appreciate that. And, of course you're invited. I guess I'll see you on the ground in a few minutes."

"It's a date. I'll turn you back over to Mr. Gamble, then." Galway's voice disappeared as if it had never been, and Lucy shook her head at the incongruity of the conversation.

Twenty minutes later, Lucy's Mamba floated into position above a white security car, yellow lights flashing, and followed it to an out-of-the-way spot at the end of one of the concourses. The car stopped for a few seconds and then shot out from under the sleek, black apparition from outer space. Lucy looked around, saw a motorized boarding ladder waiting at one side of the designated area, and slowly cut her power. The deadly little vessel drifted lower until its landing skids touched the pavement, and she slapped the last few switches, cutting the last of her power to all systems.

She pulled the actuator key out of its slot, sliding it into place in a belt newly designed for that purpose, and opened the cockpit to find the ladder slowly being moved into position.

Feeling totally exposed even though she knew she was being monitored seven ways from Sunday, Lucy finally lifted her helmet off and set to one side of the instrument panel, climbed out onto the ladder, pulled her overnighter from the space behind her, and turned around. It was at that moment that the smoked-glass doors flew open and a tall, gangling youth vaulted the low fence that normally kept spectators away from arriving aircraft.

"Luce!"

She recognized the voice, although the form was a lot taller than she remembered. "Brucie?" she asked incredulously as the young man connected with her, knocking her bag flying. She finally disengaged from the hug he inflicted on her and pushed him far enough away to get a good look at him. "You've grown, squirt. You're taller than I am now." She grabbed one arm, turned him toward the terminal, slid one arm through his, and said, "Let's get inside. I want to see the folks before they have a cow."

"They won't," Bruce proclaimed positively, snagging his sister's bag. "Mom keeps saying, 'How did my little girl get into this?' but I think she's secretly pretty proud. And, Pop! You should hear him! 'That's *my* daughter running things up there.' So, what's it like to fly one of those things? Can I sit in it sometime? When do I get to join up? The word I hear is that you only have to be eighteen, and I'll be twenty in a couple of months."

Lucy laughed out loud and finally got a word in edgewise. "Let's save that for later, okay? I've got stuff to tell you and show you that you'll just *die* over, Bubba," she said, using the diminutive that came so easily as she led him to the darkened glass doors. She stopped just before them and said, "Oh, yeah!" Turning back to face her ship, she pulled the key from its special pocket, pointed it at the craft, and pressed a button on the side. The cockpit closed of its own accord, and she pressed a second button. Immediately a shimmering bubble formed around the vessel. "Okay, let's go."

"What's that?" her brother asked.

"Meteor shield," Lucy answered matter-of-factly. "Also works real well to keep intruders out."

"Oh, wow," was his only response as he opened the door and Lucy walked into her past.

Or as far into it as she could, considering her circumstances. Mom and Pop were the first ones she recognized in the crowd, the people she'd turned to for guidance on all of the big things for as long as she could remember. She knew her brother, Bruce, of course, who'd moved over to stand beside a pretty brunette. His girlfriend? Half a dozen or so of her closest friends from Coverdale, an upscale community just across the Ohio River that helped make up the Greater Cincinnati area, were there, and a few less well-remembered faces, along with some she frankly didn't know at all, the last group probably being those who just happened to be in the "right place at the right time."

And Brandon Galway. She watched as he discreetly showed his wallet to a man trying to approach their group. As she hugged her mother, she saw the man walking away, frustration evident in his shoulders and gait.

Darla Grimes pushed her daughter away to arm's length and held her there. "I didn't understand any of this when I first heard about it," she said meaningfully, "and I really don't have a grip on it now. Hopefully, *you* can put this in perspective for me."

"I'll try, Mom. Really, I will." She turned to her father. "Hi, Pop," she said and delivered a lighter hug, knowing his feelings about public displays of affection.

"'Hi, Pop?' I want to be there when you explain to your mother just what you've gotten yourself into. And I *guarantee* you," he said with a grin, "that I'll have questions." Her father was the total antithesis of her mother. Where Darla Robinson had grown up with June Cleaver as a role model, John Grimes was enamored of Albert Einstein and his ideas about the universe. Where Darla wanted to cushion and protect, John knew that learning life's lessons had to come with at least a modicum of suffering, or the lessons wouldn't stick. And his daughter didn't seem any worse for her experiences. *She moves with more assurance than I remember*, he thought. *And she stands straighter, too*. Aloud, he said, "Go see your friends. This morning and afternoon are for them. But I want you to remember that dinner will be on the table promptly at seven. Understand?"

The First Captain of the Terran Alliance meekly

said, "Yes, sir. And, Pop?"

"What?"

"Thanks."

Lucy took a deep breath and waded into the group of well-wishers, friends and quasi-friends, knowing what was coming. Five minutes of hugs, handshakes, and one surreptitious pat on the butt later, the group began to break up.

As people drifted back to their vehicles, Lucy was left with a half dozen people—two friends she'd kept from grammar school, her parents, her brother, and Galway. The residents of a community as small as Coverdale (population hovering around seven thousand), tended to stay close for most of their lives unless someone moved away. The few who chose to move off into the great, big wonderful world were balanced by the folks who thought a small town was the perfect place to raise a family, so things never changed all that much.

"So, what do you guys want to do?" Lucy asked, knowing the answer ahead of time.

"Well," Carmen LeBoy said, jumping in, "we want to know everything, of course."

"But we thought we'd take you to Martello's," Amy Sparks said. "We got the back room, and the Pasta Primavera will be flowing freely."

Lucy couldn't remember a time when the three women hadn't been friends. Thinking back to her first day of kindergarten, she remembered how glad she'd been glad of Carmen's presence. Carmen claimed to remember even earlier.

"Martello's! Guys, that's too expensive!" Lucy

started.

"No, it isn't," Amy said. "Remember, we all worked for Martello, and he's just as anxious to see you as anyone else. When we asked to rent the back room, he wouldn't hear of it. Said it was on him and started to prepare his Primavera." Pasta Primavera on Martello's menu was a treat. It was rarely advertised, and whoever happened to pick a night when it was being served considered themselves among the luckiest people in the Cincinnati area.

"Okay, guys, you've sold me," Lucy said, remembering the nights when there was enough left over for the waitstaff to have some. "But let me talk to someone for just a sec, okay?"

She walked away without waiting for an answer, making her way to where Galway was leaning against a wall. On the way, she caught her father's eye and motioned him over. "Hello, Brandon," she said as her father arrived, an expectant look on his face. "I want you to meet my father, John Grimes. Pop, this is Brandon Galway. You have him to thank for helping put an end to your... troubles. Don't blow a gasket, but he's with the FBI. And as agents go, he's one of the better ones. As a matter of fact, I think his job title is Special Assistant to the President of the United States. I think he's more like a troubleshooter."

A cloud passed over John Grimes' face, but he finally put his hand out and said, "I guess I need to say thanks. If it was through your efforts that my wife and son were released, then I owe you."

"No thanks are necessary, Mr. Grimes. You can think of it as payback to your daughter. I owed her. Besides, I don't always agree with what my government does, and detaining you folks was wrong.

Questioning you, I can understand. Hauling you in, no."

Galway released Lucy's fathers' hand and turned to Lucy. "Commander Ross said you'll be here for three days?"

"Yeah. Training schedules will be winding down by then, and I need to get the *Norton* out of orbit. Why? Are you going to be my babysitter while I'm here?"

"Just think of me as a facilitator, Lucy," the agent said. "Go have fun. I'll just be a ghost in the background, trying to see that you're not disturbed."

"Like you did with that guy a while ago?" she asked, smiling.

"Just a reporter," Galway said, waving his hand dismissively. "When I tried to shoo him off, he showed me his press card and started spouting first amendment rights at me. I just showed him my badge and spouted jail terms back at him. He wasn't too happy, but he left. Oh, by the way, do you really think it's necessary to carry that?"

Lucy looked down at the pistol strapped to her thigh. "As long as I feel that our people are safer with them than without, yes. Besides," she said leaning in toward Galway and her father, "it's been rigged by our techies. It has a sensor that won't let it fire for anybody but me. Something to do with our wristbands. Besides, as soon as I change my clothes, it's gone. As an accessory, it doesn't go with anything I've got except the uniform. I'll see you at dinner, Pop." Lucy spun on her heel and made a "move out" gesture toward the parking lot.

The three women headed toward the main entrance to the terminal, seemingly leaving all their worries behind. Most law enforcement agencies requested and received reports on a regular basis about celebrities and dignitaries who passed through their areas, and Lucy, thanks to Galway, was no exception. Most times, just a plainclothes officer or two were needed to deter annoyances, but in Lucy's case, an extra level of care was being taken, and she was able to spot some, if not all, of it.

"So, who was the older guy? Kinda cute if he was younger," Carmen commented, oblivious to the several officers and agents shadowing the group.

Knowing the answer would floor her friends, Lucy took great relish in saying as matter-of-factly as possible, "Oh just the Special Assistant to the President." She waved her hand, dismissing the subject.

"The president? *Our* president? Have you met him?"

"No, but it's a distinct possibility sometime in the future. After all, one of our embassies is here on American soil, and who really knows who was behind the ambush at Camp David." She pulled herself up short. "Sorry guys. One of my pet peeves. I'm giving him the benefit of the doubt, especially after meeting one of the operatives who was influential in the attack. We're supposed to be having fun, but I have my buttons, ya know?"

Amy looked around the crowd. "Aren't you supposed to be incognito or something?"

"Yeah."

"Then we need to get you out of that... outfit. Besides, a woman carrying a gun on her hip is going to draw attention." And it was true, but the stares the three women drew on their way out of the building stemmed as much from their differing looks as from Lucy's somber uniform and weapon.

"I was gonna change when I got home. Seems like Bruce took off with my bag," Lucy said, looking around helplessly.

"We'll stop at my place," Amy said. "I've got something that you will kill in, and it doesn't need a gun to do it!" She giggled at her own joke as the trio walked across the parking lot, drawing stares from passersby, as well as a few unnoticed photos from a photographer with a long-distance lens. They climbed into an old Futura after Carmen unlocked the doors.

"Isn't this your Mom's?" Lucy asked.

"Yeah, but my Firebird got totaled by a drunk driver. No insurance, of course. And, no, I wasn't hurt. I wasn't even in the car. He plowed into it right in front of our house at two-thirty in the morning. So, I got Mom's hand-me-down until I can come up with the down payment on another car. At least it runs."

As has been known to happen when two women get hold of a fashion basket-case and have all the tools of the trade at their disposal, a simple change of clothes turned into a full makeover, no matter that the victim went kicking and screaming to her doom. At least she looked good.

A full hour and a half after they arrived at Amy's house, Lucy stared into the full-length mirror. Carmen and Amy's attack had been well planned. A complete stranger looked back at her. Her long blonde hair had been taken out of its habitual ponytail and fluffed and curled, framing her face and softening the lines. Her nails, both fingers and toes, had been painted a brilliant red, and she'd been poured into a pair of hip-huggers made from something akin to parachute fabric. A low-backed, low-cut white blouse just this side of legal matched a pair of open-toed platform shoes, and the ensemble, coupled with the expertly applied make-up, caused Lucy to yell, "I look like a hooker!"

"Well, maybe you do. But you certainly don't look like the woman who walked out of the airport two hours ago!"

That was true, so after one more long look in the mirror, she said, "Oh, what the hell. Let's go!"

Four years and then some of being separated from the greater mass of humanity had left Lucy a little unprepared for the super-entity that was Cincinnati, even though it was early. The mere crush of bodies was enough to give her the shakes, and she thanked the stars above that she didn't have to cope with the traffic!

Martello's private banquet room had been *the* status symbol for graduating seniors for over a dozen years now, and Lucy, Amy, and Carmen had been able to steal it away from several competing high schools when they graduated due to the fact that the three of them had worked for Martello as bussers and waitstaff. Now, on this afternoon almost eight years later, the room was almost as crowded as it had been then, and the faces were all the same. The difference was that then, everyone had gathered to celebrate a shared accomplishment. Now, they were all here to see *her*—not an unusual circumstance these days, but these were people she knew personally, and she'd have been a liar if she said it didn't matter to her.

She began "working the room," as someone had once put it to her, shaking hands and renewing old acquaintances while Carmen and Amy stuck close at all times. The rounds had nearly been completed when Lucy heard a familiar voice from the back of the room holler, "Speech! Speech!"

The demand was taken up by all in the room until she finally stood up. She looked around the room for the first voice, but with this crowd, anyone who wanted to stay out of sight easily could. "First things first," she said. "I want to apologize for all the trouble you guys have been put through over this. None of you should have been bothered by the FBI or anyone else. All I can say is that the difference of opinion as to who's going to control the technologies we've got our hands on has been settled at the highest levels. Things are progressing differently now, and no one should be bothered again." As the last word left her mouth, the room broke into applause.

She waited for the noise to die down and continued. "I'm only in town for three days, so I'm not going to have time to renew old friendships right now. Please don't feel slighted. We have a very tight schedule to keep. I guess you guys have been following the news and stuff, right?" When a few voices affirmed her guess, she went on. "Okay. We've got three ships in orbit right now that need crews." She held up her hands to stop the buzz that started at her words. "This is *not* a recruiting speech, guys, but if any of you want to join, we'll be happy to take you. Anyone who can be personally spoken for by a member who joined before we started taking specialized applications has an advantage over those who come to us off the streets, so to speak. Just so you know." Again, the buzz of conversation started up and died down seconds later.

Lucy gazed at the staring faces. "You know, I was

our class valedictorian, and I've spoken before the United Nations Security Council, The Swiss Parliament, and the Japanese Legislature, and I've never been more at a loss for words than I am right now. I guess it's because I know all you guys, and it's a little spooky. Basically, Simon and Kitty Hawke found the ship, recruited about a thousand of us for the first crew, and went out to the asteroid belt to build the first space dock. The reason for was that if we wanted to keep the technology, we needed to get it duplicated. They believed the original owners—we call them the Builders—would come looking for their ship and take it back.

"One thing led to another, and when the first dock was done, we headed back to Earth to get more crew for the next dock. I was just third shift crew supervisor at that time, and I made captain right after Kitty got promoted to *her* captaincy after we finished the third base, I think. Anyway, it wasn't until Simon got invited to Camp David that things went sour. Simon was killed, or so we thought at the time, and Kitty was critically injured. At the time I was the choice to succeed Simon and Kitty because I'd been promoted to ship captain right after Kitty and was next in line.

"Simon's vision was for us to distribute the technology aboard the *Galileo* to the people of Earth in such a way that not too many got hurt in the process. Had we given the ship to our government, Simon and Kitty believed, no one would have seen anything of the technology until our government milked it for all the military stuff it could get. Plus, given our current level of espionage, someone would have found out about it and started a nuclear war rather than let us keep the ship. Doing so would have changed the balance of power too greatly.

"Personally, I think Simon was right. How many of us have had to deal with a bully who says pretty much the same thing? Anyway, the *Galileo* is out in the belt right now building the fourth and final dock, which we've already named Taurus Base. We have four active ships, three more waiting for crews, and more coming off the assembly lines every six months.

"Our first base was attacked right after we left for home, and we lost ten crew to the attack. We believe we've found and destroyed the ship that did it, but we also think a sister ship managed to get away. It's the opinion of most of us that the attack was perpetrated by a second race, so we're in a real race to build up what we have in order to protect ourselves, and quite possibly the entire planet. I'm not really happy to be in charge of this mess, but I keep hoping Simon will recover enough to take back the reins. All I want is to be a ship's captain. Besides, the paperwork is *awful*!"

As Lucy sat down, the doors opened, with Martello leading a procession of carts and waiters into the room. Plates full of Martello's famous dish were unloaded onto the tables, and Martello himself served Lucy.

"Ah, mia Angelina! Too long have you been away. For you, my specialty! And for all your friends. In your honor, I am having new menus made up! Now and forever, this dish will be known as 'Primavera Angelina.'"

Martello, a very pious man, had taken it as a sign when Lucy applied for a job one summer. Seeing her middle name, he hired her on the spot, saying, "Whoever is named after the angels cannot be bad!"

And from that day on, he'd called her by her middle name, to her complete and total dismay.

As Martello grated fresh parmesan onto her plate, he asked quietly, "Would it be possible, mia Angelina, for poor Martello to get a picture before you leave?"

Lucy sat there, stunned. Martello had one whole wall devoted to the famous and infamous who'd dined there over the years—presidents (three!), politicians, movie stars, athletes and authors giving mute testimony to the quality he insisted upon. "Martello! Thank you! But not like this. Wouldn't it be better if I had my uniform on?"

Amy leaned over and put a hand on Lucy's arm. "Gotcha! I figured we wouldn't have time to go back to my place, so I put your stuff in the trunk of Carmen's car. Your gun is there, too."

"So!" Martello said triumphantly. Lucy gaped at the heavily laden plate sitting in front of her. "Martello, there's no way I can eat all of this. I have to have dinner with my parents tonight and explain all of this to *them*, too."

The grey-haired owner placed both hands over his heart. "A mother *must* come before Martello. Any less and you wouldn't be mia Angelina. You are a good daughter and forgiven. But taste and tell me what you think!"

Lucy made a show of taking a bite. "It's been almost four years and you still serve heaven on a fork! My compliments. And thank you for understanding."

"I'm a poppa, too," he said, moving condiments around on the table. "I'll have the camera set up when you're ready to go." He clapped his hands together. Let's go, you lazies!" We neglect our other customers."

An hour later, Lucy looked at the watch embedded in her wristband and said, "It's about time, girls. Pop will skin me if I'm late, and you know he'll skin you for *making* me late!"

"One step ahead of you, girlfriend," Carmen said. "Here's your uniform and gun."

Lucy remembered Carmen excusing herself earlier but had thought it was just to go to the ladies' room.

"Try a shot from the waist up. There are a few of those on the wall, and the rest are mostly people seated at a table. All you have to do is put the shirt on for a few, and then we can go."

And so, Lucy Grimes, once a bus person at the famous Martello's Italian Restaurant, wound up on the wall with her arm draped oh-so-casually over that worthy's shoulder.

Carmen's Futura wheezed to a stop in front of Lucy's house with fifteen minutes to spare. Lucy picked up the lump of clothes wrapped around her pistol and slid out of the car. "Tomorrow, okay?" she asked. "We'll go shopping and then I have to get back to work. Right now, it's out-of-the-frying-pan time." After the three women exchanged hugs and comments, Lucy asked, "Hey, I thought for a minute there, earlier, that I heard Jack Potter's voice, but I never saw him. Did either of you guys see him or invite him?"

Carmen said, "He's still getting greasy rebuilding engines for one of the circuit racers over at Rick's Rods. I spoke to him personally yesterday, and I thought I saw him, but we didn't speak, so maybe not, ya know?"

Lucy shrugged. "Oh, well. I *had* kinda hoped..."

"Yeah," Carmen said, commiserating. "But who can figure guys? Go!" she said changing the subject. "I see Bruce peeking around the shade. See you tomorrow."

"I'll get your stuff cleaned and back to you then, Amy."

"You can keep 'em. You make 'em work better than I ever could!" Amy said, laughing. The old clunker rattled to life and groaned around the corner, leaving Lucy with the hard part of her night still ahead. She trudged up the walk and onto the porch, and as she reached for the knob, the door swung open.

Bruce stood there, door in one hand and the other out for her load. "Go wash up before Mom has a kitten. I'll put these in your room."

"Be careful," she admonished. "I've got my pistol in there."

Lucy slipped into the guest bathroom that was tucked under the stairs. Minutes later, scrubbed clean of all makeup, she walked into the dining room. She stood there, just listening to the sounds that had given her solace during all the trying times of her life, and two tears inched their way down her cheeks. As smells began to intrude on her perceptions, she started to register them.

Pop's famous meatloaf! I am in such *deep shit!*

There was, as well, the smell of her mother's mashed potatoes, the ones with the secret spices and lumps. The smell of beef gravy also wafted out of the kitchen, along with the smell of steamed veggies, probably from the little plot out back. And banana pudding! *They've pulled out all the stops,* she thought, grateful that she'd only tasted the Primavera.

Her mother backed into the dining room carrying a serving tray loaded with slices of meatloaf covered in beef gravy. Turning around, she set it on the table and inspected her daughter. "That is not appropriate dress for the dinner table, young lady."

Her father, entering the same way, carried potatoes and veggies to the table and set them down. "I think, just this once, we can overlook that rule, Mother." He walked past Lucy and stuck his head into the living room. "Bruce!" he said, raising his voice just enough to be heard upstairs. "Dinner is on the table. Two minutes or you don't eat!" Lucy had heard that threat all her life but never seen it enforced. Still, her brother took the stairs two at a time to get there.

"Sorry, Mom," Lucy said. "Thanks, Pop."

Dinner at the Grimes' house usually consisted of all four members discussing their days and getting feedback on decisions made or help with decisions or just talking about whatever newsworthy item had been presented, sanitized, on the nightly news. On this particular night, with Lucy home for the first time in almost four years and a family conference coming up, no one was really interested in small talk, so dinner was consumed in an uncomfortable silence with very little effort to liven it up.

For the first time in recorded history, no one had seconds of Pop's meatloaf or Mom's banana pudding. As Lucy dutifully scraped the last of her pudding from the cup, grateful again for her earlier abstinence, John Grimes said, "Bruce, help your mother with the dishes. I want to have a short talk with your sister before we all sit down."

"Sure, Pop." Everyone attended to the ritual of stacking dishes for removal to the kitchen, and when there were two stacks, John looked at his daughter and inclined his head toward the living room door.

"They're going to take a few minutes to get that done," he said, sitting down in the overstuffed recliner. "You know how I like to keep the bad things from your mother. The nightly news is bad enough with all the killings and wars and such. Is there anything you want to tell me that your mother shouldn't hear?" Never one to beat around the bush, John went straight to the heart of the matter.

Lucy, ever her father's daughter, had the same failing. "Well, you were never in the service, Pop, so I don't know if you'll understand..."

John raised a hand to stop Lucy. "Not in any of the services, no. But I was involved in some top-secret armament development in the sixties. Popguns by today's standards, I'm sure, and even less than that to you if what some of the people who came to see me said is the truth. Regardless, I think I can understand a lot of what you have to say, so don't try to sanitize it for me."

"Pop," Lucy stared. "I never knew you were involved in that kind of stuff."

"Classified," he huffed. "I've never been fond of that kind of security, but there it was. I'm sure some of the developments I introduced helped kill a great many people more efficiently, and I don't sleep well some nights, but I consoled myself with the thought that my kids wouldn't have to face that. Or I did until recently."

"I'm sorry, Pop. I never knew," Lucy said softly. "But I have the same problem. Only, in my case, I *know* my actions have caused deaths. And not just of human beings. Can you get a grip on that concept?

My problem is that I think of those beings as people. And I gave the orders that killed dozens of them, if not hundreds. No matter that they attacked us first and then went into hiding to either wait us out and escape or attack again. I still go to bed at night and wonder if I'll ever sleep soundly again."

"I've never had any problem thinking of alien beings as an intellectual concept," John Grimes said flatly. "After all, I am a physicist, daughter. But having intellectual concepts come to life and try to kill my daughter, yes, I'm having trouble. And it scares me."

Hearing the man she'd looked to for guidance all her life admit to being afraid didn't exactly rock Lucy's worldview, but she did feel it quiver mightily for a few seconds. "Scares me, too, Pop. But a girl's gotta do what a girl's gotta do."

Her mother chose that moment to come into the room carrying a tray with four glasses and a pitcher. "Ginseng," she said. "Helps with the intellectual processes, or so says Mary Fellows. So, what do you have to do that scares your father, Lucy?" She sat down next to her daughter and placed a hand on Lucy's leg. "You know we're here to turn to."

"I know, Mom," Lucy said, looking at her brother as he sat down on the arm of the couch. She was surprised not to hear either parent order him down onto the cushion. "I guess what scares me is that I get to be the one who oversees the next step in human evolution," she said, astonished at the words coming out of her mouth. "I don't mean mutants or anything like that, Mom. I mean, we've been looking at the stars since we stepped out of the caves, and now we have a chance to go there. A *lot* sooner than we would if we'd had to invent this technology ourselves."

"So, what's it like out there?" Bruce got in.

"Wide, empty, scary, dark, exhilarating, deadly, and full of promise all at the same time," she answered. "We can go to the stars now, although none of us have done so yet. Partway to Alpha Centauri is all we do on our training cruises, so far."

"How about the moon and Mars and stuff?"

"Well, we haven't had any reason to go there yet. They're kinda like steppingstone for a race just starting out, and we've started out past that. Oh, there'll be reasons to go there—colonization and such—but it brings up one of the things we find so... unusual about the ship and its database."

"What's that, daughter," John asked quietly.

"There are... disparities. For example, they have these fields built into their ships to capture an asteroid and move it from one place to another. We adapted those fields to be used inside the ship. We also have blueprints on board for some pretty powerful missiles, but we converted the principles behind our engines and made missiles even more powerful than even the Builders imagined. They can speed up healing and even clone body parts, but it still requires a skilled surgeon to replace a bad organ or whatever. Our radios operate on principles we still don't understand, which helps to prevent being overheard, but a lot of information is still delivered by old-fashioned fiber optics. Kinda weird actually. But what Brucie said made me think about it again. We don't have spacesuits. Never have. We have these things we call construction pods that let us move around outside the ship but not on a planet's surface.

It's like the Builders never conceived of going to a planet that has a hostile environment. So, no exploration of the moon or Mars, not yet. Hey, Brucie, go get my bag from upstairs. I've got a present for you."

Leave it to a mother to get to the heart of the matter while her son sprinted for Lucy's bedroom. "Why do you need missiles at all? Much less more powerful ones, Dear?"

"Mom, it's like somebody having a gun. You should have one, too, just to make sure they don't try to use it on you."

"Mutually assured destruction," John said, absently. He huffed into his mustache. *Letting me dig my own grave*, she thought, not knowing how to prevent it.

"But if you didn't have a gun in the first place, there wouldn't be a problem."

"Mom, the problems with that statement are so many that I don't have enough days left to go into all of them. But let me give you just two reasons." Bruce arrive with Lucy's bag and sat down expectantly. "First, if there were no guns and I had something somebody wanted, they'd hit me over the head with a stick, or stab me, or something else. I know you don't like to hear this stuff, but it leads to reason number two. There are people out there, on Earth and elsewhere, who will go to any lengths to get what they want. I know it's simplistic, but there's no other way to look at it."

"Well, I don't have to think about it. There're people who are paid to think like that, and I'm not happy with my little girl being one of those people. Why don't you just come home and get married like that nice Buffy Barton did? She married a doctor, you know."

"And had a kid, a tummy-tuck, a nose job, and a boob job by the tender young age of twenty-five. No thanks. Not right now, Mom. I don't see how I could, even if I wanted to. Can you understand the thrill of being the first person to do something? Or being the person who goes somewhere first? I swear, it's... intoxicating."

"I wish you wouldn't glorify this in front of your brother," Darla Grimes said, finally. "He's been talking about nothing else since we found out about your travels. I won't have him following you into outer space, do you hear me?" Her voice rose a full octave, and she stood up. "I won't have it!"

"Mom! Pop, tell her. I'm over eighteen. That's the age they were cutting recruits off at when they got started. Luce, you tell her!" Bruce implored.

"Not another word about it!" Darla stormed out of the room and the sound of clattering pots began to emanate from the kitchen.

John looked each of his children in the eye and mouthed the word "porch." Aloud, he said, "I'm going to see your mother."

The siblings picked up their glasses and quietly let themselves out of the house onto the covered, oversized porch, Lucy carrying the bag Bruce had brought down.

"What do you think he'll say to her?" Bruce asked.

"How should I know?" Lucy set her glass on the porch rail hard enough to splash tea out of the glass. "I'm the one who's been gone for almost four years, remember?"

"Yeah, I remember," Bruce said with irritation.

"Off saving the universe, right? Which is cool, don't get me wrong, but did you know I made All State?"

"That's great, Brucie! Really. Sorry I wasn't there. I missed you guys a lot, though. It's hard not knowing what's going to happen next," she said, looking deep into her glass. "I guess I missed a lot, huh?"

"You missed Mom going into the hospital last year. She got diagnosed with early-onset Alzheimer's."

Lucy's head shot up as his words struck like lightning. "Oh, God!"

Bruce looked up from the spot on the floor he'd been studying. "They say it's not your common, ordinary kind, though. Treatable with medication. She just forgets stuff, sometimes. They had to take her driver's license. I think that hurt her the worst, not being able to just get up and go to the store or whatever. She tries to joke about it. Calls it 'part-timers,' but you can see how she hurts when she forgets something."

"She seemed so…"

"Normal?" Bruce said, finishing her sentence for her. "Today's one of her better days. Just so you know, okay? I was almost a father last year, too," he said, changing the subject. The shocks just kept coming. The idea of herself as an aunt brought a small smile to her face. Misunderstanding the smile, Bruce said, "I'd have married her, too, but her folks thought she was even less ready for parenthood than I was. As soon as she told me, we went to see her parents together. I offered to marry her, but they thought it best if she was shipped off to 'boarding school.'"

"I know George Cook sent his daughter off to boarding school last year," their dad said as he walked around the corner of the wraparound porch. "Should I talk to him?"

"No, Pop. I handled it. Was about the hardest thing I've ever had to do. Her folks were pretty upset, of course, but I guess I got points for taking responsibility for my actions. At least they didn't kill me. We got the 'kids and raging hormones' lecture and then were told we weren't allowed to see each other for a while. Then they shipped her off. They even invited me over for dinner to say goodbye."

"Was this just before graduation when your grades dropped?" John asked his son.

"Yeah. I was kind of a mess there for a while."

"I don't know whether to be more upset that you *didn't* tell me or that you didn't *need* to tell me. Would you really have married her?"

"I asked her father to let me when we went to see him. I told him I was ready to accept responsibility for my actions and that I really did love her, but..." His voice trailed off and he began studying the same spot on the floor again.

"This appears to be a day for surprises." John sat down in his favorite chair, set two cans of beer on the small table, and asked, "Do you drink these days, Luce?"

"Only off duty," she said with a smile.

"Mother has gone to bed," John said quietly, "so I guess the floor belongs to you."

"So, I guess the best way is to start from the beginning." She popped the top off her beer can, took a swig, and said, "We had a few weeks to go before midterms, and there was this sci-fi convention in Denver. I went with a few of my friends, mainly to look at the crazy costumes some people can come up with, you know? But there weren't as many as I thought. Then we saw this seminar advertisement. It was about transporter technology in the here and now. We all knew it had to be some kind of gag, but we went in just to see what kind of special effects they had..."

"So you assumed command as senior line officer due to the incapacitation of your superiors," Lucy's dad said, boiling it down to its basics.

"Assumed, hell!" she exclaimed. "Sorry, Pop. I didn't assume anything. I got shanghaied! All three of the base commanders refused, saying they were 'just engineers,' and the other captains kept saying, 'You got promoted first so you're in charge.' Then it was, 'Tell us what to do,' as if *I* had any idea. I was winging it just as hard as the rest of them."

Bruce stood up and headed into the house. "Bathroom," was all he said by way of explanation. "Two more beers?" When both father and sister declined, he went inside, making sure not to slam the door.

"We each have to bear up under the loads we're given, daughter," her father advised. "I can deal with the burdens here at home, and you have the unique opportunity to advance the human condition in a positive way that few will ever have in history. I know that's preachy and really doesn't comfort you, but how can I advise you on something like *this*?" He spread his hands helplessly. "Tell me, do you think things would be better if the ship had been turned over to the government?"

"Of course not, Pop, but I can't tell the whole

world to go to hell! I'm just plain Lucy Grimes from Cincinnati, Ohio! And bearing up under the load is just what I'm doing. Barely. And that with a full team of advisers. It's not like I asked for any of this."

"Your Simon sounds like an interesting individual, Luce. What did you say that he said? 'These are things no human has done before, so everyone is equally qualified'? It seems to me that you've acquired more qualifications than anyone else at the moment, so it falls on you to do the job." He sat quietly for a time, packing the old briar pipe that sat beside his chair. "Unless you want to chuck it all and move back home?"

Bruce stuck his head out the door. "Uh, Luce, I hate to interrupt, but your bag is making noises." He handed it out the door and slipped back inside.

The bag was chirping insistently. "My comm unit. Uh, can you excuse me for a minute, Pop?" she asked, digging into the offending luggage. Not waiting for a response, she activated the unit. "Grimes." Lucy looked at her father and shrugged.

"Lt Commander James aboard the *Niven*, First Captain. I have a message here. Captain Morgan advised that you be informed."

Lucy looked at her father. "Go ahead."

"Message reads: Daily report overdue. Contact Commander Ross at Training Command."

"Set me up a link, please, Commander."

"I anticipated your request, First Captain. Link established... now."

Lucy recognized the change-over from direct connection to an assisted link and said, "Diana?"

"Yes, Captain. Your daily report is overdue. Are you all right?" The anxiety in her voice came through the connection.

"I'm sorry, Di. Things are a little intense here at home, but I'm as right as rain. I'm in the middle of a discussion with my father at the moment. Can we do this tomorrow, or is there something else?"

Relief evident in her voice, Diana signed off with only a perfunctory, "No, ma'am. Tomorrow will be fine. I'll be expecting your call at about four p.m. local time. Ross out."

John Grimes smiled around the stem of his pipe. "I guess I can give you one piece of advice now. It's my firm belief that bosses are as much at the mercy of their subordinates as the other way around. That one sounded worried, and you just brushed her off."

"Not really, Pop. The 'right as rain' part was our code for everything's fine. If I hadn't said it, there would have been a flight of Mambas here within fifteen minutes, homing in on this," she said holding up her wristband.

John looked down as Lucy slid her comm unit back into her bag. "Is that a gun? I saw you wearing it when you arrived but didn't have time to ask."

"Not your garden-variety pistol, Pop," Lucy said, affirming his suspicion. "It's a laser pistol. Wanna see it?"

"You know I do. A piece of alien technology sitting right beside me? I think I'm getting the same bug Bruce has."

Lucy pulled the pistol out of the bag. "You don't have to worry about firing it accidentally, Pop. You can't fire it at all without one of these," she said, indicating her wristband again. "We've made modifications to a lot of the technology. Things like that safety, for instance. And the same system on shuttles and Mambas now, after... We had to modify them to fit human hands, too." She handed the weapon over to him as Bruce came back onto the porch.

"Too cool! What's it do?"

"It's a death ray," Lucy said jokingly. "Actually, it *is* that in the technical sense, but it's actually just a laser pistol."

"'Just' isn't a word I'd use, Luce," her father said. "What can it do? What kind of range does it have?"

"It can burn a hole through six inches of steel plate at five hundred yards in about two seconds if it's set on needle beam. It has the capacity to do that about seven times before it needs to be recharged. If you think of it as a regular pistol, you can get about two hundred shots out of it if it's set on a wider dispersal," Lucy said, reciting from a manual printed for trainees.

"A variable focus laser beam in a handheld weapon," he said to himself as he studied the pistol. To his daughter he said, "I can see why the government was after you and why they gave us so much trouble trying to get to you. But I'm glad you held out. I believe your Simon is right. Things like this don't need to be spread out on Earth. We're not ready for them yet."

"Thanks, Pop. You don't know how much I needed to hear that." Her father handed the weapon back to her, and she weighed it in her hand for a second before holding it out to Bruce as he sat back down. "Here, squirt. See what a laser pistol feels like."

The remainder of Lucy's vacation was, on balance, uneventful, considering her situation. Reporters, getting wind of her presence, haunted the area around her house until a call to the police ran them off. The more persistent and inventive ones found ways to follow Lucy to the mall when the old Futura pulled up to take her shopping on her second day home. A reporter and cameraman bedecked with all the paraphernalia of their trade cornered her outside a Foot Locker.

Lucy, tired and caught off guard, tried to duck the pair by slipping away into the masses of people swirling around her but to no avail. As a crowd formed to see what the commotion was all about, a vaguely familiar figure stepped between the two groups. Facing the reporters, the huge man said, "The lady wants to be left alone! If you two don't beat it right now, I'm gonna sit on the both of you!"

Recognizing the voice and knowing that the threat would never be carried out, Lucy watched with amusement as the team slunk off. When the man turned around, Lucy punched him in the stomach as hard as she could, with no visible result. "Just as buff as ever, Jackpot. But you've grown!"

"Late growth spurt," he said sheepishly. "Now I'm better suited to be a lineman." Jackson Potter, once the star quarterback for their football team, had been a big boy even in high school. His agility and speed had earned him the top spot on the squad, and he led his team to All State their senior year with an unbroken string of victories, a record never before achieved. Those tackles he couldn't break, he just rolled over. Now he'd added at least six inches and fifty pounds to his already massive frame, and the difference between their heights was giving Lucy a sore neck just looking up at him.

The small crowd began to disperse as Lucy and her friends ignored the incident and moved off as a group.

"Carmen, go buy me a bat, will you? I need to whup this boy, big time." Lucy crooked a finger at the big man and walked over to a bench bolted to the mezzanine floor, climbing up on it. She still had to look up at her old friend. "When Carmen gets back, you are in such trouble! Why didn't you stick around yesterday? I *wanted* to talk to you."

"Aw, come on Angel," the huge man said, actually scuffing his foot on the floor. He was the only person outside of her family with the right to call her by her middle name, save Martello. "You were busy giving a speech and meeting old friends. I knew I'd get my chance. You three never could resist a chance to shop."

"So you admit to stalking me today?" she asked, getting a sheepish nod. "And it was a speech *you* called for! I looked for you the rest of the evening. Where were you?"

"In the little room Martello uses to spy on his banquet guests. I heard everything, and then I left."

Martello's room, known only to his employees, past and present, allowed him to know when something needed to be done for his guests, and the instant and unasked for service had earned him the reputation that kept him head and shoulders above his competition to this day.

Lucy reached up and pulled Jackpot's head down by his ears, kissing him soundly. "That should cover the kiss I promised you on prom night," she said. Never given, the kiss had gone wanting when the two graduates had come around a corner in Jackpot's GTO to find the mangled wreckage of George

Beacon's restored '69 'Cuda wrapped around a tree. Both George and his date, Millie Scott, had died in the collision, and no reason had ever been found. Lucy remembered that the coroner had finally issued a report saying that neither alcohol nor drugs were related to the accident.

Due to the cloud that had fallen over the evening, the class had drifted farther apart than most small-town graduating high school classes. Not many wanted to reunite and relive that night, until this weekend. Lucy's return as something of a celebrity helped to dispel the old cloud, and for the first time in five years, most of the old gang had been found in one place.

"So, what's next?" Jack asked.

"Got a trailer?" Amy asked with a grin. "We've bought way too much stuff for Carmen's beater."

"Let me offer the services of my Humvee," the ex-jock said. "Plenty of room for us and your stuff."

"Humvee?" Lucy asked incredulously. "How did you… I mean, uh…" she finished lamely.

"Stockbroker," Jack said simply, which answered the question adequately. Jackson Potter had eidetic memory, which he'd used ruthlessly to win more poker games than was strictly possible according to the laws of chance, earning him his nickname before his victims found out and quit letting him play. "You know, it's just numbers and patterns, so I make money. For me, for my clients, and my boss. Everybody's happy, and I'm well off."

"'Well off' is hardly how I'd put it," Carmen said appreciatively when the olive-green monstrosity came into view. "I hear each tire costs over a grand, and there ain't no such animal as a used Humvee tire."

"Now there's a scary thought," Jack said, laughing. "I just got this baby, and the last thing on my mind was new tires." He opened the rear and began loading packages inside. The job finished, he turned to the three women. "Well, it's not a spaceship, that's for sure, but it gets me where I want to go. Speaking of which, who's riding with me and the packages?"

Lucy looked at her companions, who just looked back and shrugged. "I guess it's just me," she said, giving her friends a chilling glare that would have frozen any first-waver in their tracks.

Amy winked at Lucy. "We'll stop by later to divvy up the loot, okay?" Without waiting for an answer, she turned and hurried after her cohort.

Lucy turned back from her friends' retreating backs to the man who'd just faced down two wild and ferocious reporters for her. "Why do I get the feeling that this was a setup?" she demanded, unable to repress the hint of a smile that crept onto her face.

"Because it was," Jack admitted as he opened the door for her. "Step up and in. Carmen and Amy wanted time alone with you, and I did, too. I agreed to help keep the curious away, and they agreed to let me have part of this evening. I figured on dinner. But not Martello's," he said quickly.

Lucy stared at him as he walked around the front of the vehicle and climbed into the driver's compartment. "What?" he demanded as she continued to stare.

"You goof!" she laughed. "You could have joined us and, heaven forbid, shopped with us! Besides, there are enough undercover cops and FBI agents in the area that your help really wasn't needed. If you hadn't jumped in when you did, I'm sure some local

Fed would have put a stop to it pretty quick." At his stricken look she said, "Just take me out to eat and watch for cars that become familiar. Make a game out of it if you want to. This kind of thing happens to celebrities and dignitaries. They have to let the local authorities know they're in the area for their own protection, and then they get quiet escorts. I kinda happen to be both right now, I'm sorry to say."

Jack thought about it for a few seconds, shrugged and asked, "Are they gonna come in and eat with us, too?"

"Oh, certainly," she said lightly. "But probably not at the same table." At his sharp glance, she said, "I don't know, Jack. They eat, too, and have to do something so they don't look too conspicuous. Just pretend they aren't there. I had actual bodyguards for a while, and you just have to put them out of your mind and do your job while they do theirs."

Still looking unconvinced, Jack looked in his rearview mirror. "I think I spotted one."

"That's one point for you if you see it again. Tell me, what got you into being a stockbroker?"

"I fleeced a guy once too often, and he caught wise to my memory thing," he said slowly. "And you know? He wasn't even pissed. Just asked me if I wanted a job. I'd seen how much he could afford to lose and what he drove, so after a while I said I'd try it. I think he got his revenge. I've never been as miserable as when I have to deal with some of my clients. If the money wasn't so good..."

They pulled off the road and into two spaces away from the building. "In a rig this big, you look for doubles and take what you can get," he said, apologizing. As he handed her out of the passenger side, he asked, "Any chance I could get to fly one of those ships of yours sometime?"

Lucy looked up at him as they crossed the parking lot. The smells coming out of the Mexican restaurant made her mouth water. "One of the shuttles or even the bigger ships, sure," she said as they walked into the diner.

The conversation continued once they got settled at their table. "I went out to the airport and looked at your ship just like about a zillion other people. The little kid in me said, 'That's what I'd like to get my hands on'".

"I'm insulted!" Lucy teased. "I'm gone four years and all you want to get your hands on is my *spaceship*?" Louder she complained, "You don't love me anymore!" Her eyes were drawn to two men in suits four tables away, one of whom looked quickly away when she made eye contact. "Don't look now, but we've been made, Clyde," she said with a bad imitation of a gangster's moll. "We've got shadows."

The shadows remained for the rest of the afternoon. At least the human kind were less obvious to the two high-school sweethearts as they talked about the past few years. Jack had married not long after Lucy "disappeared," stayed that way for six months and, with no prenuptial agreement, lost half his worth in a messy divorce. No matter that he was worth ten times now than he had been then, the pain still ran too close to the surface. "I wish things had been different, Angel. Really, I do. But here I am, an ex-jock with a mind trick that lets him make money, and here you are, boss of your own space navy, about to drag the human race into the twenty-fifth century, kicking and screaming."

Lucy thought about that for a time. "It's not like either one of us set out to wind up where we are today. I'd say, 'No harm, no foul,' and try to move on. I do think we could try to see if things would work out between us, from the perspective of our new lives, of course. In the meantime, if you want to learn to fly, I can teach you, just not a Mamba. You're... they're built for smaller people, Jack. I'm sorry, but I just don't see how you could fit into a cockpit."

"That's what the Air Force said, too," he said, smiling. "Them, I turned down. Your invitation sounds a lot better though."

"Good!" Lucy exclaimed. "I like to see things finish up on a positive note. And that means," she said when his expression changed, "that I still have to have a talk with Pop and get some sleep. I have to fly back to New Mexico tomorrow. Say, in return for those flying lessons, how would you like to use your little mind trick for me?"

"How so?"

"Well, we have funds coming into our treasury now, and investing seems like the way to go." Lucy shifted uneasily in her chair and lowered her voice. "See, if we can intertwine ourselves more deeply into Earth's finances, it's going to be harder for them to cause us trouble. I've always felt that the more money you control, the more control you have. I've just never had the money to test the theory."

Jack laughed out loud. "Not a theory. Fact. And, sure I'll help. How much are we talking about?"

"Millions, for sure. Billions, maybe. Poor Jack," she said when his eyes glazed over. "Just take it one day at a time. I do, these days."

Lucy and Jack pulled up in front of Lucy's house and found Carmen's old Futura waiting at the curb. Both women piled out and headed for the back of the bigger vehicle. Ten minutes later, with both vehicles gone, Lucy wandered up the walk, across the porch, and into the living room. "Pretty fancy rig you pulled up in, Luce. Was that Jackpot?"

"Yeah, Pop. He's a stockbroker now. Seems to be doing well, too, if his mode of transportation is any indication."

Father and daughter made their way into the living room and sat down. "Your mother's at church, so we can talk freely if you want to."

"Actually, Pop, there's not a lot more to talk about. You've let me know that you don't disapprove of what I'm doing, and that's enough for me. Like I told Jack earlier, I just take things one day at a time. Oh, I make *plans*, but..." her voice trailed off.

"So, what are your plans when you get back?" her father asked.

"Well, I have to go over the training reports, pick captains for two ships sitting in orbit, and pick the crews if we have enough qualified to go out on their training cruises. Follow that with another wave of volunteers and another after that. It won't be long before that kind of decision is out of my hands though. I'm trying to get a personnel department set up to handle things like evaluations, promotions, transfers, and such. It's finding the right people to do the job, you know?"

"I do," he agreed. "I have an idea for you. I know a man who's retiring soon, and he'd be perfect to head up a department like that. He could take a preretirement vacation, come down there, and test the waters. What do you say?"

Lucy picked up a piece of paper and started writing. "I'll take help wherever I can find it. Anyone recommended by you will be welcome anytime, Pop. This number will get you through to my private secretary." Seeing his eyes widen slightly at her statement, she smiled. "I have a little trouble with it, too. I was always able to juggle everything in my life, but now I have a secretary, support staff, gofers, aides, personal pilots and drivers. I have department heads, ship captains, base commanders, three embassies, and headaches out the wazoo. Some of the load is picked up by Diana, of course, but I have to make the final decisions."

"I have one piece of advice, Luce. Any CEO of any major corporation learns it early or he burns out—learn to delegate. Once you pick someone, let them do the job you set them. If they don't do it well enough, replace them. But let them try! Otherwise, you'll get bogged down in minutia and never get the overall plan accomplished, whatever that plan may be."

Father and daughter sat in companionable silence for a time until Lucy looked at her watch. "I think I should get to bed, Pop. Long day tomorrow. Tell Mom goodnight and I'll see her for breakfast. Besides, I need to check in with Diana before she has kittens." She heaved herself up out of her chair and headed for the stairs. Halfway there, she turned back and walked to where her father sat, bending to hug him. "Thanks, Pop. You don't know how much I needed this vacation."

Lucy made her way upstairs, got undressed, and

picked up her comm unit. After a short talk with Diana to let her know all was still well, she signed off and lay down to sleep. The process was complicated that night, for some reason, by the sounds the old house made. Sounds that should have soothed her to sleep kept her jumping. An hour after she lay down, she heard her mother coming in from church. A few minutes after that, she heard steps on the stairs that padded into her parents' bedroom.

Drifting in that half-awake state just before sleep finally comes, she heard a door open, another close, and a few seconds later water began running in the bathroom sink. This set of sounds ended, and the bathroom door opened. Lucy was listening for the sounds that would tell her that whoever was up had gone back to bed when her door opened. She reached over and touched the base of the lamp once, bringing the light on to its lowest setting.

A short, slender figure stepped into the dim light, resolving itself into the form of her mother. "Did I wake you up, honey?"

Lucy sat up and slid over, patting the side of the bed. "Sit down, Mom. No, I was just kinda drifting in and out."

Wringing a handkerchief in her hands, the elder woman sat slowly on the edge of the bed. "I remember buying this bed for you," she said incongruously. Lucy groped for a response, and her mother continued. "But I can't remember my own address or phone number."

"Mom..."

"It's okay, honey," Darla Grimes rushed on. "I have your father. He tries to protect me, shield me, but I know what's happening to me. They *say* it's controllable, but will I know if it isn't? I'm not looking for pity, baby," she said, reaching out to stroke Lucy's cheek. "I just want you to know that no matter what, somewhere down deep, I will always love you."

Lucy squirmed uncomfortably on the bed. "Mom, you're going to be fine."

Legs crossed under her, Darla looked her daughter in the eyes. "Don't patronize me, young lady. Your father and I have always taught you to look trouble squarely in the face. What kind of example would I be if I folded at the first hint of trouble in my own life?" She laid her hand on top of Lucy's. "Like I said, I have your father. I think that sooner rather than later, he's going to have his hands full with... me. You and Bruce are going to have to look out for each other from now on. You've flown the nest, and your brother isn't far behind. That's as it should be, but I know what he's going to do, and I want you to see that he's safe. You have to promise me that, Lucy."

The intensity in her mother's voice shut all else out of Lucy's awareness. "Mom, I *can't* make that kind of promise! I have no way to keep it. Sure, I could keep him out of the Alliance, but would that keep him safe? Not in this day and age. Besides, my baby brother is stronger than you imagine. I think he'll grow up just fine. Trust me, Mom."

The older woman squeezed the hand of her daughter. "The world belongs to the young, Lucy, and one of the jobs of the elders is to know when to step aside. The future belongs to you, and all your father and I can hope for is that we've trained you well enough to cope with it. I wish it hadn't landed on you as hard as it has, but fate deals us our hands and we have to play 'em. At least that's what your father says." She leaned over, kissed her firstborn on the forehead, and stood up. "I should get back to bed. If he wakes up and finds me gone, he frets." Darla Grimes walked over to the door and looked back at her daughter. "I want you to remember, even if *I* forget—I love you and am as proud of you as any parent could possibly be." The door closed, leaving Lucy alone with her thoughts.

FUGUE

From another plane, a presence looked down on the tortured, writhing mind it held in Its grasp and chose to grant her Peace. The distant, benevolent entity watched in satisfaction as Oblivion wrapped her arms around the mangled remains of Kitty Hawke's psyche and separated her from Pain.

CHAPTER SIXTEEN

The seasons came and went, finally becoming a full turning at the matriarch's estate. Rentec had succumbed to temptation and moved onto the estate to facilitate the language lessons he'd suggested should be given. The matriarch, in her infinite wisdom, had declared that since he was the only one astute enough to see the necessity, he should be the one to learn the alien's language. Everyone agreed that their sounds could be made by a Shiravan mouth, so it remained to be seen if complex concepts could be conveyed between the two species.

Rentec made slow progress with the two aliens during the first turning he spent at the des Harras summer estate, although some things had become obvious from the outset. One was that the two aliens actually were members of the same species. They were male and female, Derek Carter and Maggie Spencer. Rentec had a bit of trouble there as the male would sometimes refer to the female as "Margaret," until he realized that "Maggie" was a nickname, much like his mother calling him "Rennie." Some concepts, such as "walk" and "sit" were easy. It was the abstract that caused all the problems. And getting to the concepts of good versus evil and right versus wrong was going to be a headache.

Right, now. Wrong, later. A little bit wrong. What's wrong for one person isn't necessarily wrong for another. The concepts made Rentec's head spin even without trying to describe them to someone whose frame of cultural reference was so different from his. He called Parlo and talked at length with him. The result was an addition to the matriarch's extended family—a bewildered Parlo. "You just waved your hand here I am. Just how much power do you really wield in this new age, cousin?" Parlo gazed about himself as he was escorted to the waiting transport.

"Power? None to speak of, cousin. I make recommendations, and sometimes they're heeded, but sometimes they're not. In this case..."

Minister Foran, on loan to the Ministry for Spatial Affairs, graciously agreed to fill the Spatial Ministry post until Rentec's return. His exceptional administrative skill had turned a minor post, the Ministry for Colonization, into a major cabinet post over the years. Now that his own ministry had been relegated to the shadows for the duration of the crisis, he was happy to lend his not-inconsiderable skills to the now-prominent cabinet post Rentec enjoyed.

The turning Rentec had spent at Cho-An, the jewel of the Stala Mountains, invalidated Maratai's prediction that he would see less of her. Almost from the moment he agreed to move to Cho-An, Maratai was there, hinting at the proper form for this function or that, helping him get settled into life in the home of the matriarch, and working to see that he wasn't disturbed during his sessions with the humans. This, of itself, was a help all the way up until she told him Ramannie was on the grounds.

"She just showed up on the suborbital, so I put her in your quarters until you decide what to do."

Rentec walked into his quarters to find Ramannie looking out the windows at the Stala's in all their glory as the sun shed its last light on their peaks. "What brings you here?" he asked more brusquely than he normally would.

"I came to see my betrothed," she answered with asperity, "and to get some answers. Do you realize that since you moved out here, we've seen each other only for social functions that you couldn't get out of? If you'd rather that I leave..."

"No! I just wasn't expecting you. I've been so busy..."

"Doing the bidding of the matriarch and sel Garian, of course. And have you thought about me?"

"Of course," he avowed. "I think about you constantly."

"Enough to keep me squirreled away in a tiny apartment in Quillas for almost a full turning with no one to escort me to functions except those you choose to attend. I'm losing my standing, Rentec. The only time I get to go out in public is when I go to work. You certainly aren't around to do your part." Ramannie gave vent to the feelings she'd been keeping pent up for the past turning. Even in Shiravan society, and even on a wartime footing when rules were relaxed, a young woman promised as consort wasn't allowed to be seen in public unescorted, with the exception of making her way to her workplace. And since Shiravan society had such a strong matriarchal flavor, a young woman who was kept from attending social functions for whatever reason soon fell out of sight of her equals. "When will we be joined, Rentec? Then I can attend functions with just a family retainer. *Someone* needs to keep the do' Verlas name in the spotlight, else you will rise no higher than you are now. And how high *have* you risen, consort-to-be? I see your old mentor, Minister Foran filling your post while you hide out here. Nowhere does your name appear on any of the ministry announcements. It's 'Minister Foran this' and 'Minister Foran that' all the time now."

"I'm not sure just what my status is these days, Ramannie," he confessed a bit uncomfortably. "I'm performing a vital task for the matriarch, and I can say no more on the subject." He was all too aware that of late he'd been given no other tasks than communicating with the aliens. "It's possible I've gotten too involved with what I'm doing. Perhaps a vacation is in order."

A thought that had been floating around for a full turning came to the fore. "We can move you out to the do' Verlas estates. It is accepted for a consort-to-be to be escorted by family members, and with so many cousins in residence, you should have no trouble getting to social events. And with my mother along, well..." He thought for a moment. "I can call and set up everything, including a time for our Matrimonial Reading. Mother has found a Reader to sit for the occasion, you know."

Setting up the trip was a matter of two calls, one to his mother and one to Maratai, who seemed to be acting as his intermediary whenever necessary.

Rentec stood with Maratai and watched Ramannie board the suborbital. "I should be gone only a few days," he said. "I want to try an idea that I think Dom' Carter has been trying to get across to me. If I understand him correctly, he wants me to live with the two of them constantly, hearing and speaking nothing but their language, a process I interpret as total immersion. The concept has merit, I believe." He said no more, as his proximity to Maratai constantly caused him to lose his focus, almost as if she were deliberately... *No*, he thought, *she can't* possibly *be interested in me*. Without another word, he followed Ramannie up the ramp.

The suborbital circled the do' Verlas estates four hundred miles to the south of Quillas. A thoroughly angered Ramannie turned to Rentec. "I thought we were going back to Quillas first! What about my clothes? My things?" she asked sharply, pulling Rentec's arm until he turned to look at her. "I have only what I'm wearing!"

Before she could get even more worked up, Rentec said, "I took the liberty of having your apartment boxed up and moved here. Staying here has enormous benefits socially, and to give your address as the do' Verlas estates cannot do you any harm. Besides, once we've gotten the Reading out of the way, all else is just formality." The female of any species hates to be uprooted and replanted without her knowledge, at the very least, and Ramannie proved to be no exception. Hardly mollified by the explanation, Ramannie finally consented to the abrupt change in her life literally moments before the suborbital landed.

It wasn't until breakfast of the second day that his mother finally made an appearance. "Sorry, Rennie, I had to make arrangements for your Reading this afternoon. Rala kep Simther has agreed to officiate. Until Morath has spilled his blood across the sky, I will be in consultation with our elders." With this pronouncement, Tira do' Verlas, Reader Prime, gave notice as to the time and place of the Reading and swept from the room.

It was customary for Readings to be overseen by a Reader of another line who had no ties to any of the interested parties. While the empathic link established during a Reading was able to give a Reader a glimpse into the future, it was the overseer who kept the Reader tied to impartiality. Tradition said that total ignorance of the pair being Read was best, so Rentec's mother, an accomplished Reader herself, had to scramble to find someone to fit the equation.

Rentec commed Ramannie in her suite. It was necessary for the two to stay apart until the Reading so the Reader didn't stumble upon the pair prematurely and taint the Reading. "Sunset at the family shrine," he told his consort-to-be, correctly deciphering his mother's instructions. Some Readers tended to wax poetic as their particular gift was activated. Emotions flowed close to the surface as the time for a Reading approached and hormones kicked in.

By the time the Reader got escorted into the room with the hopeful pair, she'd mastered the vagaries of her body and arrived at a state approaching catatonia. This was the condition Rentec saw his mother in for the first time in his life. He'd heard of the phenomenon, but until today, he'd never seen it. He sat there, arms around his consort-to-be and hers around him, entwining their auras as intimately as their physical bodies, and waited for the next step in the Reading.

Ramannie, for her part, sat woodenly still, posed with her intended as instructed by the overseer. Fear tingled in her like an electric current, and she ground it under a mental heel, dragging her emotions back under control.

For a time, the participants in this drama remained as if fixed in place. Then Tira do' Verlas, leaning limply on the arm of a servant, seemed to find strength from some inner reservoir and stood alone. The servant stepped back and, hands outstretched, the Reader approached the combined auras of the pair in front of her. She recognized the cool blue (surprising!) of her firstborn instantly and rejoiced at the feeling. The lime-green aura entwined with his she didn't recognize. Approaching, hands still outstretched, she allowed her aura to mesh with the entwined auras before her. She moved around the pair, examining them from all angles, arms around but not quite touching the supplicants. Her aura pulled one direction and then another in a dance that would, under other circumstances, seem erotic. However, presently, at sunset, surrounded by the remains of ancestors going back forty-two generations, the Reader, in her simple peasant dress, moved with grace and majesty in a dance that at its end should leave no doubt as to the rightness of this possible union.

A questioning feel began to assert itself into the dance of Tira do' Verlas. A hesitation appeared. Time passed while the last of Morath's blood fled from the skies, and still the two lovers sat frozen under the stars as their every aural nuance was examined. Finally tiring, Tira slowed to a stop. Her head fell forward and her arms to her side. Alarmed, the servant stepped forward to assist her, but pushing the offered arm away, she stood straight and faced her opposite number. "I can get no clear picture," she said at last. "Never before have I seen such auras. They mesh here and not there. They combine as one in this place yet remain separate in others. What say you, Rala kep Simther?"

Called from her position on the sidelines of the event, the overseer, equally entwined in the aural dance while it went on yet separated from it, admitted, "I see no outcome. It is as if a small part of one of these two is rejecting the other. But I cannot tell which."

"Nor can I," Tira said, defeated. "This must be studied." Motioning for the seated pair to get up, she turned, distracted, and walked slowly back to the house and her rooms, leaving the others to make their uncertain ways back as best they could.

Rentec flew back to Cho-An, seething with an inner turmoil he had trouble putting a name to. Of course, he was upset by the inconclusive results of the Reading, as was his mother. She'd gone into seclusion, studying her books and aural charts, and calling other Readers to discuss the finer points of the Reading, looking for any similarities she could use to get hold of the situation. To say nothing of Ramannie. She'd suffered for at least a full turning before getting to sit for Tira, and the results were, if not shattering, at the very least disconcerting.

"What will I tell my friends?"

"Tell them the Reading was delayed," he said testily. "Another will be done, I'm sure of it."

It was the attitude she directed at him that made Rentec so angry. Ramannie acted as if he were personally responsible for the results. He spent the entire flight trying to put the final confrontation out of his mind and return to the business at hand, and it was with relief that he watched the compound of the matriarch come into view. At this time of morning, the gava-stone walls gave no hint of their unique properties, and all he saw were the plain grey walls of the dozens of main buildings, each with their own set of support structures, the whole somehow harmonizing and drawing the eye even without the special nature of the stone.

Maratai kep Parrasine waited at the bottom of the ramp. "How was your vacation?" she asked politely.

"A waste of effort and energy," he said as he strode beside her to the waiting hovercar. "I would have gotten more rest if I'd walked off alone into the Stalas. I've heard nothing on the war front. Has there been any change in the situation?"

"We have successfully killed two more raiders, at a loss of seven ships of our own, and taken two more systems complete with their entire populations and infrastructures."

"We need to do something to even the odds," Rentec mused, "but what that would be, I don't know."

"The matriarch wants to find the homeworld of the humans," Maratai said. "Of course, that means you need to make some kind of breakthrough." She let the thought die. "Dinner in my quarters, tonight?" she asked quietly. "We can discuss your total immersion idea. When do you plan to start?"

"Tell Doma des Harras that I'll begin tomorrow. I have an idea that I think will get this experiment started in the right direction." The hovercar pulled up at the entrance to the main compound and Rentec got out, carrying his bag with him. "Dinner at the eighth hour. I will tell you my idea then."

He tossed his bag into the sleeproom and made his way to the comm panel for the compound. Picking up a directory, he glanced through it until he found a particular listing. When a voice answered his call, he asked, "Is it possible to get a car for a camping trip with provisions for two groups of two for five days?" He listened for a moment and said, "This is Minister do' Verlas. Have the vehicle ready tomorrow morning. I'll take full responsibility for all damages." Shaking his head at the pomposity of clerks and accountants, he lay down to let his body adjust to the new time zone.

The short nap adjusted Rentec's body-clock, and he found himself knocking on the door of the kep Parrasine quarters. Actually a small compound within another compound, it supported several dozen of Maratai's relatives at any one time.

Dinner was with all of Maratai's clan-in-residence, and surprisingly, the matriarch was in attendance as well. Small talk kept the diners busy discussing everything from daily activities in Cho-An to Rentec's ambivalent Reading.

"Amazing, really," Linnas des Harras said around a mouthful. "An inconclusive Reading from Tira. And with her own son! Are you sure she is well, Rentec?"

"Tira do' Verlas is in fine form, Linnas," he said, using the matriarch's first name to acknowledge the informality of the occasion. "The overseer says that one of us has some reservations but was unable to determine which of us it is. Mother is studying the situation. She sends her regards and promises a visit in the near future."

Dinner over, Rentec followed Maratai and Linnas out onto the patio to watch the sun bring the gava stone to life for a short time as it sank out of sight. Sitting down at a low table, Linnas picked up a waiting pitcher and poured into three kemwood cups. "Now, Rentec, Maratai tells me you have an idea on how to help with your language lessons?"

Rentec waved his hand dismissively. "The idea was Dom' Carter's. I merely embrace it out of frustration. The concept is simple, really. I will hear nothing but their language—Eenglits, they call it— for five days. Children grow up learning to speak one word at a time. I must do the same but in considerably less time."

"You propose to lock yourself up with them for five days?" Linna asked.

"No, Your Grace," he said, moving back to formality. "I propose a vacation, a first for our guests and a second for me," he added sheepishly. "I propose a camping trip into the Stalas for five days, in which no words will be spoken unless they are in Eenglits. We have often said that it would be a show of good faith to escort our guests around our world. And it would be good for the morale of our people, as well. This will be a first step in that direction, I think."

Linnas des' Harras twined her fingers around the cup and gazed at the mountains as the glow faded from the stone. "I will agree with this idea, Rentec. It has merit and should be tried, provided you can find someone else to go as well. The Stalas are wild, and our guests are unprepared for our world. Security comes with numbers, after all. But who would go?" she mused aloud. "It must be someone who already has knowledge of the humans, and someone who will keep a level head. Someone good in a crisis, and trustworthy, as well..."

So it was that the following morning, Maratai kep Parrasine found herself strapping on a laser pistol from a survival pack at daybreak. Her fury at being manipulated by both the matriarch and Rentec, and apparently without collusion, caused her to fumble with the fittings. And the conversation she remembered from the night before did nothing to alleviate her frustration.

"You expect me to go off into the wilderness for five days with an unattached male without a chaperon?" she had fairly yelled at him.

"*I* expect nothing, Maratai. And there will be two chaperons along, unless you've forgotten—a male to keep me in line and a female to watch you."

"And what sleeping arrangements have you decided upon?" she had asked belligerently.

"Why, the most innocent of arrangements, really. The males will share one tent and the females the other. It will give you a chance to try the total-immersion technique, as well. You'll be with them almost as much as I, after all. Unless you'd like to tell the matriarch you have other responsibilities? I'm sure we can find someone else."

Now, with dawn turning the Stalas into a shimmering dreamscape, there came Rentec with the two humans in tow.

"I had a hard time explaining the purpose of the

trip, but I think I got through to them," he told Maratai cheerfully. He climbed into the driver's seat, raised the vehicle on its repulsors, and waved his passengers into their seats.

As the floater and attached trailer moved out of Cho-An and into the Stala Mountains, Maratai said "I'm familiar with survival packs and camping trips, Rentec, but I didn't recognize the long skinny case stuck in the back of the trailer.

"Oh, that," he said with a smile of anticipation. "That's my fishing pole."

Derek and Maggie's hope that experience in total immersion would push Rentec over the edge to understanding their language took almost the full five days Rentec had allotted to the experiment. The four beings had found many mutual points of contact, but a language breakthrough seemed as far away as ever until the group rounded a bend that deposited them on the edge of a high mountain meadow that Maratai had pointed out on the map. The two humans were in the lead, eager for each new visual experience on this alien world, when the silence was broken by the scream of a tortured soul.

Rentec, clawing for his laser, yelled, "Danger! Down! Now!" Derek dove for the cover of a boulder, dragging Maggie with him. Rentec's speed was offset by his clumsiness, and two beams lanced out as one to catch the shaggy beast in mid leap. Dead before it hit the ground, the creature slid twenty feet and stopped at Derek's feet.

"Your aim is good," Maratai said coolly, "but your reaction time needs work. You let yourself get flustered. It could have cost your life, or worse. What was that you yelled?"

Stung by the criticism, Rentec started to respond but stopped, a thoughtful look on his face. "I think I spoke Eenglits," he said in wonder. "Derek, Maggie," he said to the two humans. "Danger gone. Seerka dead. We go back now."

"Nirsa," Derek said, using one of the few Shiravan words he and Maggie had positively identified. He tapped himself on the chest. "I came to fish, and I'm going to fish." He made casting motions with the hastily fashioned pole in his hand, turned his back on the two Shiravans, and headed off toward the lake beckoning from the far end of the meadow.

"What did he say?" Maratai asked.

"He told me no."

"I got that part." Maratai's ire showed in her voice. "I mean what else did he say?"

"He said that he came to fish, so he is going to fish." Rentec picked up his old perlwood pole and followed the human along the path. Over his shoulder he said, "Perhaps our peoples have more in common than we thought. I feel the same way."

Linnas des' Harras, Matriarch of the Shiravan Polity, clapped her hands together once to show her extreme pleasure. "It is well that this has happened at this time, Minister. I will authorize the departure of two Contact Fleets as soon as possible. They will be cut in size due to Korvil activity, but you will still have ten ships of the line, plus two corvettes to send word back. It remains to find the homeworld of these people. What have they to say on the subject?"

"Linnas," Rentec said, emboldened by his success and the informality of the matriarch's garden, "that's one of the first things Maratai had me ask them. It seems that they're common laborers trained to use the equipment and were transported to their asteroid belt to build a space dock. They have no concept of where their star is in relation to other stars and have no way to show us."

Maratai spoke up. "We have a few clues though. Their system has an asteroid belt between the fourth and fifth planets, and the sixth is ringed as well, and our scientists have determined that their sun is younger and hotter than ours. The spectra it puts out gives a brighter, more yellow glow than ours does. Placed in a special chamber, Derek Carter has said that a particular wavelength is what he sees when he stands outside on a clear day, and Maggie Spencer agrees, so we can discount a great many stars and concentrate on those with the correct spectra."

Rentec had one other matter he wanted to bring up. Fortunately, it was the matriarch who did so. "Minister Foran," she said, "is going to need to be rewarded for his unflagging duty to his people. I had in mind to bestow a landed title upon him. It is, of course, necessary for someone from a major family to sponsor him."

Rentec, knowing that this was the right thing to do for his father's old friend and his own mentor in the political arena, instantly agreed to sponsor him. "It would be my great pleasure to offer land to this endeavor, Your Grace. I have in mind several parcels along the Kugarin River."

"Excellent choice, Rentec," the matriarch said with a smile. "I see that we chose wisely. It leaves me with the happy duties of adding several parcels from my own clan's land along that same river and informing him personally. Minister Foran will have a very comfortable and beautiful estate to retire to after all of this is over. It's my understanding that Mondel has no living elders?"

"That is my understanding as well, Your Grace. Two ex-wives, several children, and a few grandchildren. He is the eldest of his line now," Rentec confirmed.

"Very well," the matriarch said firmly. "From this day on, he shall be known as Mondel kep Foran, beholden to the do' Verlas clan." She thought for a moment. "There's one other thing that needs to be done, and that is to confirm him as Minister for Spatial Affairs. This will leave you free to accept the post of Ambassador to the Human Race, Rentec. Do you accept?"

"Cousin," Rentec said to Parlo, "it seems that the matriarch has plans for us." The two men sat on Rentec's patio, watching the Stalas throw the sun's final rays back at it.

Parlo do' Nallen poured drinks into the kemwood cups on the table between them. "I wonder if I'm going to like the direction this conversation is taking, cousin," Parlo said. "But sitting in Cho-An, drinking zintha from kemwood, and watching the sun make all this gava stone shine is bound to affect my judgment. And that's probably what you want, isn't it?"

Rentec nodded. "Greater receptivity is what I hoped for, cousin. Linnas has decreed that the Contact Fleets will set out in half a cycle. That gives you just over ten days to better your knowledge of the English language." With the success of the experiment, Rentec was daily adding words and phrases to his vocabulary and improving his pronunciation at the same time.

Parlo took a sip from his cup. "And why do I need to better my understanding of Eenglits?"

"English," Rentec corrected. He got up and walked to the railing around the patio. "Because I suggested to Linnas that you'd be the best person to head up the contact team in the second fleet."

"You what!" Parlo sat stunned after the revelation. "You know I don't like space travel! I've never even taken the tour of Shabbas and Grinnas!" Parlo said, referring to a tour of the two moons of Shiravi that almost all children took as part of their schooling. "How could you do this?"

Rentec turned around and faced his cousin. "Parlo, it's time and past for you to get beyond your irrational fear of space. The matriarch requires your expertise and assistance on this mission to approach the humans."

"*What* 'expertise and assistance' do you refer to, cousin?"

"Why, it's well known that you are, or were, one of the best negotiators on the staff of the Ministry of Defense. And after you spend a few days with Derek and Maggie, you'll begin to be fluent in their language. These two traits alone guarantee you a place on one of the fleets." Rentec waited for the news to sink in and added the final enticement. "There will be a new position added to the existing order of things, as well, cousin, and there will be two persons posted to this new position. I'll be one of them, and you'll be the other."

Parlo carefully set his drink on the table and looked at Rentec. "And what is this new position to be, cousin?"

Rentec savored the moment. He knew he had Parlo hooked, and he drew it out. "The new position is that of ambassador." He used the human word, since there was no equivalent in Shiravan. The Shiravans had only met one other race in their four hundred and fifty years in space, and the enmity between the two had precluded any concept of ambassador. "The word means one who speaks with the voice of the matriarch, Parlo. When we meet the rest of the humans, one of us will have to be there to speak for the matriarch and try to work out a preliminary treaty. It will be best if you can speak their language, and you'll be able to practice on the voyage since one human will be with each fleet."

During the next half-cycle, while the Contact Fleets were preparing for departure, Parlo and Maratai spent their time with the two humans, and while they weren't quite as fluent by the end of that time as Rentec was, most simple concepts were being openly discussed, as well as a few esoteric subjects if simple words were used. Each day the verbal database grew, and conversations with their new friends became more complex. The humans were taken on a whirlwind tour of Shiravi and introduced to the populace at large, and most aspects of Shiravan culture were open to the visitors.

"It is of prime importance," the matriarch said, "that these people understand our culture and can accurately report to their superiors just what kind of people we are and what our situation is."

The disturbing aspect of the new conversational circumstances was that Shiravans were learning about humans as well.

"Linnas, I don't think you realize just how different these people are," sel Garian said, holding a brief report from Maratai in her hand. "They don't have a unified world, and most of their sub-cultures are run by *men!* How are we to relate to such a situation?"

"That same report states that women are beginning to have a greater influence in their culture, Manura," the matriarch returned. "There are women in their military forces, in their governmental processes, and in their business affairs. It's not as if they're second-class citizens."

"In some of their subcultures, they are, Linnas," sel Garian argued. "Maggie Spencer volunteered that information without coercion, and in such a way that there can be no doubt that she knew what she was saying and that we understood. While she seemed less than happy about the plight of her gender around their world, she seemed resigned to it as well. I have to wonder about the mindset of a people like that. Can we ever have a common ground?"

"I'm betting that we have a fear of the Korvil in common with them, Manura. That should bond us together for a short while. At least until the Korvil situation can be resolved. You know our scientists are working on ways to neutralize the Korvil. Ever since we were lucky enough to finish off that raider nest on our borders and were finally able to get a few bodies for study, they've been working night and day to find a solution to the problem. And," she continued before the older woman could interrupt, "we also have samples from Maggie and Derek if the humans try to replace the Korvil."

"I still think the situation is too delicate to allow such youthful idealists to dictate policy for you from such a distance, Linnas. It is madness to allow such a thing!"

Linnas des' Harras smiled at her friend and adviser. "And that is why you'll be going along as well, Manura. We need a voice of reason tempered by wisdom and experience. Impetuosity has its place, but there are times for restraint. A calmer head to steer things in the right direction, don't you think?"

"Me? Linnas! What about my duties here? Who will watch out for your interests in the Forum? Who will be there to watch your back? You know the Isolationists who killed Kirel do' Verlas were never caught. They bragged that they could get to *any* Expansionist, and you are chief among those. Your safety is paramount!"

Linnas raised her hand, effectively cutting sel Garian's protests off. "You have trained any number of people to do the jobs you do, Manura. It's unfortunate that it takes so many of them to do what you alone are capable of, old friend, but that's what we have to live with."

"Or die with," the Policy Minister muttered to herself.

It was almost a full cycle before the Contact Fleets were ready to move out. Twenty-four ships in all, twelve for each fleet, they had to be completely inspected and overhauled before the voyage ahead. Minister kep Foran, now confirmed in his position as Minister to Spatial Affairs, used his new position to commandeer all the files on any explored stars with the proper spectrum. Finding that none of them had any chance of harboring a native population that matched the human race, (not unexpected), he broadened his search to include the locations of all stars cataloged carrying that stellar signature. Even leaving out the obviously unpopulated systems, the number of stars of the proper spectra that they were concentrating on was daunting for the commanders of the two fleets.

Rentec, knowing that the situation with his consort-to-be was rapidly deteriorating, asked a local Son of Morath to perform a ceremony confirming his marriage to Ramannie.

"Now, my love," he said after the priest took off his vestments and joined the festivities, "you have your status. And you have the responsibility you asked for of keeping the do' Verlas name in the public view."

Rentec had revealed his new status to Ramannie only the night before. After her initial shock, she asked, "An ambassador has more power than a mere minister, is that not so?"

Shaking his head, Rentec said, "I'm not sure. It will have a lot to do with how well we get along with the humans. If all goes well, I think I'll get credit and prestige, but if not, I'm sure I'll get all the blame. Who can tell the future?"

CHAPTER SEVENTEEN

The three, soon to be four, space docks of the fledgling Terran Alliance had formed a loose amalgamation, with Captain Daniel Baylor of Orion as senior captain. An engineer had to be able to handle a variety of systems, and in most cases, apply the proper principle to a given situation to bring it under control. Dan Baylor had long before seen the need to have a universally accepted command structure, and when it devolved upon him, he accepted the responsibility with the same aplomb that he'd demonstrated when he agreed to Orion's captaincy. Still answering to Lucy as the head of the Alliance, the subcommand structure that grew up around Dan Baylor was more of an information-sharing system that began the official sharing of any innovations dreamed up by the crews of any of the bases as they went about the various duties assigned to them.

Carefully choosing among the crew of Orion Base, Dan had recruited anybody to his staff who had any engineering training at all—systems engineers, flight engineers, stationary engineers, electrical engineers, etc. These crewmembers came to be known as the Research and Development Department of each base and reveled in turning up new and innovative uses for the technological toys they were playing with. He'd prevailed upon the commanders of Libra and Gemini to implement similar programs, and by the time Lucy's order came down requiring the personal histories of the crew, the task had already been accomplished.

Since Daniel agreed with Simon that design improvements needed to be shared between the bases to allow uniformity, keeping in touch was of vital importance. They agreed that it would be a shame if a ship couldn't get proper servicing because it had to go to a particular dock that may not be able to accommodate them for some reason.

Daniel also saw to it that another task was performed by all the bases along with construction of new ships—placing sensor buoys throughout the solar system. A number of small, single-burst, omnidirectional buoys that would send out a pulse when triggered, as well as other more sophisticated kinds, had been loaded onto any passing ship and dropped off into deep space whenever feasible. The "smarter" buoys would record as much data as possible, and when the coast was clear, they'd locate the nearest base and send a compressed burst transmission. The problem as Daniel saw it was that there were just so many areas to cover.

"It would take hundreds of years to cover the entire sphere of our system with buoys," he said, "so we'll concentrate first on those areas where someone could come directly from another star and their counterpoints, and fill in the blank spaces as we get to them." He smiled at his small joke.

It had, admittedly, been an expansive project but one that needed to be started as soon as possible, and it had paid off.

"Sir, we have incoming traffic," Communications

Officer of the Watch, Lt. (jg) Sarah Rogers said, breaking into the middle of the racquetball game Captain Baylor was losing to his second in command.

"Make it brief, Lieutenant, I'm in the middle of something here." Breathing hard, he picked up a towel from a bench near the door and wiped the sweat from his face as he sat down heavily.

"Sir, standing orders require that the captain be informed whenever a buoy has been triggered."

Sometimes I think the military mind grows out of thin air! Dan thought. *Quoting orders at* me! Aloud he asked, "Which buoy and what possibility of error?" An unnamed fear raised the hair on the back of his neck.

"Sir," the young, shaky voice replied, "Buoy two-four-four-one, placed on-station seven months ago by the *McCaffrey* near the Oort cloud. Possibility of error nearing zero, sir. The data transmitted carries a power spike, and none of our ships are scheduled to be in that area at this time."

Dan glanced at his exec, one eyebrow raised slightly. It was his classic "what the hell" look. "Is that all, Lieutenant?"

"Uh, no sir, it isn't. The, uh, computer went nuts when the message came in, sir. Lights and bells all over the place. I had to hit the override to shut 'em down. Sir, the computer has issued a threat assessment."

"I'll be right up." Turning to his partner and exec, Dan said, "Tom, jiggle that memory of yours. Where and what type of buoy is two-four-four-one?"

All thoughts of the game forgotten, the two men headed for the comm shack. The hapless junior grade lieutenant handed over the papers that had poured out of the printer and made herself as inconspicuous as possible.

Several seconds went by as the two men poured over the papers, and Dan was the first to speak. "Well, the shit just hit the fan, Tom. Ninety-nine percent probability that the energy signatures of that drive match the one we recorded after the first attack. And the same for the ship in the asteroid belt but slightly less if it was the one that got away. At ninety-four percent, it's still well within the limits of an overhaul or refit. Now we've got an idea where to look for our playmates."

"We've also got the spike of a small ship here, boss," Commander Tom Caudell said, waving one of the papers. "Look here. Not as much energy as the *Heinlein* puts out and way less than the *Galileo* but more than a Mamba. My guess is that there's a mothership out there somewhere, looking to pick it up after its recon. If the *Heinlein* can make six lightyears a month, then these guys have probably been out here a long time. *If* it's the same ship. It would have had to limp back to base, report in and refit, and return. It's been two years or maybe a little more since Orion was attacked. Out and back, say seventy-two lightyears."

"A good working hypothesis, Tom," the captain agreed. "But it could be just an outpost, too. These folks have been in space a long time, and we just got here. I'll be very interested to learn how large each civilization is. Remind me," he said, changing tracks, "to get a message off to First Captain Grimes. We should try the U.S. Embassy first, but we can't stop until we have her reply. I'll be in my quarters."

"Captain," Tom said, a preoccupied tone in his

voice, "the bogey was powering down and headed straight in, not vectoring across the system." He shuffled papers around in his hands. "We're guessing at the size of the vessel from its power signature, of course. Since it shut down its drives, we can't get any other information about it, and it's going to coast through the system gathering all *kinds* of information. I'd say that it's somewhere around the orbit of Saturn right now. And if it followed a direct course, then it came in from the direction of Alpha C."

The two men walked out of the comm shack still discussing the problem. "Aren't you going to notify Libra or any of the ships?" the exec asked worriedly.

"We don't know their intentions or temperament. If we make an unscheduled comm call to the base nearest them, it could trigger the very thing we don't want to happen, which is a repeat of what happened here. I'm playing the odds, and it's with people's lives. *Not* my job. I'll gladly pass the buck on this one."

Departure was less eventful than arrival, though tears and hugs were shared all around again. Lucy called Galway just before leaving the house to inform him of her return to New Mexico. "I'll meet you there and see to the guard detail around your ship," he said.

Lucy's goodbyes were just as heartrending as she'd known they would be. She experienced fear and concern for her mother and father, and worry about Bruce's plans, although she was pretty certain she'd be seeing him soon. Regret at leaving her friends behind made her say, "You know, you guys are welcome to join up. We wouldn't get to see a lot of each other but more than if you don't. Bruce won't be far behind me. He's almost twenty, and the folks can't hold him back if he wants to go. You three could make a trip of driving down to New Mexico together."

With the last tear shed and the last hug given and received, Lucy turned to the smoked-glass doors that led onto the tarmac where her ship waited, but a tug at her sleeve turned her back. "Here's your bag," Bruce said, handing over the black nylon satchel. "And you *did* promise me a look inside your cockpit, Luce. Mind if I walk out with you?"

Expecting the request, Lucy nodded and pushed the door open. She eyed Carmen and Amy, but they both shook their heads. The cool morning air made her glad she'd worn her long-sleeved uniform, but the weight of the laser on her hip was unaccountably bothersome. "Sure, let's go." Stepping out into the bright morning light, she looked around and saw several vehicles with that "cop" look to them, and at least half a dozen silhouettes of men either atop nearby buildings or in the shadows not far from the Mamba. To one side, a motorized ladder stood waiting, its engine idling and a driver at the controls.

Reaching into the pouch on her belt, Lucy pulled out the key and pointed it at the ship. Seconds after she pressed the recessed button, the shimmering field around the Mamba vanished and she waved the ladder driver to move up to the craft. She touched another button and the cockpit opened as if on its own as the stairway came to a stop mere inches from the skin of the ship. Climbing up first, Lucy stood to one side so Bruce could look inside.

"Can I . .?" he asked, gesturing at the seat.

"Sure," Lucy said indulgently. "Just *don't* touch anything. You could deactivate the magnetic containment field and blow up half of the airport."

"Yeah, right," Bruce muttered as he slid into the cockpit. "What am I looking at?" he asked, hands conspicuously on his legs.

"Far right panel is environmental controls. Next to the left is the armament status board. Center front are the actual flight controls. Radar is a holographic display projected on the inside of the cockpit window. Next to the left is the engine status board, and on your far left is the comm panel. We simplified some of the controls so they act almost like computer games with joystick controls, but it's not really set up for atmospheric flight. These engines make it much more suited to what it was designed for—a space fighter."

Bruce looked around at the controls and the helmet sitting atop the panel. "If I've got a choice," he said, "I'd like to learn to fly one of these, but Mom..."

Lucy put her hand on her brother's shoulder. "Brucie, Mom's all right with it. Trust me. We talked last night, and she's not real *happy*, but she knows, deep down, that you're about to leave the nest. She also knows that whatever you do in life has risks to it. She's okay with this if you go in with your eyes open. And if you *do* show up in New Mexico, I'll make *sure* your eyes are opened before you get accepted. Now, just about everybody who signs up wants the glamour of being a Mamba pilot, so sooner or later we examine them all, but I do have some pull," she said, smiling up at him, "and I'll get you bumped up the list. After that, you're on your own. If you wash out of pilot training, I'll find something else for you to do if you decide to stay with us."

Bruce looked at the controls for a moment longer, then climbed gingerly out of the fighter to stand beside his sister. "You said, 'if you decide to stay with *us*.' Do you think of things as 'us' and 'them' now, Luce?"

Lucy stood on top of the stairway and thought for several seconds. She looked around the airport and, in her mind's eye, beyond, to her one-time home and her past. Bruce leaned down and picked up her helmet, turning it over in his hands.

"Yeah, I think I do, Bubba," she said taking the helmet and letting it dangle at her side. "At least for now. The world needs to grow up some before we can turn everything over to it, I think. Simon had the right idea about getting the food processors out first and free. End the hunger and then people have time to grow, as individuals and as groups. As long as you have to worry about your next meal, you can't think much beyond that. Now, they can. All we have to do now is fight man's basic greedy behavior. In the long run, I think that will be the hardest battle of all. If we can win that one, then the 'us' and 'them' can go away."

She smiled ruefully at her brother. "The last thing you needed was a speech from your big sister as she's about to leave. Sorry 'bout that. Look, I gotta get the show on the road. When you get ready, call the number in your top desk drawer and get your butt down to New Mexico." She punched him on the shoulder, then hugged him, hard. "Now go. Love you, Bubba. Tell Mom and Pop to come visit. It's about time they took a vacation anyway, isn't it? Oh, and by the way, under the right circumstances, you *could* blow up half of this airport, no joke."

She watched the look of amazement cross his face as she waved the ladder driver back and stepped into the cockpit of the Mamba. As the platform moved slowly back away from the black ship, Bruce carefully walked down the steps, and when it stopped, he stepped off.

Lucy slid the actuator into its slot and the systems came alive, one by one. She pulled the helmet down over her ears and lowered the canopy before she thumbed the comm panel. "Cincinnati Control, Terran Alliance One requests permission to take off. Destination, New Mexico."

"Terran Alliance One, Cincinnati Control," a strange voice answered. "We advise caution. There is severe weather between here and New Mexico."

"Not a problem, Control. I can fly above anything out there. And what I choose not to fly over can't hurt this ship."

"Terran Alliance One, what are your takeoff parameters?"

"Just tell me when I have clear airspace and my takeoff parameter will be straight up, Control. I can be out of your airspace in a matter of seconds."

"I doubt that, but it will be interesting to watch, Alliance One. Wait for clearance."

While Lucy waited for Control to clear the airspace above her, she brought each system on-line and double checked it. The antigravs whined into life and the sleek ship lifted off the ground. She slid the craft out over the taxiway where she floated about thirty feet off the ground.

Since she was still waiting for word from the

control tower, she called Diana in New Mexico.

"I'll put you through to your office, ma'am," the tech on duty said.

Almost instantly, the circuit connected, and Diana's voice came through her speakers. "It's good to hear your voice, Lucy. Did your trip go well?"

"As well as can be expected, I guess. How are things on base?"

"Running like clockwork, really, thanks to Abernathy and his people. But we do have a situation that needs your immediate attention. Dan Baylor just brought us a packet by way of the *McCaffrey*. It's marked urgent."

The tower chose that moment to give Lucy permission to launch, so she said, "Hold on, Diana." She switched frequencies. "Cincinnati Control, this is Terran Alliance One. You said you doubted my ability to be gone in seconds? Well, watch this."

"All eyes are on you, Alliance One. You are cleared for takeoff. Good luck and have a safe flight."

She poured more power to the generators and the ship rose another fifty feet. Tilting its nose toward the sky, she pulled the joystick back hard toward her and the ship almost literally vanished from sight. Keeping her speed down below the sound barrier, she still went from zero to almost six hundred miles per hour in under half a second, vanishing from the radar screens of anyone who had an interest in her departure.

CHAPTER EIGHTEEN

Somewhere deep inside the proto-organic gel that was the brain of the *Galileo*, a metaphorical switch was thrown, and Consciousness began to return to Kitty Hawke. That gel was most intimately connected to the occupant of the chamber in the medical bay through the sensors embedded in the pedestals under the table. It recognized a crewman in distress, and when its sensors confirmed that the crewman had a chance of survival, it began procedures that had been set down in its primal conditioning—first, insulate the body and then induce the body to repair itself.

Wiped of all its secondary programming by the virus that had killed the original crew, its primary programming remained intact. Ship functions were unimpaired, as were medical functions and logic circuits, all of which took up a tiny fraction of the organic mass and had been shielded by layer after layer of protection. Now that its new occupants had removed the last trace of the virus, it searched the remainder of itself and found appallingly little about the bodies of its new owners. Following hints, it learned of a larger database concerning the human body on the planet below. It tied itself into Earth's satellite system while all was in chaos and downloaded everything it could find on the human body.

It began comparing what it "read" with what it

sensed of the body in the regeneration chamber. When it got to the cellular level, the computer came as close to a feeling of joy as it was possible for it to get. Comparing the genetic coding in the database with material taken from the chamber, the computer began testing each of the billions of combinations it was possible to twist the human code into. It had long been known to science that reputable cases of spontaneous regeneration of an organ or even a limb existed, but the process had never been isolated. Until now.

Time, it has been said, heals all wounds, and the greater the wounds, both physical and mental, the greater the time needed to heal. Time was all that was necessary for the computer to repair the genetic damage, and Kitty's body was induced to grow nerve cells, skin cells, bone, and blood cells in the insular gel surrounding it in the chamber. But Time was going to have a harder job ahead when it came to healing the tortured psyche in the computer's care. Each time the computer's "attention" wandered even a bit in its quest to find a solution, the mind it was trying to heal fought to the surface, and each time that mind showed itself unready to return. Each time, the computer flooded the body with narcotics manufactured in its central core to calm the mind and ease the pain.

Some ten months had passed since Kitty had received her wounds at Camp David, and under the watchful care of the computer, six of those months were all that were needed to bring the body back. Electrical stimulation of the muscles helped keep them in tone, blood was flushed of waste and toxins, and nutrients were added to keep the body alive, but the mind was beyond the scope of the immense computer. Hidden behind the barriers constructed to hold the now non-existent viral attacker at bay, the computer, realigned to serve its human element, had adopted a wait-and-see policy toward the occupant of its regeneration chamber for four additional months.

The first clue that the "Kitty situation" had changed came at shift change when Lt. (jg) Heather Crawford walked into the sick bay carrying a stack of study material, preparing to take over the monotonous shift of watching the never-changing container holding the body of Kitty Hawke. Following procedure established months before, she checked the numerous dials and gauges attached to the outside of the semi-transparent material housing the body of one of the Founders of the Alliance.

"Temperature's up on the chamber, Colin. Did you get it documented?"

Performing a classic double take, Lt. Colin Hampstead said, "Everything was normal when I came on. What is it now?"

"Up six degrees from normal," Lt Crawford noted. "Procedure says to notify the captain immediately."

"Don't quote regs at me, Lieutenant," Lt. Hampstead said. "Everything was normal when I came on. I've got it logged."

"Well, I've got the shift now, and I'm notifying Captain Morgan immediately," Lt. Crawford said. She pulled her comm unit from her belt and pressed a button. "Lt Crawford to the captain," she said. "Please contact me in sick bay immediately."

The voice that came back was not the captain's.

"This is the Exec. What's the problem, Lieutenant?"

"Sir," she replied, "I just took over duty in the sick bay and found the chamber up six degrees. It's risen another degree since then, and other vitals are up as well. Heartbeat is up, respiration is up, and alpha waves are up, and I don't know what to do other than notify the captain as ordered."

"Good job, Lieutenant. I'll notify the captain and the doctor immediately. Make sure you have everything documented. Someone's going to want that information later. Exec out."

Ten minutes later, Mustafa Morgan, Captain of the *Galileo*, strode briskly into the sick bay, belying the fact that it was the middle of his off shift. "Status, Lieutenant," he ordered as he entered the room.

"Sir," the nervous lieutenant said, "temperature is up to ninety-six degrees. It's stayed constant at eighty-six since the beginning, and now this!"

Dr. Jeffers entered the sick bay looking as if he'd been sleeping in his clothes, which to all intents and purposes, he had. He went straight to the chamber that was holding Kitty's body and began studying the dials and readouts. "A full ten degrees up," he noted. "Respiration is up from eight breaths per minute to fourteen, and her alpha waves show normal sleep patterns. Has Simon been notified?"

The young lieutenant, unused to so much brass around, found a corner to make herself inconspicuous in as she listened attentively to every word. Recruited right after the Camp David affair, she'd never known Kitty and was understandably curious about the individual she'd heard so much about and been keeping watch over for the last few months.

Simon, who'd been summoned by Mustafa as

soon as heard the news, entered the room at that moment. For the first three weeks after his rescue, Simon had spent every waking moment in the sick bay, convinced that his presence would get through to her and cause her to awaken. Even the list of injuries didn't deter him from his belief that his presence would have a positive effect on the woman with whom he'd shared the last seventeen years. Finally, Dr. Jeffers had convinced him that for his own benefit he should find something to occupy his time rather than sitting around pining and accomplishing nothing. "There are plenty of people out there who would benefit from your expertise," he said to Simon. "When there's a change, you'll be notified, I promise you."

Wandering around the *Galileo* as it went about its task of building the fourth base, Simon spent considerable time feeling sorry for himself and Kitty, not really knowing who needed his sorrow the most. But he eventually began to take an interest in the engineering problems involved in building the more massive Taurus. Throwing himself into the project allowed him to hold his grief at bay, although it was always just under the surface and erupted at the most inopportune moments. All aboard came to recognize when his moods were most volatile and left him alone or just agreed with him and went ahead and did things the way the supervisors ordered, ignoring any suggestions he gave in times of stress.

Now, notified as promised, he stood, shifting from foot to foot as the doctor moved from one sensor to another, making notes. Finished with that process, he turned to the two captains and announced, "It looks like *some*thing has decided it's time to wake her up. I don't have any more control over the process than you do, so I know just how helpless you both feel, Simon in particular." An idea occurred to him. He turned to the junior duty officer and said, "Lt. Crawford, right?" At her affirmative nod, he ordered, "Go to the captain's quarters and bring back a set of clothes. It doesn't matter what as long as it covers her warmly." Dismissing her from his thoughts, he went back to his instruments. "Ninety-seven now, and respiration is up to fifteen per minute. I'd have to guess that something is about to happen, gentlemen."

As if in response to his words, the chamber began to clear a bit, showing the naked form of Kitty Hawke floating in a suspension that was suffused with glittering particulate matter of some indeterminate material. The young Lieutenant made haste to get out of the room on the errand she'd been set, leaving the three men alone with the slowly changing chamber.

Mustafa, a bit nonplussed by seeing Kitty nude, asked, "Should I be somewhere else, Simon? I don't see how I can be any help here."

Simon answered from a distant place. "I'm sure you've seen naked women before, Stafa, and I don't think Kitty is going to be worried about it. I'd rather have you here if we need you. Let's just make sure that no other sightseers get in, shall we?"

Taking the suggestion as an order, Mustafa commed his security chief and ordered a full security detail to the sick bay to guard against that occurrence.

The cloudiness continued to dissipate from the container and the three men could clearly see the hoses and other contraptions attached at various points to Kitty's body. "Well, there won't be any bedsores to contend with," Dr. Jeffers said as he noted that Kitty's body was supported about four inches off the table by the sparkling substance that surrounded her body.

One by one, the various fastenings attached to her body began to separate themselves and retract into receptacles in the tabletop, leaving only a demi-mask over her nose and mouth and another covering her eyes. By this time, the three men could see the definite rise and fall of her chest, indicating that she was breathing more or less on her own. After an indeterminate time, the level of the fluid in the container began to recede, showing a marked line along the sides of the clear cover. Finally, Kitty's body rested firmly on the tabletop, and the rest of the fluid was sucked out of the chamber. At this point, the connection over her nose and mouth detached itself, followed by the one covering her eyes, both tubes sliding into a hole in the flat bottom of the chamber.

The tension heightened as nothing further happened for several minutes. The young lieutenant returned with an armful of clothes and said, "I hope this will do, Doctor. You said warm, and this is what I could find."

Simon's thank you was aborted when a sound like hydraulic brakes bleeding down sounded in the room, accompanied by a three-tone descending chime. Immediately following the third repetition of the chime, the transparent cover slid back into the wall as if it had never been, the endcap dropping down into a recess at the end of the table. The four people in the room watched, fascinated, as Kitty took an extra-large breath, opened her eyes, and stared blankly at the ceiling for several seconds as if getting a feeling for her surroundings. Comprehension dawned on her face, and before anyone could speak, she asked no one in particular, "Why am I still alive? I don't *want* to be alive. I don't have any reason to even *be* alive with Simon dead."

Simon moved to her side and said, "Kittyn, I'm not dead." Reaching out, he slowly pulled her hands from her face and said, "Honey, look at me. I'm alive, and so are you. Come on. Let's go to our quarters. I'll explain how I made it, and we'll try to figure out how *you* did it. Truth is, dear, we should *both* be dead, but we're not."

Eyes squeezed tightly shut, Kitty refused to look in the direction of the familiar voice. "Look at me, darling. I'm alive," Simon reiterated. "Come on, let's get some clothes on you. People are gonna talk enough as it is." He pulled on her arms until she came to a sitting position, bits of sparkling goo dripping from her arms and hair, which was now no longer a golden blonde but rather the purest white. Simon's eyes wandered lower and noticed that the same condition applied there as well.

He looked back up in time to get slapped in the face. "How could you do that to me, you bastard!" In the next breath, his wife, miraculously delivered to him whole and apparently healthy, went on long enough to become embarrassing to the viewers.

Stafa said, "Uh, folks, I've got a ship to run. Welcome back, Captain Kitty. We all missed you. I'll stop by to see you as soon as you're up to having visitors. Lieutenant, it looks like we won't be needing an officer on duty here anymore. Let's move." Junior officer in tow, Captain Morgan left the sick bay, already planning the calls he needed to make.

The Hawkes spent the next two days alone in their quarters, having meals sent in. "That's one of the prerogatives of rank, my dear," Simon told Kitty, enduring constant interruptions by the doctor and fending off calls from friends and well-wishers.

"When we're ready, we'll come out. Until then, thanks for your thoughts, one and all," Simon said in a curt but heartfelt message to everyone who tried to get past the security team detailed to prevent just such occurrences.

Kitty sat on the edge of the bed, an apple in her hand a pensive look on her face.

"What's up, love?" Simon asked. He hadn't let her out of his sight except for bare necessities for the entire two days, and overall, he was happy with her recovery, but there was something troubling her. Sooner or later, it was going to have to come out, but he wasn't sure he was the one to deal with whatever it was.

"Simon, if I tell you, you're going to think I'm nuts, and then it'll be a different kind of doctor. I don't think I could endure that," Kitty said mournfully. "I know we've never kept anything from each other, but this is so... weird." She shook her head in bewilderment. "I'm not sure I believe it myself except for this," she said, twitching her hand through the snow-white hair falling past the small of her back.

"Whatever it is, we'll deal with it, hon," Simon said, sitting down beside her. "Look at what we've managed to survive already. Both of us have been all but dead, and here we sit."

"Yeah, but this..." Kitty looked at her husband sitting beside her and felt the confusion and frustration welling up in him. "Look, if I tell you, you've got to *promise* me that it goes no further than the two of us for now." When she saw the expression his face, she slapped his thigh. "I'm serious, Simon! No telling anybody! Not Gayle, not the doctor, nobody! Promise me."

"Okay," he agreed finally. "Nobody. I promise."

"On our wedding vows, Simon, you promise, or I won't say another word about it," Kitty warned.

"On our vows? Are you serious?" At her look, he said, "All right, on our vows. Now what is it?"

"When the ship took over for the doctor, it thought I was going to die. And I would have, I'm sure, without more attention than he could give. The computer, or whatever, didn't know that he planned to send me downside for more treatment, so it sorta took charge. It's something in its primary orders, I think. Anyway, it raided Earth's database for information on the human body and started repairs. As we know, the Builders are way ahead of us in that department. It programmed itself to do what was necessary to fix my injuries, mostly regeneration of things and slow growth of broken bones and things."

"How do you know all this?" Simon asked. "I'm not doubting you, but it seems kind of fantastic, you must admit."

"No more fantastic than the reality of this damned ship!" Kitty retorted. "Just listen. I don't *know* how I know, I just *do*. But that's not all. It's enough, but not all." Her voice died and she looked at her lap long enough to start Simon worrying again, but before he could speak, Kitty went on. "I think the computer put the information in my mind somehow. And there's more. One more thing, and this is the part you better not tell. Not for a while, Simon. It *has* to be a secret. The computer re-sequenced my DNA. It looked at it, decided that some things needed to be 'fixed,' and went ahead and did it. We knew the Builders could clone things, but we didn't take it any further than that. They can actually affect some things on a molecular level. And this is just the byproduct of the computer 'fixing' me," she said, waving a handful of hair in Simon's face.

A chill ran down Simon's spine. "What else did it fix?"

"Apparently the computer decided that getting old isn't normal, so it increased my lifespan by doing something to my DNA that prohibits aging. It can't *stop* the process, but it can certainly slow it down drastically."

"The computer *told* you all this while you were... being repaired?" Simon asked carefully.

"It didn't tell me so much as put the information there, Simon. It's not like we talked or anything. I had a lot of weird dreams, and most of 'em I can't remember, but this is no dream."

"Okay, so how long will you live?"

"I'm not exactly certain, but something around three times the usual for humans. Like about three hundred years."

Lucy shut off her comm unit and laid it on her desk with a feeling of wonderment. Her flight back to New Mexico had gone as well as the trip out, and she was still shaking her head every time she thought about it.

It seemed as if the fates had conspired to give her only one day of relief at a time. Shortly after walking into her office, Communications sent word that Dan Baylor had commandeered the *McCaffrey* to come to Earth.

Lucy met him at the landing field when his shuttle touched down. "We were just finishing up the torpedo upgrades when the news came in," he said as her skimmer carried them back to headquarters. He looked around at the ex-military base as Lucy followed the roads back to the parking area. "I sure didn't expect to see a sight like this again," he said, "at least not as a 'ranking officer.' It's almost spooky."

The two officers stepped over the low sides of the grounded skimmer and walked into the main building. Four secretaries were seated around the large outer room, each one handling the next-to-last daily interview for recruit hopefuls, so their trip across the foyer and through the door marked "Communications, Authorized Personnel Only," went almost completely unnoticed.

"I wasn't about to trust this to the comm system since we don't know anything about what these... invaders have in the way of communications systems of their own or whether or not they can decipher our language."

She opened the packet he laid down on her desk and started to read. A chill started at the base of her skull and traveled down her spine. There'd been an incursion into human space that was apparently still going on. The kicker was the percentages the computer assigned to the probability that it was the same type of ship that had attacked Orion, not to mention the possibility that it was the *same ship!*

"Communications, this is Captain Grimes," she said into her comm. "Raise the *Heinlein*, the *Niven*, and the *Clarke*. I want to know *exactly* where each one is at this moment. Mark it 'urgent, top priority,' and get back to me as each ship reports in." She stood up and walked to the door. "Let's get to the chart room. I want to get these coordinates into the computer and see what we can do to isolate this fucker." The two officers walked across the outer office, and just before leaving the room, Lucy turned to Diana. "Bad news—we've got company in-system, probably the same bunch that jumped us before. Captain Baylor and I are going to the chart room to see what we can do about it. Route all calls there as they come in, will you? And get word out to the *Galileo* and all bases to go on full alert. I don't want a repeat of Orion."

As Lucy started out, Diana asked, "Could you do with a bit of good news, Lucy? I really think this would be a good time to hear it."

Hand on the doorknob, Lucy said, "Give. And I sure hope it's something that can help us right now."

"Well, I don't see it being a help in this particular case, but word just came in from Captain Morgan on the *Galileo* that Kitty is awake and *apparently* sane and healthy. She slapped the shit out of Simon for 'dying,' then hugged him. The two are recuperating in their quarters."

Stunned by the revelation, Lucy could only stand there holding the knob until she felt the world start to spin again. Dan Baylor's hand on her elbow brought her back to herself and the situation at hand. Kitty, awake! After ten months! Lucy felt a weight lift from her shoulders that she hadn't known was there until it disappeared. She hadn't even thought of her friend in over a week, and her relief at the news was immense. Still, the state of affairs as they stood pushed that relief to the side.

"Send word to Simon and Kitty telling them how happy we are that she's back and that I'll get in touch personally as soon as this mess is straightened out."

The chart room was just down the hall from Lucy's office and, in fact, had no real paper charts in it at all. The computer—a duplicate of the one aboard the *Galileo*, the bases, ships, and the other two embassies—projected a three-dimensional hologram of space surrounding Earth's sun. As data was added, the "picture" grew in complexity and could be rotated in any axis, or one could walk around or even through the display and view it from another angle entirely. Dan Baylor walked over to the controls and, with several stops to consult his hard copy, began inputting data.

"Right now," he said as he gave the keyboard a final tap, "I've got the last reported positions of all three ships not in orbit and their courses plotted in green. The bogey is shown in a solid red line before he cut his drives and went dark, and the red dotted line is the projected course if it doesn't change. It will pass by Libra and come within a few million miles of Earth on its way back out of the solar system. Judging by its signature, we feel it's not capable of interstellar travel because of its size. We could very well be wrong, of course, but we can only go on what we know of our own ships and technology. This is all just best guess."

Lucy studied the holodisplay. "You said you'd just

finished upgrading the *McCaffrey*. How about the other three?"

"The *Niven* needs her upgrades, but she's carrying a full complement of the high-yield antimatter torpedoes. If we can box the bogey in, the three of them should be able to handle the problem easily. Of course, we don't know what other weapons they could have, so we might get our butts kicked. But three against one?" Captain Baylor shrugged. "This reminds me of street fighting when I was a kid. You never knew what the other guy had until you started fighting. Did he know karate? Was he packing? You just toughed it out until the answers came in. Sometimes you won; sometimes you didn't."

"That makes the odds fifty-fifty, and I don't like 'em at *all*."

Dan sat at the computer desk, slowly rotating the display. "Well, it may not be as bad as all that," he said. "Remember, this is all hypothesis, but we think that *these* guys," he said, waving at the glowing display, "are the enemies of the Builders. If that's true, they probably think we're allied with them since we're using their technology. They will probably think we have the same type of weapons and tactics used by the Builders and will react accordingly. And even though the weapons types *are* the same, we've done some major upgrading, as you know. Ships have shields unknown to the Builders, lasers are much stronger, and our torps are the real kicker. We've made 'em smaller so we can carry more, and they have antimatter warheads. The Builders didn't have that capability built into theirs. Also, we've tapped the antimatter engines to increase propulsion. Our torps can accelerate to almost light speed in a fraction of the time that the old-style torpedoes could get up to half of that. Oh, and here's another item for the 'new weapons' department. R&D says that our capture fields can be focused a *lot* tighter than we've been able to get them down to before now. It's thanks in part to our use of miniaturization."

Lucy looked away from the display slowly rotating in midair. "That means what to us, Dan?"

"Tractor beams! One of our ships can lock onto something smaller than itself and pull it into range. Then, its lasers can cut it to ribbons. Or lock on and hit the brakes, so to speak, keeping it from jumping out of our territory until we're ready to let it go, if ever. And the other side of the coin is that reversing the polarity of the fields will create a 'pressor' beam. Using both at once will be like taking a wet dishrag and wringing the water out of it. Messy but effective when it comes to combat. The drawback to that one is that it brings you into range of whatever the enemy has to deliver to you. Calculated risks, I grant you, but that's what we've been taking for the last four years now. You know, it was my intention to quit after we got Orion up and running, but I just couldn't resist the challenges. I don't see how any engineer could. Anyway, that's the situation as it stands now. The bogey should be crossing the orbit of Saturn soon, so if all goes well, and it seldom does, it should continue to follow an unpowered trajectory at the same speed it was traveling when it went dark. Then, in two days, it should be about here," he said, indicating a position about two million miles short of Libra.

"Awful close to the base," Lucy noted, "but to me it looks like the best place to intercept. Plus, Libra has several dozen Mambas stockpiled, doesn't it? And I'll just bet there are enough qualified pilots to put them in space at the same time, right?"

"You read my mind," Dan said with a small salute and a large grin. "I don't know if these alien bastards have an alien equivalent, but they're about to stir up a hornet's nest."

Signals flashed back and forth between Earth and the Alliance fleet, detailing all the information Captain Baylor had brought. Ships began shifting positions to intercept a vessel that was running silent, which meant that all scans were on full, giving away the fact that Alliance forces knew about the intruder.

The *McCaffrey* sat in stationary orbit above Zurich while Marsha Kane paced her command deck in frustrated circles. "Another ship would increase our chances of catching the son of a bitch, Lucy," she insisted when she finally got Lucy to answer her calls. "Plus, we've already got combat experience. You should maximize your resources."

"As Captain Baylor pointed out to me, Marsha, everything we do here comes under the heading of calculated risks. I want a ship in orbit in the event that there's something out there we *haven't* detected yet. I can't let Earth go without any defenses at all. Just call it the luck of the draw that you're here and the action is out there. Besides, two of the three others were involved with the action in the belt in one way or another. And we've got all those Mambas at Libra for backup. Our visitor won't get far with his scheme or his data. It's what comes later that worries me. Will we be left alone? Or is whoever sent this expedition using it to judge our strengths and responses? I know it's hard, Marsha, but you've got to sit this one out. Keep your sensors on full though. I'm putting you in charge of the defense of the entire inner system."

With that sobering thought in mind, the two women chatted about goings-on in the fleet and especially about Kitty's recovery. "Did you hear that whatever happened to her caused her hair to turn white?" Marsha asked. "God, but that is going to take some getting used to."

"True," Lucy responded. "Word has it that whatever the process is that she went through, it not only regenerated tissues in a manner we have no way of reproducing on Earth, but it seems to have reversed her aging process somewhat. Simon swears she looks at least ten years younger. Of course, she had ten months of beauty sleep," she quipped.

Changing to more serious topics, she said, "Captain Morgan estimates that construction is just a bit ahead of schedule and the *Galileo* will return to Earth orbit in just over a month before going out to Vesta. I intend to start bringing in recruits from both other embassies immediately. I want to get that last ship crewed and out of orbit before we get another batch in. As soon as this intruder is dealt with, I'll be bringing each ship in one at a time and transferring some of each experienced crew to the new ship. That will give us a cadre of trained personnel. Then, I'll fill out the crew with the latest batch of newbies. As it stands now, I have one ship ready to go, but all of the crew are new except the command staff. I'm not exempting the *McCaffrey*, either. Just a friendly warning so you won't get caught by surprise. You're gonna lose a few people after we settle this SOB's hash. The newbies you get will have more than a little training, though, so it won't be too bad. I think they'll integrate well."

Pleasantries concluded, Lucy signed off and waited. Knowing that people she knew and cared about were out there in deep space chasing their own possible deaths at her orders caused her no little concern, and she cursed the day Simon "died" and left her in charge of the fledgling Alliance.

Time lags between transmissions over the distances inside a solar system being what they were, Lucy had returned to her office before her first call was returned. Those same time lags prevented idle chitchat, so she detailed the course of action each ship was to take as the calls came in. Finished with the last call, she looked at her watch and realized why she felt so tired. "Almost midnight! Damn!" She recalled sending Diana away only moments before, or so it seemed, but that had actually been hours past.

She stood up, feeling each individual vertebra in her back pop as she did so. She waved to the night duty officer as she walked out of the building. Stopping at the bottom of the steps, she looked up into the clear New Mexican night and stared at the stars as they slowly made their stately way across the firmament.

"So beautiful it takes your breath away, isn't it?" The unexpected question made her spin around in shock to see the shadowy figure of a man sitting on a nearby bench, smoking a cigarette.

"Beautiful, yes. But that same beauty has a dark and violent side, I've learned," she replied to the stranger. "Who are you?" she asked peering hard into the shadows. "And don't you know smoking is bad for you?"

"It also relaxes me after a hard day, and I've had a rough one," he replied. "Besides, I only smoke when I get stressed, and it beats getting shitfaced. The name's Tom Breen. What are you doing working so late, and can a guy buy you a drink?"

Realizing he didn't recognize her in the dark, Lucy said, "My job has a lot of detail and stress, too, Tom. I was just going to bed, but a drink sounds good. I think I'll take you up on your offer."

They'd walked almost a block before a streetlamp revealed Lucy's face and the insignia on her collar. When Tom Breen saw who he'd been trying to pick up, he paled. "First Captain! Uh, ma'am, I'm sorry. I didn't know..."

She saw his face flush under the harsh glare of the light and laughed, her tone showing him that she harbored no ill will. "It's all right, Tom. Relax. We're both off duty, so I'll let you buy me that drink. And call me Lucy, please. I let all my captains call me by my first name when we're off duty."

They walked another few steps before the meaning of her words got past Tom Breen's embarrassment. "Wait. You said 'all your captains.' You mean..."

"Yes, Tom," she confirmed. "The positions will be posted tomorrow anyway, so what's a few hours advance notice? Anyway, it's customary for the newest captain to stand for drinks for his or her buddies. And while I don't quite qualify as a buddy, I *did* approve your promotion, so that should earn me one drink, right?"

I was an idiot to turn him down, she thought later

as she walked alone into what had once been the home of the former base commander. *He really is a hunk, but the complications! Oh, well.*

An hour later, as she wandered through the three-bedroom house wondering what she needed so much space for, her comm jangled. Still feeling the buzz from the two drinks—one she'd bought for her newest captain in return for the one he'd bought her—she said, "Grimes," with a touch more roughness than she otherwise would have done.

"Ma'am, I have an urgent message from Captain Miller on the *Clarke*. Should I have a runner bring it over?"

Shocked into total sobriety by the thought of Gayle sending her an urgent message so soon after receiving orders to intercept the bogey, she asked, "Is it marked any way other than urgent?" Getting a negative, she said, "Just read it to me, please."

"Yes, ma'am," came the reply. "It reads: Captain Miller to First Captain Grimes. Subject: interception of alien craft in Earth space. Give me the coordinates it will occupy in two hours. The *Clarke* will micro-jump in and finish this now rather than two days from now. Arguments for this course of action—total surprise and an immediate resolution of the crisis. Arguments against—none. Respectfully, Gayle Miller, Captain, *Arthur C. Clarke*. That's all there is, ma'am. Will there be a reply?"

"Not at this time, Lieutenant, but there will be soon, trust me. Connect me with Captain Baylor, please." *Now, why the hell didn't I think of that?*

"What?" a sleep-strangled voice barked after the third chime. "This had better be good."

"It's Lucy, Dan, and I think you'll find it very

good. How soon can you meet me in the chart room?"

"Ten minutes. I just need to get dressed."

"Make it five and show up naked for all I care," she responded. "We both missed a bet, and I think we can have our bogey under control a lot sooner than we first thought."

Six minutes later, a bedraggled Dan Baylor showed up in tee-shirt, slacks, and slippers sans socks. Lucy looked at the slippers and grinned. "All they need is to be pink and fuzzy, Dan." Turning serious, she asked, "Where is our bogey now, and where will he be in two hours?"

Still blinking sleep out of his eyes, Orion's commanding officer asked, "Two hours? I can figure it out in no time, but why the hell do you need to know that? Shit!" He jumped for the computer console.

"Exactly. Shit. We transmit the coordinates to all three ships and have 'em micro-jump in and solve the problem before it gets any worse. The only drawback is that we won't have the Mambas from Libra for backup."

"Unless you have them leave first under high boost," he said over his shoulder. "One, it will make the bogey give itself away by powering up to either attack or escape. Two, the three main ships show up almost instantly, powered up and ready for either eventuality, and three, they can act as tenders for damaged ships and pick up any survivors and injured." During all this, his hands were flying over the keyboard, entering figures and computing results. Silence descended on the room, broken only by the clicking of keys and the occasional muttered oath.

Finally, he finished his computations. "I make just

over three hours if you start the Mambas now. Send these coordinates to each ship in this order," he said, handing over a piece of paper. He collapsed into a chair and sighed. "I'm really getting too old for this, you know. Bridges and buildings are one thing, but space stations and ships are another thing entirely."

Lucy stopped in the doorway and looked at her friend. "I know how you feel, Dan. I'm what, about half your age, and I feel the same. And it doesn't look like it's going to get better any time soon," she said and started to head for the communications office.

"Lucy," Dan said, stopping her in her tracks. She looked back at the man who seemed so much older than he had an hour before. "You know that people are going to die, don't you?"

She leaned against the doorjamb and looked down at the paper as if it was about to bite her. "Yes, I do. And this time tomorrow I'm going to be so drunk you won't admit to knowing me. A lot of those people will be ones I've known for years now. And some of them will be people I call friend." She stood up resolutely. "But what choice do we—do *I*—have, Dan?" She took one step away from the chart room and turned back. "The only thing I'm going to add to this list is a notice to Libra to expect casualties. I think they're going to have to act as a hospital station for a short while." She straightened up and turned to leave the room. Speaking loud enough to be heard as she walked away, Lucy said, "What I don't know is how I'm going to face myself once I sober up."

Lucy walked into the communications room feeling like she'd just stepped into a death chamber. In one way, it was, but not for her. Orders flashed out to four different locations in the solar system, ordering ships to converge on a certain spot just inside Saturn's orbit. The Mambas from Libra were the first to launch, leaving their station under high boost, each pilot knowing that he or she might not return from the mission but knowing, as well, that the mission they were on could define the course humanity would follow for centuries to come.

On three other ships, the clocks ticked down to zero and, from widely separate locations, they jumped into a space that contained themselves, forty-one Mambas, and one alien ship. Two of the ships, the *Heinlein* and the *Niven*, jumped in behind the guesstimated position of the alien ship, and the *Clarke* jumped directly into the projected path of the bogey. So close was the timing that mere minutes later, the squadron of Mambas passed her. Sensors tuned to their highest degree, the three major ships began quartering the area, looking for the proverbial needle in a haystack. But thanks to the engineering expertise of Dan Baylor and his counterparts on the other stations with building and launching the sensor drones, and thanks to the computations derived from those same devices, the spatial haystack had become more manageable.

Barely an hour after the forty-four ships arrived at the projected coordinates, a lone Mamba pilot called, "Target lock! Sensors indicate alien metal composition similar to data in my computer. Probability ninety-eight percent. Request assistance!" She followed this with a string of numbers indicating her position.

Forty other Mambas turned like a swarm of guided

missiles and began to converge on the spot where they could now make out the alien craft. It was two thirds the size of the Alliance's own cruisers, like the *Clarke,* and oddly similar in style but with subtle differences.

"Target powering up!" the first pilot announced. "Instructions!"

Seconds later, a message arrived on the *Clarke's* bridge. "Wait for them to fire first," Gayle ordered. "We will *not* initiate hostilities! If fired upon, all bets are off, and good luck to you all." Switching frequencies to her bridge crew, she said, "Comm, send to the bogey on all channels: 'You are in Earth space. This is interdicted territory. Stand down or be fired upon.' Send it three times and report any response."

Her exec, Commander Scott Newman, "Captain, what if they don't speak English?"

"I don't expect them to speak English, Number One," she answered, using the title from a sci-fi series she'd watched years ago. "What I expect is for them to see an overwhelming force and hear *something* being said to them. If they have the smarts of a doorknob, they'll figure out that we mean 'stop.' Otherwise, we're about to fire the second or maybe third shot in an interstellar war. Whatever, it won't be the first shot. We will be defending ourselves with prejudice." She stared at the computer plot. "I also expect to be saying goodbye to some of my friends in the next few minutes," she said softly.

"No response to our message, Captain," Comm said.

"Damn. What I wouldn't give for a universal translator. Too bad they only exist on television,"

Gayle lamented. She fingered her command panel. "Eagle One, fire one torp across the bogey's bow and detonate it manually well short of the target, then repeat the warning. Report results." Seven flights of five Mambas and one of six made up the forward assault force against the intruder. Now sitting squarely in its path, the lead ship, Eagle One, fired a single torpedo as ordered and repeated the order to stand down.

While she waited for the results of the Mamba pilot's attention-getter, Gayle called another section of the ship. "Forward Fire Control, this is the Captain. Arm a full spread and load all tubes. Prepare to fire on my order. Code alpha, alpha, prime."

The response came back immediately. "Arm a full spread, aye, Captain. Load all tubes. Code alpha, alpha, prime acknowledged."

Gayle swallowed hard. "Helm, bring us directly into the bogey's path. Hold your course." She hit the all-ships button. "All hands, this is the Captain. The bogey has refused to answer our hails. I expect to engage within the next few minutes. Lock down all stations and prepare for combat."

The bridge loudspeaker crackled to life. "Flotilla Leader, Eagle One. No response torpedo or hail. Request further inst—" The transmission broke off mid-word as the lead Mamba exploded, leaving only the hiss of interstellar space as her epitaph.

Immediately a gabble of voices came through.

"Oh, my God, she's gone!"

"The Bogey has returned fire!"

"They're attempting to run!"

Studying her battle plot, Gayle ordered, "All Mambas, attack pattern delta. Attack, attack, attack!"

The plan she ordered sent the remaining forty ships into attack mode in waves of ten, flushing their tubes of their full loads of torpedoes, now eight per vessel, followed by laser assaults until they passed their target. After being disarmed by their passes, the Mambas moved to regroup and return to Libra at just under maximum speed to preserve their engines and crew.

Four times, ten ships sent a total of eighty torpedoes at the enemy, the pilots recklessly careening close to the target to get the best laser shots possible. The attacks proved of little use as they blew up on the shields they hadn't expected the enemy ship to have. Since the lasers were set up to fire forward only, this left each Mamba open to return fire while their only protection was their speed and maneuverability. Gayle's battle plot showed most Mambas making successful passes and moving off into space to regroup, but a significant number didn't as the enemy ship returned fire. Gayle's heart ached with each wave that threw itself against the unknown might of the alien invader with little effect.

"Helm," she said, a catch in her voice, "come to attack speed and follow the fourth wave in." Switching frequencies, she called the other two ships in her fleet. "*Heinlein*, *Niven*, you are cleared to attack. Code alpha, alpha, prime. We have the point and will hold the enemy until you arrive. Good luck and God bless! Miller out."

She went back to internal frequency. "Forward Fire Control, on my order, fire all tubes and reload." She watched the plot, and just as the fourth wave of Mambas was reaching attack position, she ordered, "FFC, fire, fire, fire." She felt the now-familiar lurch as her ship expelled twenty missiles, each tipped with more megatons of explosives than had been released in all of World War II. "FFC, reload and prepare to fire," she ordered. On another channel, "Flight decks, prepare to launch both flights. Attack plan echo." This plan would have the ten Mambas that were an integral part of each ship launching as the *Clarke* passed the enemy ship, trying to attack from the rear with the twenty Mambas from the *Heinlein* and the *Niven* as those two ships poured their immense firepower into the backside of the hopefully fleeing invader.

This last order proved to be unnecessary as the combined torpedoes of the last flight of Mambas and the *Clarke's* first salvo met the target vessel almost simultaneously. Gayle watched as the ten little ships peeled off and went to join their fellows awaiting the outcome of the battle. The *Clarke*, however, much larger and harder to turn, was not able to escape the whirling, white-hot vortex created by one hundred missiles and the explosion of the enemy ship's power core. Speeding right into the center of that unimaginably intense man-made inferno, the *Clarke's* Mambas launched and moved away from the artificial sun, trying to come up behind it to contact any survivors of the attack. The *Clarke's* shields, powered by the same principles that had destroyed her quarry, failed under the onslaught of the inferno she'd helped create.

Twenty missiles, still in their tubes, vaporized when the shields failed, taking out the entire forward half of the ship. Airtight doors sealed off the damaged portions of the ship as critical systems failed, leaving only the red emergency lights burning dimly, a fitting illumination for the hellish interior of the crippled ship.

Anything not nailed down became missiles careening around the interior of the doomed ship, killing or wounding almost as many as had died outright in the attack. Control consoles, unable to handle the high-energy backlash, erupted in showers of sparks, sending parts of themselves throughout whatever room they happened to be situated in. Four hundred eighty souls sailed the *TAS Arthur C. Clarke* into battle, and barely one hundred twenty survived the destruction that followed the trip through the artificial sun they'd created. The bridge, situated in the center of the ship, barely survived, as did the engine room, rear torpedo rooms, and life support. Crew quarters, most of the flight deck, engineering, astrometrics, sick bay, hydroponics, communications and many others did not. Thirteen Mambas and their pilots never returned to base, adding to the total dead.

The missiles set off by the passage through the inferno caused the ship to begin tumbling, adding to the casualties. The *Heinlein* and the *Niven*, as soon as they were sure the enemy had been destroyed, moved in alongside the stricken vessel, using their capture fields to stop the tumble and move her back toward Libra, almost two million miles away.

Victor McCord, Commander of Libra Base, ordered the half-completed ship being assembled in his dock to be towed and set adrift near the base. More intimately acquainted than most with the construction of these ships, he knew that opening this can of worms was going to be a major undertaking. For whatever reasons, the Builders had neglected to provide airlocks for most parts of their vessels, a condition that had been noted but not considered a necessity until now. Another oversight of the Builders was the lack of spacesuits. It had been surmised, in innumerable bull sessions, that the Builders either relied solely on the construction pods or just never set down where there would be a need for that type of protection. So, with the *Clarke's* flight deck gone, there was no way for an individual to gain access to the savaged remains of the ship that had so proudly sailed from this base mere months before.

Hastily assembling his staff, Victor began issuing orders for the fabrication attached directly to Libra herself. The base would have its own airlock, already under construction, and the other end would be open to space until the *Clarke* could be pushed into place and held there by the capture fields of the base itself. Construction pods, positioned in the tube, would first seal the ship and tube together, then cut their way into the shattered hulk, allowing for the offloading of any survivors.

During the agonizingly long hours that it took the *Heinlein* and the *Niven* to transport their sister ship to the dock, no word was received from any of the *Clarke's* complement. Mambas from both escort ships reported that all external antennae had been lost, leaving no way to communicate even if the comm center had managed to survive.

Word flashed to Earth almost as fast as it had to Libra, considering the distances involved, and Lucy, beside herself with grief and fury, raced to the spaceport, climbed into her Mamba, and left a double sonic boom behind her as she made for the ship in orbit.

"Marsha, this is Lucy," she said as soon as she cleared the atmosphere. "Prepare to leave orbit for Libra Base as soon as I dock, and you're elected."

She arrowed directly for the bigger ship, slowing finally as she drew near. "First Captain, this is the *McCaffrey* Flight Control," she heard an unfamiliar, no-nonsense voice say. "Come alongside the flight deck, cut your engines, and be prepared to be pulled into the bay."

Cutting her power and turning control over to the crew operating the capture fields, Lucy sat through the procedure of being pulled through the force field and into the *McCaffrey's* bay. She released the cockpit controls and, as the canopy slid up and back, grabbed the quick dismount rail above her head. Allowing it to pull her bodily from the cockpit, she rode the bar just far enough to clear her ship and dropped to the deck, in complete disregard of all safety precautions, many of which she had instituted. Both feet hit the deck together, and she let her knees bend, taking up the shock of her landing, with only one hand going out to lightly touch the deck for support before standing up to her full height.

She turned around to find a full commander waiting for her with a look of disapproval on her face. "Permission to come aboard?" she requested.

"Permission granted, First Captain," the woman ground out frostily. "Captain Kane is expecting you on the bridge. If you will come with me, please?" She led Lucy to the elevator, and when the door closed on the two officers, she punched the hold button and said, "I'm glad none of my pilots saw that stunt you just pulled, First Captain. I have enough trouble keeping them from pulling dumb stunts without having them see *you* go all cowboy on us."

"Which is a polite way of saying to follow my own rules, right?" Lucy said, contrition in her voice.

"I don't know how polite it is, ma'am, but I have enough on my hands as it is," the commander, whose nametag read Valentine, said. "Besides, do you know how much trouble I'd be in if the boss got hurt on my deck on my watch?"

"I'd feel the same way in your position, Commander," Lucy said. "I helped formulate some of the rules I just broke. I apologize, and the only excuse I have is that I need to get underway as quickly as possible."

"Apology accepted," the commander said, apparently expecting anything but that from the First Captain to a mere commander. Emboldened by her success in chastising the boss, Commander Valentine pressed the bridge button and added, "I'd like to point out that whatever has happened has already happened, and that kind of haste won't help at all."

As the elevator began its ascent to the bride, Lucy said, "While I agree with you in principle, you're about to see another rule broken, Commander. And I'm not going to apologize for this one."

Seconds later, the door slid open and Lucy strode down the short hall to the command center of the ship, the perplexed commander following in her wake.

Setting foot just inside the bridge proper, Lucy saluted Marsha and asked, "Permission to enter, Captain?"

"Permission granted, First Captain," Marsha

answered. "I assumed you'd want to get underway immediately. Engines are online, and we're ready to break orbit on your command."

"No, Captain. On your command," Lucy corrected. "Can I see you in your ready room first?"

The door closed, cutting the two friends off from the rest of the ship, and Lucy began immediately. "Your Commander Valentine just chewed me out for breaking a flight deck rule, and rightly so," she said, sitting down in one of the chairs in front of Marsha's desk. "And now I'm going to ask you to break a bigger rule. I need to get to Libra soonest. I want you to micro-jump into the belt, Marsha, but I won't order it. This is your ship and crew. It's a risk, and you have to make the final decision. But as a friend, I'm asking you to consider it. I ordered the action, and I need to be on the scene. I figure if you jump to a point just *above* the plane of the belt and Libra, I can take my Mamba in the rest of the way. That way, I can get there before Victor can get the *Clarke* opened up, and you can either come back to Earth or I can send Jerry or Robert back here," she said, referring to the captains of the *Heinlein* and the *Niven*.

Lucy made a helpless gesture with her hands, letting them fall into her lap and slumping down into the chair. Marsha looked at her friend for a few seconds and began to call figures up on her desk comp. She made several false starts, clearing her screen each time, until she finally got the results she wanted. Picking up her comm link, she called her Helm officer. "Bunny, I need you to run us up to jump speed as fast as possible. I'm sending coordinates to Nav. Just go with 'em. I know what you're going to say, but the rules just changed. There will be quite a few things done differently for a while, I'm afraid. Let me know when we're about to jump." Lucy heard a muffled response, and Marsha set the comm down, stood up, and asked, "Something to drink?"

Lucy waved her hand indifferently. "Pepsi if you've got it. I think I want my caffeine cold."

"Nothing stronger?" Marsha asked, skepticism in her voice.

"I'm flying soon, remember? That's one rule even I won't break."

"Glad you've got some of your wits about you, girlfriend," Marsha said, opening the refrigerator at the side of the room. Peering inside, she said, "Coke's all I've got here."

Lucy flopped her hand in her lap again and Marsha popped the tab on the can and set it in front of her. "Look, you can't beat yourself up over what's happened, Luce. It's turned into a war out here, and somebody has to make the tough decisions. You can't blame yourself."

The ship shuddered as it got under way, settling down to a smooth purr. Lucy picked up the red and white can and took a long pull. Setting it down hard, she asked angrily, "Who the hell can I blame then? Simon for getting shot? The people who shot him? Kitty for getting hurt? The same people who caused *that?* How about some faceless aliens who lost a spaceship? Or some other faceless aliens who probably don't want us to keep it? You tell me who to blame, Marsha. Somebody's to blame for so many lives lost on the *Clarke*! Who do you think the families of those people are going to blame? *I* sent those ships out there." She stared absently at the brown liquid bubbling up out of the can she'd just slammed down on the desk.

Unable to answer the questions Lucy posed, Marsha sat there, wishing she could do something, anything, to ease the pain her friend was feeling but knowing she'd probably feel and react much the same way under those conditions. She also knew that at some future date, she just might. The silence lengthened, and both women felt the ship continue to change its subtle vibrations until Marsha's comm chimed. She picked it up and listened for a few seconds.

"Thanks, Bunny. I'll be right out." Hooking the device on her belt, she placed a hand on Lucy's shoulder. "Time to go, Luce. We're about to jump. You've got to get to the flight deck."

Lucy picked up the can from the desk, looked down at the ring of drying liquid, and asked, "Bunny? For real?"

"For real," Marsha confirmed with a grin. "Bunny Bradshaw, a real whiz at Helm, but watch what you say around her. She's kinda sensitive about it. There've been a few black eyes I've had to overlook, but nothing serious, and not a one lately."

The two women walked out into a scene of quiet efficiency, though with some slight apprehension in the air. Marsha said, "Report, Number One."

Her executive officer responded, "We're almost ready to jump, ma'am." In a quieter voice, he added, "The crew knows the destination and seem a little tense, but there haven't been any incidents."

"Very well, Number One. You have the bridge. I'll be on the flight deck for a short time."

"I have the bridge, aye, ma'am," the exec

acknowledged. Apparently dismissing her from his thoughts, he turned to the rest of the bridge crew. "Helm, how long until we reach jump speed?"

"Sir," Lt. Commander Bradshaw replied, "five minutes. Ten, tops."

Lucy and Marsha walked onto the flight deck and found it to be a place of furious activity. Commander Valentine, having returned to the flight deck when Lucy and Marsha had gone into conference, turned away from the crewmen she was giving orders to, tucked a clipboard under her arm, and saluted. Lucy, as senior of the two being saluted, returned it.

"Problem with my ship, Commander?" she asked, nodding at a pair of legs dangling out of an open hatch near the rear of her Mamba.

"Not to speak of, ma'am," the commander replied. "I ordered a diagnostic run on your systems and found a wobble in your grav compensator. Not dangerous yet, but without attention…" she let her voice trail off and shrugged.

"How much longer do you figure, Commander Valentine?" Marsha asked.

The pair of legs turned into a full body as the technician wriggled his way out of the access hatch. "I can answer that, ma'am," he said. He reached inside, pulled a small tool case out, sealed the hatch, and said, "All done. Just needed to recalibrate the sump sensors. They were throwing off the compensators just enough to register as a glitch on our diagnostics."

Commander Valentine said, "I noticed that your ship only carries four torps. That makes it one of the older models. I suggest that you have your power core replaced sometime soon, ma'am."

Lucy nodded. "Sentimental attachment, Commander. Thanks for your attention to detail." At that moment, the triple tone that indicated an upcoming jump sounded. "That's my cue to lock and load," she said.

Marsha said, "Safe trip, First Captain. I'll see you on Libra. Think about what I said, okay?"

"I'll keep it in mind, Captain," Lucy answered. She saw Valentine signal the Ops officer to lower the dismount rail. As the bar came within reach, Lucy grabbed it with both hands and nodded at Valentine, who then waved her hand, thumb up. Immediately, Lucy's feet left the floor as she was carried up and over her cockpit. Looking down, she slid her feet forward as her butt met the seat. She slid each arm through the crash webbing, locked it in place, put her helmet on, and hit the power button. Once her systems were live, she called Launch Control.

"Comm check," she announced.

"Loud and clear, First Captain," came through the speakers built into her helmet. "Stand by for jump." A pause, then a short countdown. "Four, three, two, one, mark." On the last word, the familiar queasiness that signaled a jump through the mathematical anomaly humans had started to call "otherspace" twisted her stomach and then disappeared. "Jump complete. Prepare for launch."

"Prepare for launch, aye," Lucy replied, and the ship, lifted by the interior capture fields, slid smoothly to the open bay doors and was pushed through the force field into space. When the last of her status lights turned green, she powered up her side thrusters and moved effortlessly away from the *McCaffrey*.

Lucy queried her onboard computer for information about nearby space, and moments later, objects began to appear on her radar screen. First, the slowly receding blob that was the *McCaffrey* showed up, followed by several small asteroids. *That's why we don't do this!* She thought to herself. Finally, the conglomeration of blobs that was the complex known as Libra Base showed up on her screens. She locked the center of the base into her computer and fired up her engines, allowing the little ship to pick its way through the clutter surrounding the base.

Less than a minute after she'd done so, three Mambas appeared on her screen headed straight toward her, and a hail came over the speaker. "Solo Mamba, this is Libra patrol. Identify yourself or be fired upon."

"Libra patrol, this is First Captain Grimes. Request an escort to Libra Base. I believe I'm expected. Isn't your reaction just a bit overstated?"

"You're a bit ahead of schedule, First Captain, and no, our reaction isn't overstated. We have no idea who could have possession of a Mamba or Mamba-style craft, so we take no chances. Neither will any other base anymore. Anyway, welcome to Libra space. If you'll follow me, ma'am, I'll lead you in. Just stay a bit to starboard to clear my engine wash."

Almost immediately, a Mamba passed above her and slowed as it moved into position. Her screens showed two other ships flanking her, but since neither of them spoke, she ignored them and followed the patrol leader as requested. Ten minutes later, she was warped into the docking bay of Libra Base and being greeted by Victor McCord.

"Permission to come aboard?" she asked formally.

"Granted, First Captain, and gladly. Good to finally meet you," Victor said, reaching out to shake her hand. "I'm sorry that it's under these conditions."

"Me, too, Commander. But we've met before. Back then I was just a third-shift watch officer and you were concerned with setting up a deep space manufacturing facility for spaceships, so not remembering me is understandable," she answered. "What's the status on the *Clarke?* I saw her on the way in. God, what a mess. Can you tell me what happened?"

"We haven't gotten her opened up yet, ma'am, so we don't have any word from the survivors, if any. But the sensor data from the *Heinlein* and the *Niven* seems to show that the last wave of Mambas and the *Clarke* fired on the bogey at the same time. Most of the Mambas were able to veer off from the explosion, but the *Clarke* either couldn't turn in time or Captain Miller felt she could ride it out. What we've recorded is a second explosion *after* the enemy vessel was destroyed. So far, that's all. We've just warped her into the boarding tube, and I have three construction pods welding the two together right now. We should be able to cut through within the hour."

Two pods welded the hastily constructed boarding tube from the outside while a third worked from the inside. Welded to the hull just forward of the engine compartment, it was thought that the cutting process from the single pod inside the tube posed the least danger to both the remaining crew of the *Clarke* and to the base in general. The specially constructed airlock on the station side of the tube was kept closed until the inside pod could cut through to the inside of the stricken ship and poke a camera inside to assess conditions.

Lucy chafed at the slowness of the process, calmed only slightly by Victor as they watched the pod on a monitor set up just outside the airlock. "One step at a time, or we could do more harm than good," he cautioned. "I want to go charging over there, too, but one thing I've learned is that you have to let people do their jobs and trust that it'll get done. Sometimes, like now, you can supervise the process, but it still gets done by someone else."

Lucy and Victor, along with a growing crowd of people, watched as the pod operator turned off the cutting torch and checked a gauge he had attached to the outside of the *Clarke*. "Positive pressure," he announced. Lucy watched as an extension arm threaded a small tube through the hole. Victor tapped a command into the monitor's console and the view changed to a surreal view of the inside of the ship. Lit by a dim red glow, the camera showed several people floating to one side of the picture, most oriented with their feet toward the floor but a few at odd angles to the camera. The posture of three or four indicated that they were injured, while two others held crewmates and a third held a laser trained on the camera snaking into the ship.

Victor pulled his comm from his belt and spoke into it. "Relax people. We're the good guys. This is Commander McCord of Libra Base. You've been towed to the dock, and we're cutting our way in now. What's your situation?"

The man holding the laser lowered it to his side. "I'm Chief Engineer Gordon Conners, Commander. We have fourteen still alive in this section. I have no idea about the rest of the ship. All airtight doors are closed down and all communications are out. Life support seems to be operating, just barely, but no other sections answer our calls. I can't even get into the engine room to check on my crew. I've banged on the bulkhead, and I do get a response, but I can't tell much more than that. There are dozens dead though, mostly due to stuff flying around from exploding equipment."

"Very well, Chief," Victor answered. "Stay back while the operator cuts a bigger hole. We'll get you out and to medical attention as quickly as possible."

The view cut to the skin of the ship as the pod operator pulled the camera out of the small hole he'd cut, and Victor switched to the wider view offered by the exterior camera. Sparks flew as the torch began to cut a swath inches from the edge of the tube.

Working quickly in the weightless environment, the hole was soon finished, and the section of hull was pushed inward by the extendable arm of the pod. Seconds later the pod disappeared inside the ship, allowing room for the swarm of people moving from Libra to the *Clarke* to assist in the rescue process.

Lucy tried to move across as well, but Victor held her back. "There's only room for one pod and so many people over there right now. You and I will wait until the pod cuts through to the bridge."

Distraught, Lucy took Victor's implied order with ill grace and watched as the first casualties began to emerge from the boarding tube and were whisked off to make-shift infirmaries around the base.

The watch on her wrist slowed to a crawl as the pod's cutting tools sliced through door after door and the pitiful few survivors trickled in. Finally, the pod operator reported that he'd arrived at the door to the bridge. The flow of people had ended, leaving room for Lucy and Victor to cross to the stricken ship. Gliding through the interior, reddened by the emergency lighting, Lucy shivered as she saw the mangled bodies of the dead that the rescue teams hadn't yet had time to remove. She stopped and looked at the face of one as she passed, and wept, then closed the staring eyes and followed Victor down the once-familiar corridor. Hovering in the gravity-free hallway with the tech team, all of whom were as shaken as she, Lucy watched as the final barrier was breached and the heavy door was pulled away and set to one side. She steeled herself and pushed to the front of the gaggle of people, pulling herself into the command center and burning her hand on the hot metal of the opening as she did so.

For the rest of her life, Lucy would remember the sight that met her streaming eyes. Ten positions had been occupied at the time of the disaster, and seven limp bodies floated in various positions around the room or sat strapped in front of their exploded consoles as if ready to perform their duties. Two of the three survivors hovered over the central seat from which the *TAS Arthur C. Clarke* had been commanded. Lucy, gagging at the smell trapped in the room from the failing ventilation system, floated over to the command chair to find Gayle's first officer and navigation officer trying to remove her from the straps holding her in place. Both officers showed evidence of their harrowing ordeal, but they single-mindedly kept at their grisly task until the medical officer from Libra ordered them back. Beckoning an assistant to bring a light to bear on the captain of the *Clarke*, he began an inspection that finally produced a groan of pain from Lucy's friend.

Gayle's eyes fluttered open to see Lucy watching worriedly. "Did we hold 'em, Luce?" The question was so quiet that Lucy almost missed it but for the movement of her lips.

"Yeah, you held 'em, Gayle. You held 'em good. Now let the doctor take a look at you, okay?"

"Sure, Lucy," the injured captain mumbled. "How's my crew? And the ship? How did she do?"

Tears floated from Lucy's eyes as she saw the wound in Gayle's side, hidden until now by her hands, the spreading stain of red on black being wicked away from the wound by the material of her uniform. A piece of one of the exploded consoles had pinned her to the chair she sat in. The doctor reached into the bag held for him by an aide and looked up at Lucy. "I need to put her out for a while. We're going to have to cut the chair free and get her out of it back on the base."

"Do it," was all Lucy could say.

The doctor pushed up Gayle's sleeve, slid a hypodermic under the skin, and pressed the plunger home.

"Lucy," Gayle whispered, her hand drifting out to rest lightly on her friend's arm, "how is Stephen?" Her eyes closed as the drug started to take effect.

"We'll talk later, Gayle," Lucy said, grief strangling her voice.

The doctor motioned for the pod operator to start cutting the chair free as the captain succumbed to the narcotic he'd injected into her arm. Lucy slowly turned around and surveyed the room again. Floating over to the science station, she found the body of Stephen Walker still strapped in his chair, his heart pierced by a piece of his console that had blown apart during the energy backlash that had destroyed so many other systems throughout the remains of the ship.

At the same moment, millions of miles away, another ship quietly moved away from human space, undetected by the still-unfinished surveillance net being constructed around the system.

CHAPTER NINETEEN

The *McCaffrey* one-jumped Gayle and thirteen other seriously wounded survivors to the *Galileo* to be seen by Dr. Jeffers. The remaining survivors, just over a hundred, were either loaded aboard the *Heinlein* and taken back to Earth or were given berths aboard Libra until such time as they could be sent back to Earth as well.

Lucy, feeling like an interplanetary hitchhiker, stowed her Mamba on the *McCaffrey's* flight deck and waited out the jump while standing behind Marsha's command chair. Less than an hour later, running at speeds that would make the Builders themselves shudder, the *McCaffrey* lay alongside the huge factory ship at the nearly completed Taurus Base.

Dr. Jeffers, alerted to the arrival of so many wounded, triaged the entire group himself, assigning crewmen to attend to the less seriously injured. One amputated arm and three surgeries later, he walked out of the sick bay to find half a dozen anxious people waiting for him. Sitting wearily in a chair, he looked at the row of faces. "I said it the day I came aboard, and I'll say it again—we don't have enough adequately trained medical personnel for a really serious incident. This just points the fact up. I need to find a donor with B-positive blood for a transfusion for Captain Miller, but the others will be fine as they are now. Lieutenant Morrison needed an O-positive transfusion, but I found several of my assistants who helped in that department. She's going to have to learn to do things left handed, I'm afraid. Her hand was crushed when one of the airtight doors closed on it. The other three will have some interesting scars, but the B-positive is considerably rarer and needs to be found as soon as possible."

Captain Morgan stood up. "That will be my job, then. With the *McCaffrey* and the *Galileo* here, I should be able to get someone here pretty quick." He turned to leave but then turned back. "Unless B-positive is *really* rare?"

"Not all that rare," the doctor said. "About seven percent of the population have it. Out of what, some thirteen hundred plus, you should be able to find at *least* a couple of dozen who have B-positive."

Captain Morgan nodded and said, "I'll put out a ship-wide bulletin right away."

He'd started to leave when Marsha stopped him. "Call my exec and have him put out the same notice, will you, Mustafa? Can't hurt." The *Galileo's* captain nodded and left without a backward glance.

Simon, standing next to a transformed Kitty, asked, "So, exactly what is Gayle's condition, Doctor? Not to disparage the others, but Gayle is a personal friend, and I… we all," he said, waving at the room in general, "want to know."

"Well, to tell you the truth, she was in the best condition of the four who needed my attention. The piece of metal that pinned her to the chair had wedged itself between two ribs. No internal organs were damaged, but she did suffer a lot of blood loss, hence the transfusion. If she wears a bikini, she is going to have an interesting scar to explain. But I understand that we may still have a problem, and that's in the department of mental health. Is it true that her boyfriend or lover was aboard and died in the attack?"

Lucy answered, "Yes he was, Doctor. As a matter of fact, he was in the same room. Died instantly, we believe, sitting at the science station."

Dr. Jeffers shook his head. "That's a rough one. I thought it might be something like that from some of the things she said while she was under sedation. She's going to need the support of all her friends in the months to come, as will the others," he added. "This is a new experience in the human condition, people. Participating in space battles isn't something that happens in 'real life,' and the trauma, both physical and mental, is going to be severe."

Simon spoke up more confidently than he had in almost a year. "We didn't expect a cakewalk, Doctor, but I had hoped that after taking out whoever attacked Orion, we'd have a longer breathing spell than we got. Distances being what they are, we figured we'd have more time..."

A white-haired, still not completely up-to-date Kitty spoke up. "Dr. Jeffers, is it? I don't know you, but I know what Simon told me, and if he trusts you, then I do, too. I guess you know about me and my condition." She self-consciously fingered her hair. "*I* sure as hell don't. But Gayle and I have been friends for almost thirty years now, and if anyone can even come close to understanding her loss and helping her, I think it would have to be me."

Brian nodded slowly. "I was briefed on your condition when I took over Dr. Penn's position, and

I'm as much at a loss to explain what happened to you as anyone else. According to all medical data and experience, you should be in a vegetative coma, at best. Still another case of technology getting the upper hand—for the better in this case, thank God. But just for everybody's information, none of the patients were left on any of the tables. I don't want another occurrence of what happened to Captain Hawke. Anyway, none of these are suffering from life-threatening injuries. I did *think* about leaving Lieutenant Morrison there to see if we could give her back her right hand though."

Kitty asked, "So, when can we see her, Doctor?"

"I think this time tomorrow will be soon enough," he replied. "I'm going to keep her sedated for a while to let the stitches set and to let her to gain some of her strength back. I'd like you there when she wakes up, of course, so I'll let you know a bit in advance."

"None of us are going anywhere right now, Brian," Simon said familiarly.

"All right, then," the doctor said with a touch more joviality than was really necessary. "I should get back to my patients. I'll leave you folks to your reunion." He stood up and shook hands all around. When he got to Kitty, held her hand a bit longer than the others. "I'd like to give you another quick exam sometime tomorrow, if you don't mind. After you see Gayle would be a good time. I can check out your stress levels as well."

Sixteen hours passed, allowing all concerned to let their body-clocks adjust to the *Galileo's* time while they came to some kind of terms with the situation. The "reunion" consisted of Simon, Kitty, Lucy, Marsha, Victor—who'd also hitchhiked to the

Galielo—and Mustafa when his shift ended. The group made their way to Mustafa's ready room, and on the way, Lucy laid her hand on Kitty's arm, slowing her down a bit. The action caused the two women to be the last two to enter, and as the door closed, she hugged Kitty gently.

For her part, Kitty hugged back fiercely and said, "I'm not going to break, okay?"

Marsha took her turn, and the six sat down around the table.

Mustafa, playing host, brought a pitcher and glasses to the table. "Tea," he said. "Technically, I'm still on duty."

"Sounds good to me," Kitty said. "Simon had a beer in our quarters last night, and the smell almost made me gag. I guess I was out way too long."

Lucy sipped from her glass and asked, "How much did he tell you about what happened?"

"Pretty much everything, I think," Kitty replied soberly. "I gather I was pretty messed up, like one-foot-in-the-grave kind of messed up." She sat quietly for a time, twirling the glass in her hands. "He didn't think I should see the footage of what happened at Camp David, but after he fell asleep, I found it. Some pretty rough stuff. Our guys did a good job. I just wish, you know, that fewer people had died, like none of the bystanders. And the changes!" She flipped a hand through her hair. "I don't just mean me, this I can get used to after a while, but I mean the embassies, the ships, *you* in charge. It's a lot to take in and process in forty-eight hours, you know?"

"I know," Lucy said, nodding. "And I apologize for what I'm about to say. We have six captains present. As far as I'm concerned, that's a quorum, and I'm making this a Captain's Call." She looked around the table. "At present, there's one topic up for discussion, and that's Simon taking back the reins. I feel that since the Alliance was his vision in the first place, he should be the one to lead it. *Especially* right now, with what has just happened. He has the military mind among us, and he's best suited to lead us through this."

"'Military mind,' my ass!" Simon exploded. "I was just a sergeant, for Christ's sake! And I made that rank three times. Insubordination, I believe the charges were both times I got busted. And I haven't forgotten how to *be* insubordinate, either. How about, 'No way in *hell* am I taking this job back!' I didn't 'die' on purpose, you know," he said more reasonably. "You just got stuck with the job. And you're doing a good one, too. We need an administrative type at the top, and you've got the mind for it. Look at what you've accomplished so far." He stared across the table at Lucy. "I just got my wife back, dammit, and I'm not going to let anything get in the way of that for a while. I say, let's not change horses in midstream. It'll just confuse the troops. And more importantly, it'll confuse everybody on Earth at a time when we need to have them see us as more stable than we know ourselves to be. I know I wasn't acting responsibly most of the time Kitty was out of it, but I did keep track of what and how you were doing. I couldn't have done any better. Remember, we're winging it here."

Simon wound down when Kitty laid a hand on his arm. "I agree with Simon, Lucy. And not because he's my husband. God knows, I've stood up to him before, but right now, you're our best hope. Not necessarily as a military mind—those are a dime a dozen—but as an overall administrator." Simon settled back into his chair and Kitty put her hand back on the table. "We talked a long time ago about the occupations we were going to need out here, and tacticians and strategists were on the list. I remember that. So, go looking for some. Put one in charge of military matters and let him or her do it. I hate a sports analogy, but you're the coach. Make someone the quarterback and let them run the plays. You set overall policy, and we'll do what needs to be done."

"I don't know if I can do that," Lucy said quietly, her voice cracking. "Hundreds of our people died yesterday, and I'm the one who gave the orders. Do you know how that *feels?*"

"Yes, I do," Simon said gently. "And if that gets easier as time goes by, *then* you aren't the right person for the job. But as long as even one death hurts you, your compassion is intact, and you can't do any worse than anyone else. Plus, you're known and liked. Me, I'm a tactless SOB who'd rather tell someone else *they're* an SOB and watch the defecation hit the oscillating air movement device." He was interrupted by a wave of laughter that rolled around the table, and even Lucy's mouth turned up faintly. "Is that who you want running this show? I always said that all I wanted was a ship of my own, and being the boss won't get one for me."

Marsha had sat back to watch the sparks fly, and she finally spoke up. "Are you really calling for a vote on this, Lucy? I have to go with Simon, here. You've done a damn good job. You can't blame yourself for what happened to the *Clarke* and her people. If there *is* anyone to blame, it's the damned aliens who won't leave us alone. Twice now, we've slapped 'em down for being where they shouldn't be. The first time we were lucky, the second, we got our fingers burnt. We're learning as we go. If we dump someone because they feel bad about a battle they *won,* we're in deep enough that we might as well kiss our collective asses goodbye. I'm not ready to do that."

Mustafa chimed in, agreeing with Simon and Marsha, and Victor took his turn before Lucy could start over.

"I agree with the rest, Lucy. You've done first-rate work, and you've got all five of us of one accord. Even if you think that all five of the other captains and commanders would vote your way, the tiebreaker is still under sedation but will be able to vote in the not-too-distant future. Do you want to drag this out or give in gracefully?"

Lucy sat silently, eyes twitching left and right, looking for an escape route.

Wild animals caged for the first time have that same look, Simon thought. *The next words we hear are going to be interesting, one way or the other.*

"So, you want me to be the boss? Is that what you're saying?" Lucy glared around the table. All five facing her nodded, some a bit more affirmatively than others. She stood up and placed her hands on the table, fingers splayed. "Okay. But there will be changes, and the first is that I will not be called First Captain any longer. And you won't have a president, either. What my position will be called is yet to be determined. Here's another—every one of my captains will follow my orders, or I'll quit so fast it'll make your heads spin! Am I understood?" When she got a few weak nods in response, she asked again. "Am I *understood?*" The volume rose substantially as all five answered aloud.

Her glare included all present and stopped when it got to Simon. "You're going to regret this, Simon Hawke. And I hope you live a long time so you can regret it *in detail*." Lucy stood there, chest heaving for a few seconds longer. "There will be one more meeting before the *McCaffrey* takes me back to Earth." A transformed Lucy stood up straight and said, "I'll let you know when." Only a hint of the trapped beast remained, hidden behind a stern look and new resolve.

Twenty-four hours went by before Lucy summoned the five conspirators together again. The fact was that they'd spent a considerable amount of that time together already, trying to guess what was going on in the head of the woman who'd gone into total seclusion.

"I don't think she's eaten at all in the last twenty-four," Mustafa said. "She's either been in her rooms or in the comm shack. All I know for sure is that she's ordered that all her incoming and outgoing traffic be kept secret."

"She sent word to me that the *McCaffrey* is on a five-minute departure notice," Marsha announced. "Has anyone heard anything else?"

"All I know is that Dr. Jeffers has pushed Gayle's visitation back by a day. Says she needs more recovery time before we inflict ourselves on her," Kitty said.

The door opened, stopping any further discussion, and Lucy walked over to the table wearing a uniform shorn of all insignia. "This meeting is called to order," she said without preamble. Looking down at a piece of paper she had placed on the table in front of her, she said, "First order of business: I will no longer be called First Captain. My new title is 'Herald' from this moment on.

"Second, since we're forming a government, I will choose a deputy herald and other members of my cabinet, who will be known as 'wardens.' Below that rank will be the secretaries of various parts of our new nation—Treasury, Commerce, Foreign Affairs, Extra-Terrestrial Affairs (which will become shortened to ET Affairs anyway, so let's just do it now), Trade, Production, Defense, State, etc. Below that will be elected representatives of our populace, modeled on the good ole U.S. of A, of course, and our charter or constitution will be a direct steal from theirs, too. Those called to serve, *will* serve, or they will be dropped back on Earth without wristbands.

"Third, as soon as this present crisis is over, specifically, the threat from an unknown alien source, elections will be held to determine who the next herald will be. I'm taking a page from Simon's book here, and the next herald will *not* be me.

"Fourth, there will be a massive personnel buildup beginning as soon as I get back to Earth. Ship production will increase to maximum without over-stressing our people, work on Vesta will be started, and we'll keep a closer watch over each base to prevent any further attacks on our less well-defended assets." Lucy looked down at the paper before her. "We'll have another ship ready to go in about a month and two a month thereafter. From that point on, we'll be getting roughly eight ships a year unless we use Taurus to build something bigger. Your guess is as good as mine as to whether or not that will be good enough, but I do have some good news. I've spent most of the last day talking with Libra's engineers. They've been going over all the data accumulated from all sources, and it seems that Stephen," she said, choking on the name, "left us a legacy."

The assembled officers stirred at the mention of Stephen's name, but said nothing. Lucy went on, "He was using his station to assess the effectiveness of each wave of Mamba attacks and was making notes as he went along on what we could do to make it easier to knock out one of these craft. As you know from our only other assault in the asteroid belt, we had a harder time taking out the enemy craft than our engineers had assumed. The situation was much the same this time. It appears that our energy release, while devastating, isn't as effective as we'd hoped." Lucy closed her eyes for a few seconds before she continued. "Stephen was working on equations that would let us build a type of shield nullifier. I don't understand the physics at all, but I'm assured by our engineers that the project is feasible—something about opposites canceling each other out. What that means is that a missile carrying a wave generator would leave a ship on course for an enemy ship, followed microseconds later by standard antimatter missiles. The generator would produce, for lack of a better term, an anti-shield—energy that cancels out the shields of an aggressor. This would make a hole in his shields long enough and big enough, hopefully, to let the following antimatter missiles through to do their jobs. All sheer speculation at this point, but we've gotten a push in a direction that we may not have even seen without Stephen's contributions."

Stunned by the revelation, Lucy's audience still said nothing, watching her as if she were a specter come alive. Lucy's lips turned up mirthlessly at a stray thought. "I never figured this group would ever be speechless over anything. I guess I was wrong." She looked down at the paper before her. "Then, you add the still-to-be-built-and-tested shield penetrator missiles to the possibility of tractor and pressor beams for grappling onto a ship in space, and I believe we have a chance to do more than just give a black eye to whoever it is we're fighting. The engineers on all bases, as well as the *Galileo,* have been given copies of all pertinent information and will be working as closely as the distances will permit. It has been postulated that the destruction of the *Clarke* was due to the fact that her shields weren't sufficient to handle the sudden onslaught of energy she faced as she flew through the destruction zone of the enemy ship. A new addition to all future ships will be the ability to crosslink any two of the three power cores to double the available power to the shields as necessary."

Switching tracks at a lightening pace, Lucy added, "Enough to keep you thinking for now, I would guess. Happier subject—I've just come from the sick bay where I talked with Gayle. She's awake and waiting for you to visit. Dr. Jeffers does say that you should keep your visits short."

This welcome news brought the most response to anything Lucy had said up until that point, and everyone sat up straighter and looked around.

"Last note," Lucy said, picking up the paper. "It's

my intention to get the best possible use out of all our assets, and that includes personnel. Some of you will be receiving new assignments in the near future. Remember, refusal means expulsion! You made me the monster; live with it!" Her right hand balled up the paper, and she turned without another word as she stalked to the door, tossing the paper in a basket on the way out. Stopping at the door, she turned back, stemming the sudden gabble of voices. "Marsha, make a visit to Gayle. She's expecting you. After that, the *McCaffrey* will return me to Earth. One hour."

The silence went on for thirty seconds before Marsha stood up. "Well, guys, I'm off to the sick bay. Who else?"

The group followed Marsha out the door, and Simon stopped long enough to retrieve the paper Lucy had thrown away. Following the others down the hall, he smoothed the paper out and stared at it, incredulous.

His low chuckle made Kitty slow down and walk beside him. "What's up?"

He passed the paper over. "Looks like she's learning even faster than *she* realizes," he said.

"What do you mean?" Kitty asked, glancing down at the paper.

"I mean," Simon said quietly, "that Lucy was just using that as a prop. She kept referring to it during her little lecture back there, and it's just some doodles. She walked in knowing what she wanted to say and used that to keep us just a bit off balance. Now she's laid down the law, and we better fall into line, or else."

"Or else what?"

"Or else we get ourselves a new herald. And it's almost too late for that."

A pale and haggard caricature of the person they all knew lay propped up in a makeshift bed as the small crowd entered the sick bay. Gayle's eyes slowly opened as the sound of feet shuffling across the floor penetrated her consciousness. "'Bout time you guys got here," she mumbled. "I was beginnin' to think I'd been forgotten."

Kitty knelt beside the bed and hugged her friend gently. "The doctor was supposed to call us… me, before you woke up, hon. I'm sorry I wasn't here."

"Hey, it's not like I'm goin' anywhere," the petite blonde declaimed. She looked closer at Kitty. "Wow. The Doc must have given me some really good stuff."

Puzzlement on her face, Kitty asked, "What do you mean?"

Gayle's face screwed up, and a tear trickled from one eye. "First, you got hurt, then you got sucked up by the ship, then Simon died, and Simon came back but you didn't, then we got to go fight this ship, ya know? And I wrecked the ship and Stephen died, and now you're back, and I think I remember somebody saying so, but right now, I'm not sure. And I'm not surprised by your hair, and Stephen being dead doesn't hurt. Must be some really good stuff to make me see things like that. It's your hair that's the giveaway though." Her voice trailed off and silence reigned for a time.

Kitty looked helplessly over her shoulder at her four equally miserable companions. Seeing no help coming from that quarter, she turned back to her stricken friend. "Gayle, hon, we need to talk. But I don't think this is a good time."

"Why not?" Gayle demanded. "Cuz you think I'm loopy from the drugs the doc gave me? I'm with it enough to know that Simon came back to life, and that you're really here, so you did, too. And I know that Stephen *won't* be." Her voice cracked on the last word, and she descended into bone-shaking sobs.

Dr. Jeffers chose that moment to come over and inject a needle full of something into the IV drip going into Gayle's arm. "You need to leave now," he said protectively. "She's lost a lot, both physically and mentally. She needs her rest."

Kitty stood up and Marsha quickly slid into her place. "Gayle, listen up, girlfriend. I'm headed for Earth in about an hour, but I'll keep in touch and stop in to see ya when I can. You just remember what friends are for—to help when they can and listen when they can't help."

Gayle's hand shot out and closed on Marsha's arm. "It's not *fair!*" she wailed. "He asked me to marry him!"

Marsha gently disengaged Gayle's hand from her arm. "Now I'll agree that the drugs are kicking in," she said lightly. "Stephen, propose on his own? He'd have to be drunk. That man couldn't make a proposal in committee."

"No!" Gayle said, less adamant as the sedative kicked in. "Well, he was, a little. But it's *not* a dream." Her voice began to lose clarity and strength as the drug took effect. She struggled to get her left arm out from under the light blanket covering her. "See?" she crowed in triumph as her arm finally came free and fell to the bed, revealing a small gold band with a huge stone.

The group filed out the door and milled around in

the corridor, not having any specific destinations for the next few minutes. Before they could break up and go their separate ways, the doctor stepped out. "Captain Hawke, Kitty? May I speak to you for a moment?"

"Of course, Doctor. What can I do for you?"

He hesitated for a few seconds. "It's not for me. It's for my patient. She's asking for you, even through the drugs. I think it would be a good idea if you could stay for a while. Quietly, mind you. Stay clear of stressful topics. She's going to fall asleep soon, but she's fighting the sedative. A friend nearby will help her relax."

CHAPTER TWENTY

The loss of the *Clarke* and her crew was a blow that left the Alliance stunned, but like determined people everywhere and in every time, they mourned and then made a commitment to see through 'til the end a course of action that, in retrospect, seemed inevitable: the digging in of heels, the effort to first deny and then blame, moving on to acceptance, and ending finally with a dogged resolve to persevere.

The year that passed after that disaster had transformed the Alliance in ways even Lucy hadn't foreseen. Six ships were added to the active roster—two of them, the *Canopus* and the *Aldebaran*, being the carriers Simon had envisioned in the beginning. Now, the ships, bases, and Project Vesta carried a total personnel count of over forty-five hundred. Planet-side, another five hundred served in three embassies, while hundreds were training at any one time in preparation for a ship assignment or to replace a downsider finally moving up to space.

The Alliance entwined itself into the fabric of downsider economics by investing as Jackpot Jackson, Lucy's old boyfriend and now Secretary of the Treasury, advised. More funds began to enter the Alliance coffers to pay personnel, now being called "citizens" more often than not.

Almost two thousand Alliance personnel were on "rest shift" or simply taking vacations, able to be tapped at need to fill positions on the various ships and installations. None were allowed to talk about their jobs or missions except in the broadest terms, allowing for more exposure, and finally the media started getting used to this new phenomenon and began leaving the Alliance alone.

Research and Development began turning out "shield-killer" missiles, sending the plans to the bases to begin construction and deployment. Ships' personnel received training in the use of these new weapons, and the tractor and pressor beams were being actively researched. A few hundred plasma bombs, like the one used when Simon was rescued were built and put through their paces. This was not a weapon that could be stockpiled, as their power was drawn directly from one of the power cores of an individual ship and needed to be used then or allowed to bleed off safely by firing it into the depths of space, thereby squandering a measurable portion of the core itself.

Earth began to see Alliance technology on a more personal level as solar power systems began to make their presence known by reducing the emissions from fossil fuels, food processors were still being given away to anyone who could demonstrate a need for one or more, especially in third-world countries. Anti-gravity began to revolutionize the transportation industries, whether it be bulk goods or simply a cab to get from one part of town to another, and, unexpectedly, the Japanese began to impact the timber and mining industries world-wide by beginning to export a cheaper, far superior building material. Based on the Alliance's "plastics" technology, it was stronger and less brittle than steel and lighter than an equivalent piece of wood.

Lucy moved her permanent base to Zurich, chafing under the handicaps imposed upon her not long after she released the list of her appointees to the various cabinet positions created for the fledgling government. That meeting still caused her distress whenever she thought about it. Simon had led the "delegation," she remembered, a look of satisfaction his face even before he spoke. "So, you're going to go ahead with the full nationalization thing?" he asked casually.

"Of course," she had replied. "It's what you were going to do before... We have the full support of all our people, and you agreed to it too, Simon. Why would you ask?"

"Well," Simon said, all innocence, "a few of us were having drinks the other day, and we came to the conclusion that the offices of the herald and deputy herald are just too important to go without a proper security contingent any longer. So far, you've been lucky, but what's to stop someone from assassinating our top officials?" His tone took a more serious bent. "The only thing standing between you and an assassin's bullet at the moment is pure luck. We took it upon ourselves to create a new cabinet position— one we're sure you won't approve of, but one that you won't be able to overrule. We've got the votes to back this up."

"So, you're all in on this?" Lucy asked, looking the group over from the depths of her chair. "Okay, what is this new position you've created?"

"Yes, we're all in on it, Lucy, as well as every captain you have, every warden, every secretary, and even the base commanders. The vote was unanimous.

The position is Office of Herald Protective Services, and since it's a cabinet level post, the person filling the position will be awarded the title of warden, as well. Its function is, overtly, to provide personal protection to the persons of the herald and deputy herald, but it will be charged with a secondary mission as well. They are going to be our intelligence group. In effect, it will be used as our FBI, CIA, NSA, and Secret Service all rolled into one. Prevents a lot of jurisdictional disputes, I'd think."

Lucy stared at Simon as if he'd suddenly grown a second head. "You don't think I'm going to take this lying down, do, you?" she said, finally getting the words past her clenched teeth. "Why are you doing this to me?"

Simon grabbed his chest, feigning a wound. "I'm only concerned with the safety of the herald. We've managed to locate and reassign several dozen ex-military or former police personnel to fill out a unit dedicated to the protection of the person of the herald. About forty in all. That will be the nucleus of the new office. As intelligence needs are recognized, people will be hired to keep track of, or in some cases, influence the event or events."

Lucy, feeling control of the meeting slipping away from her, asked, "And who do have in mind to head up this new position? I imagine the qualifications would be rather hard to meet."

"They were rather hard to *define*, much less meet," Simon answered. "I really wouldn't want to drop the ball on this one, now would I? Especially since this office is dedicated to the protection of yourself as well as my wife."

"So that's your reason!" Lucy exclaimed. "You're

just pissed because I split you and Kitty up, keeping her here on Earth and you in space."

"That's not it at all," Simon denied vehemently. "My wife is in charge of her own destiny. She accepted the position of deputy herald willingly, and there's nothing I can or would do to influence her decision. I can only applaud and support her. But if there *were* a reason, you might say that it would be that you wouldn't give me a ship. Promoting me to admiral and putting me in charge of all the ships just doesn't cut it. I'm still not in the captain's seat."

Simon stood up and paced around the space in front of Lucy's desk. "I'm really getting tired of saying this, but I'll do it one more time. I realize that if I hadn't gotten 'killed,' I'd be sitting where you are right now, and I *still* wouldn't have a ship of my own. But you picked up the ball and carried it at a crucial time. I know Kitty and Gayle and I found the *Galileo* and got all this started, and I know you're just following the ideas I set out while Orion was being built. My original vision called for this outfit to be set up along military lines because I believed, and rightly so it seems, that space is a dangerous place, even with all of our new toys. It was intended that, sooner or later, a government would be set up, and I would *not* be a part of it."

Simon quit pacing and stared at the carpet. "It's not like any of us had any idea where things would lead, ya know? Figuring that the U.S. Government, as well as others, would try to take it from us wasn't a stretch of the imagination, and thinking that the Builders would come looking for their missing hardware wasn't a much further stretch. That they'd be openly hostile about it *was* a surprise. Or that their enemy would find us. Whatever. We've taken casualties from all sides and managed to survive it. So far."

Simon visibly shook himself out of his reverie and faced Lucy. "I don't know that I would have made the same choices you did or gone an entirely different route, but what you did worked. That's what counts. My problem with you is that I think you stuck me with this job because I wouldn't take *your* job back. Now, *that's* what I call petty and vindictive. Just remember—I'm one of those people who think that what comes around, goes around."

He strode to the door and opened it. "So, you've got yourself an admiral, and now you've got a security detail to keep you safe at all times. On embassy grounds, you'll have no fewer than two guards with you. That is paramount, Madam Herald, and you'll just have to accept these new security guidelines." The ends of Simon's mouth turned up in a mirthless grin seen only by the herald. "And the chief of the new Herald Security Detachment is going to be Mike Abernathy," Simon said, referring to the sergeant who'd arrived at the New Mexico embassy shortly after it opened. "Remember him? I think you're going to have a very hard time subverting him, Lucy. His job description has him answering to me, not you." Simon bowed slightly to Lucy and said, "Have a nice day, Madam Herald."

Pulling the door closed, Simon crossed the outer office, paying no heed to the secretaries or the two guards he left behind.

That conversation in her office only bothered Lucy

these days when the consequences impinged on her as they had today, reviving the memories. Scheduled to appear in southern Germany at an automobile factory where the first of a new breed of vehicles was due to "roll off the assembly line," she boarded the shuttle along with Kitty and ten armed escorts. Ignoring the armed detail as much as possible, she engaged Kitty in small talk until the shuttle was airborne, then closed her eyes and napped until she was awakened by changes in the internal noises of the shuttle as it settled down on a grassy expanse just outside Stuttgart, Germany.

When the herald and her deputy were finally allowed to exit the shuttle, they found themselves on what appeared to be a soccer field, surrounded by about two thousand onlookers, including several camera crews. The babble of sound produced by all those voices began to make itself heard as the shuttle's systems started shutting down, and Lucy felt a gentle poke in her ribs.

"Wave, Luce. We're here to put on a show, remember? Let 'em see the Alliance working hand-in-hand with Earthbound industries for the betterment of mankind."

"So why wasn't I at the opening of the plant putting out the first food processors?" Lucy asked petulantly.

"Because," Kitty said in her third-grade teacher voice, "we decided to put the plant in Afghanistan, remember? Even though they're happy about the infusion of cash, jobs, and food, there are just too many extremists still running around over there. You know how well the United States is thought of over there after the pounding they took, and we have too many ties to the U.S. Somebody would try to kill you, and that can't be allowed to happen. So we take our photo ops where we can find 'em."

Met at the end of the ramp by the German chancellor's deputy, the Alliance group was driven to the nearby factory complex where they were invited to freshen up before meeting Daimler-Chrysler's upper-level management team. Limiting themselves to one ceremonial glass of wine apiece, Lucy and Kitty circulated among the executives, making small talk until the PR people felt that the press and guests had suffered long enough.

Lucy and Kitty were ushered to one side of a low stage at the end of a huge auditorium-style room. Along with about a dozen members of the upper echelon of Daimler-Chrysler and four of the guards assigned to this particular outing, Lucy and Kitty suffered through several speeches extolling the virtues of the newest-production vehicle for model year 2015. The other six guards circulated through the hundreds of people present for the unveiling of the first consumer-oriented vehicle built using the combined technologies of Earth and the Alliance. People moved out of the way as the solemn-faced, black-clad security officers passed by, many warily eyeing the unusual weapons strapped low on their thighs.

The reason for all the attention sat placidly in front of the stage under a red-velvet, gilt-edged cover, and after all the obligatory speeches, it was finally exposed to the general public for the first time. Even Lucy and Kitty, knowing what to expect, felt their breaths catch in their throats. The sleek, ultra-modern shape spoke of speed while standing still, but it was the *lack* of a heretofore necessary item that caused the crowd to begin to mutter. Letting the vehicle sit flat on the concrete floor for a few seconds longer, the Daimler-Chrysler chairman listened as the crowd's noises began to grow.

"Ladies and gentlemen," he said into a microphone produced by an assistant. When the crowd subsided, he smiled and said, "We thought to call our first offering the 'Jetsonmobile.'" He waited while the uncertain laughter died down. "But some thought it too clumsy, and some thought it too cute. Therefore, we present to you the Daimler-Chrysler Quasar. This vehicle embodies the best of both Earth engineering and Terran Alliance technology blended into a functional and, we hope, pleasing vehicle."

At this point, the driver, unremarked upon until that moment, chose to bring the automobile's systems to life. First, a barely perceptible hum penetrated the ears of the audience as the vehicle rose off the ground about sixteen inches. As it settled into its new position, the hum disappeared and the car began to slowly spin clockwise, giving everyone a full view of all sides.

"Powered by sunlight, this revolutionary vehicle is freed from the restraints of both gravity and fossil fuels. Equipped with the latest in proximity-avoidance equipment, one of the benefits of the Quasar is the lessening of the loss of life as the onboard computer reacts to the presence of other vehicles in its vicinity. Internal safety fields, adapted from the force fields supplied by the Alliance, will automatically deploy in the event of an accident, effectively cocooning the passengers and preventing injuries. In the event that the solar charging system fails, a backup system will allow the Quasar to be plugged into household current and run for about a week before needing another charge."

The chairman continued to talk, but it was mostly to hear himself finish his speech as the driver moved through a preset course around the outer edges of the big room, allowing one and all to see that there were no mirrors, illusions, or hoaxes being perpetrated. The vehicle came to a stop back in front of the stage, and the cameras followed it. Lucy and Kitty endured twenty minutes of questions and answers before being able to make an unannounced departure as attention was diverted back to the new Quasar.

On the trip back to Zurich, Lucy watched Kitty talking with Sarah Parker for ten minutes or so before coming over to sit down at her side. Dropping limply into her seat, Kitty said, "Sarah will release the news about the Montana base while you're talking with the president. That'll let her get a short jump on her competition. Here's what I told her..."

President Drake, nervous at his first meeting with Alliance personnel after the Camp David affair, greeted his guest in the Oval Office, bypassing the usual press conference and photo session. "First, let me say how happy I am to finally meet you, Madam Herald," the President said. "And let me also say that you are causing our security chief to have fits over the armed guards you insist upon. Protocol dictates that we, that is the United States, are to be responsible for your safety while you're our guest."

"I'm no happier than your security chief," Lucy said sourly. "But I must point out that I'm hampered by the strictures of my office, just as you are. My people are still too close to the loss of three of our own at Camp David at the hands of U.S. troops, not to mention the injuries sustained by Admiral Hawke, as well as the attempt to shanghai him. If we hadn't received warning, there's no telling where he'd be right now. So, I'm accompanied by armed guards." Lucy held her hands out, palms up, indicating resignation. "I realize Camp David is still a sore spot with both our groups, but it needs to be out in the open."

Drake nodded. "Sore to a lot of Americans, most of whom blame me for the disaster, Madam Herald. I was actually surprised to find out that I'd won the election. But what's past, is past." He waved his hand dismissively. "That's not meant to diminish the death of the vice-president or any of the others lost that day. Their efforts to form a union with your Alliance were only in the beginning stages, and I want to make sure that they didn't die in vain. So. Let's change the subject. I'm given to understand that you want to negotiate for a different base on U.S. soil?"

Lucy smiled slightly. "I wouldn't use the word 'negotiate,' Mr. President. Actually, this is a courtesy call to inform you of something so you don't get caught with your pants down." A single raised eyebrow and a slight nod filled the moment of silence. "I'm sure you're kept apprised of just about everything the Alliance does, Mr. President, so it should be no surprise to you to find out that we've bought several thousand acres of land in Montana. What we plan to do is move our embassy there as soon as we can build a new facility, one more appropriate to our needs. We'll use the *Galileo* and her factories to manufacture whatever equipment we can't hire from on-planet to construct a training facility for our new citizens. But this facility won't serve that purpose for very long. As you probably know, since we've made no secret of it, we've hollowed out the asteroid Vesta and are in the process of fitting it out as a permanent headquarters facility. All of our administrative staff will be moved there, and the training of new personnel will be conducted there as well. This will leave the three embassies here as recruitment, pre-space training, and spaceports."

The president leaned back in his chair and looked closely at Lucy. "And tell me, Madam Herald, how do you see that affecting the economy of the U.S.? Not to mention other economies around the world," he added hurriedly.

Lucy smiled. "That's the beauty of it, Mr. President. The Alliance Embassy in Zurich will be our Earth-side headquarters, shipping recruits to our embassy in Montana, which will also be accepting recruits from the Americas, and Alliance Embassy Asia will be our financial center, as it were, sending recruits here as well. The recruits will be quartered in Montana and receive their initial pre-space orientation and training. From there, they'll be moved onto ships, to Vesta, or the space docks as personnel requirements dictate. The U.S. will get a small boost because there will be more people here, but it will mostly affect New Mexico and Montana—a loss of income for New Mexico and a gain for Montana. And whatever monies we have will still be rooted in Earth's economies. Mostly, they'll stay in banks and be used to purchase luxury items we don't care to manufacture, which will put the money back into circulation. And pay salaries to our citizens, which will also go back into circulation as Alliance citizens come home for vacations or to retire. As for the rest of the world, they'll fall in line or get left behind."

President Drake, obviously not pleased with the direction the meeting had gone, glanced at his watch and stood up, saying, "We really should be leaving if we're going to make the press conference on time."

As he led her out of the Oval Office and down the corridor to the conference room, he said, "We've studied you, you know, Madam Herald, everything we could find, and nothing in any of it would lead someone to think that you'd turn on your country like this."

Lucy stopped so quickly that the Secret Service agent following her almost ran her down. Her own security detail had trouble keeping their hands off their guns, but one managed to insert herself between Lucy and the errant agent.

"Mr. President," she said to his retreating back, her voice replete with venom, "did any of the information you managed to dig up on me happen to include my grades?"

The leader of the free world, noticeably greyer than when he'd begun his term, stopped and turned, surprise at the distance between the two leaders showing on his face. "Why, yes, Madam Herald, I believe it did. Public knowledge, you know."

"Public knowledge be damned, Mr. President," Lucy said, sparks flying from her eyes. "If the knowledge had been confidential, you'd have gotten it anyway. So don't go getting all holier than thou on *me*."

Set back by the verbal assault in the middle of his

own sanctum, the president could only respond, "Why do you ask?"

"Because," she answered, walking toward him, "if you'd *really* looked at my records, you'd have seen that I got straight As in history, sir. And I find it totally hilarious that the leader of a country that got its own freedom by refusing to obey constituted authority would have the nerve to say what you just did." Pausing when she drew even with the president, Lucy said, "Face it, Mr. President, we're never going to be each other's greatest fans. But we *do* have to work together upon occasion, so let's just smile and say nice things for the next few minutes, shall we?"

Simon, Kitty, and Gayle stood on a small bluff overlooking the site of the new Alliance Embassy about an hour's drive east of Helena. Casting a critical eye over the area, Simon said, "It's not on high ground, but it *is* a defensible location."

Kitty looked up at her husband. "Defensible from whom, dear? If Lucy and I have done our jobs, we won't need to defend against anyone here on Earth except the occasional psycho. And if aliens get this far, then we're screwed anyway."

"You do have a way of putting thing into perspective, hon," Simon said, a slight smile passing across his face.

The three friends watched the activity as transports arrived with raw materials destined to be dumped into the converter copied on a smaller scale from the big one aboard the *Galileo*. They followed the process as the converter passed its output to the extruders where transports waited to move a finished product to a building site. There, grapplers would move a prefabricated section into place while other machines welded, nailed, or otherwise attached each new part to the whole. Five other similar sites were under construction in the same area, to be covered by walkways, eventually forming the headquarters. Housing was being constructed to one side of the area for the personnel expected to be living there while awaiting assignment, and other structures were being laid out. A small town was planned, to include training facilities, mess halls, recreation areas, and entertainment facilities. Already, the smooth, flowing lines that had been envisioned were beginning to show as the main buildings went up. In the distance, the world's third antimatter power generation plant was being constructed to handle the requirements of the community, as well as the generators that would power the defense shields.

"Strange how it is that the three of us are here together after all this time," Simon mused aloud. The inspection of ground-side facilities wasn't on his mind, and only the insistence of Kitty made him show his face at this semi-event. He'd felt that his time would be better spent keeping tabs on the ever-growing fleet of ships flying the Alliance banner, but the women had other ideas.

"Right back where we started," Kitty noted. "This isn't far from where the first shuttle landed. Hey! Do you guys know that you... we," Kitty said, waving her hands expansively, "have become folk heroes or legends or something? You should hear how the 'Firsters' are talked about by the new recruits, and how *we* are regarded! And that includes the general public, too," she added, her circling finger indicating the three of them. "There are a bunch of folks who haven't seen much of the famous Simon Hawke yet, and you need to make your presence known to all, Admiral." Her bantering tone took much of the sting out of her comment.

"Not to mention the Deputy Herald and the famous Captain Miller," Simon added.

"Don't call me famous, Simon," Gayle protested bitterly. "I got over three hundred of my crew killed. I shouldn't even be here."

Kitty stopped in front of the huge windows that looked out of what was going to be one of the cafeterias. Simon and Gayle stopped as well and glanced at each other behind Kitty's back. Staring at the valley below, Kitty raised her voice to be heard by her companions. "I want you to tell me with certainty that someone else would have done a better job, Gayle. And I want you to tell me that you wouldn't do the same thing again. Who would you wish this experience off on?"

"I wouldn't want anyone to have to live with what I do, Kitty. You know that!" Gayle protested. She stood frozen for several seconds, trying to find some way to answer the demand her friend had made. "I can't tell you that, and you know it." The agony was evident in her voice. "Why are you torturing me? We're supposed to be friends."

"We *are* friends, Gayle," Kitty said, turning and hugging her long-time pal. "That's why I said what I did. You did as good a job as anyone else could possibly have done. Remember, we're learning as we go along. The technology just bit us again, that's all. Sure, a lot of people died. You were almost one of 'em, you know. And it's really shitty about what happened to Stephen, but we can't just stop because of it. We're in way too deep now, and we need all our people at their best. We need *you* back, Gayle. I hate to ask, but you've managed to heal pretty well physically. It's time to get back on the horse. I know it hurts, but you need to do it. We've got another ship arriving in Earth orbit in a couple more months. That'll give you some time to think it over."

Letting that particular conversation drop, Kitty finished touring the new facilities, followed by Simon, Gayle, and the ever-present gaggle of armed guards.

CHAPTER TWENTY-ONE

Torlan Garpal stared at the communications console for several seconds before the full implication of what he was hearing hit him. When the shock wore off, he hit the emergency call to the commander of the small Korvil fleet. Within minutes the summoned individual entered the bridge. Taller than most Korvil, Fleet Lord Formug Gavrit, second cousin to The Korvil himself, ducked his massive head as he strode into the confined space. Having worked with this team for almost two cycles now, he knew this would be no false alarm. "Report, Communications Second."

"Lord, we are currently in the fringes of a trinary system. No signs of the Humanz or Shiravi, but I *am* picking up signals that appear to be less than random. I have the computer checking now."

Gavrit sat heavily in his command chair and waited while the comm officer refined his data. At last the computer blinked and Garpal read directly from the screen, "Lord, there is no indication that any species has visited this system—no message traffic, no signs of any construction—but the computer reads intelligent signals emanating from the yellow star nearest us." He pointed to an image on his screen.

Fleet Lord Gavrit transferred the images to his own screen and compared them to information he'd been given before beginning this hunt. "That is indeed the system we're searching for. All information from previous visits to this region has been made available to me, and our attempt to search out the Humanz from a second angle appears to have been effective. Make course for the new system cautiously," he ordered the navigator. "I will not have our prey spooked before we're ready to pounce. How long to reach the fringes of the system?"

"Lord," the navigator responded as his finger flew over his own console, "it appears that we will spend four more periods before we reach that point."

"So long? This creeping through the dark can sap the patience from a Hunter's bones, no? Very well. Continue with standard protocols and regular reports. I will guide us into our final position." Not waiting for verification of his orders, the fleet lord returned to his chambers to prepare a message to be sent to Homeworld that would arrive months after any possible engagement with the Humanz took place.

CHAPTER TWENTY-TWO

Derek Carter stood behind the navigator's station aboard the Shiravan flagship *Light of Dawn* and stared intently at the battlecruiser's display. "That's got to be it!" he exclaimed. Five months crammed into the overstaffed ship with nothing to do but wait to be called to identify Earth's system had taken its toll on him. The relief that flooded through his system threatened to drag him to his knees. "I'm home," he whispered.

Rentec do' Verlas, first Ambassador to the Human Race, looked at the human sympathetically. "Are you so certain, my friend?" he asked. Many times, he'd tried to imagine what it would be like to be stranded lightyears from home, the sole representative of his race, and totally at the largess of aliens to get home. He admired—and secretly feared more than a little bit—the drive and internal fortitude that had allowed his friends Derek Carter and Maggie Spencer to maintain their sanity. Somehow, he doubted he would have fared as well.

As he looked at the long-range scan on the navigator's console, Derek felt a connection form between himself and the image on the screen almost instantly. Something primal, buried deep in his genes at the dawn of time, recognized the configuration of the system. On a more rational level, he pointed at the sixth planet. "How many planets have you seen that are ringed like that?"

The navigator responded, "I know of two ringed planets and one ringed moon, but none so large as this one appears to be." His fingers flew over his instruments, trying to eke out any more information at this distance.

"Eight major planets, an asteroid belt between the fourth and fifth, and the sixth is ringed. It is as you described, Derek," Rentec agreed. A true comradeship had grown between the two disparate aliens over the last half-turn, and Rentec felt a wave of joy wash over him at the expression on Derek's face. He placed his hand on the shoulder of the crewman seated at the console. "Navigator, set course for that system. Standard approach, and stop at the outer edges until we can get a full scan of the system."

Rentec decided a gamble was in order. Trusting in Derek's feelings, he turned to *Light of Dawn's* Captain and said, "Download the coordinates of the target system to the corvettes, Captain. Brief the crews and let them complete their missions." One six-man corvette would head back to Shiravi while the other searched out the second Contact Fleet. The matriarch would have the coordinates of the human homeworld, and the second fleet would immediately head this way, operating as either a relief force or under their original orders as a reprisal fleet. Both Contact Fleets had a human with them to act as interpreter and to ensure safe passage, if such was possible. Both fleets were composed of two battlecruisers carrying five interceptors and a long-range scout, four destroyers carrying three interceptors each, two destroyer escorts, and two heavy cruisers. The corvettes had been attached for just this purpose due to their extreme speed and the ability of their crew to endure the extended flight. Now, they flashed away on their separate missions, leaving the ten ships of the Shiravan Contact Fleet to make their way to human space.

Marcad Korvil listened to the summation of the report as it came from the captain of the *Fist of Vengeance*. "It is my conclusion, Lord, that this situation is different than most others we've encountered. If this is truly the home system of this new race, these *Humanz*, and if they truly took possession of a derelict ship, as has been surmised, then they've taken that technology in an altogether different direction than the Shiravi do when starting a colony world."

Marcad had paced through the entire debriefing and now froze into the preternatural stillness that allowed a Korvil to become all but invisible to prey. "And how did you proceed?" he asked.

"Lord, I followed standard mission protocols all the way in. When we were first able to define their entire system, we stopped and scanned it in all bands. Two different types of transmissions were detected. One, a series of low frequency types, carried audio signals only, or visual data mixed with audio. This type was found to be coming exclusively from the third planet. The other type is what we find whenever we encounter the krath-Shiravi. It was found that this second type was coming from a variety of places throughout the system. We identified a hand, three of major sources and uncounted hands of minor targets."

Marcad spoke as to a cub. "The norm is to set up a

colony before building ships. Do you have any thoughts as to why it's different in this case, Captain?"

Hesitating for a second, as though choosing his word carefully, the captain answered, "I turned my attention to the matter fully on the voyage back to Korvilene, Lord, and it is my opinion that these Humanz already have their power base, their homeworld. All they need to do is begin building a fleet."

Marcad nodded. "War Minister Darmag and I are of the same mind. What did you do next?"

"Lord, the captain of *Hunter's Pride* one-jumped into the system for a more definitive look. They attempted to coast through the system unpowered and under full stealth, recording all they could using passive scans only."

"You said 'attempted,'" Darmag said before his captain could continue. "Were you seen by the Humanz?"

"Until the Humanz attacked the *Pride*, War Minister, I would have said that we were not detected. We recorded signals being sent, but since we have no working knowledge of the language, we were unable to tell if any of it referred to us until the Humanz short-jumped within their own system. *Pride* made it halfway through the system. They were attacked and destroyed, along with any knowledge they may have gleaned."

Darmag stood up. "Lord, it is my duty to tell you that I think we should attack these Humanz now, before they can build up any further. Only a hand of seasons have they had this ship, and look what they have done."

"With packs of krath-Shiravi roaming our space,

decimating entire *clans*, we now have the added insult of these puny Humanz destroying ships!" Marcad roared. "Now we must split our forces to prevent any further attempts by these upstarts to claim our rightful space. Until now, the Humanz had no certain knowledge of our existence and therefore no reason to expect attack from us. Now they are alerted, Captain! I detail you and your entire clan to watch these Humanz until such time as we are ready to act. My orders: assemble all ships except for those of Clan Prandalk into hunter packs. Most will begin harassing any krath-Shiravi they can find. This will make the krath-Shiravi send out their ships to protect their worlds, tying down their ships defending against attacks that might or might not come. Take out *all* ships wherever they are found. Leave them with no way to attack Korvil worlds or ships. After our warriors have honed their skills against these krath-Shiravi, they can turn their attention to these Humanz."

The hulking figure of the Korvil monarch loomed over the smaller captain. "The loss of any ship is of utmost concern to all Korvil. But to lose a hand two to the krath-Shiravi and now another to these Humanz is not to be tolerated. I give your life, Captain, because you bring the news of the loss and of the abilities of these new enemies. The fact that they are willing to one-jump *inside* their own system, shows their faith in their abilities, or a lack of fear for the consequences." Marcad backed up a pace before continuing. "But *you* were in charge of this mission. On your head lies the responsibility for the loss of the *Hunter's Pride*. For that, you and your entire clan will pay with your Honor. You will skulk like the vergas of the field, waiting for the leavings of the true predators. You will search out the weaknesses of these Humanz and report them to me." Marcad paced back to his throne and sat, looking into the eyes of his subject. "Know, too, that I know these new enemies can detect our presence at a longer distance than the krath-Shiravi, so what *other* tricks do they have to surprise us with? Study well, Captain. Learn the weaknesses of your enemies, and you can defeat them."

An exaggeratedly casual wave of one hand sent the hapless captain back to his clan, plans already floating through his mind to restore the Honor of his clan, even if it be at the cost of his own life. Some of those plans foundered when The Korvil added one final bit of news.

"I am putting at your disposal two transports. They will be loaded with sixty light attack craft, and you will launch them through the Humanz system on a slash-and-destroy mission when I send the word and not before. The transports will wait and depart the system just before the raiders show themselves. This should have the effect of siphoning off any defenders who might see the drive traces of the two transports. Two other transports will be waiting on the other side of the system to pick up any survivors of the three waves of ships that we will launch against these Humanz."

Eventually, over a hundred raider ships formed into groups of five to ten and spread out through Shiravan space, looking for the less well-defended planets and lone ships ferrying supplies in one direction or the other, while the ten ships of Clan Prandalk, including *Fist of Vengeance* plus the four transports and their deadly cargo, headed to the refit yards to prepare for such an extended voyage.

CHAPTER TWENTY-THREE

Kitty messaged Simon with her suspicions concerning Lucy. Since Alliance scientists still hadn't found a way around the light-speed limitation for messages, answers could take hours to arrive, depending on what the recipients were doing and where they happened to be in the solar system. In Simon's case, he was beyond the orbit of Saturn aboard the new flagship *Rigel*, engaged in fleet exercises with the *Asimov* and the new fleet-carriers the *Canopus* and the *Aldebaran*.

Pulling himself away from a planning session with the newly promoted Captain Miranda Lee and several of the top Mamba pilots from both carriers, Simon opened the sealed communiqué in his quarters. After getting through the "missing you's" and "I love you's," the main reason for the message became clear. "I'm sorry to have to tell you this, Simon," the letter read, "but I have the distinct impression that Lucy is losing her ability to cope with situations as they present themselves. Ever since the destruction of the *Clarke*, she has become more distant and dictatorial. We all thought it was her way of coping right after the tragedy, but now it appears that she's trying to deny or avoid troublesome issues. More and more over the past few months, I've found myself making the hard decisions while Lucy spends more time in isolation. I've spoken with Dr. Jeffers, and he suggested a few good psychiatrists. I confronted Lucy with my thoughts and observations, and she admitted she didn't feel up to her job. While Gayle now seems to be able to cope with the losses she incurred, Lucy is still blaming herself as the person who ordered the action in the first place. 'Morose and combative' is the way one doctor described her."

Simon scanned the rest of the message and then sat back in his chair and closed his eyes. Raising his hands to his temples, he massaged them for a minute. Picking up a pen, he started to write. "I don't know what I can do from out here, but it would seem that you have the situation under control. If Lucy needs time off or therapy, then see to it that she gets it. We're coming along as well as can be expected out here. Fleet maneuvers are progressing satisfactorily, but the sheer number of ships is daunting as more arrive each day or so. As you know, we have one hundred Mambas on the two carriers, as well as ten each from the *Rigel* and the *Asimov*, plus each ship of the line and its Mambas as well. We're looking at almost two hundred individual vessels at any one time."

He sat back and looked at what he'd written. Steering his thoughts back to Kitty's problem, he wrote, "Lucy has finally reached the dark side of command decisions. If she needs to be sidelined until she can get her head back on straight, then that's what she'll have to do. I'm sure you're thinking, 'Oh shit, that leaves me in charge!' like it's a bad thing, but trust me, honey, there's no one I'd rather have calling the shots. Remember," he added with a smile he hoped she would mirror, "I'm used to taking orders from you. Just keep me fed with updates and I'll get my job done. I feel that our jobs are almost done out here anyway. The Alliance isn't going to die out now. Somehow or other, no matter what happens to us, it will go on." Adding a personal thought or two to the missive, Simon took it to the *Rigel's* comm shack. "Send this out with the next packet, will you, Lieutenant?" he asked the comm officer behind the counter.

"Yes, sir, Admiral!" the young man responded. "I have a packet going out as soon as the results of today's training exercises are posted. That should be about two or three hours."

Kitty stood at the window of the newly built spaceport outside Zurich and watched as the shuttle carrying Lucy and her party took off. One of the harder decisions she'd to make of late, it was a group consensus that had sent Lucy off to Vesta for a period of working recuperation. Dr. Jeffers had suggested the name of a psychiatrist specializing in what most people would call nervous breakdowns, and Kitty had placed the call. Visions of a paper on space-related stress in his head, he'd jumped at the chance to work with Lucy. Kitty had informed him that the problem wasn't space related, but he agreed anyway, hoping that once he was attached to the Alliance, he could find a way to *stay* attached. Private talks with Dr. Jeffers pointed to that exact scenario as the Alliance was still woefully short of trained medical professionals in all disciplines.

Two months of work with Lucy had convinced the psychiatrist, Dr. Mark Emmanuel, that she shouldn't make a total break with the Alliance, so she'd been allowed to sign aboard the Vesta Project for an unspecified period of time. It had taken considerable thought among all parties concerned to come to this decision. Compromises had been made along the way that resulted in the Alliance getting its first fulltime psychiatrist, who held out for a position aboard the ship, taking Lucy and her party out to the asteroid belt. Dr. Emmanuel would have to find a replacement for himself before he'd be allowed to leave Lucy and start practicing aboard ships of the fleet.

Lucy's party consisted of five people in all when it finally matched orbit with Vesta. Kitty, searching for a way to keep Lucy close to the Alliance, had finally called the Grimes family for assistance on the problem and came away with three new recruits—her brother, Bruce, and her two best friends, Carmen LeBoy and Amy Sparks. The three would act as anchors to reality for Lucy, along with her doctor, while the three newest recruits helped with the construction of the interior of the asteroid.

Kitty Hawke, now the Herald of the Terran Alliance and surrounded by her inevitable security detail, turned away from the window that looked out onto the Zurich spaceport. Feeling like she'd lost an important part of herself, she turned to Commander Diana Ross, Aide to the Herald. "I know you've said that you have no problem with the changeover, Diana," Kitty said as she paced slowly back to the parking facility. "I just want to ask again if you think you should've gone with Lucy or if you'd like to take a different assignment."

"And I have to say again that I'm happy right where I am at the moment, Madam Herald," Diana said slowly. "I just have a different boss. One, I might add, that I don't have any problem working for. Not being an ass-kisser," she added hastily. "It's just that I've heard so much about you from Lucy and from a lot of other people as well, that I almost feel as if I know you. And it does help that we've met a time or two, you know."

"Thanks, Diana," Kitty said. "I'm going to need to lean on you for a lot of what goes on in the embassy until the facilities on Vesta make it possible for me to move our permanent headquarters there. Actually, I've been thinking of promoting you to Head of Embassy for some time now. You've been doing most of the work anyway, so you might as well get the recognition and rank."

Kitty had self-consciously taken her seat at the head of the table for her first council meeting as herald, and during the meeting, she presented the motion that the heads of embassies be given the rank of captain. It had been debated and passed, with the result that now, with eighteen active ships, including the *Galileo*, there were twenty-five captains, some of whom did double-duty by filling cabinet positions in the Alliance government.

CHAPTER TWENTY-FOUR

The slash-and-destroy mission Marcad Korvil had ordered was designed to test and hopefully destroy the defenses of the Alliance, as well as gauge the effectiveness of their offensive capabilities. When it finally descended on the Alliance, it came with almost no warning at all, catching the Alliance with its collective pants down. The first of the three waves didn't show up on scan until they were less than ten minutes from Earth's orbit. The fact that they'd been launched on a ballistic course from far outside Uranus' orbit and remained at minimum power for the weeks it took the ships to reach their destination spoke volumes for the tenacity and fortitude of the crews of the light attack craft, hunters that they were and needing more space per individual than humans. It also spoke volumes for the relatively few sensors that had been deployed to cover an area of space that could only be expressed by a higher math understood by very few people, Alliance or otherwise.

The newest addition to the fleet, the *Mira*, had made Earth orbit the previous day and was still waiting for her assigned crew to come aboard, allowing the transport crew to be released for reassignment. The helm officer, a veteran of two other transports, was testing the scans when all hell broke loose. "Ma'am, I'm picking up *dozens* of drive traces! They all just came up in the last few seconds and are just outside the moon's orbit. The computer has no record of anything with this particular signature."

Transport Captain Heather Reed looked up from the manual she was studying. "Probably just a glitch, Deb. Recheck your short-range calibration. Make sure you aren't picking up background radiation."

"Ma'am, I've done that twice now, and they're still there!" Real panic sounded in her voice. "Starting to separate from a compact group, and the traces are very distinct. I think we should notify Command." Lt. Commander Deborah Waterman chafed at having her word questioned. She'd helped install most of the consoles on this particular ship and had dreams of getting a ship assignment herself. She'd filed the transfer request long enough ago that it should be in the mail packet brought back from Libra Base and could be undergoing evaluation even now. "All my information is routed to your scan now."

The young woman looked over the information transferred to her screen and began crunching the information herself. Seconds later, she hit the all-ships. "All hands, prepare for evasive maneuvers! Engine room, I need full power. Now!" Turning to her abbreviated bridge crew, she said, "Carla, get over to Tactical and get our shields up as fast as you can. I don't like the looks of this." She opened a channel to Alliance Command, explaining the situation tersely. "I've downloaded all of our scans and slaved our sensors to your computers, for whatever good it's going to do. What are your orders?"

The thirty ships of the Korvil's first wave attacked before an answer could be formulated and sent. At the speed they were traveling, the Korvil raiders were essentially manned weapons platforms with limited mobility. Able to pick one, maybe two, targets and fire before passing out of the system, the thirty ships managed to make a mess of a large part of the orbiting hardware mankind had put into space.

Almost instantly, most military and governmental communications systems went silent. Civilian systems fared no better. Global positioning systems went down, leaving ships, planes and individuals to rely on dead-reckoning to get to their destinations. An unexpected and frustrating side effect of the attack was the jamming of all land-based telephonic communications as irate television and radio addicts tied up all lines trying to find out why their favorite shows were no longer being aired. Only the Alliance, operating on a frequency not dependent on satellites, was able to mount any kind of defense at all.

Kitty, returned to Alliance Headquarters, Zurich, read the reports in the chart room just off her office. Ten minutes had gone by since the first wave had passed through Earth's system. It was plain luck that let the *Mira* get her shields up in time to sustain only minor damage. It was a shame, however, that they didn't have enough crew aboard to put up a fight.

"So," she said, "we've got about forty percent of Earth's satellites down and the *Mira* reporting slight damage. It could have been a lot worse, but they will pay for this. Those guys can't go but a few places. Communications," she said to the young man sitting at the comm console, "Message to Captain Lee: Earth under attack. Bring your battlegroup to Earth soonest. Deploy Mambas on arrival to interdict any further attacks. Message to the *Spica*, the *Niven*, the *Capella*, and the *Norton*: Short-jump to the following coordinates," she said, reading off a series of numbers, "to intercept retreating attackers. Approximately thirty in number. Terminate with prejudice. Message to all ships: Sensors on full. Continuous scans on all bands and frequencies. Report any discrepancies immediately. You are cleared to use any necessary force to stop invaders. Shoot first and ask questions later. Alliance Command out."

"Are you sure we should be shooting at whatever we see, Madam Herald?" Diana asked from the doorway. "What if there are friends out there?"

"Friends wouldn't come in shooting," Kitty responded. "And especially not in such a way that we didn't have any warning. How the hell did they get so close before we saw them? That's not a trick I want to see twice. Who can we get here fast?"

"Ma'am," answered the comm officer, "both the *Heinlein* and the *Castor* are close enough to get here within a half hour."

"Very well," Kitty said, looking into the battle plot. "Send to the captains of the *Heinlein* and *the Castor*: Earth under attack. Short-jump to Earth orbit soonest and deploy Mambas screening force. Place yourself under the command of Admiral Hawke as soon as he arrives with the carrier group. Send to the *Shasta*: Rendezvous with Orion Base. You are assigned as mobile security until further notice. Send to the *Regulus*: Rendezvous with Libra. You are assigned as mobile security until further notice. Send to the *McCaffrey*: Rendezvous with Gemini, etc. And send another to the *Vega* for Taurus. Send the *Pollux* and the *Deneb* to Vesta."

The comm officer turned from her console.

"Madam Herald, Captain Ross, I just copied a message from the International Space Station to NASA. It was on an open channel. I think you should hear it."

"On an open channel, you say?" Kitty asked, intrigued. "That's unique enough that I think we should at least listen to it. Go ahead, Lieutenant, play it." The playback made both Kitty and Diana wince.

"NASA Control, this is ISS. We have sustained severe damage from an unknown source—not meteors, but beyond that, we have no ideas. Solar panels are gone, and power is fading fast. The station is venting air, and we are going to suits. Escape module is damaged beyond our ability to repair it. I estimate that we have six to eight hours of air left. Request immediate evacuation. ISS standing by."

Simple inertia had kept Earth's first cooperative space station going over the past four years, but ever since the revelation of the Alliance's existence, enthusiasm for the project had been waning. The point had finally been reached where the ISS was experiencing the same troubles the old Russian Mir space station had gone through before its demise a decade before—parts failures, slow repairs, less frequent supply missions. Not from lack of money or resolve, but from the simple knowledge that the station was now an anachronism.

A chill ran down Kitty's spine as she listened to the response. "ISS, this is NASA Control. Be advised that we have nothing that is even near ready to launch at this time. We are currently checking with the Russians to see if they have a vehicle nearing launch. We will advise soonest. NASA Control clear." The preceding two years had seen a decline in the use of rockets to launch satellites into orbit. Even the launch systems themselves were beginning to fall into a light state of disrepair despite the attention of technicians working for downside governments. Earth-based companies with ties to the Alliance had begun to place satellites into orbit at a fraction of the cost of government launches. A shuttle could carry a satellite into space with its capture field and deliver it to its proper orbit or pick up a malfunctioning unit the same way and bring it back for repair. The net result was a lessening of ready launch vehicles for governments too stubborn to avail themselves of the Alliance's services. Now the piper was being paid.

Kitty, alerted to the attack, found herself in the Alliance chart room, staring into the slowly rotating solar system display trying to devise a strategy. With Simon working with the soon-to-return carrier group and all of her top advisers in widely flung positions around the solar system, as well as not having named a new deputy herald, she had no one to bounce ideas off of.

"We need to find out where they're coming from," Diana said.

"More to the point, we need to find out if there are any more of 'em out there." *And I want to know just* who *the hell they are, damn it!*

By this time, the drive traces of the thirty alien attackers were headed out of the system and almost to Mars' orbit, having made mincemeat out of Earth's satellite net. And not one shot had been fired in return.

With the communication time-lag, only now were some of the ships she'd messaged beginning to return her calls and starting to move as she'd directed

Diana stared at the screen in consternation. "Is that

going to be enough, Kitty? If there's another attack, we're going to get our heads handed to us on a platter."

"We're going to do the best we can. That's all anyone can do." Kitty stared into the holographic display and watched as ships finally began to move according to her directions. "Remember, Di, humanity has conquered almost an entire planet and made it safe for a person to go wherever she wants, barring interference from other humans, of course. It's high time that we made sure the same thing is true for our entire solar system And next on the agenda is to warn Libra Base about those ships." She turned to the comm officer and rattled off a message with an "urgent" tag, informing Commander McCord that he had hours at the most to prepare for a possible attack.

Kitty paced the floor, feeling as if she'd forgotten something. Finally, she said, "The ISS! We can kill two birds with one stone here. Comm, send to the *Mira*: Proceed to the ISS. Pick up stranded astronauts and set course to rendezvous with the *Galileo*. You are under-crewed and are not able to mount an effective defense of your ship or assist in repelling any further attacks. Once you arrive at the *Galileo's* position, both ships are to go silent and await further instructions. Hawke out." Kitty turned to Diana. "That's all we can do from here. The only thing left is to ride it out. But first, I think we should let NASA know that their people will be taken care of."

The *TAS Heinlein* flashed into Earth orbit a mere hundred thousand miles above the surface, violating every safety protocol the young Alliance had envisioned and enacted. Only after all ten Mambas, fully armed and looking for trouble, had been ejected to screen the planet did the captain of the battlecruiser call headquarters.

Kitty uploaded all the data from the now-departed *Mira*. "Captain Chapman, until Admiral Hawke arrives with the carrier squadron, the *Heinlein* and the *Castor* will be Earth's only defense. I expect the *Pollux* to arrive momentarily. I regret the necessity of dumping this on you, Jerry, but I have no choice."

"Madam Herald, we'll do the best we can. The *Heinlein* has all sensors on full and all weapons hot," Captain Chapman responded. His voice didn't betray the massive case of butterflies that was trying to tie his insides into knots. "We are at full alert and all sensors are double-manned. I received a message from the *Castor* just before making orbit and expect her to arrive at the same state of readiness."

"I know you'll do your best Jerry, and I… we all, appreciate the efforts of your crew and Captain Dahlquist's."

Kitty had barely finished her sentence when the sensor alarms went wild. The *Castor* followed the *Heinlein* into orbit, broadcasting on all channels. "Incoming craft! Incoming craft! Approximately one hour out and headed straight for us. We were moving too fast to do more than register their drive traces on our sensors. All ships prepare for attack!"

Shirley Dahlquist's voice sounded tense but controlled as she reported in. "Madam Herald, the *Pollux* is at your disposal."

"I'm glad you're here, Shirley. Follow Jerry's lead until Admiral Hawke and the carrier group arrives.

It's going to be a close thing, I'm afraid. The group was on maneuvers and had to pick up too many Mambas to jump quickly."

"Yes, ma'am," came the instant reply. "But may I respectfully suggest that we meet the attackers as far from Earth as possible? It would seem the wise thing to do, especially knowing where they are, and it would lessen the risk to Earth."

Kitty pondered for no more than a few seconds before agreeing. "Jerry, get a fix from Shirley's data and jump as close to the enemy as possible. Good luck. I'll see that the Admiral is informed so he can move to assist you."

"I anticipated your orders as soon as Shirley made the suggestion, Madam Herald. My Mambas are already docking. We'll be ready to move five minutes after we get Shirley's data. Got it! *Heinlein* out."

The second, smaller wave of Korvil ships had powered up at almost the same instant that the first had begun its attack run. Counting on the fact that the Alliance would be either too hurt to respond or busy chasing the receding first wave to notice them, the second wave planned to use the higher velocity attained from starting farther out to blast through any remaining defenses. Each of the eighteen ships in the second wave carried a secondary power core attached to its outer hull. Of a size to power a mothership, each core was, in essence, a bomb capable of destroying thousands of square miles when it hit its target.

None of the Korvil ships, intent on the blue-green target just outside their grasp and equally intent on bringing their systems back up to full power, noticed the Alliance ship as it sped toward Earth, coming in from behind and below. It was, therefore, a complete surprise when two Alliance battlecruisers suddenly appeared directly in the path of the raiders, disgorging a swarm of Mambas in response to the data the *Pollux* had managed to pull in as she headed for Earth.

Even Korvil response time wasn't up to stopping the twenty tiny ships that darted in and out among the fleet, especially once the two bigger ships moved off to either side of their formation and began pounding them relentlessly.

Unable to penetrate the shields of this new enemy, these Humanz, the raiders began to concentrate their fire on the lighter craft even as they moved inexorably closer to the destination their Honor demanded.

The Mambas expended their torpedo tubes and returned to their ships for reloads as the two battlecruisers continued their relentless assault. Eighteen raiders were now only fourteen, but twenty Mambas were now only eleven. Unhesitatingly, each pilot returned to the battle as soon as her ship was rearmed. The comm net was full of chatter among the surviving pilots as they devised and tried new strategies, literally on the fly. One that seemed to have the most success was to come upon a raider from the stern and shoot for the engine pods. The shielding was minimal to allow for the expulsion of the energies that moved the ships, but those same energies were potent weapons in their own rights. And the Mamba pilots had to meet the raiders head-on at least once each time they went out just to get into position for their stern shots, then pass the enemy *again*, this time unarmed and with their *own* sterns exposed, in order to get back and rearm for yet another run.

Two more passes and five Mambas returned to the fray, pitting themselves against eight of the Korvil six-man light attack craft. The distance to Earth had closed to just outside the moon's orbit, some two hundred forty thousand miles. Suddenly the comm net, which had been nearly silent for the last twenty agonizing minutes while the surviving Mambas grimly threw themselves at their larger foe, came alive. "*Heinlein, Castor*, break off, break off!" Simon and the carrier group had managed a coordinated short-jump that placed all four arrivals directly between the raiders and the object of their attack. "Reform on the carriers. *Aldebaran* and *Canopus* will launch all ships and stand off. *Rigel* and *Asimov* will hold the center, *Heinlein* take the left flank and *Castor* the right as soon as you pick up your Mambas. Do *not* redeploy them! They've done their jobs and then some."

As the *Heinlein* and the *Castor* picked up their pitifully few surviving Mambas, Jerry Chapman called Simon aboard the *Rigel*. "Admiral, we've found that the enemy is most susceptible from the rear." Even as the information was being passed, swarms of Mambas were emerging from the two carriers and orienting on the surviving raiders. With so many targets to choose from, the targeting systems aboard the raiders overloaded and would only lock on when a ship came within a minimum defense perimeter, which allowed the smaller, more agile Mambas to evade most of the weapons fire directed their way.

Still, two raider craft managed to make it through the line drawn by the Alliance ships. Followed closely by the pursuing Mambas, the attackers dove on the helpless planet below, intent on whatever mission they'd been given. That mission became apparent when one raider, passing over the Sea of Japan, changed its course to take it directly over Tokyo. Fearing the worst, one lone pilot pushed his ship's systems to their limits, and as the Earth's atmosphere slowed the two combatants, it managed to get off a double shot led by a shield killer. Only fractions of a second passed between the impact of the first missile on the raider's stern and the release of a slowly falling object. The swiftly expanding shockwave of the raider's own engine exploding and the missiles that destroyed it caused the object to veer away from its intended target and land in the Pacific Ocean about five hundred miles east of the main island. Plummeting beneath the waves, the errant antimatter bomb exploded about a half a mile beneath the surface, sending a gout of superheated water vapor, biological material, and rocks miles into the atmosphere. The resulting tsunami nearly washed away an entire nation but for the Alliance embassy turning on their shields, separating the murderous waves and blunting its force. South Korea and Russia had almost as little warning as Japan, and the later report on loss of life came close to the twenty million mark in those three countries alone.

Hawaii fared almost as badly, although the tsunami took longer to arrive. The mutilated satellite system prevented warnings that would ordinarily have arrived within minutes of any disaster. In

Earth's information age, the loss of her satellite system was particularly advantageous to any enemy with the resources of the Korvil. The United States' West Coast was subjected to waves over forty feet high, washing everything away as if it were made of paper mâché. In places, the water wormed its way hundreds of miles inland, depositing fish and debris wherever it chose.

The second raider, caught above South America, was destroyed before it had time to release its deadly cargo. The double explosion of its power core, along with the bomb it carried, left an area of devastation that was reminiscent of the Tunguska meteor of the early 1900s. A single meteor had exploded above the Russian countryside with a force approaching later-day nuclear weapons and flattened thousands of square miles of forest. Now, South America had a scar just as horrible to gaze upon.

Military communications nets, among the best on the planet, were the first to begin to come back online. Kitty, through the transmitters aboard the six ships in orbit, was able to inform all the governments of the world of the events that had just transpired, averting a nuclear exchange that would have succeeded where the Korvil had failed on their own. Those same governments, feeling the powerlessness of their positions, began to berate the Alliance for allowing the Korvil to come within range of Earth at all. Some were even calling openly for the arrest of anyone associated with the Alliance.

Stunned by the vehemence of the response to her announcement, Kitty turned to Simon for advice. "I was only trying to keep everyone from blaming each other for what happened, Simon. How could they blame *us*?" The anguish in her voice carried through to her husband aboard the *Rigel*.

"It's the nature of the beast, hon," Simon answered. "The human animal has to have a scapegoat. Someone to blame. I'll take care of this."

"Simon, don't back us into a corner," Kitty chided. "I know how your temper can get the best of you at times. And this isn't the time to let yourself lose control."

Simon didn't immediately make the announcement he had intended. Kitty's plea had caught him in the deepest part of his being. The one time their nearly seventeen-year marriage had almost come apart was due to his volatile temper. Shame was one of the factors that led him to subject himself to anger management counseling, but the most compelling reason was his fear of losing the only woman he'd ever really loved.

Now, he was able to recognize that same atavistic anger and fear in the communications coming from Earth, and knowing he couldn't stop it, he sought to redirect it. "People of Earth. I am Simon Hawke, Admiral of the Terran Alliance Fleet." Even now, his ire at being forced to take the position he occupied still rankled him, and those who knew him heard it in his voice. "It is my sad responsibility to report to you that unknown enemies from beyond our solar system have attacked us without provocation. In this new age of weapons of mass destruction that are magnitudes more advanced than even the nuclear weapons stockpiled on Earth, it only takes a few in the right spots to put an end to an entire species. Regrettably, two attackers got past our defenses in a sneak attack much like the one the United States suffered with the destruction of the World Trade Center some years back. Nothing I can say will bring back any of the lives lost due to this attack, or lessen the pain of that loss, but you can rest assured that we will do all we can to put an end to the menace that faces us all.

"I realize that the attacks are aimed at the Alliance, and the Earth is feeling the effects of those attacks, but we are of Earth as much as you are. There are some who say that we are responsible for the attacks in the first place, merely by having taken the technology we found and using it. That could well be true, but we, the Alliance, are no more to blame than would be any government we could have turned the technology over to. We still believe that the best way to get that technology into the hands of the general populace is as we are doing. Hunger is being eradicated all over the world, with a corresponding decrease in violence. Energy costs are going down as more and more homes come equipped with the new solar power converters, and automobiles that run on solar energy are even now beginning to hit the world markets.

"I cannot guarantee that there will be no further attacks. Rather, I have to work under the assumption that there *will* be more attacks. We of the Alliance stand ready to defend Earth and ourselves from any and all enemies, wherever they may be found and at whatever the cost. We are expanding our fleet and personnel base as fast as we can to meet the crisis before us. This enemy from the depths of space has been harassing us from the first and shall not be allowed to go unpunished for this heinous act. Root and branch, we will find and destroy his ability to persecute us. Look at your night sky and know that we stand between you and the unknown."

Feeling like he'd left something out, Simon ended the transmission abruptly. He sat staring into the holographic display of the solar system as it floated in the air to one side of his desk until his comm unit chimed. "Admiral, the herald is calling."

He leaned forward and activated the channel. "Well, how'd I do?"

Kitty's chuckle came through as if she were right beside him. "Remarkably well. You only threatened the entire planet once. Are you learning restraint in your old age?"

"Well, you do bring out the best in me, my love," Simon retorted. "I know, I know. It's taken something going on over sixteen years now, but better late than never, right?"

Twenty-seven hours after the second attack, the threat assessment level was dropping steadily, not for further attacks but for an imminent attack. Sensor scans had gone back to one person per scan per shift. Vigilance was beginning to waver as no further evidence of enemy action presented itself. It was assumed that the enemy would have to go home, report, receive new orders, and make their way back to continue to press the attacks, giving the Alliance many months, if not a year or more, to prepare for more hostilities. It was a universal truth that unfounded assumptions had a way of coming back to bite one on the nether part of the anatomy.

It would have been better if mankind had known about a small pest native to the Korvil homeworld. Analogous to Earth's ant, the thukira would dash about with no apparent plan, looking for whatever had disturbed the nest, and calming down after the attacker had been dispatched or after an extended period of time had passed. Over time, it had become customary to wait a full day before venturing within range of a violated nest.

It was a flight of Mambas that was unlucky enough to be in the way of the third wave of ships as they powered up for their attack run. The flight leader ordered his ships to attack without hesitation and called in the alert. "*Rigel* Command, Dragon leader. Be advised we have seven drive traces on our scans. Same MO as previous attacks. Same direction. We are moving to interdict. Assistance would be appreciated, guys."

Manned by Korvil desperately seeking to restore lost Honor to clan names, these seven ships were quite literally suicide ships. Each crewmember had already been listed among the Honored ancestors of their clans. Desperation, determination, the effects of the long separation from their species, and the certain knowledge that they were already dead to their families, gave an impetus to the attack that was almost impossible to avert.

All five Mambas went down under the massed firepower of the larger raiders, but the alert had been sounded. Operating on data dumped to the *Rigel* before Dragon leader died under a three-way crossfire, two battlecruisers short-jumped into range and offloaded their Mambas. Adding their heavier firepower to the lasers and missiles of the smaller ships, the battlecruisers accounted for two of the seven invaders. Wildly veering one way then another, the remaining Korvil ships closed on their target, as one by one, they went down under the massed fire of the Mambas and battlecruisers arrayed against them.

Fatalistically charging the swarm of Mambas launched from the *Aldebaran* and the *Canopus*, the five remaining ships of the third wave managed to fight their way through the screen, giving up three more of their number before breaking through into clear space above their cerulean destination.

One raider, engines damaged by a near-miss, swerved off course and added a new crater to the lunar surface, while the final ship, seeing a clear path to its destination, dove for the surface as Honor dictated.

The crew of the last raider, studying their scans in an effort to find the most effective target to expend their lives on, didn't see the three Mambas scramble from the surface. It wasn't until the ship took repeated hits on its outer skin that they had any intimation of another bar to their progress. High-powered lasers punched through metal designed to repel inert meteoric rock, and two Mambas died in the upper reaches of the atmosphere.

The last pilot, glancing at his weapons display and seeing only one missile left—and that one a shield-penetrator—aimed his ship at the raider's midships hull and accelerated onto a collision course. Fingering two buttons on his control yoke, the pilot closed the distance, taking advantage of his superior maneuverability to get close enough to ram the larger vessel. Fractions of a second before impact, he pressed first the launch button, sending the penetrator ahead of him, and then raised the forward shield strength to full. As he passed through the last few meters between him and the raider, he let out a scream of primal rage and fired both lasers, gouging a hole deep into the body of his opponent.

The raider, all power cut off from the control section by the smaller ship, began to fall to the ground miles below, dragging the Mamba with it. The Mamba's nose, aided by the cutting power of its twin lasers, had punched completely through the mortally wounded raider, stopped only by her stern control vanes.

Amazed to find himself still alive, the pilot looked to the wildly careening ground, then to his altimeter. At a height of fifteen thousand feet, he activated the self-destruct timer and fired the explosive bolts that separated his cockpit from the rest of his stricken vessel.

On board the Mamba, a timer counted down to zero, and a double-sun was born high above the Earth. The falling cockpit/escape module was thrown farther from the scene of devastation by the shockwave, blaring Mayday on all frequencies. At two thousand feet, the antigravs cut in, slowing the pilot's module to a safe landing on the Korean peninsula where he was picked up, battered but alive, less than an hour later.

Elsewhere in the solar system, four Alliance ships chased the retreating first wave. The *Spica*, the *Niven*, the *Capella*, and the *Norton*, along with their complements of Mambas, harried the invaders as they tried to rendezvous with the motherships waiting to take them home. The taskforce had whittled the Korvil light attack craft down to a mere dozen ships when the *Capella's* Nav officer reported, "Captain!

I'm picking up two new drive traces directly ahead of the enemy! Powering up and outbound. And these are big mothers!"

No sooner had this announcement been made than the fleeing raiders turned en masse and headed directly for the Alliance fleet. Mambas started to disappear from the battle plots as the two fleets engaged. Robert Greene, Captain of the *Niven* and senior captain present, ordered all four capital ships to assist the Mambas at the expense of the escaping larger ships. "If we don't assist our fighters, we'll be losing at three-to-one odds, and I won't allow that."

The last Korvil raider, obviously fighting to the last to give the larger ships time to escape, was finally destroyed, and Captain Greene ordered all hands to stand down from battle stations. "Sensor stations remain on full alert," he commanded over the all-ships band. "I won't take the chance of another sneak attack."

The grisly business of searching for surviving Mambas began, scans reaching deep into space looking for distress calls. It was as the four ships had begun to widen their search pattern that the *Norton's* senior scan tech sounded the red alert. Robert Greene, jolted back into full awareness from a state of post-battle euphoria, called the *Norton*. "What's the fuss about, Anna?"

Captain Zandt looked into her viewscreen and said, "Nav has just picked up new drive traces. They apparently just jumped in. There are ten of 'em, and the smallest is about half our size. I think we're screwed, Bob."

ABOUT THE AUTHOR

Bob lived in Montana for over thirty years, since late '85. He fell in love with the state almost instantly (who wouldn't after spending the previous twenty or more years trapped in Houston, Texas). Out in the Big Sky Country, he found the "elbow room" he didn't even know he was looking for. He lived quietly with his two cats and library of nearly two thousand books—about 95% Sci-Fi. He discovered that he liked to write as well and could often be found doing just that. Bob passed away in November of 2019 and is survived by his younger brother. Before he passed, he finished his writing project of more than a decade, The Stellar Heritage series, and he will live on in the hearts and minds of his readers.

Learn more at:
bladeoftruthpublishing.com/bob-mauldin

MORE FROM THE PUBLISHER

Blade of Truth Publishing Company specializes in science fiction and fantasy stories that change the way you view the world.

To find more great books head over to:

bladeoftruthpublishing.com/books

Bringing truth into the world, one story at a time.